Contra _____ :
a baseball novel

Bee Hylinski

For Rose,

Hope you enjoy Larry's Journey!

Bee Hylinski

Sept 2012

Andrew Benzie Books
Orinda, California

Published by Andrew Benzie Books
www.andrewbenzie.com

Printed in the United States of America

First Edition: March 2012

10 9 8 7 6 5 4 3 2 1

Hylinski, Bee
Contract Year: a baseball novel

ISBN 978-0-9852229-1-8

www.contractyearnovel.com

Cover and book design by Andrew Benzie

For Ralph, Ginger, Cliff, Natalie and Ryan,
all of whom give me great joy.

Note to readers: A list of baseball lingo and definitions can be found at the back of the book.

Chapter One

The sunlight beats down through the master bedroom window and onto my face, bringing me back to consciousness. Bats seem to be flying circles in my intestines as I roll over into the fetal position and try to escape life's reality for at least a few more minutes. I close my eyes, but have to open them again because the earth is spinning out of control. Sleep is out of the question.

No use fighting it, so I stumble out of bed and over to the fireplace. I swallow down the bile that's in the back of my throat, and rub my hand over my stubble, which is as rough as sandpaper.

I flip on a light and stare into the large rectangular mirror above the mantle. Brown bloodshot eyes look back at me, empty and longing. I remember when they used to shine. Before my world went to hell.

I take a swig of the hefty glass of scotch that I left on the mantle about eight hours earlier, the better to wipe the taste of bugs off my tongue. My head pounds like a jackhammer, and my heart skips a staccato beat as I stumble into the bathroom and turn on the shower.

The steam rises, but today it's no comfort. My body aches everywhere. I stick my head under the steady stream of water and close my eyes.

How did this happen?

Gina Green, my girlfriend of the past five months, stormed out of my house and perhaps my life last night. All because I let slip that I slept with other women on the road while I was seeing her. Of course, I medicated the pain of her leaving with booze, my drug of choice.

As water runs over my head and down my cheeks and shoulders, I can picture her premium legs, hips, and curves, her long blonde hair, and her eyes the color of the noontime sky. Everything about her—her looks, her taste, and her smell—made my problems fade into the background and brought me to heaven. Have I mentioned that she's a pediatrician?

1

I take another sip and balance the glass on the top of the shower door. She's what we in my profession would call a five-tool talent. And now, she's gone. Just like everything else in my life that used to be good.

My name is Larry Gordon, and not so long ago I was perfectly content with being one of the best pitchers in the major leagues with all the extended adolescence that comes with it: chasing tail in every city, partying to all hours, ego running out of control. That was pretty much life in a nutshell, and, well, life was good.

Gina came into my life last fall, as I was putting the finishing touches on another sensational season for the Oakland Renegades, the team that drafted me out of college when I was still a hayseed from Texas. I don't like to talk about my accomplishments, but I spent less than three years in the minor leagues. I struck out the side in my first major-league inning, and I have eighty-four wins in my first five seasons in The Show, including twenty-one last year. I've won at least fifteen games every year I've been in the majors, something nobody else in baseball—hell, the Earth—has done.

Once I met Gina, I realized something had been empty inside of me. I don't know what it was, but being with her filled it up. I used to drink a lot, blowing off steam, screwing the groupies, but when I was with Gina the booze didn't seem so important anymore. But last night I stepped back into drowning my sorrows in alcohol, and now I'm suffering the after effects. But somehow through my alcoholic haze, I know that drinking isn't a long-term solution. At least being with her made me see that.

Gina, what am I gonna do?

Something else has changed recently. The calendar just turned to February, meaning I have to report for spring training in two weeks. Usually, I can't wait. Now, I don't want to think about it, because every mention of the upcoming baseball season puts me in a state of panic.

You see, this season everything changes. It's the final year of my contract—my "contract year."

I wish I could stay with the Renegades after this season. I grew up in Midland, a small west Texas oil town. I don't play this game to be in the spotlight. It just sort of finds you sometimes, so this organization is a perfect fit. The guys keep it light in the clubhouse and they have my back when I'm on the mound. I'll miss that if I'm on a different team next year.

The melodic tones of "Take Me Out to the Ballgame" sound from my cell phone on the sink, bringing me momentarily out of my mope. I step out of the shower, dripping shampoo foam on the bathroom floor, and look at the name in the display.

Bob Jacobs.

Shit! Just what I don't need.

Bob is my agent. I hired him last summer on the recommendation of Jason Giusti, our superstar first baseman who departed as a free agent this winter. Jacobs works with some of the biggest free-agent names in the game, and I'm going to be one of them, so it seemed like the prudent thing to do.

But almost from the moment he came on board, my love for the game has been streaming toward the drain. For Bob, it's all about working my brand, and my market value. If I'd strike out eight in a game, he'd want to know why it wasn't ten. I went five and one last August, but he wanted six and zero. He's never happy, and I get the sense that when it comes to me, all he cares about are the dollar signs I can generate—for him!

Still, he's the best, and I've done pretty well in my career. I've already had an All-Star appearance, and I won the Cy Young award last season. With Giusti gone, I'm the most marketable guy on our club. The best deserves the best.

I ignore the ring and step back in the shower. I remember taking showers with Gina here. It was so good to be naked with her, the water sluicing over us while we soaped each other up. She'd always smile up at me and light up the whole bathroom. Those sessions usually ended up... no, I can't go there.

I've lost her, and the future looks like a yawning abyss that stretches into the next millennium. I feel so sad and alone, with spring training staring me in the face and crushing pressure from Bob Jacobs to be lights out. I hate this shit.

Why can't I be like my buddy, Rick Wycliffe, one of our relief pitchers? We've been teammates for seven seasons, going all the way back to our rookie year in A-ball. Rick is married and has three great kids. His contract runs out this year, too, but he won't get huge dollars like I will. Middle relievers are a dime a dozen.

And yet, Rick still seems to enjoy the game. Still wants to be one of the first guys to arrive at the ballpark and one of the last to leave. I used to be the same way, but that feeling changed last summer after I hired Jacobs to be my agent.

Rick says to me all the time that we're just on borrowed time in this profession anyway, and we'd better enjoy it for the right reasons rather than play it for the wrong ones. What can I say? Rick is a bit of a straight arrow. But he's my best friend in the game, a brother not linked by blood. So maybe he's onto something. Worth thinking about.

Rick's also been trying to get me to marry Gina, but I'm not ready for that, at least not yet. I'm miserable without her, but is that love? I don't know. I've mostly focused my attention on doing well on the mound. Women were just a means to an end—getting laid. Until Gina. She was so much more than that to me. I've always felt so alive when I was with her. That's all history now.

So I can't dwell on something I can't have. Gina or no Gina, I literally have the world at my feet. I've achieved what I've dreamed about since I was six years old. I'm twenty-eight years old, a year away from having a sixty- to eighty-million-dollar contract. I live in one of the greatest places on earth. I have super teammates. My parents are both healthy, and I can get laid with all the effort it takes for me to throw a curveball for a strike.

I should be happy, but I'm not. I guess Gina meant more to me than I realized.

Chapter Two

For the first week after Gina left, I called her almost daily, but her machine always picked up. I left messages as often as not, but she hasn't returned any of my calls. I'll keep trying until I head to Phoenix for spring training next week. I don't know what else to do.

After my workout this morning and a solitary lunch at Prima in Walnut Creek, I'm headed to Boundary Oak with the top down on my Lexus convertible to hit some balls at the driving range. It's a clear sunny day, warm enough for just a sweatshirt. I retrieve my clubs from the trunk and walk up the small hill to the driving range office. Armed with a large bucket of balls, I head down the row of stalls past the other golfers until I find and empty one.

I put my bag down and fish in one of the pockets for my golf glove. When I look up, I check out the people I just walked by, to see if anyone has recognized me. So far so good. Then I turn to look toward the other end of the row of tees, and my heart thuds to a stop. At the end of about five empty stalls, Gina is driving golf balls. She is blasting shots beyond the 200-yard marker, swinging hard and fast as if she hates the balls. She probably sees my face on them.

What should I do? This is such a public place. I'm not sure how she will react when she sees me.

A war breaks out inside my head and my gut. I've got to try to straighten out what happened when she walked out on me. But I don't want to cause a scene. Yet I probably won't get another chance. But I don't want to see the anger that was on her face ever again.

I can't help myself. I start walking toward her. She looks so beautiful, intently concentrating on the ball. She takes a swing and hits a beauty about a hundred seventy-five yards out. She reaches down to get another ball and places it on the rubber tee, her blond hair covering her face. I want to put my arms around her and make

5

all of her anger go away, but I realize that would be a colossal mistake.

She must sense me coming, because she looks up quickly when I get about ten feet away from her. Hurt, anger, and sadness march across her face before she turns away.

I take the last few steps toward her and say to her back, "Gina, I really need to talk to you about what happened between us."

She turns around slowly and plants her feet wide apart. Looking at me defiantly, her hands folded across her chest, she says, "I have nothing to say to you, Larry."

"But I have a lot I need to say to you. I want to apologize for how I behaved the last time we were together."

She stands frozen in place. "Larry, nothing you can say will change what you did. So leave me alone and let me hit my bucket of balls in peace."

"Please, Gina. Just give me a few minutes." I motion to the bench behind her golf bag. "Sit with me, let me talk. If you don't like what I have to say, I'll leave you alone from now on."

She drops her arms and shakes her head. After a couple of deep breaths, the last of which comes out as a loud hiss, she turns and sits down on the bench.

"My body tells me this is a huge mistake," she says, "but I'll give you a few minutes to say what you want. Then I'm going back to punishing these balls, and you'll leave and won't contact me again. Understood?"

"If those are the ground rules, I'm okay with that." I don't want her to see my concern, so I look out at the yardage markers on the driving range. What if I blow this? What if I can't communicate how I feel? This is like the last out of a tight game and the bases are loaded with two outs. I have one chance to end this with a win. I've got to say this right. I clench my hands into fists, so my fingers don't shake.

I look back at her, but her face doesn't give any clue as to what she is thinking. As if she can feel my eyes on her, she drops her head so I can't see her face behind a blond curtain of hair. This is my last chance, and I have to take it. Right now.

I move her golf bag, the one I gave her last fall, and sit down on the other end of the bench and face her, my back to the other golfers on the range.

She looks up at me and says with ice in her voice, "Okay, you've got two minutes. Then you're leaving." She crosses her legs and her arms, her armor firmly back in place, and nods for me to start talking.

I look into her eyes and say, "I've thought a long time about what I said, and I can now see that my saying I was not monogamous on the road was the wrong thing to say, and I'm really sorry."

She looks up, sparks shooting out of her eyes, "Larry, it's not that you said the words. It's that you weren't faithful to me. I can't forgive you for that."

"I understand you can't forgive me, at least not right now. It's just that I've never been faithful to any woman. I don't know how to do that."

"Well, you'd better figure it out or you'll die a very lonely old man, if some woman doesn't kill you first!"

How do I salvage this? I think for a few moments, trying to conjure up the perfect thing to say that won't end this conversation.

"You're right. I want to try to figure out how I can be the kind of man you want. I really miss you, and I miss what we had together. I'm a wreck without you."

"How do you think I feel?" she asks, glaring at me. "This hasn't been easy on me, you know."

"I know. Just talk to me, Gina. Tell me what you are feeling and how I can undo what I did?"

With anger still blazing in her eyes, she says, "Tell you what I'm feeling? Since when are you at all concerned about what I'm feeling?"

"Since you left me and I've had a lot of time to think about what I said, and what we had, and I realize I'm willing to do anything to get that back."

She looks at me for a few moments and then folds into herself, shoulders rounding, shaking her head slowly.

I feel her slipping away. "I'm so sorry," I say. "I don't mean to make you uncomfortable."

She looks up and straightens. "Okay. Since you seem to want to know, I'll tell you how I felt after what you said to me that day."

"Good. I'm listening," I say, trying to sound patient, but, with my whole world teetering on the edge of a cliff, I'm anything but calm.

She looks down at her clenched fingers, and says, "Larry, you need to understand that after I first met you last August, I gradually let down my guard and allowed you into my life. I took a risk and decided to enjoy the company of a man—you—for the first time in a very long time. I'd been hurt pretty badly about five years ago, and vowed I'd never let that happen again."

"Gina, why didn't you tell me about this before?" Would it have made a difference? I don't know.

"Maybe it was unfair, but I didn't think you were ready to hear about my inner feelings, so I kept them to myself for a long time."

She's right. I wouldn't have wanted to talk about feelings with her. But I have no idea how to respond to her, so I stay quiet, my heart pounding like a machine gun.

"Over the course of the next few months, Larry, I gradually allowed you into my heart. I thought I saw more in you than the macho ballplayer façade, but I realized that you weren't in touch with that part of yourself yet. I thought I could help you to see who you really are, and you would grow to love me."

There's the dreaded "L" word. Was I—am I—in love with her? Hell, I don't know.

"I thought we were both falling in love," she says, with a tremor in her voice. "You'd let me have glimpses into the real Larry—the fun-loving guy who enjoys some of the same things I do and cares about something other than playing baseball. But then you'd clam up, or change the subject. I was willing to be patient. I just tried to love you as best as I could."

No one—especially a woman—has ever spoken to me this way. Shit. This conversation is terrifying me.

"My only mistake was expecting you to love me back. I didn't need the words. But I thought you felt what I felt, and that was enough for me."

"I guess I don't know what being in love is."

She ignores that comment, still looking at her hands. "When we were making love that last time, I thought it was time to start talking about how we felt, so I suggested we talk about the idea of marriage. I knew it would be a surprise to you, because we hadn't spoken about love yet." She hesitates a moment. "But never did I think that you'd admit that you'd been screwing other women while you were having a relationship with me."

"I... I..." I say, but I can't find the rest of that sentence.

8

She takes another deep breath and lets it out slowly. "Larry, you hurt me deeply. With one thoughtless sentence, you destroyed the happiness I had found with you and made me doubt who I am. I hate you for that."

"Wow. Hate is a strong word." My hands start to shake, and I feel a pang of nausea. This isn't going well.

"Yes, it is, Larry. I hate what you did to me, what I allowed you to do to me. I was miserable for about a week, but after getting past my initial hurt, I decided to stop feeling sorry for myself. I've picked up my life where I'd left off last August, and have immersed myself in my work at the hospital. That's all I can handle right now."

I hate all this talk about feelings, so I run from it, and ask, "So where does this leave us?"

"'Where does this leave us?' That's all you have to say about what I just told you?"

"I don't know how to respond to what you just told me. This is all foreign territory for me. I don't know whether what I felt—feel—for you is love. I've never been in love. I just know that I miss being with you."

"Larry, this isn't getting us anywhere. I'm sorry, but I will need more from you, if I ever consider seeing you again. Right now, I don't think you are capable of giving me what I need."

"And what you need is for me not to screw other women?"

She looks at me for a few moments and a tear escapes and rolls down. "Larry, it's so much more than that. You would have to love me so much that you wouldn't consider touching another woman. I don't think you're anywhere close to making that kind of commitment, or if you're even capable of it. So I think we are done here."

She's right. I'm not capable of making that kind of commitment. Maybe I'll never be. I guess it's time for me to leave and let her go back to her life while I try to figure out what I do want.

"Maybe you're right. I can't give you what you want right now, even though I want to. I don't know how to love. I suppose I'd better find out."

She stands up and grabs her three-wood and turns to go to her tee box. She turns back to me and says, "Good bye, Larry. I hope you find what you want."

9

I sit on the bench for a few minutes, watching her. Finally, I realize that there is nothing more I can say, so I go back to my golf bag, pack up my gear and walk to my car.

Shit. I feel like I've just been lit up by the Yankees and sent to the showers.

*   *   *

During the next week, before I have to leave for spring training, I try to get on with my life without Gina. I try to forget about her when I'm in the arms of another woman, but it doesn't work. Gina's still in my head most of the time. I guess I'm not over her yet.

This could be a problem.

Chapter Three

M_y flight arrives at Phoenix's Sky Harbor Airport an hour late. I've spent the winter trying to keep my body and arm in shape, and the last two weeks ramping up my conditioning while trying to adjust to life without Gina. Now our flight is late. The airlines treat you like they're going to throw you a brush-back pitch when you're looking for the ball out over the plate. Hard, up and in, with little regard for your welfare.

While our plane sits on the tarmac waiting for our gate to clear, I stare out the window at the heat rising in waves from the pavement. Warm Phoenix weather will be a welcome change from the near-freezing cold we've had in the Bay Area.

Now that I've been firmly banished from Gina's life, I pull out my cell phone and dial a couple of women I know in the area. All I get is their voicemails, so I leave messages. I'll hear from them at some point. When, not if, my ego is telling me.

When we finally pull up to the terminal, I put on my suit jacket, gather up my gear, and exit the plane. My contract year is about to begin.

At baggage claim I see a limo driver holding a sign that simply says "Larry." I wave to him and he retrieves my bag from the carousel. Inside the limo's cool, I ask him to take me to the Enterprise rental car office on 44th Street.

Thankfully, the rental office is devoid of customers. I use this out-of-the-way location because I don't have to deal with throngs of people here. I claim the Cadillac Escalade I have reserved, and after the obligatory tour of the midnight black vehicle, I head off to the condo that Rick Wycliffe and I have rented in Scottsdale.

Rick and I have talked in the past about buying a condo together here in the Valley of the Sun, but Rick says he'd rather not invest the money. He will be a a free agent at the end of the season, too. So he's gun-shy about making any investments until he knows how much he'll make and where he'll be playing next year.

As for me, I don't like making commitments, even to real estate. Gina flashes across my mind.

"Go away," I say out loud to the windshield. "I am not ready to get married, and you're no longer in the picture anyway, Gina. So fuck off!"

I grab my luggage out of the back of the Escalade and let myself into the condo. Rick comes bounding down the stairs and gives me a big bear hug. "Hey, Buddy. Great to see you!" He looks at his watch. "I guess your plane was late. You could probably use a beer." He reaches into the fridge and shoves a cold bottle of Heineken at me without waiting for a response.

"Thanks. You're a star." I chug a few swallows. "Man, it's nice to be in warm weather."

"Yeah. It's perfect for baseball, and the paper says it will stay in the seventies for the next week or so. Then it'll get warmer and we'll wish we had this weather back."

I grab my bags and head upstairs to see what room Rick has left for me. He follows me up the stairs, holding our two beer bottles. It's so good to be back in the baseball world with my best friend. He doesn't carouse around with women or do drugs like some of the other married guys do. He's a good role model. In my current state, I could do worse than to emulate him.

"Hey, Larry, wanna grab some chow later?" he asks, dropping onto the other bed in my room. He's wearing Bermuda shorts, and a faded Rolling Stones tee shirt. He kicks his flip flops onto the floor and looks like he's hanging out at the beach with his hands behind his head and ankles crossed. All he needs is a pair of shades to complete the picture.

Rick drove in from California this morning in the Hummer 2 he bought last year in a moment of weakness. Cindy was really pissed, so he drives to Arizona to avoid airfare and spending money on a rental a car.

"Sure," I say. "Dinner sounds fine, if I can't line up some female company for the evening. I'll let you know by six, okay?"

Rick shakes his head, his thick eyebrows forming a frown. "You and your fuckin' stones! Aren't you ever going to settle down?"

"Yeah, Yeah. You're a broken record."

He starts to say something, hesitates, and then plows ahead anyway. "Hey, how are things going with Gina?"

"Next subject," I say, with more irritation in my voice than necessary.

Rick just shrugs. He gives me a look but keeps his mouth shut and unrolls a *Sports Illustrated* that he retrieves from his back pocket. He buries his face in the magazine, but lowers it when I drop my game console onto the dresser. "Oh good. You brought your Madden game." He smiles wickedly. "Are you sure you want to take me on?"

"Are you kidding? Bring it, bro. A hundred dollars a game? Fifty?"

"Shit, a dollar is about all I can handle. It's early in the year and Cindy will have my ass if I gamble away any serious money. Three kids are expensive now that they're getting bigger. Geez, every week there is something else they need for school, sports, or new clothes, and it all costs a ton of money. Not to mention the thought of three college tuitions in the future." He shivers at that expensive thought.

By six, it becomes obvious that I am not going to hook up tonight. Rick has moved to his bedroom and is snoring, obviously tired from his long drive. I don't have the heart to wake him so I settle back against my stack of bed pillows and read the copy of *USA Today* that I took from the plane. When he comes to, we order pizza from a take-out service and turn in early.

Chapter Four

The next morning, after a good night's sleep, we head out in my Escalade to the Renegades' minor league spring training facility at Papago Park, where we'll work out for the first week or so. The complex is located in the middle of a huge desert landscape surrounded by Phoenix's urban sprawl and appears suddenly as you round a curve in the middle of the desert scrub. Big red rocks punctuate the skyline, and saguaro cactus and weird trees look like they were dropped from another planet.

I park under a smoke tree which offers very little shade. The sun's reflections off the other players' cars dance in the waves of heat radiating from the black hood of my Escalade.

On the way in from the parking lot we follow a bunch of young guys I've never seen before. One of them turns, sees me, and asks, "Aren't you Larry Gordon?"

The rest of the young players turn around in unison and smirk, probably waiting to see if their fellow rookie gets skewered by me. My reputation precedes me.

"Yeah. Who are you, rookie?" I ask him.

"Name's Darren Clarke, Mr. Gordon." He thrusts out his hand.

When I don't respond in kind, he quickly withdraws his hand and looks embarrassed, undoubtedly afraid he's broken some unwritten rule.

I've never heard of him so he must be a non-roster invitee. He probably got called-up to Triple-A near the end of last season because he impressed one of our scouts.

"Where'd you play last year?" I ask, trying not to sound too interested.

"I finished up with the Sacramento River Dogs," Darren says.

A non-roster newby. Knew it!

Because rookie hazing is an art form on this team, a put-down almost jumps out of my mouth, but I was in his shoes not that long ago, so I decide to go easy on him. What's happening to me? Last year I'd have cut him to shreds.

Instead, I say, "Great! Let me know if I can help you in any way, and call me Larry," and offer my hand.

"Gee, thanks... uh, Larry. Thanks a lot!" His eyes are big as quarters as he shakes my hand and blushes to the roots of his fair hair.

I turn and head into the clubhouse, leaving him there to take the ribbing from his friends. Once inside, I find my locker near the other starting pitchers and stow my gear. We give each other high fives and man hugs all around.

"I just met a rookie named Darren Clarke," I say to no one in particular. "He fucking called me Mr. Gordon!" We all have a good laugh at that.

Our pitching coach this year, Bud Tanaka, overhears this and stops by my locker. A paunchy Asian in his early fifties with straight salt and pepper hair, Bud always has a smile and a good word for everyone. He used to be a scout, and for the last few years he's been the pitching coach for the Sacramento River Dogs, our Triple-A minor league affiliate. He scouted me at the University of Texas and considers me one of his successes.

"Hey, Larry, that's not just 'some rookie.' Wait until you see him throw. I worked with him last year at Triple-A. He has a decent fastball and slider, but a truly wicked curve." A smile splits his face. "He reminds me a lot of you six or seven years ago. You could be real valuable to the kid. Cut him some slack."

Not! Watch out for the shaving cream, rookie. I remember my first year at spring training. It seemed like every time I turned around I was met with a towel full of the stuff.

I head off to the weight room and spot Darren jogging on a treadmill. "Hey, Darren," I say, trying to be nice. "Did you get any sleep last night?"

Sleep is difficult the first night at spring training. Nerves and worries keep your mind fizzing until dawn. It suddenly hits you: Oh, my God, I'm actually at spring training with the Big Team! It's enough to make you shit your pants.

"A little, I guess, uh... Larry." He reddens again, and ups the speed of his jog.

I smile. "A word of advice. Don't forget you're a rookie. And watch your backside at all times while you're here."

15

I head off to the other end of the weight room to stretch. Next I do squats and lunges to tone up my legs. Then I move on to rotator cuff exercises. Bud says he swears by them to protect his pitchers' shoulders. Next I run thirty minutes on the treadmill and lift some weights.

Even though it may not fit my macho veteran persona, I also do some Pilates and yoga. Pilates strengthens my core muscles, giving me more velocity on my fastball. I can certainly use that. Yoga helps me to be calm and relaxed, especially on the days I pitch. I take some shit from the guys for doing the New Age stuff, but it works for me, and I could use some calm right about now.

Soon our head trainer, Jake Martinelli, calls me to the training room for my assessment. A tall, muscular guy with a toothy grin, he extends one hand for a shake and claps me on the back with the other. "Hey, great to see ya, Larry. This is your big year. How are you feeling about that?"

"Okay, I guess. I'm a little worried about the contract thing. And there's a possibility I might not be here next year."

Damn. I hate thinking about maybe playing somewhere else next season.

"Sorry to hear that," he says with a smile. "I wish I had some good advice for you."

"It would be a huge change for me not to wear this uniform. I'd miss the fun and games in our clubhouse, and I'd really miss the guys." I give him a friendly punch with my non-pitching hand. "I'd even miss you, Jake!"

"Yeah, well I'd miss you, too." He slaps the examining table and motions for me to climb up.

Jake puts me through his assessment routine of muscle and frame analysis, stretches, and strength moves. I've followed my workout program this winter better than I have in the past. And what else was there to do in the last two weeks after getting dumped by Gina?

"You're in the best shape I've seen you in at this time of year," he says. "Just keep doing what you're doing, and follow your usual strength and conditioning program. You should be good to go for the season."

"Easy for you to say." My eyes follow the crack in the opposite wall that looks like the Dow Jones index having a bad day. Jake's not staring at free agency, I think, while toweling off my sweat. He

16

doesn't have to play day in and day out under the constant pressure to perform.

"Chill, Larry. You're not the first guy to go through a contract year, and you won't be the last. You'll be fine."

Jake pats me on the leg and pronounces me assessed.

I walk back to my locker to suit up and head out into the warm sun. I trot out to Field Number 1 to shoot the shit with the other veteran pitchers who are hanging out in shade of the dugout area. Our strength and conditioning coach, Don Farley, trots out, interrupts our fun, and sends us jogging around the warning track.

I shake my head and take off at a slow jog.

Chapter Five

When we're done for the day, Rick and I drive back to the condo. I check my cell phone to see if I have any calls from women. "You have no new messages," drones the electronic voice in my ear. Damn. No one has returned any of my calls. I feel like throwing the cell phone across the room, but Rick catches my arm in mid-pitch.

"You're going to need that if someone does call you back," he says, ever the voice of reason.

"Yeah. Yeah." I toss the phone onto the bed instead.

Rick just shakes his head at me and gets us each a beer from the fridge.

"Let's go to the Round Up," I suggest, thinking maybe I can hook up with someone there.

Rick gives me a funny look, but swallows his thoughts once again. With resignation in his voice, he says, "Okay. I guess I'll tag along. I gotta eat somewhere."

We leave the condo around six-thirty and head to the downtown area of Scottsdale. I gotta have wheels if I get lucky, so he follows me in his Hummer. Visions of gorgeous long-legged beauties dancing around naked flit through my brain. I could get a hard-on just thinking like this.

I shake my head clear and watch the streets of Scottsdale flash by. This place used to be one of the Southwest's original cowboy towns. Today it's the opposite, with upscale shops, restaurants and art galleries, and the San Francisco Giants' spring training facility. The Round Up is a throwback to the town's roots.

We all used to love the Pink Pony before it closed down a few years ago. Apparently, it's reopened but I hear it's gone upscale and expensive, and the food is not that good. The old Pink Pony was part of Scottsdale's long history and a great place to hook up. I have many fond memories of steamy nights of sex that started there. The Round Up, though fairly new, pales in comparison. However, it's the only real action in town now.

As we drive into the parking lot, I banish all thoughts of Gina and vow I will play the game of hooking up for the evening enthusiastically, just like old times. I salivate as I survey two well-endowed young women walking up to the front doors, both blondes with long strait hair and curvaceous bodies encased in tight-fitting short dresses. They look like twin sisters. With a smile on my face, I hear Aerosmith's "Back in the Saddle" playing in my head. "Come easy, go easy. Ridin' high already."

I pull into the space next to Rick, hop out and lock my Escalade. When Rick emerges from his Hummer, I say with a broad grin, "Damn Bro! This place draws beef like a magnet."

Rick winces at my metaphor and says, "Yeah. Whatever."

He locks his Hummer and turns to face me. "I hate that expression. Cindy would be all over you in a fury for calling a woman 'beef.' Can't you come up with something less offensive?" Rick goes back to what he's been doing a lot in the last twenty-four hours—shaking his head at me in disgust.

"Well, she's not here, now is she?" I look longingly at the door of the restaurant.

Rick sighs and says, "Okay, let's wade into the herd. Remember, man, this is your gig, not mine. I'm just along to get some dinner and try to keep you out of any real trouble."

"Gee, Rick. I'm sorry I dragged you along tonight. I don't need a lecture on metaphors or trouble. I'm just looking to get laid."

"Dude. I just care about you getting your sorry ass home in one piece."

"Give it a rest, Rick. I'm twenty-eight fuckin' years old, for Christ's sake. I can take care of myself!"

"The jury's out on that," Rick says, just loud enough for me to hear.

He looks like he has more to say, but he starts walking toward the restaurant.

After two strides he stops and turns. "Besides, bro, this time next year with your big contract you're going to have paparazzi all over you. Are you prepared for that?"

Paparazzi? Shit, I never thought about that. Can't worry about that now. This year it's all about my next start and my next piece of ass. I'll think about the fucking paparazzi at the end of the season.

Rick looks worried. He puts his hand out to stop me.

"Buddy, we've got a lot of history together, most of it terrific. But from where I sit, it looks like you're running as fast as you can, but you're not getting anywhere at the moment. I'm just looking out for your backside, bro. If I didn't think there was some hope you might grow up sometime soon, I wouldn't waste my time trying to mother you." He shoves his hands in his pockets, and his big brown eyes look at me with concern.

"Rick, I know you're worried about me, and I appreciate what you're trying to do. But I have to sort this out myself... so, let's go inside and see what happens."

I don't have to look at him to know that his head is shaking. I just blew off his advice again. I hate that he worries about me so much. Hell, I worry about me sometimes too. Well, not that often.

We walk through double oak doors into the restaurant area which is jammed. The décor is pure cowboy, lots of rough-hewn wood and bandana-print. Spurs, lariats, and steer horns adorn the walls and sawdust is liberally sprinkled on the floor. Families and tourists dressed for summer are eating gigantic platters of ribs or burgers and fries. It's obvious there's no action in this part of the place, so we continue on to the cocktail lounge.

Some of the Giants players we know are huddled near one end of the rustic bar surrounded three-deep by girls in very short sun dresses or tight tank tops and skimpy short shorts. Most have legs I could get lost in.

We find two empty stools near the middle of the bar and order drinks—Rick his usual Heineken, and a Gordon Biersch Hefeweizen for me, both of which they have on tap. I settle back to survey the young women trolling the crowd, lovely young things looking to hook up with a ballplayer, or failing that, a ballplayer wannabe.

"Thank God this place doesn't allow smoking," says Rick, who gave up that nasty habit over the winter. He breathes in and seems satisfied with the aroma of stale beer and competing perfumes. He looks wistfully at a tall brunette with large brown eyes and a curvaceous silhouette, and catches me watching him.

"I can still fuckin' dream, can't I?" His face reddens.

"Dude, Cindy wouldn't like to hear that."

"And she won't unless you tell her," he responds, glaring at me.

"Not me. My lips are sealed." My hands shoot into the air like a thief with a gun to his back. I know I look like an idiot, but what the hell. The Hefeweizen is providing its friendly buzz.

Rick settles back to pull on his beer, shoulders rounded, and shaking his head at me yet again.

I down a few swallows of my beer, surveying "the herd," as Rick so aptly called the female portion of the crowd.

"Now there's a tall drink of water that looks like just my type," I say, rising up to my full height with my feet on the bar rail. "I bet she'd fit my six-foot-four frame just fine."

I hop down and make my way over to the tall lanky confection in bright red jersey that hugs her body like skin.

"Hi. I'm Larry Gordon. Nice to meet you." I extend my hand while my eyes wander up and down, appraising the merchandise. She looks so hot in her chili-red tube.

Gina? Gina Who?

"Hi, Larry," she says, placing her slender manicured hand in mine. "My name's Gail Ostrofsky. I'm a big fan of yours."

Hell, I bet she doesn't even know who I am.

"Well, hello, beautiful, I've just become a big fan of yours." God, I sound like such an asshole. "Why don't you come sit down and let me buy you a drink."

She lets me guide her over to the bar. I indicate my barstool and say, "Sit right up here and make yourself comfortable."

Gail manages to get up onto the stool, revealing miles of shapely leg. Oh, Mama, how did I luck into this? Thank you, Rick! Now get lost.

Rick looks at me and smiles, grabs his beer and wanders down toward the Giants' end of the bar, relinquishing his role as reluctant wingman. I'm on my own now.

"What do you do?" I ask.

"I'm a lawyer, a civil litigator to be precise," she responds.

Oh, oh. Should I be worried about that? Too late.

"Well, you don't look like any lawyer I ever saw before." I feel like a cat about to pounce on an unsuspecting mouse. "Is this your first time at spring training?"

"No, I've been coming for a long time."

"I've never seen you before, and I'd remember you." I hope I'm not looking too predatory, because that's how I'm feeling.

21

She seems not to notice as she lets her gaze wander around the bar.

"I don't usually come to places like this," she says and looks down at her silver purse in her lap, its skinny strap hanging from one shoulder.

"This place is great. Aren't you enjoying yourself?" I sure am, running my eyes over her curvaceous body.

"Sure. I'm here this year with a couple of my college roommates, and they said I needed to loosen up a little. They took me to a boutique here in Scottsdale to 'modernize my look.' I don't know. It may be a bit much. What do you think?"

She hops off her barstool and twirls around for my benefit. Sure she doesn't know. She's workin' it real good.

I try to maintain my cool. "I think you look deliciously modern. What can I get you to drink?"

"A gin and tonic would be great." She regains her perch on the barstool, flashing even more leg.

She looks so hot swathed in tight red jersey that I'm starting to get a hard-on.

The bartender appears with her drink and I watch her raise it to her ruby lips. Um. Um. I'm looking forward to this.

We chat for a while, sipping our drinks, until I can't restrain myself any longer.

"How about we blow this place," I say, warming to my quest, "so I can get a better view of your 'new look'?"

"Well, I don't know." She looks around, probably scanning for her girlfriends. "I only just got here."

"Oh, come on. It'll be fun. There are way too many people here. And I want to see more than just your packaging up real close." I give her my winningest lustful smile.

She looks at me for what seems like an eternity. My grin broadens as I hear the Final Jeopardy theme playing in my head. The song ends abruptly as decision flashes into her eyes. With one swift motion, she launches her gin and tonic into my face.

Dripping wet, with a slice of lime and ice cubes now in my lap, I am unable to locate a single word to say. My neighbors at the bar are trying to suppress laughs. The room grows suddenly quiet and all eyes are on Gail and me.

She looks at me and says, loud enough for everyone to hear, "Nice to meet you, Larry Gordon. Now grow up!"

22

She whirls away from me, her swinging purse nearly slapping me in the face, and marches off to applause and catcalls. Her girlfriends materialize from the crowd and follow her out of the bar in lockstep.

After the girls make their exit, all eyes swing back to me.

Crap! I just made a fucking ass out of myself in front of a whole shitload of people, who, thanks to Gail, now know who I am. I'm so screwed.

The hundreds of eyes trained on me feel like little pin pricks as I try to blot the liquid from my face and clothes with a pile of cocktail napkins provided by the helpful bartender.

Feeling very alone and the center of much unwanted attention, I say to the guys near me at the bar, "Shit. The beeves are getting grouchy around here."

"Yup," offers one. "They're getting more uppity every year."

"There are plenty more where she came from," says another, gesturing toward a group of lovelies down the bar a bit.

Other guys offer more sympathy and wise cracks about beeves and broads, and I relax a little, enjoying the familiarity of testosterone in the air.

I look around for Rick who is still talking to some of the Giants down the bar. They're looking at me, obviously amused by my dousing. Rick, shaking his head in disgust, detaches himself from the group and walks toward me.

He plops down on the stool vacated by Gail, but only after wiping it off with some more of the cocktail napkins. "Gees, Larry, I guess you weren't very subtle."

I order another beer, and study it, watching the amber liquid catch the light, not wanting to attempt a believable explanation, but I can't help myself.

"Shit, Rick, all I did was suggest that she come back to the condo so I could get a better view of her 'new look.' Chicks are usually looking to score when they come trolling in a place like this, aren't they?"

I pick up my beer glass again and drain it. I say, mostly to myself, "It's always worked like a charm before. Maybe I'm losing my touch."

Rick just shrugs his shoulders and sips his beer in silence. I'm sure he'd like to give me a tongue lashing, but he swallows it with his brew.

I signal to the bartender for another Hefeweizen, taking several large gulps when it arrives. Staring at my glass, I watch the foam undulate as I swirl the liquid around. Who knows? Maybe I'm not in the mood for hooking up after all. That would be a first.

Gina pokes her way into my thoughts, and though I try to get her out of my mind, nothing banishes her.

Finally, I turn to look at Rick, and say, "Okay. You asked about Gina." My stomach contracts violently. "What do you want to know?"

"Well, I really like her. So does Cindy. We're hoping that you and she will join the ranks of us married folks."

The dreaded "M" word. I keep quiet, hoping he'll drop this train of thought, but no such luck.

"You know, Larry," he says. "Gina's pretty special. She's the best thing by far that's ever happened to you."

I shake my head, and say, "Rick, I guess I really don't want to talk about it."

"Hey, you could have fooled me," he says. "You brought her up."

I order us each another beer and chug about half of mine. What is this by now, three beers? Four? This had better be the last one. I have to drive myself home.

I put my glass down with a thud. "What the hell, I might as well get it out in the open."

I tell him how Gina and I were lying naked after some amazing sex when she dropped the marriage bomb.

"I can just imagine how you took that," he says.

"Yeah, I freaked out."

"What did you say to her?"

I take a deep breath and look at him. "All I said was something like, 'I've never lied to you or tried to mislead you. I'm a happy bachelor. I love what we have, but I've never promised you I would be monogamous, so I'm just not ready to settle down quite yet.' It sounded reasonable to me."

Rick looks at me for a long time and then shakes his head. "Jesus, Larry, did you just come out from under a rock? Don't you know that women really don't want to hear that their guy has been screwing around on them?" He takes a sip of his beer. "I can't believe you said that."

24

"Well, she shocked the hell out of me by bringing up the "M" word. We'd never even talked about love, so I was caught completely off guard." I take a deep breath and let it out with a whoosh. "I guess it was the wrong thing to say."

"Ya think?"

This is embarrassing. I feel my face flush bright red.

"So what did she do?" he asks.

"She went ballistic and told me I was a typical baseball player. 'Fit and gorgeous, but with no substance' were her exact words, and she stormed out the door. Since then, she won't return any of my phone calls.

"Any possibility of resurrecting it?"

"I don't think so. I saw her at the driving range a week ago and we talked. She made it pretty clear that unless I can make a commitment to her that includes my not fucking anyone else, she doesn't want to see me again. I couldn't make that commitment, so we went our separate ways."

Rick swivels his barstool around to face me. "You know, buddy, maybe it's time you settled down with one woman, and Gina's really terrific."

"Me? Settle down? Besides, she wants way too much from me." My shoulders drop in defeat. "Every time I think about a more permanent relationship with her, my stomach twists into knots."

"Yeah, but hear me out," he says, and takes a sip of his beer. "Buddy, you've been chasing tail for as long as I have known you. Hell, I used to chase tail right along with you until I met Cindy." He takes a swig of his beer.

"You've said Gina's different than your usual eye candy, and you've enjoyed her company a lot," Rick lets me chew on that one for a minute.

Then he grins. "Every time I see you after you've been with her, you certainly have the shit-eating grin of a happy man. Maybe you should give it some thought."

I look down at my beer. "I dunno, Rick. Could I do that? Be true to one woman?"

He swirls his remaining beer around in his glass as if the right words will appear there. After a minute, he looks up, and says, "You know, Larry, for a relationship to last, it can't be just about the sex. There has to be love, companionship, respect, trust. Do you love Gina?"

25

I let that hang in the air for a few seconds.

"I don't know the answer to that," I say, finally. "I've never been in love before. I don't know what that feels like. And Gina wants all that stuff you mentioned. Sex and having fun together has been enough for me in the past. And I don't know any other way to behave with women."

I take a few more swallows. I'm really feeling the beer all of a sudden. Maybe it's this conversation, not the beer. He's still looking at me, and he's probably not going to let me off the hook. After all, he's right. I did ask for this.

"Okay," I say, clearing my throat to stall. "Since you seem to need to be in the middle of my personal life, let me ask you a question. How did you know when you were in love? And when did you decide that you wanted to spend the rest of your life with Cindy? You were as big a hound as the rest of us single guys. What made you change your mind?"

He thinks a minute. "Hell, damned if I know. It wasn't any one thing. But after I'd dated Cindy for a while, all other women began to be less appealing. Once my feeble brain recognized that, I realized that I wanted only her, and I asked her to marry me."

I slouch down on the bar stool even further. "Well, my gin and tonic facial tonight was definitely a new low for me. I've always been Larry the Stud. Chicks used to fall all over me. It was never this hard to get laid before. What's happened to me?"

"Sounds to me like Gina's gotten under your skin and you can't get her out of your mind."

I let that sink in before responding. "So what do I do about it?"

"I don't know, man. But you'd better figure something out or it could mess you up on the mound."

That brings the conversation to a halt.

Why do I avoid any kind of commitment, except to baseball? My parents have a great relationship, but my older brothers aren't married either. Why have all three of their sons turned into sex hounds and haven't settled down by now? I really wish I knew the answer to that.

I decide to change the subject. "Maybe I'm just not cut out to be married, at least not yet," I say.

Rick looks at me for a long time then signals to the bartender for the tab. "Let's blow this place and I'll beat your ass at a game of Madden."

"In your dreams," I boast, though with this much booze on board, he probably will.

The bartender hands Rick the bill. I grab for it, but Rick's too fast for me tonight. "It's the least I can do for my best friend who's had an unexpected shower tonight," he says, smiling, and plunks down two twenties.

We leave the bar scene behind in Ricks car. I've had way too much to drink and drive. We can pick my car up in the morning. On the way back to the condo, we stop for some takeout burgers, since we never got dinner at the Round Up. We attack the food as if we hadn't eaten in days.

Back in the condo, Rick relieves me of forty dollars by cleaning my clock at Madden. I guess we're about even on the night.

Chapter Six

I'm starting the first exhibition game of spring training against the Milwaukee Brewers at our home field, Phoenix Municipal Stadium. My bullpen sessions the first two weeks this spring were very erratic—pitching so-so one day and positively awful the next. But I've worked a lot with Bud Tanaka, our pitching coach, and have begun throwing my pitches for strikes consistently. My last few bullpens have actually been quite good. So I'm looking forward to getting the ball today.

During my three innings, I allow a hit but nothing more, and the defense does everything right. We win the game, but it's really irrelevant. Winning isn't the goal at spring training. Pitching and playing well are. And the coaches want to see lots of guys, especially some of the minor leaguers, so no one plays more than three or four innings, and starting pitchers are lucky to get three this early in the spring.

As I gather my gear to head to the clubhouse, Bud Tanaka grabs my arm. "Chill a minute. Darren Clarke is coming in."

I think about blowing him off, but something makes me drop my stuff, and sit down next to Bud.

Just then the stadium announcer drones: "Now pitching, number 68, Darren Clarke." I watch Darren trot in from the bullpen and take the mound. He throws a few fastballs and curves, and then signals he's ready.

I watch as he goes into a full wind-up, with a high leg kick, and good movement forward, and delivers a fastball into the waiting mitt of Jason Gardelli, our catcher. The batter swings hard and misses, way behind the ball, almost screwing his feet into the ground, and falling awkwardly.

"Stee-rike one!" The umpire yells.

Dusting the dirt off his uniform, the batter steps back into the batter's box. Darren delivers the second pitch, a hard back-door

28

slider that crosses the rear corner of the plate as the batter watches helplessly, unable to pull the trigger. He glares at Darren.

"Stee-rike two!"

"Wow, this kid is good." I say to Bud.

"I told you so. Now wait for his curveball."

Darren throws a couple of fastballs away hoping that the batter will take a swing at a pitch outside the strike zone, but he doesn't take the bait.

Darren walks back up to the top of the mound and looks in to Jason for the sign.

"Here it comes," Bud says.

I watch Darren rear back and go through the identical windup of the previous few pitches and deliver the ball toward the plate but high. Right in front of the plate, the ball runs out of gas and drops down through the strike zone. Uncle Charlie. A thing of beauty.

"Stee-rike three!"

The batter, a veteran, turns to the ump and inquires about the location of the pitch.

When the ump ignores him and leans down to dust off the plate, the batter retreats to his dugout, shaking his head.

When the three-up-three-down inning is over, Darren walks off the mound, hiding his smile behind his glove.

I wait until he gets his accolades from Bud and the few guys still on the bench, mostly scrubs, guys who didn't start and who are not veterans. The others are already in the clubhouse or have left the facility. I waive Darren over to join me.

"Great job out there, Darren. And the curve that rang that guy up was awesome. Bud here says that you remind him of me five or six years ago. That's pretty lofty praise, Kid!"

"Thanks, Larry... Bud," nodding to each of us in turn.

"A word of caution, Darren. You may feel a little cocky now but it won't always be this good. You'll have days when you take the mound and you just won't have it."

"I know. I'm just enjoying this one for now," he says, while putting his pitching arm into the sleeve of his warm-up jacket.

"You keep on feeling cocky, Darren," I say. "But sometime soon you'll put a couple of guys on with walks or hits, and a number four hitter will swagger up to the plate and dare you to throw him a strike. You'll nibble around the strike zone and get the count to three balls and have to get it over the plate. The guy will send it to the seats and you'll be lifted for another reliever. You won't know what hit you."

Darren's shoulders round a bit, as some of his euphoria fizzles away.

"Taking a shelling is part of growing up in this game," I say. "It's not the end of the world. It's how you learn from those situations that will make you a great pitcher. You learn to stay sharp any way you can. Never underestimate the hitters. And Darren, always be cocky, even when you're losing."

Darren's shoulders slump further and he looks like I have completely deflated him after his good outing.

What can I say? The big leagues are a bitch.

"Darren," I continue. "I learned a mantra from Sandy Koufax when I was a kid and my dad took me to an event to meet him. He told me to 'Treat every pitch you throw as if there are two outs in the ninth inning of the seventh game of the World Series and the game is tied.' I wrote it down and kept it. I've shortened it to 'Ninth inning. Seventh game.' Saying it to myself during a game keeps me focused on what I need to do."

"Okay, Larry. Thanks for the advice. Maybe I'll try it."

"Be my guest. I hope it works for you."

Darren gets up, throws his shoulders back as if he is shaking off a heavy coat, straightens up a little taller and walks towards the clubhouse. To his receding back I say, "Hey, Kid. Watch yourself on your way out today. Career major leaguers like that last batter don't like a rookie making a fool of them." He waves an acknowledgement as he steps through the door into the cool air of the clubhouse.

I sit in the dugout for a while, reliving some of my most embarrassing moments on the mound.

Chapter Seven

We have a rare day off today and Rick and I decide to venture out in my Escalade to the Boulders Resort in North Scottsdale to play some golf. It's a beautiful course with lush fairways surrounded by all things desert. If you're not careful, your ball careens off one of the course's namesakes and winds up who knows where, totally unfindable. This makes for high scores and long afternoons. Rick says he likes the challenge. He's a better golfer than I am.

I learned to play golf only after I came up to The Show, and I struggle mightily through the first five holes, sacrificing dozens of balls to the golf gods. Rick doesn't fare much better.

When we get to the sixth hole, we stop at the refreshment stand and order hot dogs and a couple of beers. The booze may not make me play better, but when I can't find my ball, I won't care so much.

Just then the tee clears and it's our turn to hit. Rick strokes a laser shot down the middle of the fairway. I'm not so fortunate. My ball ends up behind one of the many boulders, and I have to take a penalty stroke and move my ball two club lengths. Story of my life these days. Why not the same on the golf course?

When I get back into the cart after hitting my approach shot, Rick drives us to his ball. He hits a nice three-wood shot which ends up in a bunker in front of the green. He gets back into the cart and asks, "Have you thought any more about trying to get back together with Gina?"

"Yeah, that's about all I've thought about. She is pretty special, I guess." I shake my head and look at him. "She's really great but after our conversation at the driving range last week, it's over."

He stops the cart at my ball and takes his pitching wedge and putter and heads up to the bunker where his ball resides. I grab my eight iron to hit my approach shot which lands on the green but rolls about thirty feet away from the pin.

I move the cart up to behind the green and grab my putter. Rick chips out of the bunker, his ball rolling to a stop two feet away from the pin. I take my time over my long putt and stroke the ball toward the pin. It stops about a foot short of the cup.

"Nice putt, man," Rick says, and claps me on the back. We sink our final putts and head to the next hole.

My head is still working on what Rick said. "Maybe it's better if I just sample the groupies and keep moving on," I say, while we are driving.

"Bro, you can't think like that. Gina clearly means something to you. She's got you tied up in knots. Either she's right for you and you work it out with her, or she's not. You need to find out."

We turn the corner and golf carts are lined up six deep waiting for this tee. Rick drives off the cart path and parks in the sparse shade of a smoke tree.

He gets a bottle of water from the cooler in the back of the cart, and after brooding for a bit, says, "Tell me why you're so bent out of shape about making a commitment to Gina?"

I look at him for a while without answering. Finally, I say, "I'm afraid if I commit to Gina, I'll slip with one of the groupies on the road. I don't want to see the look on Gina's face when she finds out. I saw that look in January and it's heartbreaking."

"Well, you're going to have to find out if you can keep a commitment sometime in your life. Why not now? With her?"

"I dunno, Rick," I say, and think about that for a few moments. "I know I need to make some sense of this thing with Gina. No woman has ever gotten under my skin the way she has. I don't like it, but at the same time I do. I'd really like to see her again, but I don't know if I can give her what she wants." This is so far out of my comfort zone that I'm sweating a lot more than the warm air warrants.

"I don't know what to tell you, man. Just keep an open mind and try to figure out what you really want. Until then, try to have some fun."

"That's what I'm doing, but I don't seem to be getting any closer to an answer. And dating is definitely not as much fun as it used to be."

Rick stares off into the distance for a moment and looks back at me, concern showing in his eyes. "I have been wondering if you are ever going to tell me what happened to you a few nights ago when you came back to the condo looking like someone had worked you over pretty good. I was worried about you."

Oh, God. How do I tell him about that fiasco? I grab a bottle of water from the cooler and gulp down several swallows. "Well..." I take another sip to stall as long as I can. "Some of the guys and I went back to the Round Up. I met a woman named Crystal who came on to me. We had a few Mojitos and ended up at her house." Man, I hate thinking about this, let alone telling it.

"Anyway, right in the middle of having sex..." I sigh and look hard at my water bottle. "... everything... sort of... shut down."

My face is hot and my hands are shaking. I look up for a second to see Rick's reaction but I can't read his expression.

Finally he says, "What did you do?"

"What could I do? I was so embarrassed that I got the hell out of there as fast as I could."

"Maybe it was something about her, or just a fluke," he says, always the optimist.

"I dunno, Rick. I just don't know."

"So does this mean no more trolling the herd?" Hope shows in his eyes.

"Not necessarily. I went out with the same guys the following night and hooked up with no problem." I smile. "Well, except that I bagged a real nympho who took me out to her pickup truck which had a camper shell on it and a bed in the back—a mobile crash pad. Everything worked just fine that night."

"That must have been a relief," he says with a big smile on his face.

"Yup. But afterward she asked me to autograph her tee shirt. I complied, but shit, her shirt already had quite a few autographs on it. I thought I was bad. That girl made me look like a virgin."

"Maybe you could learn something from that encounter. Did it ever occur to you that women that you fuck and ditch might have the same feeling about you?"

That stops me cold. Do I really make women feel like that?

I look at him and then down at my golf shoes. "I guess it's possible. I never thought much about what they think." I turn to him and smile. "Kind of selfish, isn't it?"

"Uh, yeah!" He says, and moves the cart to the tee. "Look, I don't know what to tell you, buddy. But I'm here if you need to talk."

"Thanks, bro."

We finish out our round of golf and grab some dinner at the resort. Over our delicious meals we try to solve all the problems of our potential contracts for next year, about playing baseball, and what's going on in the world. Anything but my botched relationship with Gina.

Driving home through the pungent night, each of us is lost in our own thoughts. As we pull into the parking space in front of the condo, I put the Escalade in park and look at Rick.

"I guess we'll both be striving for the same thing this year, getting a good contract. You and me getting lots of money and staying in the Bay Area. Let's hope it works out that way for both of us."

"Amen!" Rick says, and opens his door.

*   *   *

During the rest of spring training I pitch well. My performance in bed is back to Cy Young status, though I don't hook up nearly as often as I have in the past. Most nights Rick and I have dinner at a different restaurant and turn in early.

I work with Darren and he has a good spring. He's going back to Triple-A Sacramento. Hopefully, he has a good year and when the team needs to call up a pitcher, he'll get a shot. As we gather our gear in the clubhouse after the last game in the desert, I wish him well and tell him I hope to see him in Oakland.

Chapter Eight

I watch the late March rain course in rivulets down the floor-to-ceiling windows behind my agent, Bob Jacobs. He's the founder and head of Jacobs Sports Management, whose offices are located in the Transamerica Pyramid in downtown San Francisco. He's in his mid-forties, short and potbellied, and his scalp glints through the sandy blond hair on top of his head. He has a reputation for being a tough negotiator, which is why he's now my agent.

After the few pleasantries Bob can manage, he sits down and puts his feet up on his black lacquered desk. He looks at me for a long time before saying, "I'm sure you're probably aware of this, but there's no way you'll be staying with the Renegades. They can't afford to keep you after this season."

Bob's words hit me like a sucker punch. I've played ball with some of these guys since my Single-A days. So much for Rick and me staying in the Bay Area together. And what about Gina? This is not good news.

He notices. "Why the long face, Larry? With your record, every team should be dying to sign you!"

He drones on about my Cy Young award, my career 3.12 career ERA, and my eighty-four wins. Blah, blah, blah—just like every agent does, but what he's saying doesn't make me feel any better.

"It's just that I've played my entire career in the Renegades organization. I've made some good friends here." I take a deep breath to try to settle my nerves, and ask, "There's no chance of my staying?"

He smirks. "This is Major League Baseball, Larry. You know that."

"Maybe, but I wasn't expecting to have to face it quite so soon."

This conversation feels like the time I was called into the manager's office at Single-A and told to pack my things, that I didn't play there anymore. It meant a step up to Double-A Midland, but my feelings of exhilaration and doubts were at war with one another. Yahoo, I'm called up! I'm going home to Texas and Mom's home cooking. But can I succeed at the next level? Why do I have to leave my best friend Rick behind? This session with Bob feels like that one, but with major-league anxiety. Maybe a couple of deep breaths will stop my heart from hammering.

He grins broadly, his loafers still crossed on his desk and his clasped hands now mashing down his blond hair. "You're sitting in the catbird seat, Larry."

"What are you looking at in terms of money?" I ask.

His smile acquires a Cheshire-cat look. "I'm confident I can get you more than a hundred million dollars for four or five years with any number of teams. We'll probably start there and hope for a bidding war. I think I can position you to be one of the highest-paid pitchers ever, if not the highest."

Now my heart really races. Highest-paid pitcher ever? Is he serious?

His feline smile confirms that he is.

"Damn. That's a shit load of money!" I say.

Suddenly, excitement wins out over the doubts. I could buy a mansion, get a really fast car, a new set of pro-level golf clubs. I could give my mom that new kitchen she's always dreamed about. I won't have to worry about money ever again.

I can't believe this is really happening.

My mind wanders off again. I did succeed at Double-A, staying at first in my old bedroom at home, and getting to spend lots of time with my parents. Rick got called up a month after I did, when one of our relief pitchers went on the disabled list—the "DL" to us guys. Rick and I rented an apartment, even though Mom and Dad said he could stay at our house too.

We were both promoted the following year to the Triple-A Sacramento River Dogs, where I spent almost two full seasons. My confidence level grew along with my abilities, but it was nerve-wracking waiting to be called up to the Majors. I have always lived in the moment on the field. I tune everything out. The chaos of the present fades away and I'm in the zone. That's as close to God as I know how to be.

The pressure to perform that comes in one's contract year is a whole new thing. I've seen it eat at a guy's core, undermining his focus, and screwing with his mind. One of my coaches once said, "No one ever thrives under pressure. Some just learn to survive it."

Can I survive this burden and perform well this season? Or will I crumble?

Bob snaps me back to reality by clearing his throat. "So what's going on inside that big head?"

"Sorry," I say. "This is all mind-boggling. I had a good year last year, but I also had my moments of disaster. I wasn't thinking quite that high."

"The market's escalated a bit over the winter." He takes a swig of his coffee. "I've had general talks with the Red Sox, Dodgers, Cubs, Yankees, Rangers, Mariners, and the Giants, and there will be others toward the end of the season. Some of those teams should be willing to talk big money when the time comes, providing they're still interested in a premier starting pitcher."

Those are all great teams, especially the Red Sox, Yankees and Dodgers. Visions of playing in pinstripes in Yankee Stadium flash through my brain. Or pitching in Dodger Stadium. Or Fenway. Any of them would be so cool. And, if I could sign with the Giants, I wouldn't have to move away.

I shake off these jumbled thoughts. "All this is super news, Bob, but kinda mind blowing."

Emotions and memories clamber again for attention, causing my heart to pound. When I was finally called in to talk to the River Dogs' manager five years ago, I was raring to get to the majors. I was confident—even cocky. I knew I could succeed. I was going to The Show.

I had my share of stumbles early on in the big leagues as most guys do, but the prospect of going back to Triple-A was enough to keep me focused on my job. In the last five years I've achieved all those things that Bob rattled off, and now I'm about to reap the benefits of that success.

So why do I feel like I might have a heart attack?

I lean forward, elbows on knees, and look at the floor. I hope I can live up to all that money and the pressure to perform that will come with it. My gut contracts to the size of a pea. I try to stuff my feelings in the vault in my brain where I park my thoughts while I'm on the mound, and focus instead on the fact that my dad will be so proud.

Bob drops his feet to the floor with a thud, which pulls me back to the present again.

"Come on. You should be happy," he says. He's sitting forward, smiling as if talking to an insecure child, which at this point is pretty close to the truth.

"Look, you've had a great run with the Renegades. You deserve to get a big contract." He looks at me and chuckles. "Hey, the big bucks are what you hired me for, aren't they?"

His broad grin widens and all I see on his face is dollar signs, so I take a deep breath and force all doubts back into the vault and slam the door. Sitting up, I throw my shoulders back, and look him in the eye. Confidence restored, at least for now.

"Yup. You're my pit bull." I say, with a smile.

Bob looks at his watch and stands. Guess it's time for me to leave. "Knock 'em dead this season, Larry," he says.

I shake his hand, and say, "Thanks for doing this for me. I'll get my head around what you said and do my job."

Highest paid pitcher ever, I muse, as the elevator glides down to the parking garage. I can't wait for the season to begin. Pressure or no pressure. Playing baseball is what I do and who I am. Bring it on.

Chapter Nine

Yesterday we finished up the annual pre-season series with our cross-town rivals, the San Francisco Giants, taking two games out of three. The team flew up to Seattle last night. We open the season tonight against the Mariners, so Rick and I have some time to relax in the Emerald City before reporting to the ballpark to begin a new baseball season.

This morning Rick and I are doing the tourist thing. Rick is decked out in faded jeans, a well-worn Grateful Dead tee shirt, and a beat-up brown leather bomber jacket. I'm in my usual uniform: khakis, a navy polo shirt and a dark green Ralph Lauren sweatshirt. We both are hiding behind our sunglasses, as much because of the unusual bright sunlight as our need for a disguise. We look like the odd couple but try to blend in with the other tourists out on the town.

Seattle is a beautiful city. Lots of water. Not too hot. And plenty of gorgeous women.

We decide to wander around the downtown area. It's a rare sunny morning and the air smells clean, having been washed by last night's rains.

Pointing to the Space Needle, which is visible between the buildings up ahead, I say to Rick, "I bet the view from up there is spectacular today. Wanna go?"

"Sure," he says, and we take off at a brisk pace in the sparkling sunshine. We purchase our tickets and take the elevator up to the top, five-hundred-twenty feet above the ground, according to the brochure we got with our tickets. Out on the observation deck we stop every few seconds to look at the sparkling panorama of Seattle's wonders visible in the crystal clean air.

Mount Rainier wears a cap of gleaming white, dwarfing the rest of the Cascade Range to the east and the Olympics to the south. To the southwest, Puget Sound is a deep blue, dotted with whitecaps in the fresh breeze. Ferry boats slice through the waves, taking people and vehicles to various places. Further to the north, float planes take off and land on Lake Union, looking like ungainly birds.

Rick leans down and looks through one of the telescopes and is pleasantly surprised to find it works without having to insert coins. He points it to the south and chuckles. "Look. There's our home for the next three days."

I look through the eyepiece and see Safeco Field with its roof retracted, waiting for us in the brilliant sunshine. I am looking forward to getting this season under way but I'm apprehensive as well. I have to be at the top of my game this year to maximize my value in the free agent market. God, I hope I can do it. At least, I had a decent spring.

After making one circuit around the observation deck, my stomach is growling so we walk down one floor to the Sky City Restaurant for lunch. A hostess shows us to a table next to the window and we order our usual beers. I look over the menu. The food choices look great and the back of the menu has some "Fun Facts" about the Space Needle.

Rick chuckles. "Did you know that this restaurant rotates one complete turn every forty-seven minutes?"

"Nope," I say, and go back to dealing with the more important issue of what to eat for lunch.

Rick pulls down my upturned menu with his forefinger and looks at me with a wicked grin. "Hey, Larry. This is one place where the world looks like it actually revolves around you." He pokes me in the arm and enjoys his joke at my expense.

I decide to ignore the verbal and physical jabs and ask, "It doesn't feel like we're moving, does it?" I look around for any evidence that we are not stationary.

Rick replies without looking up from studying the back of the menu, "I think I can feel a faint rumbling."

He reads for a second and says, "This is amazing. Do you know that it only takes a one-horsepower engine to turn this whole restaurant? That blows me away."

Rick is a trivia nut and likes learning little-known facts and inflicting them on his family and friends. He continues devouring and sharing the tidbits of data on the back of the menu while I admire the spectacular view, happy to have such a good friend to share it with.

Watching Seattle spinning slowly below me, the color of the water causes my mind to conjure up an image of china blue eyes and long blond hair. Gina, I wish you were here to see this awesome sight.

I try to shake these thoughts out of my head and look out over Puget Sound, to no avail. Gina, you'd love this view.

Dipshit, stop thinking about her, I growl inside my head. It does you no good.

When our plates are cleared, we order coffee and dessert. Rick reads my mind and asks, "So what's up with Gina?"

"I keep picking up the phone to call her, but then put it down again. She wants too much from me. The truth is I still don't trust myself around other women."

"Hey, man, maybe you still aren't ready to make a commitment yet." He leans back in his chair and cogitates a minute or two, his brown hair blown askew from our stay outside.

Rick looks up and says, "Okay, I'll change the subject." He hesitates for a few seconds, and asks, "Has that little problem you had in Phoenix cropped up again?" His brown eyes are full of worry, which makes me even more uncomfortable.

I breathe in deeply and let it out slowly, stalling. "Yeah. It happened again the night before we flew home from spring training, while you and your Hummer were in the middle of the desert somewhere. A couple of us went out to a new bar in Tempe, and I hooked up with a really nice girl. In the middle of it, everything shut down again, just like with Crystal." This is so embarrassing, even talking to my best friend. I am sure my face is beet red.

Rick turns on his warm smile. "Got any idea why that happens?"

"The only thing I can think of is that sometimes I have this feeling someone is watching me when I'm having sex. I'm pretty sure it's Gina. But what triggers it? I'm not sure. Maybe the girl says a word that Gina uses, or she plays with her hair like Gina does, or she has a familiar scent or body language. But something conjures up Gina at just the wrong time."

Rick smiles. "Sounds to me like it's the right time. This could be a message from your subconscious."

Shit, he sounds like Dr. Phil. I ignore the psychobabble. "Since we've been back in the Bay Area, I've been so afraid that she'll appear again and I won't be able to perform, that I chicken out and go home and take care of it myself. That I can do just fine."

"Well, it proves the plumbing works. It's better than nothing, at least until you figure out what you want to do about Gina." He grins. "When Cindy was very pregnant, I used to…" He looks away and his face reddens. "Well, you get my drift."

I smile at the fact that someone other than me is uncomfortable talking about jerking off.

"So I'm living a very boring life. But it is what it is, and I'm dealing with it as best as I can," I say.

We pay the bill and take the elevator down. Rick informs me that the elevator travels at eight hundred feet per second, about the same speed as a falling raindrop. Menu tidbits again. "Since snow falls slower than rain," he says, "if you are descending in the elevator while the white stuff is falling, it looks like it is snowing up, not down."

I just shake my head.

We emerge from the elevator and head in the direction of the water, pulled there by the magnet of the magnificent blue.

We walk on in silence, my mind racing all over the place. How do I really feel about Gina? Do I love her? Scary thought. Can I be true to her? What would I do if some gorgeous girl slinks up to me and my dick pays attention? Can I resist that temptation? I've never been able to before. But I've never had a reason to say no before. Right now, I'd have to say that I'm not sure I could say no.

I know that Rick is right about this. I need to find out and the only way I can is to test myself with other women. But it's such a gamble. Maybe I'll get an answer I don't want. Shit, I'm so fucked up.

"Hey," Rick says with a smile. "Did you know that when the Space needle was built in 1962, it was the tallest building west of the Mississippi?"

It's not fair. All he seems to worry about is enjoying life. Why can't I have what he has?

Gina pops into my head and refuses to go away. Last opening night she was in the stands. I felt as if I could do anything, knowing she was there. This year I'm on my own. I'm confident I can do a good job on the hill, but there was something sweet about seeing her there as I leave the mound, something I'll have to learn to live without this season.

Chapter Ten

Great hoopla and ceremony surround the start of a season's opening game, and it's no different here in Seattle. The fronts of the upper decks are draped with red-white-and-blue swags, and the emerald green field is in pristine condition after the winter off. Rock music blares on a terrific sound system, and a feeling of expectancy hangs in the air.

Safeco Field is a great baseball venue, for the players and the fans. It's a relatively new ballpark—decades newer than ours—and the visitor's clubhouse is one of the nicest in the league. The fans are great, even though they aren't rooting for us. Here everyone is very polite, unless one of the Mariners' ballplayers screws up. Then they're merciless.

About ten minutes before game time, the resonant disembodied male voice of the stadium announcer welcomes the crowd to a new major league season in Seattle, and begins to introduce the Oakland Renegades. One by one as our names are called, the coaching staff and our guys line up on the third base line to mild applause.

I'm warming up in the bullpen with backup catcher Johnny Perez, under the watchful eye of Bud Tanaka, our pitching coach. I'm feeling good. My fastball has some pop and Uncle Charlie is dropping like a stone. Adrenaline pulses though me with the anticipation of a new season.

The Stadium announcer says, "And in the bullpen for the Renegades, today's starting pitcher, number fifteen, Larry Gordon." Adrenalin spikes through my body at the sound of my name.

I love pitching the opening game of the season, even when it's on the road. I'm amped up and raring to get the season started with a win. It's like taking off on a long-awaited vacation, full of anticipation and hope for a good time ahead. The fans give off the same vibe. We play one hundred sixty-two games each year, but opening night is really special.

With a fanfare of extra loud music, the amplified voice raises a few decibels and says with great vigor, "Ladies and Gentlemen. Here are your Seattle Mariners!"

Peppy music blares and I turn my attention back to my warm-up. I throw a few more fastballs that paint the edge of the plate, and Bud nods approval.

The booming voice tugs me back to the field when he shifts into his next gear. "And now your Seattle Mariners starting lineup." More loud music and thundering applause.

"Playing right field and batting in the first position, Takeo Shimada." The audience cheers wildly, "Ta—ke—o! Ta—ke—o!"

Shimada has been my nemesis on the Mariners ever since he burst on the scene from Japan five years ago. I have a really hard time keeping him off the base paths. He can hit absolutely anything I throw at him, and he runs like the wind. Maybe I'll just walk him. No, I can't do that. Not the leadoff hitter in the first at-bat of the season.

I force my attention back to the bullpen and throw some curve balls. They are really diving today. As long as I can get them over the plate, the batters should have a terrible time swatting at them.

The umpire calls "Batter up!" and the game begins. I can tell by the intermittent cheering that Felix Sanchez, the M's hot young pitching phenom, is dispatching our hitters easily. No surprise there. He's a great pitcher.

Before I know it, the bullpen guy tells me it's time to go. I gather my warm-up jacket and bottle of water, take a deep breath, and say a little prayer for luck. The door opens and Bud Tanaka, Johnny Perez, and I walk out on to the field. They head toward the dugout and I walk to the mound. For me, another baseball season is about to begin.

I throw a few warm-up pitches to get the feel of the mound and, with a wave of my glove, declare myself ready. I feel really confident I can beat these guys. Piece of cake, I chuckle to myself.

Shimada, the leadoff batter, walks to the plate, takes a few practice swings, and steps into the batter's box.

Okay. Here we go. Ninth inning. Seventh game. World Series.

I step onto the rubber, lean down and look in for the sign. One finger by Jason's right thigh. Fastball inside. I go into my wind-up and deliver the ball but it bends too much and crosses the middle of the plate. Takeo pounces on it and strokes my first pitch of the season into the right field seats for a home run. The crowd goes nuts, the roar deafening.

Piece of cake, my ass!

I walk around the mound on the infield grass and chant to myself. Ninth inning. Seventh game. I take a deep breath and let it out with a whoosh. It's only one run, I tell myself. I can do this.

Arlen Jones steps in and takes a few practice waggles with his bat. I waste a few pitches that run outside the strike zone to see if he'll swing at them, but his bat doesn't budge.

Jason puts down three fingers, a slider. I deliver the pitch to his glove but there isn't much movement on it, and Jones hammers the ball on the fly to the wall in deep center for a triple.

"Fuck!" I scream into my glove as I back up third base.

Jason asks the umpire for time, then trots out to the mound, and asks, "Are you okay?"

"I'm fine. I'll get this guy out." I'd better. This is fast becoming a disaster.

Jason gives me a stern look and walks back to his crouch behind home plate.

I walk around slowly and step back up onto the mound. I scuff up the dirt in front of the rubber to kill some more time and try to settle my nerves. What the hell happened to my great warm-up?

When I look in for the next sign, Jason puts down one finger and I throw a fastball in on Jackie Bell, missing the strike zone for ball one. The next pitch is a carbon copy of the first with the same result. The fingers now show slider which I throw perfectly over the corner of the plate, but the umpire calls it ball three. I step off the rubber and grab the rosin bag, then drop it in disgust. This can't be happening. I've got to focus and get this fucker out.

Jason shows fastball again and I deliver one down the middle of the plate. Bell was taking all the way and the bat stays on his shoulder.

Call that a ball, ump!

"Stri-eek!" he growls.

There that's more like it. Three and one. Runner on third, and nobody out.

Jason calls for Uncle Charlie who doesn't dive like he's supposed to and Bell trots down to first base with a walk. Double fuck!

45

Bud Tanaka, our pitching coach, hustles out of the dugout toward the mound.

"What's going on, Larry? Something wrong?"

"No. I feel fine," I say into my glove so no one can read my lips.

"Well, get it together or we are going to be down a few runs." He looks at Jason and then back at me. "There's not much movement on your pitches and you seem a little scattered. Jitters? Amped up?"

"Maybe a little amped up. I'll get the next guy out." I wish I could be sure I could deliver on that promise.

"You need to settle down. Let's get out of this without any further damage," he says. Jason nods in agreement.

When the umpire approaches the mound, Bud turns and marches back to the dugout. Now the Mariners have a run in, runners on first and third and nobody out. Helluva way to start a season.

On my first pitch to left-fielder Pablo Ruiz, Bell steals second base, eliminating the possibility of a double play. Shit!

After that, Ruiz works me hard. I throw a lot of good pitches, and he keeps fouling them off. Seventh inning. Seventh Game of the fucking World Series. I feel frustrated enough to scream it out loud. But I swallow the words instead.

With the count three-and-two, Ruiz wins the battle on the fifteenth pitch which paints the edge of the plate, but the umpire calls it ball four. I glare at the umpire. Ruiz jogs down to first, loading the bases. Well, the double play is back on the table, but first I need to get a strike out or an infield fly ball.

Ryan Campbell steps in. On a two-and-one count, he gets a piece of a hard slider and grounds to second. We turn the double play, but Bell scores from third. Now we're down two runs, and it's only the first inning. But at least there are now two outs. I can't believe this. I had such a great warm-up.

I walk off the back of the mound and pick up the rosin bag. After rolling it around my fingers, I throw it down angrily, raising a little puff of white powder when it hits the ground. Focus! Get the next fucker out.

I throw two fastballs on the outside corner of the plate to Bobby Black for two quick strikes, and then deliver a diving slider. Black takes a mighty swing and I hold my breath, but all he connects with is air. Strike three. Inning over.

Relief floods in. But I look up at the scoreboard, and my heart sinks. It says I just threw twenty-six pitches in the first inning. That's more than two innings worth.

I negotiate the two cement steps into the dugout with my head down, crunching peanut shells and sunflower hulls on the way to my seat. The guys leave me a wide opening on the blue plank bench. They look everywhere but at me. What a way to start the season!

I drop my glove on the ledge behind the bench and put my pitching arm into the left sleeve of my warm-up jacket. Slumping down heavily, I stare into space, eyes unfocused and stunned. Horrendous, just horrendous! Twenty-six fucking pitches. At this rate I won't make it beyond the fourth inning. Coop has got to be shitting his pants. Keep this up and there goes my big free-agent deal!

The bench is deathly quiet. No one talks to me, which is how I normally like it on the day I pitch. But today I feel an arctic chill all around me. I can hear them thinking: Nice going, Larry! You're our best pitcher and we're down a quick two runs in the first inning of the opening game.

Superstar, my ass!

In the top of the second, Felix Sanchez continues throwing bullets on the edge of the plate for three quick outs, and our guys go down quietly.

I come out to pitch the bottom of the second and things improve greatly. My pitches are breaking like they are supposed to, and I dispatch three batters with only seven pitches. Now that's more like it.

I'm my old self for the next three innings, getting the necessary outs and keeping my pitch count low. Unfortunately, we can't get a runner past first base, so it's still two to nothing Seattle after five innings. We keep fouling off Felix' pitches so his pitch count is getting up there. That's at least some consolation.

In the top of the sixth, we tie the game up when Frank Matson works a walk and Nick Hayner gets a hold of one of Felix' fastballs and blasts it into the right field seats. Hey, maybe I can salvage a no-decision out of this, or even a win.

I cruise through the bottom of the sixth, three up, three down. In the top of the seventh, Sanchez reaches his pitch count and the Mariners bring in Julio Ruiz. Last year we trashed him royally, so my hopes soar. Our guys score two more runs before Ruiz is lifted and Jake Creamer comes in and shuts us down. We're now up four to two. Unfortunately, my pitch count is at ninety-two. That twenty-six-pitch first inning was a disaster.

I walk out to the mound to pitch the bottom of the seventh, a little weary but happy that we have the lead. I strike the first two batters out on six pitches. As the ball makes its way around the infield, I think: Man, I can't wait for this game to be over. I'm looking forward to a hot shower, a few beers, and maybe something female. No. No. Erase, erase! We're not done yet. One more out to get.

A dull hush has hung over the stadium since we took the lead.

"Okay," I growl. "Let's do this." This is my last inning, most likely.

I look down at Jason and agree with his fingers. I go through my windup and confidently deliver the first pitch. Takeo Shimada leans in and allows it to hit him in the back. That fucker! The umpire points him toward first base.

The crowd resuscitates and cheers wildly.

Arlen Jones steps in and on the second pitch beats out an infield hit. The crowd roars. I stroll around the mound thinking: What's going on here? I'm still pitching well. That hit was a fluke.

Then, on a routine ground ball to second base, Jaime Cruz misjudges the hop and has to retrieve the ball from the outfield grass with no chance to get any of the runners. The bases are now loaded with two outs. The crowd goes nuts and the roar becomes deafening.

Shit! Sweat trickles down my face and into my mouth, tasting bitter like the anger I feel. I take off my hat and dry my face in the crook of my arm. I'm waiting for Coop to come out and yank me but he stays put in the dugout. I guess this is my inning to finish. This is why I'm going to make big money next year.

Ninth inning. Seventh game. World Series.

As I bring my hands to my belt, a flash of blond hair in the first row right behind Jason catches my eye but then disappears. It is replaced by a large sign that has my name on it.

I step off the rubber so I don't balk, and stare at the sign. It says: "Marry me, Larry!"

What the fuck?

I close my eyes and shake off the girl and the sign. Focus! Do your job!

Pitching from the stretch, I start toward the plate and the sign pops up again. Too far into my motion to stop, I release the ball, but it bounces wide of Jason's lunge and slams into the backstop, twenty feet behind home plate.

I should be covering home but I am suddenly paralyzed. Time slows to a crawl. Shimada on third takes off for home and scores easily, making it four to three, and the other runners move up one base. The Mariners' fans jump to their feet and the stadium thunders.

Rooted to the pitcher's mound, I am dumbstruck. What the hell just happened? Nothing in the stands has ever interfered with my concentration.

I come out of my paralysis when I see Jason approaching. Shit, here it comes!

"What the fuck was that?" he hisses.

"I... uh... my finger slipped. It won't happen again," I say into my glove. I can't admit I let some blond hair and a sign fluster me.

"It better not happen again!" he menaces. He looks at me for a long time, shakes his head, and storms back to the plate.

Oh, Man. Am I steppin' in it!

Back up on the mound I glance into the stands behind home plate, suddenly wondering, could it have been Gina? I don't think so. She's not speaking to me. Wait, maybe it was Lisa, that blonde who steamed up a spur-of-the-moment hotel room last September when we played here? There are a couple of blondes in that general area but no Lisa, and the sign is nowhere in sight either.

I go to the back of the mound to regroup, taking a few deep breaths. You've got two outs. You can do this.

Ninth inning. World Series.

I step back onto the rubber and stare down at Jason. Full count. Curveball in. Okay, good call. I glance heavenward, hoping for a miracle.

Looking over my shoulder at Jones on third, I come set and fix my eyes on Jason's waiting glove. Slide stepping, I deliver a perfect Uncle Charlie. The batter stands statue-like as the pitch floats down over the plate through the heart of the strike zone. The umpire punches the batter out, and the inning is thankfully over.

My heart is racing at how close I came to giving up the game. Big money, my ass. I should never have let the game get that close.

The noise from the stands evaporates like dew in the morning sun.

Rick pitches the eighth inning, striking out two, and Jud Johnson, our closer, finishes it up, neither man yielding any runs. We don't score either, so we win the game with the score of four to three, and I get my first win of the season.

When we file out to congratulate the guys coming off the field, I try to find the "Marry Me" sign or the blonde. The first row behind home plate is empty, and I scan the stands. No luck. Now I'm pissed. She almost made me give up the lead. Who was that girl? Why did she leave? And why was I so rattled?

In the locker room, I shower and dress, fending off the joking jabs from my teammates about the wild pitch and my narrow escape. I decline to join Rick and some others for dinner and get out of there as quickly as I can, grabbing something from the clubhouse buffet to take with me.

I take a taxi back to the hotel and pour myself a beer from the minibar in my room. I settle onto the fake leather couch to unwind from the game and turn on the TV, but I turn it right off again. I'm not in the mood for the eleven-o'clock news which has just begun, or anything else on TV. I should be happy with the win, but my stomach is saying otherwise.

I lean back, close my eyes and give in to my thoughts. If that wasn't Gina, who the hell was it? If it was Gina, why did she disappear? I pick up my cell phone and punch in her number, but put it back down without hitting the green talk button. I take another swig of beer and repeat the same routine, looking around at the paintings of ships and the hotel-beige curtains.

Finally, after I have drained the beer, I hit the talk button and get the same message I got in January: "Hi. This is Gina. Leave a message and I'll call ya back. Have a great day!" I wait for the beep, my heart pounding.

"Hi. It's Larry. Were you in Seattle at the ballgame tonight? I saw someone out of the corner of my eye and thought it was you. Please give me a call. I really need to talk to you."

I move on to Scotch and try to drink myself into oblivion. What do I do about Gina? I don't want to get married but I want to have a

50

woman in my life for more than one night, and I guess this episode tells me I want it to be Gina.

An irritating voice barks in my head: Yeah, well you had your chance and you blew it. What makes you think she wants to talk to you? You are not the marrying kind. Anyway, you don't need that distraction during your contract year!

"Go fuck yourself!" I rail aloud.

I hurl the glass across the room hitting the wall and sending ice cubes and broken glass flying. I get up and stumble off to bed, trying not to step on any shards of glass from my fit of anger.

As I collapse onto the sheets, drunk and spent, I lie there reeling from the booze and the events of the day. I realize that I'm going to have the mother-of-all hangovers in the morning. Serves me right!

Before long I pass out, silencing the chatter in my head.

Gina doesn't call me back.

Chapter Eleven

The sun is high in the sky this Monday in early July. The Renegades have the day off, and I'm eating a Subway sandwich by my pool in Danville, mulling over the season so far.

During April, May and June, I won more games than I lost—barely. When I'm pitching like the old Larry, I keep runners off the bases. But when I lose my concentration, I'm a wimpy bundle of nerves, and the other team scores runs in huge numbers. Consequently, I have six wins but I've also got five losses. My ERA is still way too high at 4.65, but it's down from the 6.50 it was at the end of April.

I'm in deep wallow about my disasters on the mound when my cell phone rings. I look at the display. Shit. Bob Jacobs, my agent. Should I let it go to voice mail?

Why does he always call when I don't feel like talking? I guess we players have to have them—you know, to deal with the legal shit, contract negotiations and that kind of stuff. But they're really ruining the essence of the game. It's no longer as much fun to play baseball; now it's all business. Worry about your stats. Don't make any mistakes. Keep your nose clean. All in search of that extra million bucks. It sucks.

After muttering a few four-letter words, I hit the green talk button. "Hi, Bob," I say, trying to sound upbeat, but dreading what's coming next. He says he's out my way and wants to meet ASAP, and before I know it, I tell him to come on over. I wait with a beer, trying to read the newspaper and failing miserably. My mind keeps wandering to the upcoming dose of reality.

The doorbell rings and I muster the best manners I can find and invite him in. I open a beer for him and we amble out to the back patio. It's a gorgeous day, sun blazing but not too hot and no humidity. My favorite weather for a Monday off day. Right now, I'd much rather be out on the golf course. Anything but having to deal with Bob Jacobs.

We take up residence on my two chaise lounges. The sun glints off his balding head, and sweat sprouts on his forehead. He gets up and takes off his suit coat which he hangs over the back of his chaise. After loosening his tie and sitting down again, he takes a huge swig of his beer and starts in on me.

"I gotta be honest, Larry, you're making my job fuckin' hard. You're losing too many ugly games."

Here's my ass chewing.

"And you don't act like someone in the middle of a contract year. Look at Trevor Jackson. He's ten and three. Mark Belding has nine wins. You've got six." He looks at me and shakes his head. "Your ERA has come down to 4.65, but that's not close to good enough. And those five losses are an embarrassment."

I feel like I've just been scolded by my father. Running my hands through my hair, I try to find some courage. "I'm trying, Bob. Really I am. But I can't seem to find my edge consistently. When that happens, I can't focus on doing my job, which is really unusual for me. I don't understand it."

"Do you have an injury that you're hiding? Having women trouble? Are you playing hurt? Larry, I need to know what's going on with you."

This really pisses me off. I've never hidden an injury. "No, Bob, I'm not hurt. I'm in better shape than I've ever been." A few deep breaths and my anger ratchets down. "As for my personal life, the woman I was dating last year broke up with me right before spring training, because I wouldn't marry her, and I can't seem to get her out of my head."

Bob looks all business. "Here's what I think. You'd better marry her or get over it ASAP. If you don't fuckin' resolve this, your value is gonna go way down, and the players' union is counting on you to set the market for pitchers this winter."

No pressure there. My stomach says otherwise.

He takes another pull on his beer. "You know? Your two problems could be related."

Now he thinks he's a shrink. What a tight-ass.

"Bob, I'll figure something out." I lie to myself while I study my beer bottle, not wanting to continue this dialogue. I try to rally some of my old bravado. "Hey, you know I always pull it together in the second half of the season." I try to convince myself that I can do it this time.

"Okay, Larry. I'm sorry to be hard on you, but a lot is riding on your doing well this year." He stands up and drapes his coat over his arm. "I'll take myself back to the office now and rag on some of my other clients. Thanks for the beer."

I make myself walk him to the front door and mumble a goodbye. After he's driven away, I walk out to get the mail, and sort through the stack as I amble back up the front walk. It's mostly junk, but there is one envelope obviously containing a card. Hmm, it's not my birthday. I don't recognize the handwriting.

I rip open the card which has a picture of a sad-looking bum on the front. Above the bum are the words "Cheer up! It could be worse!" Inside, the printed text states: "You could be down to your last nickel!" Very funny!

Written under that in a masculine ballpoint scrawl is, "A great pitcher once told me to focus on every pitch as if it's the ninth inning of the seventh game of the World Series and the score is tied."

There is neither a signature on the card nor a return address on the envelope. The postmark says Sacramento. It's gotta be Darren Clarke, the rookie from spring training. How did that little shit have the balls to send this to me?

I walk through the house, grabbing another beer, go out to the patio, and flop down heavily onto a chaise. I mull over what Bob said and Darren's card, as I suck on my beer.

Ninth inning. Seventh game. Score tied.

I sit for a long time, beer bottle in hand, staring at the flowers that have miraculously survived my benign neglect. I close my eyes and try to sort out this tangle. Finally, I come to the conclusion that I don't have any answers. Maybe I should talk to somebody.

I walk into the house and call Rick. Fortunately he is home. "Hey, buddy, what's up?" he asks, cheerful as usual.

"I'm not sure." I pause to take in a deep breath. "I really need to talk to someone, and I was hoping you could come over for a beer."

I hear muffled conversation on the other end of the phone.

Rick takes his hand off the phone's mouthpiece. "Sure, I can do that, but let me finish up the wall I'm painting for Cindy and I'll be over in a half hour or so. Okay?"

"Great! See you then. I'll be out in the back yard. Just let yourself in." I hang up the phone, unlock the front door for Rick, and return to the backyard, a fresh beer in hand. How many beers have I had? Four? Shit, I'm a fuckin' basket case.

Thirty minutes later, Rick wanders into the back yard, paint of various colors splashed across his clothes, face, and hair. A beer dangles from his right hand. I give him a half-hearted wave and attempt a smile. Rick sits down on the chaise next to me and takes a long chug of beer.

I look over at his splattered clothes and smile. "You look like you've painted the whole house."

"Nah. Cindy got this hair up her ass that we had to paint the living room. I wanted to hire a painter, but Ms. Frugal wouldn't hear of it."

I know he doesn't make as much as I do, but I also think he enjoys doing those things himself. He's always got some project going on around the house. Rick is wonderful to Cindy, and vice versa. I hope someday I can have the kind of relationship they have.

Rick clears his throat. "Okay, dude. Stop daydreaming. What's on your mind?"

I launch into the mess of my current life. "Bob Jacobs stopped by earlier and hammered me about making it hard for him to get me a good contract for next season."

"Ouch. I bet that was fun. Sounds like my agent. They're both pricks!" His supportive smile makes it easier for me to continue.

"Yeah. But not unexpected. My pitching has been so up and down this year. One day I'm the old Larry Gordon, lights out on the mound. The next game and I can't seem to fucking get anyone out. I can't stay focused on what I'm doing. My mind is all over the place."

"Yeah, I've noticed." Concern blooms on his face. "Do you have any idea why that's happening?"

"Not really." I look up at him. "If I knew, I'd fix it."

I take a long pull on my beer. "Bob asked me if I'm getting laid regularly. I told him about breaking up with Gina, and he said I'd better straighten it out with her or get over her in a hurry, or I'll ruin my career. At first I thought it was a bit harsh, but now I'm beginning to wonder if he's right. Maybe, like you said a couple of months ago, my break-up with Gina might have something to do with my struggles on the mound..." I take a deep breath, "... and my problems in bed."

Rick shrugs and smiles but doesn't say anything.

55

I draw an anxious gulp from my beer bottle. "I don't know. For the first time in my life, I can't think or talk my way out of this. The worst fuckin' part is I'm not having fun playing ball anymore. That's how I know I'm in real trouble."

There. It's all out in the open.

Rick sits up and looks at me, his face full of worry. "This sounds really serious."

I pick dryer lint off my shorts, trying to avoid facing him.

"Yeah. I know. I'm so not me right now. I've never experienced anything like this before." And I really hate talking about this.

"Could be time to pay Dr. Blackwood a visit," Ricks offers.

I sit up and turn to look at him. "Shit, I'm not going to a fuckin' shrink!" This I say a little too loudly. I hope no one is outside next door to hear it.

"Why not? This is exactly the type of thing the team hires Dr. B. to deal with."

Now I'm getting mad. "But I'm not crazy. What do I need a fuckin' shrink for?" I glare at him.

Rick smiles gently. "Chill, bro. You don't have to be crazy to go to a shrink."

I start to say something nasty, but it won't come out.

Rick swigs his beer and stares into the distance for a long time, a frown on his face.

Finally, he looks over at me. "I am going to tell you something I've never told anyone before."

"Okay…" I offer, wary of what he might say.

He looks at me before continuing. "After the birth of our second child, Cindy went into a deep depression. You remember that?"

"Yeah?" I say tentatively.

"We started having marital problems. I thought she ought to just snap out of it, get on with her life. Typical guy reaction. Cindy couldn't understand why I didn't get how she was feeling. We started fighting a lot, and she withdrew into her head."

He pauses for a sip of beer. "The house was a mess, the kids were out of control, and she wouldn't talk to me. On the mound, I couldn't concentrate, and I started getting knocked around. Bud took me aside during one of my bullpen sessions and asked what was going on. I told him a little about Cindy's problem, and he suggested I go talk to Dr. Blackwood."

My eyes widen. "*You* went to Dr. Blackwood?" Why didn't he tell me this before?

"Yeah, I saw Dr. B. I didn't tell anyone, and I swore Bud to secrecy. But if you remember that year, I turned my game around and finished out the season as our go-to guy in the late innings."

"I remember you got your act together, but I had no idea that you went to see a shrink." Wow. Who knew? I sit quietly with the things Rick just told me ricocheting around in my head.

He looks at his empty bottle. "I saw Dr. Blackwood about six times and he really helped me to look at Cindy's depression from her perspective. At his suggestion, I started doing all the things around the house she used to do and told her to just take it easy and work with her shrink to get better. When we went on the road, her mom came to stay with her and the kids. Cindy started taking her antidepressants regularly and gradually fought her way through her despair. She's been fine ever since."

"Man, I had no idea." I thought I knew Rick from cover to cover, but I didn't know this chapter.

"Yeah, well it's not something you go blabbing around, even to your best friend. I wanted to tell you at the time, but Cindy asked me not to. She was too embarrassed."

"That's okay. I understand. Poor Cindy. I had no idea it was that bad."

"So don't hesitate to ask Dr. Blackwood for help. That's what he's there for. It's better than dousing your troubles with beer after beer."

I look at my empty bottle. Maybe he has a point.

He looks at me and smiles. "And your secret will be safe with me, I promise."

"I'll think about it," I say. Maybe? Maybe not.

Rick puts his empty beer bottle down on the table between us and picks up his keys.

I jump up from my seat. "Thanks for coming over, Rick. I really appreciate it. Now go back to your painting and thank Cindy for springing you for a while."

His eyes bore into mine. "Think about going to see Dr. B., okay?"

"I'll definitely think about it." Why does this idea scare the crap out of me?

I walk with him into the house and pitch the two beer bottles into the trash can in the corner of the kitchen. Four points! Rick gives me a hug and departs.

I stand for a long time, staring at the phone on the kitchen wall. Hell. I guess I might as well do it before I chicken out. Rick's usually right about stuff.

I look up Dr. Blackwood's number and listen to it ring three times before I hear "Dr. Blackwood's office. May I help you?" With my stomach in my throat, I tell the secretary who I am and ask to make an appointment.

"You're in luck," she says. "Dr. Blackwood has had a cancellation for four o'clock this afternoon. Otherwise it will be next week."

So soon. Anxiety rears its ugly head.

I breathe in deeply and let it out slowly. "Okay. I'll be there at 4:00."

My hands are shaking as I replace the receiver in its cradle.

Chapter Twelve

I walk into the richly carpeted reception area a few minutes early. Dr. Blackwood's secretary smiles and says, "Go on in. He's expecting you."

Oh, God. What am I doing here? Ninth inning. Seventh game.

I push back the half-open door and settle down in one of the green leather armchairs in front of his mahogany desk. His lanky frame is bent over the desktop covered with green leather that matches the chair I am sitting in. The curly dark hair, thinning on the top of his head, reveals a shiny mahogany scalp. He is busily making notes in a file and seems unaware of my presence. I gaze around the room taking in the floor to ceiling bookshelves filled with thick medical books and a diverse collection of ceramic art.

As I clear my throat of anxiety, he looks up from his desk and says, "Boy, you're the last person I expected to see in here." He smiles, which reassures me a little, then stands up and walks to the door and closes it quietly. He settles himself into the leather chair next to me.

I wonder how much of what has been going on I should tell him.

As if he is inside my head, he says, "Our entire conversation will be held in strictest confidence. I did my Psychology dissertation on 'Dealing with the Celebrity Mind,' so the Renegades hired me ten years ago to counsel players who are having issues or problems, on or off the field. I've been doing this for a long time."

I take a deep breath and say, "I've never talked to a shrink before, and I wouldn't be here except that Rick Wycliffe told me this morning how you helped him deal with Cindy's depression." I smile sheepishly. "I made the appointment right after I talked to him before I could chicken out."

"I'm glad you decided to call. So what can I help you with?"

I look over at him. "I've got to figure out why I am all over the place with my pitching. I'm in my contract year, and I need to get it together so I can do well on the free agent market, but I can't seem to get anything right on my own. Doing the macho 'I-can-fix-this' thing isn't working this time."

"Well, I'm glad you came." He looks at me invitingly. "And for me to help you, I need to know what is going on with you in detail."

I take a deep breath and laugh nervously. "Well, my girlfriend, Gina, broke up with me in January when I wouldn't marry her. Since then, I've been having problems off and on… uh… finishing my sexual encounters." I can feel my face flush bright red. "Also, some silly things, like a sign in the stands, can destroy my concentration on the mound. I can't seem to find my edge anymore, and my stats suck big time."

"Well, Larry. It's perfectly natural to be distracted. You have a lot going on. Let's start by talking about your pitching, and why you can't get your 'edge' back."

Staring at my hands I admit, "I can't seem to focus on my work the way I need to. One game I'm lights out. The next game the strike zone looks like the size of a tea bag and I either walk a bunch of guys or give up homers, or both." The knot in my stomach twists tight.

"Do you have any idea why you can't focus? Is something distracting you?"

"I guess I don't know the answer to that. It's as if my mind jumps around all over the place, and I can't concentrate on the job I have to do. What can I do about that?"

"Let's explore that a bit. Do you have a routine that you go through on the mound? And, if so, have you deviated from it?"

"I have a routine. I try to pump myself up with a mantra I learned from Sandy Koufax when I was a kid. I usually chant it to myself, but it doesn't seem to be working anymore."

"What's your mantra?" He turns his chair so he can look at me.

I tell him about meeting Koufax with my dad, and what Koufax said to me. "I've always used the mantra when I am in a tight place on the mound. In fact, Darren Clarke, a rookie I helped at spring training this year, sent me a card this week and reminded me of it. It was then that I realized I've lost my way."

"Darren is a very astute guy," he says. "What do you think has happened to your confidence, your 'edge' as you call it?"

"I don't know. I was hoping you could shed some light on that." I shift position in my chair, trying to relieve the tension in my stomach unsuccessfully.

Shifting gears, he says, "Talk to me about your inability to perform in bed at times. What do you think that is about?"

I wince at the question. But I know I have to bite the bullet, so I tell him in more detail about Crystal and some of my other sexual disasters. "I don't know why all of this is happening, except that I keep seeing visions of Gina, and everything shuts down. I am hoping you have some answers for me, Doc."

"You know, Larry. The thing about therapy is that most likely you already know the answers yourself on some level. I can only suggest places to look. You have to find them and you will. I can help you do that."

When I don't respond to that, he continues undaunted. "Talk to me about Gina. Were you in love with her?"

"Oh, I don't know. That seems to be the big question. I have never had a relationship with a woman that was so... um... intense. I mean, I really liked her, liked being with her and the sex was amazing."

He is quiet for a moment and then asks, "Was the relationship mostly about the sex? Or was there more?"

"I thought it was mostly about the sex. But after she walked out on me, I can't get her out of my mind."

"What attracted you to her in the first place? Other than good looks, great body, things all guys want?"

"Well, she is a pediatrician, so she's a lot smarter than any other girl I've dated. And what really caught my eye was her commitment to her 'kids' as she calls her little patients. She cares so much about them, and they seem to do well in her care. She's amazing." I am smiling by now.

"Okay. And how does that relate to your feelings for her?"

"Well..." My voice trails off while I think about that.

I clear my throat. "I guess deep down inside I wish someone would care about me with the intensity that she cares about them."

He looks at me and asks, "Do you think she cared about you that way?"

"I really don't know. I was so focused on the sex, I guess I never really noticed. I would look at her and all I could think about was getting in bed and losing myself in her body." My face feels hot. This is so embarrassing.

He thinks for a long moment. "Anything else about her you like?"

"Well, she loves jazz, and we'd go to concerts when one of her favorite musicians was in town. And she's plays golf so we'd hit the links together, though she doesn't have a lot of time to devote to it."

"So it sounds like she's more to you than a good roll in the hay."

"I guess so. I mean, I really miss seeing her. And yes, I guess I have to admit that she means more to me than just getting laid."

His eyebrows shoot up. "Did you ever have any problems with impotence with her?

"No!" I blurt out. "Never."

He thinks for a minute, fingertips pressed together in front of his face. Finally, he drops his hands and asks, "So, what do you think you should do about this problem?"

"I haven't a clue." So now I'm right back where I started when I walked in the door.

He's silent for a few minutes. Finally he says "Here's what I think, Larry. You should go see Gina. Find out if there is still a relationship to be had there, or not. Because..." he pauses a moment as if forming the sentence in his mind. "... I suspect your lack of performance on the mound and in bed are, in fact, related to your breakup with her."

"I don't know..." My voice trails off.

"What have you got to lose, Larry, other than the possibility that it might not solve the problems you already have?" He smiles broadly.

I sit there for a long time saying nothing, trying to make some sense of the thoughts racing around in my brain.

The Doc looks at his watch and stands up. He sticks out his hand. "Think about it," he says with a smile. "And let's get together again in a couple of weeks. Make an appointment with my secretary on your way out."

I shake his hand and make the appointment, a battle raging in my gut. On the way home, I go back and forth: What a waste of time! Or should I go see her? But what if she throws me out?

Chapter Thirteen

While cruising east on Highway 24, I think about my visit with Dr. B.

Do I love Gina? I don't know. Maybe.

Do I want to see her? Yes.

Do I have the nerve to go see her? How bad can it be? She could tell me to fuck off.

At least that would be a resolution, and maybe then I can put her behind me. And maybe she won't keep appearing when I'm trying to get laid.

By the time I reach home, I've worked up some nerve. I jack myself up even more with a beer and decide to follow the Doc's advice. I brush my teeth and check my appearance in the mirror. Not too bad for someone about to go before a firing squad.

I raise the convertible top on my Lexus. I need camouflage for this mission.

Reaching for the steering wheel, my hands are shaking like leaves in an autumn wind. It's shit-or-get-off-the-pot time. I put the car in gear and ease out of my driveway for the ten-minute drive to Gina's house.

Parking a few doors down from her small craftsman bungalow, I sit for a long time staring at her tidy house, which is painted a warm grey and set back from the street behind a lush green lawn. Brightly colored flowers in the gardens along the foundation frolic in the breeze, as do the flowers in the two cement urns at the bottom of the steps leading up to the front porch. It looks so inviting, not at all like a place where my life might suddenly hit rock bottom.

I hunker down in my seat, pretending to sleep behind my sunglasses. Every time a car goes by I peek to see if it's Gina. I hope a cop doesn't cruise by and think I'm casing somebody's house.

I check my watch. She should be coming home from work anytime now.

63

My mind races at warp speed, mulling over what I want to happen when I see her, and it suddenly hits me. This anticipation and my singing nerves feel familiar, like the way I feel before a game I'm going to pitch against a tough opponent—adrenaline pumping, a little nervous, but hoping for a win—a mixed bag of emotions.

Ninth inning. Seventh game, I chant, hoping it will quiet my nervous system. No such luck. My heart is beating a quick staccato and I'm hyperventilating. My stomach is working its way up to my mouth. Shit. I'm a fuckin' major league All-Star but I feel like a kid on his first date.

Finally, I hear a car slow down and look up to see her silver BMW pull into the driveway. I get out of my car and jog towards her. As she gets out from the driver's seat, I say, "Hi."

She jumps back a little, and I watch a series of emotions flicker across her face like a silent movie. She stands there for a while, holding the door between us like a shield and just looks at me.

Finally, she says in a flat voice, "What are you doing here, Larry?"

God, she looks gorgeous. "I was hoping to talk to you." I put up my hands. "Just talk."

This is so hard. I want to go to her, but something tells me that would be a fatal mistake.

"Okay," she says, drawing the word out, her voice full of doubt. She stands there looking at the ground with her arms folded across her ample breasts. "Talk."

She's not making this easy on me, so I ask, "Can we go into your house so I'm not so…" I look around, "… publicly exposed?"

Hesitating a moment, she says, "I suppose. But only for a little while."

She looks like she wants me to be anywhere other than here.

I follow her up the front steps, keeping my distance. She unlocks the door and holds it open for me to enter. As I pass her in the doorway I inhale her essence, and memories come flooding into my brain. To keep me from doing something rash, I plunge my hands deep into my pockets.

The house looks the same as the last time I was here. Lots of bright white woodwork gleams in the sunlight streaming in through crystal clean windows. A couple of flower paintings increase the warm ambiance. A table by the door holds mail and keys on a little

64

silver tray. An oval braided rug lies on the floor in the foyer, and the grandfather clock ticks away like an old friend. I peek into the den and notice a huge high-definition TV which dwarfs the small room.

"Your place looks cozy as always," I say, sounding lamer than ever. "And I see you got a big screen TV."

She nods and I can feel the ice in her rigid body chilling the air.

"Have you watched any of my games?" I know it's the wrong thing to say the moment it comes out of my mouth. "No, no, don't answer that. I was being flip and somehow I don't think flip will work here." I'm sure my face is bright red. My heart is running wind sprints making me feel out of breath.

"You're right. Flip will get you an invitation to leave," she says, her look cold and defensive.

I can't think of what to say next, so I stand in front of her awkwardly and look at the floor.

She stands there with her arms still crossed, looking closed and uncomfortable. "What do you want, Larry?"

I collect my scattered wits and look at her. "I want to talk about us and…"

"There is no 'us', Larry!" she interrupts me, her voice red with anger. I feel the sting of her words on my face as if she actually slapped me.

Her eyes blaze. She looks so enraged that I want to put my arms around her to hug her into a state of calm. Of course, I can't do that now.

"Remember?" She asks. "I wanted to move to a more permanent relationship and you threw your lechery in my face?"

I can't seem to find my tongue so I just stand there, taking my punishment.

She hesitates a moment, marshaling her emotions.

"Unless you have something else to say, Larry, I want you to leave." She points toward the door. Her face is flushed and her eyes flash.

I breathe deeply and try not to react to her fury. "Gina, please hear me out."

She glares at me for a long time, but then her face relaxes a little and she shakes her head.

I plow ahead. "Can we sit down, rather than stand here in the front hall? We can sit in separate chairs. I promise I won't touch you." I attempt to muster a smile.

She looks at me askance, but turns and walks into the living room. She motions me toward one of the two yellow upholstered chairs on either side of the couch.

I sit down but she stands there, looking unsure of what to do next. She shakes her head again and sits down on the edge of the floral-print sofa as far away from me as possible, looking like she might flee at any moment.

My glance lands on a coaster with the Renegades logo on the coffee table, and then rises to look at her. She drops her gaze and studies her hands, her blond hair cascading forward, hiding her face.

I keep going. "When you stormed out that day in January, I thought, good riddance, end of chapter, time to move on. I tried, Lord knows I've tried. I've had my share of one-night…"

"Spare me the details, please," she says from behind the blond curtain.

"Gina, you're intelligent and beautiful. I love being with you and you know how much I enjoy having sex with you, but it's taken me a long time to realize that sex isn't all I need."

She looks up, and emotions flicker across her gorgeous face.

I hate to see her so hurt and angry. I wish this weren't so hard.

I take a gulp of air and decide to finish what I started. "I've found out the hard way that I need more…"

Pain flourishes on her face and she starts to get up.

"No, don't go. Please let me finish."

She settles back down on the couch slowly and retreats once again behind her blond curtain of hair.

"It's all so hollow, so meaningless," I say, looking at my hands in my lap. "I realize now that sex alone doesn't do it for me anymore."

Never mind that I can't even manage to do it at all sometimes.

She shrinks back into the sofa, still looking down and shaking her head. The grandfather clock ticks an ominous counterpoint to my pulse.

An eternity later she looks up and a smirk creeps across her face. "Are you saying that Larry the Playboy is finally growing up?" she asks with more than a tinge of irritation still in her voice.

I wince. I probably deserve that.

I breathe in and let it out slowly, and keep going. "I'm also having trouble focusing on my work. One game I pitch okay and the next game I get shelled." I shift positions in my chair, aware that I'm putting my fragile pride into her hands.

"That's not like you." She gives me a brief sympathetic smile and then retreats behind her mask of hurt. She looks so wounded and diminished that I want to hold her.

Instead, I go on. "I don't know why I can't get it together, but the team shrink thinks my personal problems and work troubles are related. That's why I am here."

Her head snaps to attention, blue eyes drilling into me, suddenly alert. "Your shrink? You're actually seeing a shrink?"

I look at her and nod slowly.

A smile flickers briefly across her face. "Never in a million years would I have guessed you would talk to a shrink."

"Yeah, I know." I smile broadly at her. "I'm just full of surprises." I hope that doesn't sound too flip.

"Yes, you are." We sit there in uneasy silence for what seems like an inning. She stares intently down at her folded hands.

The grandfather clock ticks loudly, trying to fill the void. I attempt to break the mood. "What have you been doing since... well, since that day in January?"

She looks up briefly and then down again.

I don't want to ask the next question, but out it flies. "Do you have... someone in your life?" My stomach does a back flip, but I keep looking at her.

Her blue eyes turn cold as ice as she raises her head. "Shit, Larry. You hurt me deeply. It's taken me a very long time to get over you, but I think I've done it."

My body tightens another notch.

She lowers her eyes and breathes in and out slowly. "No, I don't have a boyfriend. I'm really busy at work. Most nights I'm on call because we are short-staffed. I haven't had the time nor the inclination to look for a new relationship."

She raises her head suddenly and looks me in the eye. "I would have to think very long and hard about beginning a relationship again." She looks down for a moment and then back up at me. "And particularly long and hard if it were to involve you."

No boyfriend. I don't hear much beyond that good news.

"In January," I say, "I was happy with how things were, but you wanted more. Hell, I wasn't capable of giving you or anyone else more. I'm only now wondering if I want a more serious relationship

67

or if I even can have one. I don't know the answers to these questions. But I'm trying to figure it all out." I blush. "This is definitely a first for me."

I shift my long frame around in the chair again and my eyes wander over the room, noting all the little details I've never noticed before. She has an encyclopedia. The walls are a soft green. There's a baseball on her bookshelf, probably signed by me, and the print curtains match the sofa. Here I am, baring my very soul to her, and I pick this particular time to scan her room and actually see what's there for a change. What a piece of work I am.

She breaks into my reverie. "I think it's wonderful that you're trying to sort this out."

The clock keeps up its steady beat.

She looks up, tears shimmering in her eyes. "Why couldn't you have been this honest with me in January? Things might have turned out differently if you had."

Gina, please don't cry, I beg silently. I can't stand that. I look at her, aching to make her feel better.

"It's taken me this long to even recognize that I have a problem with relationships," I admit. "And it has taken me doing a lousy job on the mound to take a look at doing something about it."

Tick. Tock. Tick. Tock.

Her face shows indecision, thoughts apparently fighting with each other. I bide my time in silence, praying that she won't retreat behind her blond tresses and ask me to leave again.

Finally, she looks me in the eye and asks, her voice guarded but not so angry. "So back to my initial question. What do you want?"

I think about how to answer her question, stalling and listening to the ticking that continues to punctuate the silence.

Leaning forward, I look into her brilliant blue eyes. Time for the equivalent of Uncle Charlie.

"I think I would like to see if we can repair the train wreck I caused in our relationship. We can take it slowly. I want you to be my friend and nothing more for now."

Please believe me, Gina. Hell, I want to believe me.

She sits forward, elbows on knees, her eyes lowered as if trying to keep me from seeing into her soul. "I don't know, Larry," her words breaking the long silence. "Maybe I'm not over what happened in January after all. I'm still pretty hurt."

Then it all pours out of me in a rush. "Gina, I've never felt this way about anyone before. I can't get you out of my mind. I made a terrible mistake and took you completely for granted. I assumed that you would be there for me whenever I wanted you. I didn't think about your feelings and what you wanted. I was too focused on the sex and not much else."

I am afraid to look at her. But I have to get to the point of why I came.

I look up and she follows suit.

Gazing into her blue eyes, I swallow and say, "I'm extremely sorry for treating you so badly. I hope you can find it in your heart to forgive me." I am pleading now for my life.

Again silence.

"All this comes as a big surprise, Larry," she says in a small voice, her eyes fleeing back to her folded hands. "I'll have to think about it."

I sit there looking at her hunched over and closed, and watch her in silence.

Finally, she looks up at me, and says, "You'll have to give me some time. Okay?"

"How much time?" I realize this was the wrong thing to say when I saw her blue eyes register hurt. "No, you don't have to answer that."

This is a lot harder than I thought. But at least she hasn't said she never wants to see me again.

She sighs. "I don't know how much time. A few days? A week? I just don't know." Her body language says she still wants me to be somewhere else.

I put as much sweetness into my voice as I can manage. "I'll give you as much time as you need."

We sit there in silence, each lost in our own thoughts.

When I can't stand the ticking of the clock, I get up from my chair and say, "I think I had better go. Thanks for listening."

I look down at her for a second, sitting on the print couch where we've had sex so many times, and want her with my entire being. She looks so beautiful and vulnerable that I don't trust myself to stay here any longer. I smile at her upturned lovely face, wave, and walk out the door.

Driving back to my house, I think about what she just said. I just hope she doesn't take too long. She said maybe a few days.

Man, this is going to be tough.

*   *   *

I hate this waiting, not knowing what Gina will say. Days loom ahead of me like a range of mountains, and it seems like I have to claw my way over each one of them, just to get to the next one. At least we have games tonight and tomorrow to keep me occupied. I'm on the mound this evening. That will keep my mind off waiting to hear the verdict from Gina.

Somehow I manage to get through the morning, reading the paper, doing some laundry, vegging in front of the TV, trying to stay cool while it's a hundred and four degrees outside. After my boredom gets the better of me, I drive to the ballpark.

It's a nice warm evening, and although it's a Tuesday night game, there's a pretty good crowd on hand. The Detroit Tigers are in town and I am facing Justin Black, the ace of their rotation.

During my bullpen warm-up, my fastball has some pop, and all my pitches have good movement, so I am looking forward to doing battle with these guys.

Everything goes well for the first three innings. The game is scoreless for both teams, looking like it's going to be a real pitchers' duel.

In the top of the fourth, I walk the first batter, Curtis Hendersloot. Shit!

After a circuit around the mound, I step onto the rubber and look in at Jason Gardelli for the sign. Fastball in. I can do that. I come set in the stretch, look at Hendersloot so he retreats back to the first base bag, and deliver the pitch to Brandon Orry. Unfortunately, my fastball has neither pop, nor movement, and Orry sends it into the left field bleachers. Tigers two. Renegades zip.

Here we go again.

Jason asks the umpire for time and trots out to talk to me.

"Larry, you feeling okay? Your pitches are really flat all of a sudden."

"I don't know, Jason. I was going along fine and then I completely lost it. I don't know what the fuck is going on."

"You can do this. Give me more of those magnificent curve balls."

70

I nod and he jogs back to the plate.

When Emilio Consuelos steps in, Jason puts down two fingers and taps his left thigh with them. Okay, Jason, Uncle Charlie outside is what you'll get.

I wind-up and throw a perfect curve on the outside corner to the Tigers' most dangerous hitter. He watches it go by for strike one. Then I throw him a fastball that breaks back over the plate. He swings too late and doesn't connect. Strike two.

Another walk around the mound to settle my nerves, and I deliver another Uncle Charlie. Emilio flails helplessly at it for the first out of the inning.

Okay. That's one out.

Jorge Sandoval steps in and I get him to hit a ground ball to Javi Vasquez at third for the second out. Then Jamey Cox flies out to left. I walk off the mound, happy to be out of the inning, but down by two runs. On the way to the dugout, I grumble into my mitt, "Okay. I got it together. I can fucking do this."

I pitch with runners on base most of the rest of my seven innings on the mound, but don't allow any more runs. Our guys manage to score five runs before I leave the game. The bullpen does its job, so I notch my seventh win.

Everyone is enjoying the victory in the clubhouse. My music is blaring, and Nick Hayner is entertaining everyone with his dancing and terrible imitations of other ballplayers' batting stances. I stay there as long as possible, jiving with the guys and filling my stomach from the lavish spread set out for us. Anything to put off having to go home to that empty house and the endless wait for Gina to call.

When I finally do get home, I check my cell phone, but I have no new messages, so I grab a beer and plop down in front of the TV to watch a movie. I check out the HD films in On Demand and find one of my favorites, "Dances with Wolves." I settle myself on the leather couch to attempt to get through the next few hours with Kevin Costner.

Sometime in the middle of the night I wake up on the couch, shivering and a little disoriented. Then I remember my win today and the first few scenes in the movie, and stumble off to bed. One day down.

Today will be harder. I'm not pitching so I'll have more time on my hands. At the ballpark, I workout in the weight room and do laps around the warning track. Typical non-pitching day routine. And it's a day game so we'll be out of here around five o'clock.

Unfortunately today's game doesn't go so well. We get tagged for a twelve-to-two loss. Five balls leave the yard, and the guys have a bad case of rock hands and commit four errors. It's one of those days when nothing goes our way. That's baseball. It still sucks.

On the way home from the ballpark, my mouth waters for a big piece of filet mignon. But eating in a restaurant alone makes me feel too exposed, and the likelihood of meeting girls at the bar would make it impossible to live up to the commitment that I know Gina expects of me. Shit, I ought to be able figure out a way to stay celibate until I hear from her.

I decide to stop at Lawrence's Meat Market in Alamo and pick up a thick filet to grill at home. I run into the nearby Safeway and snag some veggies to grill along with the steak. Maybe I'll cook some rice. That's about the extent of my culinary abilities. It should be good if I don't burn any of it.

My dinner is delicious and uncharred. I even get out a cloth napkin, with the intention of eating in my seldom-used dining room, but revert to eating in the den so I can finish watching "Dances with Wolves" before it disappears from my saved list.

I succeed in making it all the way through to the part where Kevin and Stands With A Fist ride off to talk to the soldiers about peace with the Sioux, with the credits competing with the falling snow. Such a sad movie, but Kevin Costner is an awesome actor.

The only parts of the movie that made me uncomfortable were the love scenes. I kept thinking of Gina, and wishing I were holding her. All of my anxiety came flooding back.

Two nights in a row at home. Alone. That's gotta be a record for me.

I hope she calls soon. I'm going out of my fucking mind.

Chapter Fourteen

Today's the second day this week that we don't have a game, a very rare occurrence. I'm fidgeting around the house, doing everything I can think of and accomplishing next to nothing. I'm trying to keep busy so I won't think about the fact that Gina still hasn't called.

It has been "a couple of days." Should I call her?

No, give her the time she needs.

I put a load of underwear into the washing machine, turn it on, and walk to my bedroom to retrieve my Michael Crichton novel. On the way to the kitchen, I glance at the title, "State of Fear."

Damn! That certainly does describe my life right now. I've never dealt well with fear, and now is no exception. My nerves are completely shot.

I grab a beer and go out to the patio to read, or try to anyway. Before I can sit down, I hear the ding-dong of the doorbell. Shit! With my luck, it'll be some salesman, or a UPS delivery.

But when I open the door, Gina is standing there. My heart kicks into high gear, and I can't help but grin.

"Hi, Larry. Can I come in?" she says without smiling.

Oh, oh. This doesn't bode well.

She is wearing a blue striped tee shirt and white short shorts, and I have to pry my eyes away from her long legs.

"Absolutely!" I say, stepping aside to let her through the door, catching a whiff of her as she passes close to me. Why does she have to smell so good?

I inhale deeply and shake myself back to reality. "I was out on the patio reading. Would you like something to drink?"

"Just a glass of water, please." Still no hint of her mood.

"I don't have any limes. That okay?"

"Plain water is fine." She smiles shyly.

I grab two of the cobalt blue glasses that she talked me into buying last summer. She said they made her eyes look bluer when she held the glass to her lips. I took the bait and bought them. Who knew it would be true?

I add a couple of cubes from the icemaker to each, and pour some Brita water from the fridge into the glasses. I hand her one and we walk out to the patio in silence. I'm dying to know what she has to say about our last conversation, but I keep all of my questions inside my head.

Once seated side by side on the chaises, which allow us to talk and not have to face each other, she clears her throat.

"Larry, I don't think..." Her voice trails off and she sighs, staring at the scraggly roses in my miserable excuse for a garden. What I can see of her face looks serious and sad.

She sits like that for a long time, torturing me with her silence.

Finally, she says, "I came here to tell you that I am not comfortable with seeing you in any capacity. I am not over the hurt I experienced in January."

I feel like I'm plunging off a high cliff. What do I say now? I take a peek at her, but I can't see her face at all now behind her blond hair.

She takes a deep breath, holds it for a few seconds, and lets it out loudly.

"But... I've been thinking about what you said, that you want to repair the 'train wreck,' I think you called it, in our relationship. I don't believe I am saying this, but, against my better judgment, what you proposed sounds... I guess it sounds... well... okay."

"'Okay' is great." I swing my legs over the edge of the chaise toward her.

She recoils like a wild animal at my sudden movement, and I force my legs back onto my lounge chair.

Turning her head to face me, she says, "I won't let you hurt me like that again, Larry." Her expression and her voice are deadly serious, almost belligerent.

She turns back to my pathetic roses. "My brain is screaming: 'Run! Get the hell away from him! Remember how he hurt you!'"

She clenches her hands together, knuckles white, and takes a few deep breaths.

The tension in the air is thick, like after a brush-back pitch. She and I sit like frozen statues. She shakes her head and turns to me. "I should just get up and leave, but..."

She looks at me and smiles.

74

My heart melts.

Still smiling, she says, "I also remember the good times. And we were good together, Larry. So I guess..." Her voice trails off.

Obviously a battle is waging inside her too.

"Soooo..." she says after what seems like an hour, "I guess... I'm willing to take some very tiny baby steps toward you again." She shakes her head again and sits up to face me, dragging a finger through the hair that had been covering her face and hooking it over one ear.

"That sounds good to me," I say. My nerves are willing to believe it, and I relax a bit.

"If we start seeing each other again, Larry, it's only as friends at first. I want to be very clear about that." She looks at me with those beautiful blue eyes, and then looks down at her lap.

"Okay. Just friends. I can live with that." Can I do the friend thing? And for how long?

She looks up again. "And, Larry, it has to be me and no one else."

There it is. The sticking point. The one thing that twists me into a sailor's knot. I'm not sure I can do the celibate thing for very much longer. I have a trip coming up and I'm afraid of what might happen when confronted with a hot chick. But, I want to get back together with Gina, so I guess I have to suck it up and do what she says.

Ninth inning. Seventh game. World Series. Game tied. It's all up to me.

I will myself to keep looking into those china-blue eyes, and say, "I understand. We'll take it slowly, and I won't be with anyone else while we sort this out." I pray that this doesn't turn out to be a lie.

I swing my legs off the chaise toward her, slowly this time, and she doesn't recoil.

"Gina, I know I was a real ass in January and I'm so sorry. I'll make it up to you, I promise."

No response.

"I have been tearing myself up inside," I continue, "afraid that you would say you didn't want to see me again. I've been a useless wreck the last few days." I hate talking about my feelings.

She smiles and looks over at me. "Thank you for giving me the time to think. I knew you had the day off today so I thought it would be a good time for us to talk. And I didn't want to leave you hanging any longer."

She laughs and blushes. "But I certainly didn't come to say what I just said."

"I'm glad you came over, and I am happy you changed your mind."

Man, am I glad I didn't go to the driving range.

I want to jump up and sweep her into my arms, but I don't want to do the wrong thing and cause her to retreat, so I just look at the wilting flowers in my garden, waiting for her to make the next move. I'm such a chicken.

She puts her glass down and stands up. "I have to get going. I just wanted to let you know what I have tentatively decided."

I get to my feet and smile. "Thanks for coming over and for being open to some baby steps." As these words echo in my brain, I realize that maybe things might work out between us. I just have to take it slowly and do what she asks.

I jab my hands in my pockets so I don't do something rash. I give her a big smile and we walk into the house.

At the front door I stop and decide to take one more plunge. "How would you like to have dinner with me Saturday night? Just two friends enjoying a good meal." My hands remain firmly in my pockets.

She doesn't say anything for a long time and steps out onto the front porch.

I jump into the silence and say, eagerly and little boy like, "I'm pitching that day. I could leave a ticket for you at will-call if you would like to come to the game, too." I grin at her broadly.

"Slow down, Larry. Let's just do dinner and see how it goes. Just friends. Nothing more." She smiles at me, but her raised hands seem to push on the air between us.

"Okay, dinner it is. How about Fleming's? I'll pick you up at seven. Okay?"

Her eyes are wary. "No, Larry. I'll meet you there."

I show her the palms of my hands. "Okay. I'll see you at Fleming's at seven."

She smiles and says "Bye," with a little wave, and walks down the steps without looking back. I watch her through the narrow sidelight window as she walks to her BMW and unlocks the door with her remote. She folds herself into the driver's seat and backs down the driveway, her hand sticking out of the window for one more goodbye.

I watch her disappear from view, my heart racing at the speed of sound, happier than I've been since January.

Chapter Fifteen

I'm all cranked up today as I drive to the Coliseum. Since talking to Gina I feel better than I have in a long time. I'd never admit that to the guys, except maybe Rick. I'll just show them and the Baltimore Orioles with my work on the mound.

There's something about driving to the ballpark on the day I'm scheduled to pitch. Adrenaline zings through me, and cool jazz plays on my I-Pod. I'm trying to stay calm, taking my time behind the wheel. My heart swells as I drive through the bowels of Oakland's industrial area, make the turn onto 66th Avenue, and catch sight of the Oakland Coliseum rising from a sea of asphalt like a giant concrete bowl.

At games with the Yankees or the Giants, the place can pack close to thirty-five thousand fans, all with an opinion, and none wanting any excuses. Just wins. That's it. Life in the Bigs. By contrast, at midweek night games we're lucky to draw twelve thousand, but they're vocal and very supportive.

Today my warm-up goes really well. My fastball has a little more bite than it's had recently, and my curve drops right over the plate at the last minute. I'm feeling confident, but not cocky. I'm so up for the coming battle. Bring on these guys!

After the umpire calls, "Play ball," I take the mound and look around at the sun-drenched stands which are full today. This is what I loved about baseball before I became a head-case. It's nice to get reacquainted with the feeling of calm excitement.

Let's feed on the fans and do this right.

I go through my windup and deliver a fastball to the Tampa Bay Rays' lead-off hitter, Eugenio Juarez. He watches it cross the plate on the outside corner. "Stri-eke one!" The next two pitches just miss, one inside and one outside. Juarez swings at the fourth pitch and hits it hard down the leftfield line, but it lands just outside the foul line. Two balls, two strikes.

Time for Uncle Charlie. I shake off Jason until he puts down two fingers. I rear back and spin the pitch so it appears to be sailing over Juarez's head. Perfect. A split-second later it dives like I planned, and the umpire punches him out.

I cruise over the first six innings throwing shutout ball, but their ace, Joe Smith, is doing the same. The score remains nothing-nothing. In the bottom of the seventh, Smith begins to tire and we score three runs before he is lifted. Now with a lead, I don't let down my intensity, and pretend the score is still zero-zero. I'm on cruise control and want to keep it that way. I feel like I could pitch fifteen innings.

I take the mound in the top of the ninth with the score still three to nothing. My pitch count is only eighty-seven, and I'm calm and confident. I retire the first batter on a grounder to Javi Vasquez at third, who fires a strike to Dan Jackson at first. The next batter strikes out on three pitches. Now all I need is one more out and my day is complete.

Eugenio Juarez steps in and waves at two fastballs on the outside of the plate. I waste a change-up low and outside. Time again for Uncle Charlie, I think, but Jason's fingers say fastball inside. I shake him off a couple of times, but Jason keeps putting down one finger.

Do I really want to have a fight with Jason? No. I already got this guy out with Uncle Charlie earlier in the game, so maybe a different pitch would be better.

I walk around the mound, grab the rosin bag and decide that I can go with the fastball in. I go into my wind-up and deliver a dart that nicks the inside of the plate. The ump punches him out with a flourish. Game over. A complete game shutout in my last start before the All-Star break.

Standing on the mound while the guys mob me and the fans applaud my effort, my mind wanders back to a Little League game I pitched for the championship when I was twelve years old. I remember feeling like I could do anything. I had fought a tough battle and prevailed. And there I stood on the mound, my friends all around me jumping up and down, my coaches on the margins of the group shouting congratulations. I was in the middle looking around at the people in the stands, feeling elated and so proud of myself. At that moment, I was the happiest I had ever been in my young life.

After that long-ago celebration wound down, my parents said they'd take me to dinner at any restaurant I wanted. I chose the local steak house. I was on such a high that I felt I could eat a horse. I can see myself sitting in the back seat of my parents Buick Skylark as we drove to the restaurant, with me in the middle between my two older brothers. I smiled the whole way there. My face began to hurt with the exertion, but I couldn't let go of the smile.

"Where did you go off to, Larry?" Jason tugs on my sleeve and brings me back to today and the bouncing huddle on the mound. "Great job today," he says. "I've never seen you so focused."

"Thanks, Jason. You were a big part of it too," I say, and give him a man hug.

I still couldn't shake the vision of that Little League championship. I feel the same way after today's game. We're all just bigger kids, but the emotions are the same. It feels like winning the pennant, but we have a long way to go to get there.

In the clubhouse I stop in the training room to get ice on my arm, and head back to my locker. The media guys are waiting for me, and I give them as much time as they need, as I still have three hours before I have to be at Flemings to meet Gina. They don't ask me too many gotcha questions and want to talk mostly about my going to the All-Star Game as the lone representative of the Renegades. I almost enjoy talking to them for a change.

After making nice with the media, I head off to the workout room to cool down my muscles and do some stretching for about an hour before hitting the showers and dressing for the evening. I don't take much from the buffet that Steve Fox has laid out. I don't want to spoil my appetite for dinner with Gina.

I shower and brush my teeth. I even floss. Back at my locker, I put on a cream-colored Polo shirt, an olive green linen jacket, freshly pressed khaki pants and my good loafers. Gotta look good for my girlfr… no, just friend. That sounds so awful.

On the drive to Walnut Creek, I relive my complete game shutout and think about my dinner with Gina tonight. I'm excited, but also anxious that I'll somehow blow it. I show up at Fleming's about fifteen minutes early.

I have arranged for a booth in the private room behind the main dining area. I follow the maitre d' quickly, my stomach doing the same somersaults it does in the bullpen before a game. I keep my sunglasses on and my hand over my mouth so I won't be recognized. I probably look like I'm about to hurl, no pun intended. I have to hold back a chuckle at my little joke. When I get to the booth, I settle in so I can't be seen by the people in the main dining room.

In about five minutes, I hear the waiter say, "Here you are, Miss. Enjoy your dinner!"

Gina looks angelic in pale blue, with her shiny blond hair cascading over her shoulders. She sits down on the other side of the semicircular booth, facing me with a shy smile. A waiter appears and takes our drink orders.

After he leaves, I say, "You look ravi… very nice tonight! Did you have a good day?"

"Yes, I did, and you did too. It was good to see the old you on the mound." She smiles demurely.

The ironic thing is that in my personal life I'm trying not to be the old me right now.

God, she looks wonderful. I want to slide over to her and put my arm around her but I hold my ground. Take it easy. Don't spook her.

She takes a sip of her chardonnay. "I have to confess that I did buy the plasma TV right before we broke up so I could watch you pitch. After the season started, I couldn't stay away from the TV if I knew you were on the mound. I hated your attitude that day in January, but also I hated to see you struggle. I know how much this year means in terms of your future."

"Yeah. But if I don't start pitching like I did today regularly, I might not have a very good future, well, relatively speaking." I take a drink of my Hefeweizen and grin. "Today I pitched like I need to the rest of the season. I felt really great."

"I watched the whole game and I was really happy to see you pitch so well," she says, her face beaming.

I smile back at her. "Well, I think you and a rookie pitcher from the Sacramento River Dogs, had something to do with it."

"Rookie pitcher?" Her face grows quizzical, and her head cocks to one side.

"Yup. In spring training, our pitching coach, Bud Tanaka, asked me to take a rookie pitcher named Darren Clarke under my wing. I thought, why not. It can't hurt my reputation to help someone coming up, so I worked with him and told him some of my secrets. He sent me a card this week with some amazing words in it."

81

"Like what?"

"He wrote that a great pitcher once told him to treat every pitch as if it's the ninth inning of the seventh game of the World Series and the game is tied."

"Who told him that?" Her eyes sparkle in the light from the candle in the center of our table.

"I did."

"You did?" Her left eyebrow arches.

I nod. Man, she looks good enough to eat.

Gina smiles broadly. "Amazing." She takes a sip of wine, and turns those amazingly blue eyes on me. "And it's not a bad philosophy for civilian life either. The self-help gurus tell us we should live every moment as if it's our last. That's sort of the same philosophy—focus only on what is directly in front of you."

"Makes sense," I raise my glass to her. "Maybe this good old boy is finally starting to grow up."

Can it be true? Maybe? The jury is still way out.

She smiles at me, and I melt into her sky-blue eyes.

She finally looks down and says, "By the way, about your phone message in April? I was not in Seattle on Opening Day. Must have been someone else." A question hangs in the air between us. "You want to tell me about it?" She asks.

Shit! I don't want to ruin this nice evening, but I guess I can't avoid her question. I try to be breezy and nonchalant.

"Oh, some blond groupie held up a sign that said 'Marry Me, Larry.' She looked a little like you but then she disappeared. It's no biggie. Just one of the endless chicks that throw themselves at us ballplayers. I never saw her again." I hope she buys this. It's the truth.

Gina looks at me for a long time and then drops her eyes to look at her menu. I do the same.

She looks up, her face blank. "What are you going to have? It looks like the food here is wonderful."

"Yes it does," and bury my head in the menu.

When the waiter reappears, Gina orders the crab cakes. I decide to have the filet mignon which, when it arrives, is so tender it almost falls apart when I threaten it with the knife. It turns out to be as flavorful as it is tender. Gina says her crab cakes melt in her mouth. We decide on a bottle of Duckhorn merlot.

Both of us get lost in the delicious food. The conversation we do have is about safe topics, like what's been going on in our lives since January other than my escapades with women, and things we'd like to do together in the near future. Nothing about the nature of our relationship and where it's going. Or not.

After dinner and dessert, we linger over our bottle of delicious wine. When we are the last people in the restaurant, I pay the check and feel somehow content just to enjoy the cool evening walking beside Gina on the way to her car.

"I had a wonderful time tonight," I say, hoping I'm not going too far.

"I did too," she says, smiling.

We reach her BMW much too soon for me, and she unlocks the car door with her remote.

I don't want to let her go just yet. "I'm off to Pittsburgh for the All-Star Game tomorrow. I'll call you when I get back."

"I'll be watching the game. And best of luck to you there. And I look forward to hearing from you when you get home." She drops her eyes and blushes like I'm sure she did in junior high.

I stand there unsure of what to say.

She breaks the silence. "I hope you pitch well."

"At this point I just hope I get into the game. There's no guarantee of that, you know." She nods and looks like she wants to go, but she doesn't make a move.

I take a step back. "Well, I'd better let you go," afraid of what I might do if I stay any longer so near to her.

She puts out her hand and stops me. "Larry, thank you. This has been a wonderful evening. I'd like to do it again."

"You're on!" I'm all smiles. A feeling of relief relaxes the muscles I didn't realize were tightly clenched.

I fight back the urge to say more.

I reach around her and open her car door, inhaling her lovely scent. She turns into my arms and gives me a hug. My arms encircle her, but I hug her tentatively, afraid if I grab her I might scare her away.

Well," she says, slowly pushing herself away from me. Lowering herself into the driver's seat, she wraps her seatbelt around her with a metallic click. When she turns the key in the ignition, the German engine hums to life. I close the door and wave her off, watching until her tail lights disappear into the breezy night.

Ambling back to the restaurant, I feel like dancing. I retrieve my Lexus and drive through the cool night air with the top down and the heater running. I whistle one of Mom's favorite songs, "Got a date with an angel, and I'm on my way to Heaven," all the way home.

Chapter Sixteen

My flight to Pittsburgh, the site of this year's All-Star Game, drones on to the hum of the engines right outside my window. My dad, ever the baseball historian, emailed me a piece about PNC Ballpark, and another about the history of the All-Star Game. He also sent me the Ken Burns book, *Baseball: An Illustrated History.* Dad gets a little carried away. Anyway, I have them all tucked in my carry-on to browse on the plane. I love his enthusiasm and respect his love of the game and its historical perspective. I spend the first hour or so of the flight nursing a beer while poring over his treasures.

When I have had enough of earned run averages, won-lost records, and pictures of the all-time greats, I order another beer and think about my evening with Gina last night. I'm happy that we're seeing each other again, but I'm worried about whether I can say no if some gorgeous thing presents herself to me in Pittsburgh. I think I can stay out of trouble when I'm at home. It's when we're on the road and I'm horny as hell that I'm worried about. I want to be faithful to Gina, but I've never been true to one woman before.

The big-money question is whether I can do it now.

Somewhere over Kansas I remember that the Futures Game is being played and I check ESPN on the plane's in-flight entertainment system to see if they are covering it. Darren Clarke called right before I left, breathlessly excited to tell me that he will be playing for the US Team.

Bummer. No Game. I'll have to check Baseball Tonight when I get to the hotel.

Pittsburgh's Westin Convention Center Hotel is All-Star Central for the players and coaches from both leagues. I entrust my bags to a bellboy and go looking for Phyllis Johnson, the All-Star Coordinator in charge of the American League Players, a job she's held forever. She knows all the players by sight and name.

"Hi, Larry," she says when I find her. "Welcome back. Here's your packet. We've got quite a few meetings with the news media for you, and the players' banquet is tomorrow night. You know the drill. Anyway, you'll find a complete schedule inside."

I take the red folder from her and start pawing through it. "You're amazing, Phyllis!" I say without looking up.

She continues, "The tickets for your family are in the blue envelope. I hope you have a great time."

I thank her and find the bellboy guarding my bags. He and I ride up to the floor set aside for the AL players and coaches. When I slide my card key through the slot, we enter a spacious room with two queen-size beds, a large sitting area with a couch and two arm chairs, and a kitchenette, all in muted shades of beige and aqua. I throw my carry-on onto the nearest bed. Two American League All-Star jerseys are draped over the other bed, courtesy of Phyllis or one of her staff. The bellboy sets my suitcase on the luggage stand and I give him a twenty-dollar bill as a tip.

"Thank you, Mr. Gordon." He starts to leave and then comes back. "Are you looking for some female companionship while you're here? I could arrange something." He winks and smiles.

Hmmm. God knows, I'm horny. Damn. I can't think like that. I had a great evening with Gina last night. It didn't involve sex, but if I play my cards right, that will come. Besides, I need to stay focused on Tuesday.

I turn to the bellboy, and say, "Thanks for the offer. I think I'll pass this time."

"Okay. Let me know if you change your mind. Just ask for Miguel. Good luck on Tuesday." He pockets the twenty and closes the door behind him.

I grab a beer from the minibar in the kitchenette and notice that my hand is shaking. I actually considered Miguel's offer for a split second. Damn, this is hard.

Beer in hand, I stretch out on my bed with my marching orders for the next two days. In the blue envelope are four tickets for Tuesday's game.

Since Gina and I were not speaking when I found out I made the All-Star Team, I invited Mom and Dad and my two brothers to come. But my brothers are both scheduled to pitch in the Triple-A All-Star Game on Wednesday in Toledo, Ohio, so they can't make it. I remove two of the tickets and set them aside to give to Phyllis later.

Mom and Dad are going to try to go to both All-Star Games, leaving Pittsburgh Tuesday night and flying to Toledo for my brothers' game the next day. I send a silent prayer to the God of Flight that their plane is on time.

I wish I could spend a lot of time with my parents, but I will be very busy in the next forty-eight hours. I peruse the schedule for a few minutes. Maybe we can have breakfast Tuesday morning in the hotel. I have a little time then. I call Dad's cell phone and leave him a message.

I grab the remote and flip on the TV to see if there is news of the Futures Game, but Baseball Tonight is all about the big game on Tuesday. They do say that the US Team beat the World Team in the Futures Game, but there's no footage of the game and no mention of Darren. The local stations are no more helpful.

I check my messages and find one from Darren. I call his cell and he answers on the second ring. "Hey, Larry. Did you catch any of the Futures game?

"Nope. I couldn't find any coverage on the plane or here in the hotel, except that your team won. How'd you do?"

"It was so exciting. I got to pitch an inning, and I struck out the side." His voice bubbles with excitement, like a little kid. "I just kept thinking of you and the 'seventh game' thing, and it worked. I stayed focused and they couldn't touch me. I'm so pumped!"

"That's terrific, Darren. Any chance we can get together while you are here?"

"Unfortunately, no. That's why I called. I have to fly back to Sacramento tonight. I guess they don't want to shell out any more dough than they have to on us rookies, and I have to get ready for the Triple-A All-Star game on Wednesday. Sorry."

"I understand. Congratulations on your good outing and on being an All-Star. By the way, my two brothers are playing in the game in Toledo. Just look for the Gordon boys. Say hi to them for me. My parents will be there, too."

"I'll find them and say hi. Good luck on Tuesday, Larry."

"Thanks, and good luck to you, too." I hang up and start to unpack. I suddenly realize I'm ravenous and order room service. I drink another beer from the minibar with my steak, salad, and fries, and turn in early.

Chapter Seventeen

I make my obligatory appearance at the Home Run Derby on Monday. We lounge around, making wise cracks about the hitters from both leagues, and try to soak up the experience. The air is almost electric, and the sell-out crowd is really into the amazing show of raw male power.

I feel like one of the fish you see in the waiting room at the dentist's office, swimming back and forth as children tap on the glass. TV cameras are everywhere. You can't possibly keep track of where they all are or whether they're pointed at you. If a player scratches his crotch or picks his nose, it's likely to wind-up on the huge diamond vision screen in the stadium, or worse, on national television. I try to keep my hands inactive and in plain sight.

Home runs fly out of the park more often than not. Gradually, hitters are eliminated until only two are left. After the previous rounds, both finalists are tired and the number of dingers is way down. The winner is awarded the trophy and the keys to a huge brand new pickup truck.

After the hoopla is over, we all go back to the hotel to get ready for the big banquet. After my shower, I flop down on the cool sheets and consult my schedule which says I have to report to the third floor banquet room at 7:00 pm.

After a short nap, I get dressed and gather up the stuff I brought from home—some Sharpie pens, four hats, a couple of Renegades tee shirts, and three of our team jerseys which bear my name and number. With one of the Sharpie's I put my name inside everything so I will get them back at the end of the evening, not that there is any question as I am the only one with Renegades gear here. I fold the shirts and the All-Star jerseys and stuff everything into a gym bag I brought for this purpose.

In the floor-length mirror on the outside of the bathroom door, I check my appearance one last time. Suit pressed, shirt with no wrinkles, tie straight, hair all in place. I am a handsome dude.

I emerge from the elevator with several other All-Stars, and we follow the signs to either the American League or National League Banquet. Lots of security to keep the fans away so we can enjoy the evening in peace.

The AL banquet room is set up with red-clad round dining tables in the middle of the room, each set with white napkins and gleaming silver. Long tables march around the perimeter of the room dressed in white table clothes down to the floor. I find the table with my name on it and lay out my gear and the Sharpies as artfully as I can and stuff my gym bag out of site under the table. I wish Gina were here to arrange my gear. She's so much better at this kind of thing. Oh well. I shake off such thoughts and give my table one last tweak. I guess it looks okay in a guy kind of way.

I work my way to the bar and, in honor of my friend Rick, order a Heineken since they have no Hefeweizen. A couple of us pitchers cruise around the perimeter tables together, signing the gear brought by the other players. By the time the evening is over, everything should sport autographs of most of the players and coaches, each a priceless piece of memorabilia. Hell, if I'm ever down on my luck, I can get big bucks for them.

I wander around the dinner tables until I find my place card and sit down next to Joe Thayer, the catcher for the Twins, who regularly finds a way to get on base when I have to face him. The din in the room makes conversation hard. Before long I am hoarse. Thankfully, dinner arrives and is delicious—prime rib, baked potatoes, and a Caesar salad. My kind of meal.

I look around the room at the top guys in the American League and feel a little uneasy. On the one hand, I've been here before. I had really good seasons each of the last two years. So maybe I deserve to be rubbing elbows with these guys.

But I wish I had better stats this year, especially a lower ERA and fewer losses. Not at all the way I wanted my contract year to go.

Before dessert, Bud Stewart, the Commissioner of Baseball, steps to the microphone and the noise level gradually subsides. Bud welcomes us and congratulates us on making the All-Star team. We each are presented with our All-Star rings which are slightly less hefty than the World Series ones, and have cubic zirconia instead of diamonds. Quite impressive anyway.

After dinner, a rock band plays, and those with dates or wives with them start to dance. Now I really wish Gina were here with me. I mostly stand against the wall and watch.

The party continues louder and longer than I'd like, and around eleven o'clock I gather up the autographed gear from my table, stuff it in my gear bag, and go back up to my room to get a good night's sleep.

I call Gina but get her cheery machine. I leave a short message and turn out the light.

*   *   *

While I am dressing this morning, I gaze out of my hotel window at PNC Ballpark sitting on the banks of the Alleghany River across from the downtown area of Pittsburgh. According to the email my father sent me, the stadium opened in the spring of 2001, an intimate classic-style baseball-only stadium that embraces the city's progressiveness, while paying homage to historic ballparks such as Pittsburgh's old Forbes Field.

I tear myself away from my musings to finish getting dressed, and go down to the restaurant to meet Mom and Dad for breakfast. It is so great to have some quiet time to spend with them in the middle of the frenzy of All-Star Week. Dad has always been so supportive of me, even when I screwed up, or when my brothers ganged up on me. Mom has always been my soft place to fall when things aren't going my way. I wish I got to see them more often.

When I reach the restaurant, they are already seated at a table in the back. We exchange hugs before I sit down.

While the waitress takes our orders, I look at Mom. She's had her hair cut and styled in a modern hairdo, and she's decked out in a very trim suit of pale blue that I've never seen before.

"Wow, Mom. You look great! That suit is fabulous and very slimming. Have you lost weight?"

She blushes beet red. "Well, my son is going to pitch in the All-Star Game. I wanted to look my best. And, yes, I've been walking and taking water aerobics classes, so I have lost about fifteen pounds. Thanks for noticing."

She reaches over and squeezes my arm. "You look pretty wonderful yourself."

Dad is beaming at our exchange. He looks thinner too and very nattily dressed in a beige linen sports jacket, a polo shirt, and slacks. A carbon copy of my usual uniform. Like son, like father, I guess.

"I've been out walking with your mom and working out at the gym," Dad says. "I've shed about twenty-five pounds myself." He pulls open his jacket so I can see his achievement. "We've actually been enjoying our walks together. We really talk to each other. The rest of the things in our lives are put on hold when we're pounding the pavement. It's very relaxing." He chuckles and squeezes Mom's hand. "It's sort of like dating again."

"Gosh, it's so great to see you two," I say. "You guys look like life is treating you well. I'm so happy for you both."

"It's great to see you, too, son," Dad says. "Congratulations on being back at the All-Star Game. Are you nervous?"

"I don't know. Maybe a little. Even though I've done this before, it's still kind of an adrenaline rush. And I'm sure you've noticed that my pitching has been all over the place this year. The wins are okay, but I'm concerned about the ERA and the losses."

"Yeah, I've been following you, of course. Your mom gave me a subscription to MLB TV for Christmas, and I watch most of your games. I've hesitated to say anything because I wanted you to work it out yourself. Your last start was terrific. But some of your earlier ones... well... you looked kind of lost."

"Don't remind me. I'm all too aware of those disasters," I say. Taking a drink of the bitter coffee, I try to swallow those memories.

"What do you think is going on?" he asks. "You're usually Mr. Consistency."

"I used to be, but that seems to have deserted me this year. It reminds me of the last time when I was playing really well and it all fell apart. Remember when I was in high school and you were gone a lot? I didn't have your encouragement on a daily basis like I'd had before. It wasn't the same without you at my games. I started making errors, losing games, pitching wildly."

Wow, I hadn't thought about that in a long time. This year I've felt just like that, until Gina and I started seeing each other again. Amazing.

He looks at Mom for a long minute. "Yeah, I remember. Believe me, I felt really bad that I wasn't there for you then." He looks sad, but smiles when Mom puts her hand on his arm.

Just then the waitress comes with our food. I wait for her to leave before continuing. "I guess I might as well tell you. At Rick's suggestion—and by the way he sends his love to you both—I went to see the team shrink to help me sort out why I've been so inconsistent on the mound."

Dad smiles. "I'm proud of you, son, for being open to taking the help that is available to you. What did the doctor say?" His smile broadens a bit.

Mom looks worried. "Don't pry, dear," she says.

"It's okay, Mom. Dr. Blackwood thinks my pitching difficulties are related to my rocky personal life. As you know, Gina walked out on me in January. I thought I could shrug it off and go on with my usual flare for attracting women, but it just hasn't been the same." No way am I telling my parents about my occasional problems in bed.

Still looking worried, Mom finds her voice. "We were so sorry to hear that things didn't work out between you. She certainly was a really nice girl."

"I agree with you. She's amazing, and so genuine. And she cares so much about her work. She likes lots of the same things I do. And I've been a mess without her."

"You know that all we want is for you to be happy." She puts a hand on mine and gives me a Mom smile. "You'll work this out."

Mom is so loving, and Dad knows how to make me feel good about myself, even if everything isn't going well at the moment. I wish I didn't live so far away from them.

"So what does Dr. Blackwood think you should do about your pitching difficulties and Gina?" Dad asks.

My stomach flip-flops as I weigh how much of this I want to go into. I sure don't want to jinx the possibility of getting back with Gina, but I decide to chance it.

"Well, there's still a glimmer of hope. A couple of weeks ago, at Dr. Blackwood's suggestion, I went over to her house to talk to her. I did a lot of groveling and admitted my mistakes. She didn't throw me out and we had dinner three nights ago." I can feel a smile breaking out on my face.

Mom looks at me for a long moment. "It sounds to me like Gina means a lot to you, son. Look at that grin." She takes a deep breath and asks, "Do you think you're in love with her?"

92

"I don't know, Mom. I do know that I have never felt this way before. I think about her a lot, I'm distracted on the mound, and my enthusiasm for meeting other women has died down to non-existent." I'm horny as hell, but I can't very well tell my mother that.

"Sounds like you might just be in love, which isn't a bad thing. Go with your heart. See where it takes you."

"I'm trying to do just that, Mom, but it's hard. You have no idea how often gorgeous girls throw themselves at us ballplayers, especially on the road. It's very tempting, but I'll lose Gina if I give in to one of them."

I take a sip of orange juice and try to swallow my uneasy feelings.

"This is unfamiliar territory for me," I admit. "It almost feels like I have some kind of disease." Dickus Nonperformus? Maybe I'll tell Dr. B. I've identified a new name for my problem.

Dad looks me in the eye. "I know how hard it is, son. When I first met your mother, I was enjoying being single... a lot!"

"I'll say!" Mom laughs with a twinkle in her eye.

I'm completely nonplussed. "Gosh, Dad, I had no idea."

Like Father, like son, again. Who knew?

"Well, it's not a thing you discuss with your children exactly, but I just want you to know that I have had some experience with this." He smiles at me and then at Mom.

I really don't believe we're having this conversation, but I decide to float a question anyway. "Dad, how did you decide Mom was the one?"

He smiles and looks in her direction. "She gave me an ultimatum: 'It's either me and only me, or goodbye.'"

Gee, that sounds familiar.

"And he chose me." Mom interjects with a bright smile.

Looking at Dad, I ask, "Was it hard? Were you tempted?" I look over at Mom, who looks a little flustered. "I'm sorry, Mom. I don't mean to make you uncomfortable."

"No, problem. I know all of this by now." She gets up from her seat and looks at us both. "I think I'll use the powder room so you guys can talk."

My eyes follow her as she walks between the tables to the front of the restaurant. "I hope I didn't embarrass her," I say.

93

"Not a problem, son. It takes a lot more than that to make your mother uncomfortable. And I'd bet she really does have to use the powder room."

He takes a sip of his coffee. "To answer your question, yes, it was hard. Things were different back then. Women weren't as forward as they are now, and they dressed more demurely. But temptation still presented itself."

He takes a deep breath as if he's debating with himself about whether to continue. "After I made my choice to be faithful to your Mom, I was on a business trip, and I had dinner with a nice-looking woman I met at one of my business meetings. I could tell that she would happily go with me to my hotel room."

He looks around the room, then back at me. "We got as far as the door to my room when I suddenly realized that I really didn't want to go through with it. Right there I made my decision to ask your mother to marry me."

"So when you got home from your trip did you ask her?"

"Yes. Fortunately for me, she said yes."

"Were you tempted after that?"

"Not really." He looks at me and smiles. "Oh, I like to give a pretty woman the once over with my eyes. Nothin' wrong with looking. Your mother even started pointing them out to me."

I look at him and smile. "This gives me a lot to think about. Thanks for being so honest with me, Dad."

For a few moments I listen to the chatter going on in my brain. Am I like my Dad? Can I make it work with Gina?

Dad interrupts my silence. "I can't tell you what you need to do about Gina. Only you can make that decision. My only advice is don't do anything rash in the heat of the moment. You may slam a door that you won't be able to open again."

Mom rejoins us looking fresh.

"There! That's better. So did you guys solve all the problems of the world?"

"No, but we had a nice time talking about how good you look." Dad winks at me.

I pay the check and we leave. I have a press conference to attend with the other American League pitchers. Mom and Dad are going to go sightseeing until we have to be ready for the Red Carpet Event.

Chapter Eighteen

After the press conference, I head back up to my room. A call to room service produces some lunch and, after wolfing down a Black Angus burger, I lie down for a cat nap. I can't seem to go to sleep, but I close my eyes and mull over what my dad said.

At two o'clock my alarm jars me awake and I stumble bleary-eyed into the shower to wake up. Much refreshed, I put on my suit, a fresh shirt and tie, and perform a last minute check in front of the mirror. Still a handsome dude.

I take the elevator down to the lobby where we board a bus to take us the short distance to the Byham Theater where we are sent to the Green Room to wait for the parade to begin. It feels surreal to be here with all these guys, the best of the best. Everyone is keyed up, and testosterone is the stench in the air.

Juices and sodas are set up on a bar in one corner of the room, and a few tables of munchies, mostly finger food. I cruise the goodies and eat a few shrimp spring rolls.

At around two-thirty, we are told that we should proceed to our vehicles when we hear our name called. When I hear mine, a gorgeous young thing steps forward. Uh, oh.

"Hi. My name is Lana. I'm here to escort you to your vehicle." She's about twenty-five, very well built, with a broad inviting smile, and I can visualize myself spending some serious horizontal time with her.

No, Larry. No! I yell inside my head.

Damn this isn't going to be as easy as Dad said. I plunge my hands into my pockets and will myself to keep them there.

She reaches up with her left hand to smooth her long sandy-blond hair back from her face, and I see it—a wedding ring! Shit! Just as well.

I sigh. "Hello, Lana. Lead the way."

We walk out the doors onto a broad red carpet to the cheers of a huge crowd which has gathered there to watch us attempt to get into the back of pickup trucks without making fools of ourselves. Lana leads me to the truck with my name emblazoned on the sides, a brand new fire-engine red Chevy Avalanche. I bid married Lana goodbye and climb up into the truck bed, trying to avoid looking like a klutz.

I settle myself on the chair at the rear of the truck. My parents are seated inside the cab, Dad by the passenger window, and Mom squeezed between Dad and the driver. The back window is down, so I lean forward and try to say hi to them. The cheering crowd is so loud that conversation is impossible.

Like the Oscars, a huge red carpet is laid from the theater, across the Roberto Clemente Bridge, and comes to an end at the entrance to the stadium. They told us in the Green Room that the carpet is one-third of a mile long and forty feet wide. This is the one event this week that is free and open to the public, so fans are packed eight or ten deep behind barriers along the entire length of the carpet.

The driver pulls out of the parking space and falls in line behind a royal blue Avalanche carrying one of the mega-millionaires who plays for the Yankees. We are traveling at the breakneck speed of about two miles an hour. Gotta let those fans get a really good look at us.

What a scene! You'd think we're all royalty.

Last time I ate this up—the cheering, being a celebrity, the showing off. Today is somehow different. It all seems superficial and fake this time. I'm just a guy like anyone else. I don't need this nonsense to feed my ego. What I really need is Gina in my life for more than one date. She makes me feel like I can do anything, be anything.

Once we reach the stadium, I am relieved that my gym bag containing my cleats, two hats with the Renegades logo on them, my mitt, a change of underwear, and toiletries, are in my locker and intact. I don one of the American League All-Star uniforms hanging in my locker and pull out the folding chair and sit down to await the press onslaught. The media is allowed in for some last-minute interviews about a half hour before we have to be in the dugout.

I'm glad I play for a small market team and do not draw the attention of the majority of the media folks. But my ego is a little deflated to see the Japanese Media types ten deep around Takeo Shimada, flashbulbs popping blindingly, and Japanese chatter sounding like a flock of seagulls squawking. Smaller throngs are huddled around some of the other well-known stars.

Occasionally, a reporter stops to ask me a question and wanders off shortly thereafter. I guess I'll have to get my recognition on the mound.

Finally the members of the press are shooed out and a few minutes later we make our way down the tunnel to the dugout. The crowd starts to buzz as the dugouts begin to fill up. I can feel the fans' excitement crackle in the air.

Chapter Nineteen

The All-Star Game is truly surreal. One or more of the best players from each team get to show off for the fans here and across the country on TV. And the winner gets home field advantage in the World Series. It's a really big deal.

The American League manager, Eddie Rodriguez, whose team won last year's American League pennant, named me to this year's All-Star squad as the only representative from the Renegades. I was surprised because lots of our guys are having good years. But we play in relative obscurity so apparently none of our other guys got Eddie's attention. I was the only Renegade the last time too.

I know I will be relegated to the bullpen, as Eddie has chosen someone else to be starting pitcher. With my ups and downs, I didn't expect to be the starter anyway. I chew over all my missed opportunities, before yanking myself back to the fact that I'm here. I need to stop focusing on the negatives and just enjoy it.

Last night at the banquet, Eddie said, "I'm going to try to get you all in the game but if we need to go with someone longer to win the game, we have to do it. I hope you all understand." The thought of sitting in the bullpen for nine innings as a spectator makes me wince. I really hope I get to pitch.

There was nothing better than the adrenaline rush I had when I took the mound in my last All-Star Game. I was in awe of everything and wasn't prepared to be so amped up. I couldn't locate the strike zone and gave up a three-run homer to the Angels' Gary Richards. Man, I hung my head in shame as I walked off the mound at the end of my inning. This time I feel much more in control.

Once all the players are in the dugouts, we are each introduced with much applause and blaring music. When I hear my name called, I sprint out onto the field along the nearest baseline. Standing there my heart beats in time with the pounding bass line of Kool and the Gang's "Celebration" blasting from the stadium's speakers.

By the eighth inning, with the national League up two to one, I'm getting antsy out in the bullpen. For most of the game I've been trying to pay attention to the action, but my left knee gives me away by bouncing uncontrollably as soon as I forget to keep it still. Now some of us have resorted to joking with each other to stave off the anxiety and mask our disappointment at not being out there on the mound.

When the phone rings on the bullpen wall, we all come to attention and watch the bullpen coach pick up the receiver, listen for a moment, and nod. He turns and yells down the bench, "Gordon, warm up! You're pitching next." My adrenaline level skyrockets. The others slump down again and grumble.

I grab my glove, shrug off my warm-up jacket, and walk to the bullpen mound. I look around at the packed stands and my heart pounds as I realize I'm going to pitch after all. I caution myself that things could still change, so I tamp down on my excitement and try to chill out.

I go through my warm-up routine—stretching, wind-milling my pitching arm, and throwing to the bullpen catcher, working up to pitching full bore from the mound. The bullpen coach watches and, after a while, asks, "Ready?" I nod and stand on the bullpen mound focusing on what is going on out on the field. I throw a pitch now and again to stay warm.

When the last out is recorded in the top of the inning, the stadium announcer booms: "Now pitching, from the Oakland Renegades, number fifteen, Larry Gordon..." An electric rush courses through my body and blood rings in my ears. I thought it would be different than what I felt last time, but I'm just as excited and way more confident. Bring it on!

I jog in from the bullpen to the mound and throw a few more warm-up pitches to get the feel of the mound. The umpire calls, "Batter Up," and I will my butterflies to go to sleep. I can do this.

After getting a strikeout on three pitches, Al Jardine walks on a hard slider that breaks back across the plate. The next guy, Bryan Blaze, pinch hits for the pitcher and fouls off my first two pitches. Then I throw a ball just off the plate. Blaze almost swings at it but holds up at the last second. I waste a pitch for another ball. My next pitch, a slider, breaks too much and Blaze has to lunge out of the way.

99

The count is now full. I look in at Joe Thayer, who was my dinner companion last night, now crouched behind the plate. He puts down two fingers for a curveball. I rear back with my full windup and send the ball to the plate high. Right in front of the plate the ball falls through the strike zone into Thayer's waiting glove. A perfect strike.

Except the umpire sees it differently. "Ball four," he yells a little too loud, sounding like a threat. Blaze jogs down to first base, and Jardine moves to second.

Bullshit! How can the fuckin' ump be so blind?

I walk off the back of the mound, touching the rosin bag on the way, and rag on the ump inside my head.

I take a few deep breaths. Okay, settle down. I'm an All-Star. I deserve to be here. Getting upset will only make me careless.

I throw the ball a couple of times into my mitt and stride back up onto the mound. I put on my game face and stare down at the plate, under control once again.

Up steps Dave Brown, the runner-up in yesterday's Home Run Derby. I glare at him hard. Don't even think about getting a hit, you fucker. You can't touch me today.

Ninth inning. Seventh game.

I look in and see one finger being held down next to Thayer's leg. Fastball down and tight. I hear the crack of the bat, and watch the ball take a couple of hops toward the second baseman Mike Jones. He tosses the ball to Michael Tiner covering second, and Tyner guns it to Bobby Black at first, beating the runner by a step for the double play. Yes! Inning over.

I walk into the dugout fist-pumping lightly. The guys are up on the steps to greet me, giving me lots of butt pats and attaboys.

My day is done. I sit down on the bench, grinning from ear to ear. My heart is racing. I'm on top of the world.

In the top of the ninth with the score still two to one, the National League looks like they are going to break a fifteen-year curse and come out victorious for the first time since 1996. Our guys ground into two quick outs. Now the American League is down to its last out. If we don't score, the game is over, and the National League will have home-field advantage in October.

George Roman, the White Sox' big slugger steps to the plate and drills the first pitch down the left field line for a single. We all jump to our feet. Hope fizzes through the dugout.

100

The next batter, James Bailey from the Toronto Blue Jays, takes a few pitches, and then strokes a double. This should tie the game but the ball bounces into the stands for a ground rule double, so the lead runner has to stop at third base. Now there are runners on second and third with two outs.

The Angels big outfielder, Vern Ramero, settles in at the plate and takes a few practice waggles. Throwing from the stretch, Soley Bachman, the National League pitcher, checks the runners. Ramero swings at the first two pitches, fouling off one and missing the other. Now down to our last strike, we all stand on the top step of the dugout and hold our breath.

Ramero asks the ump for time and takes a few more practice swings outside the batter's box. He steps back in and takes his stance. We all watch the ball leave Bachman's hand and spin toward the plate, seemingly in slow motion. Ramero picks up the rotation of the ball, times his swing perfectly, and strokes a blistering line drive to the outfield. I hold my breath, willing the ball to make it over the fence. All our guys encourage the ball, waving it on and yelling, "Go ball! Go ball!" When we see it clear the fence, we all yelp and jump up and down like a bunch of school kids. Pandemonium reigns in our dugout.

The other dugout is silent. Stunned looks freeze the faces.

In the bottom of the ninth, the American League is now up by two runs, and the Yankees' closer, Marty Lucas, comes in to pitch. Everyone knows he's going to throw sliders, but it doesn't matter. They still can't hit his stuff.

The first National League batter grounds to the third baseman who throws to first for out number one. The next batter steps in and grounds to Mike Jones at second, who converts the second out. Awesome!

After fouling off a couple of pitches, the Cubs' Jim Thibaux, lifts a fly ball to deep right field which looks as if it's going to hit the wall. But the National League's luck has run out. Vern Ramero sprints toward to outfield fence and leaps. He turns in mid-air and makes a great over-the-shoulder catch before slamming into the wall. He drops awkwardly to the ground, does a summersault, and ends up on his feet, the ball firmly wedged in his outstretched glove for the final out.

We race out onto the field and mob Lucas and Ramero. It's so cool celebrating with the guys I usually try to strike out. I can suspend for one day the usual feelings I have about them when I'm on the mound in a regular game. Today I can just enjoy the fun and act like a kid again.

The post-game festivities seem almost anticlimactic and drag on and on, so I head back to the clubhouse to change. Besides, I have a flight that leaves in a few hours. I pack up my belongings in my gear bag and retrieve my suitcase from the locker-room attendant, giving him a hundred-dollar bill for being so good to us. I catch a cab to the airport to fly home to Oakland with visions of a great game playing in my mind. On the way, I call my dad to say how much I enjoyed seeing them.

While my plane is sitting at the gate waiting for our turn to get in line to take off, my cell phone rings. I can see from the screen that it's Gina. "Hi," I say, and my heart starts pounding.

"Hi, yourself! You pitched a great inning! And what a catch Ramero made! He deserved the MVP," she gushes. "Are you on your way home?"

"Yeah, we're about to push back from the gate and get in line to take off, so I'm going to have to hang up very shortly."

"That's okay. I'll talk to you when you get home."

We say our good byes and sign off. My stomach is queasy for some reason. I couldn't eat much before the game, and I didn't have time to eat more than a few bites of the buffet after the game. Maybe I'm just hungry.

Chapter Twenty

After posting my ninth win today against the Angels, I'm heading to Walnut Creek with the top down to pick up Gina. I know that sex is still off the table, but I feel like it's easier to be patient when I'm winning. Hell, everything in life is easier when I win.

Gina says she doesn't mind the top being down. She ties a soft pink scarf over her blond hair. Her dress of a similar hue covers her body more than I would like, but she looks wonderful.

I fill her in on the rest of my All-Star experience as we drive through the balmy night to Esin in Danville. I find a parking place and we amble toward the restaurant, enjoying the evening air which is fragrant with Gina's perfume.

She seems friendly but it's hard to read what she's thinking. I'll just play it by ear and see what happens.

The maitre d' greets us and takes us to a table in the back of the restaurant, a small room with subdued lighting and cream-colored walls punctuated with watercolor paintings of flowers in glass vases. We have the room to ourselves, at least for now. The waiter arrives with the menus. He takes our drink orders and then melts away.

"How was your day?" I inquire, looking for neutral ground to break the ice.

"Long. Cindy was in today with their youngest who has been coughing. Nothing serious. Just a summer cold. Then I had non-stop fevers, sprains, swimmers' ears, a couple of convulsions, and a heart murmur until five o'clock."

God, she looks radiant when she talks about her work. I admire her dedication. I hope someday she cares about me that much.

"So how did your pitching go?" she asks. "I heard on the six o'clock news you got the win."

The waiter arrives with our drinks and then disappears so quietly that it seems like he dematerialized.

"Yeah, the win is great, but I still had one bad inning when I completely lost it. I wish I could figure out why that happens. It's as if something suddenly just shuts off in my head, and I can't seem to concentrate on anything."

"Oh, Larry, don't be so hard on yourself. You can't be perfect, no one is. Everyone has a bad day or inning now and again."

"Yeah, but I can't just lose it in the middle of a game and give up a bunch of hits in a row. I can't be doing that during the rest of the season."

"But Larry, you have to give the hitters some credit. They have to hit the ball and some of them are very good."

"I know. I guess I am too hard on myself. I felt really good for most of the game today. Except for one bad inning, I was completely in control. I dared them to hit me. I probably scowled at them."

"You can be scary when you look at the batters that way. I hope you never scowl at me like that." Her face lights up and makes me feel warm all over.

Without thinking, I say, "I thought that if you and I were seeing each other again that these moments of losing it would disappear, but it's still happening."

The smile drops off her face. "Oh, so you're just using me?" She shifts in her seat, body language indicating withdrawal, a distinct edge in her voice.

I shake my head and breathe deeply. "There I go, putting my foot in my big mouth. No, of course I'm not using you. I want to be here with you."

A momentary smile flickers on her face, and then disappears.

Don't frown at me Gina, I think. I can't take that much longer.

I take a couple of deep breaths and plow on. "It's just that my shrink thought that my not seeing you and my lack of focus might be related, but I guess maybe they aren't."

"Interesting," she says, with a little more enthusiasm.

"I'll figure it out," I continue. "But it'd better be soon. We are coming down the stretch, and I have to pitch well from now on."

"I hope you do, for your sake." She smiles encouragement.

Gina sips her drink for a few moments, and then looks up. "By the way, I have an idea how I can use you. I have a little guy named Jimmy who came into the ER last week and almost died."

My heart suddenly constricts, thinking about Gina losing one of her patients. They mean so much to her. She tells me a little about Jimmy and his touch-and-go night near death.

"It turns out that he had both the H1N1 virus and TB, but we brought him through. It was such a relief when I went in to check on him at five the next morning and he was sleeping peacefully."

"So how do I fit in with all this? How are you going to 'use' me?" I chuckle, and ignore my visions of her naked in bed.

"Jimmy is a huge baseball fan and the Renegades are his favorite team. He knows everyone, all their numbers, positions and stats. I told him I know you. He said I was so lucky and wanted to know if you were nice."

"What did you tell him?" I'm almost afraid to ask.

"I told him you were very nice."

"Thanks for that. You're pretty nice yourself."

She smiles and blushes.

When she recovers her composure, she continues. "Here's where you come in. Jimmy also plays Little League and he's been champing at the bit to get back to playing. He's coming in tomorrow morning for a follow-up visit to get my okay to play."

She takes a deep breath and gets to the point. "Would you be willing to come to the hospital and meet him? It would really make his day. And it would mean a great deal to me to see the smile on his face when you walk through the door."

All sorts of excuses rush into the void in my head, but I bat them all down. She asked me a favor. It's the least I can do for her.

"Sure," I say. "What time do you want me there?"

"Nine o'clock would be great. Just tell the nurse who you are and she'll bring you in. I'll set it all up." Her smile broadens. "That will mean so much to Jimmy. Thank you, Larry."

Her eyes are radiant. I feel so good about putting the light in them. Well, a little of it anyway.

The waiter arrives with our dinners. "You two look like you're having fun."

Gina blushes. "He just promised to do a huge favor for me."

The waiter puts a filet mignon with a balsamic reduction sauce in front of me, and a phyllo-wrapped chicken breast stuffed with spinach and a trio of cheeses at Gina's place. We both take our first bites and give thumbs up to the waiter, who vanishes again. Mine is exquisitely tender and flavorful. We exchange tastes and agree that each dish is out of this world. We eat as if we haven't seen food in days.

After a few minutes of savoring the superb food in silence, Gina looks up from her plate. "You'll be fine on the mound. You always do well after the All-Star break. I have confidence in you." She winks and puts her hand on my arm encouragingly, but withdraws it quickly. I feel the electricity of her brief touch through my shirt and jacket.

"You can leave it there. I don't mind!" I say, grinning.

"I don't think so. Not yet. I still haven't determined that you're serious about having a monogamous relationship. How do I know you won't jump in the sack when the next pretty woman gives you a 'come here, sexy' smile?"

"Look, I haven't had sex since I came to your house to surprise you a few weeks ago. For me, that's an eternity. I had a couple of opportunities in Pittsburgh and I declined them. What more do I have to do?"

She looks at me and shakes her head. "You still don't get it, Larry. Do you?"

"Get what?" Where is she going with this? I've been doing what she asked me to do. What's the problem?

She gets that adult-talking-to-small-child look on her face and takes another deep breath.

God, I hope this isn't the end of everything between us. It feels like it could go that way, and that thought makes me worry that I will get sick right here.

She must see my distress, because she smiles, and says, "I don't want you to be a 'good boy,' mind your P's and Q's, or engage in a white-knuckle struggle. I want you to refrain from having sex with anyone other than me, not because you feel you are being good, but because you couldn't seriously consider having sex with anyone else. I'm not sure you're there yet."

"Maybe you're right… but I do want to have sex with you, and right now I don't want to have sex with anyone but you." I try to sound convincing but even I don't buy it.

She takes another bite of her chicken and swallows. "Sure. With me sitting across from you, that's all you can think about. What about when you are on a long road trip and I'm back here in California? You are very good at sending out messages to girls that you are on the prowl."

"I do not!" I protest.

"You most certainly do. Maybe it's pheromones. Maybe it's a certain look or a touch. You probably don't even know that you are doing it."

"If I do send messages, I'm not doing it on purpose."

"But you are sending out the messages. I ought to know. That's how we got together last August. You were broadcasting big-time at P.F. Changs'. I picked up the signal and came over to you."

"And boy, am I glad you did." I smile at her stern expression.

"So, back to the subject at hand. Can you look me in the eye and say with certainty that when you are on the road next week you won't be tempted?"

"I might be tempted…"

"Yes, but are you absolutely sure you won't act on that temptation?"

I look at her for a long time, drowning in those blue eyes, and then look away, mute and hot-faced.

"Larry," she says, "it's obvious that you're not ready to make a commitment to me. So I'm declaring the issue of sex between us off the table for now."

I stab my last bite of filet, mop up as much of the sauce as I can, and put it into my mouth, not sure of how or if I want to respond to that. I chew for an eternity, thinking about how to proceed, and finally manage to swallow.

"Why the hang-dog look?" she asks. "Nothing's changed, you know. We are trying to be friends, without the complication of sex. That's what we agreed to, or have you forgotten that?"

"No, I haven't forgotten. But Gina, I've never done this before, just be friends with a woman and not have sex with anyone else. I'm walking new territory here, and this is really hard for me."

She smiles. "I know it's not easy, but it's really important to me."

For a long time I look at her, sitting across from me looking like an angel, emotions zinging around my body. I'm so horny, and she's sitting within touching distance, but I know that reaching out to her will be a mistake. And I haven't a clue what to do about any of it. Why is this so hard for me?

Her last statement deserves some response. I decide to be honest with her.

"You're right. I need to work some more on this. I do want to do what you ask. I really do. I'll figure out a way." I wish I was as confident as I sound.

She smiles and looks into my eyes. "You're leaving day after tomorrow for eleven days back East. Why don't you go on this trip with no strings attached and see how you do. We can talk again when you get back."

I look at my plate for a long time, and then look up at her. "Okay. That's fair. We'll talk when I get back." I really don't want to do anything rash on the road. The problem is that I'm just not sure I can resist a sexy woman.

The waiter arrives and removes our dinner plates. He places Gina's dessert in front of her. I'm not having dessert. The thought of eating anything more makes me nauseous.

She looks at her plate for a very long time and finally shrugs her shoulders. She picks up her fork and takes a bite of the warm bread pudding with bourbon caramel sauce, closes her eyes, and glows in complete rapture.

"Bread pudding is one of my favorite desserts, and this is exquisite." She takes a few more bites and moans a little after each mouthful, oblivious to everything around her.

Oh, great! She goes all orgasmic over a dessert right in front of me. Apparently sex, and oral sex at that, is okay at the dinner table. And this is actually turning me on, for crying out loud.

"Are you doing this just to jerk my chain?" I say with anger tingeing my words. "You'll have sex with your dessert but not with me? That's just not fair. Shit, what do you think I am? Made of stone?"

She pauses with her fork in midair and gapes at me with a stricken look.

I push back my chair, nearly tipping it over, and head for the men's room. I hope she didn't see the bulge that has appeared in my pants. I throw some cold water on my face and try to calm down.

Is this shit worth it? Right now I'm not so sure.

I look at myself in the mirror over the sink, and say, under my breath, "No one said this was going to be easy."

Hell, I've done much harder things in my life. Making it to the big leagues, for one. And I'm pretty sure she is what I want.

"So suck it up and play the game her way," I say with resignation in my voice.

I run my fingers through my hair and show my palms to my reflection in the mirror. Okay. Okay. I give in.

I paste a smile on my face and head back to the table. I sit down and fold my hands into fists out of sight in my lap.

"I'm sorry. I kind of over-reacted. I'm better now." Yeah, right.

Her mouth is full of bread pudding, preventing a response.

I watch her finish her dessert. Happily, she eats with a little more restraint than before.

I hail the waiter and ask for the check.

Safe, light chatter is all I can manage as we drive back to her house. She seems friendly and the tension from the restaurant blows out the window into the night air.

At her door she turns and looks at me, her head slightly tipped to one side.

"Larry, as I said before, you need to decide what it is you want and then go for it with everything you've got. If I'm the one you're looking for, then you know the ground rules. If you can't live with them, then we should stop this right now before someone gets hurt... again."

She turns quickly to let herself in the door, her long blond hair flaring out around her shoulders as she turns. The door closes with a click before I can find my tongue.

My nerves are jangled and my stomach is a quivering mess as I walk back to my car and get in. I stare through the windshield into the summer night. It always comes back to the same thing. If I want her, I can't screw anyone else. Short. Simple. If I trusted myself on road trips, I could make the commitment she wants.

Gina doesn't trust me after what I did to her in January. Once trust is gone, it's really hard to get back. I'm learning that the hard way.

Chapter Twenty-One

The next morning I drive to the Medical Office building at Kaiser's Walnut Creek Hospital. Walking in from the parking garage, my turmoil is raging after our conversation of last night. Will she be happy to see me? Will I be happy to see her?

When I get up to the third floor and locate the Pediatrics Department, I tell the receptionist who I am in hushed tones. She picks up the phone and says something. When she hangs up she tells me step inside the door to the left.

A nurse approaches as I close the door behind me. "Hi, I'm Mary. I'm Dr. Green's nurse. Nice to meet you. Please come with me."

I follow her until she stops outside examining room six and knocks on the door. Gina peaks out and waves me in with a smile. That's promising.

On the examining table sits a small boy, whose face breaks into a huge grin as he lets out a whoop. A woman, who must be his mother, sits in a chair next to him.

Jimmy covers his mouth to keep from whooping again. Finally, he manages to calm down a bit and says, "Oh, my gosh, Mr. Gordon..." but he can't go on, his eyes big as baseballs. He looks at Gina, at his mother, and then back at me.

I thrust out my hand and say, "Hi, Jimmy. Great to meet you."

I turn to his mother and offer her my hand. "Larry Gordon." Now her eyes grow huge as she recognizes the name.

Jimmy is still staring, wide-eyed.

"I brought you some of my gear. Would you like me to sign them for you?" I hand him a cap, a ball, and one of my jerseys.

"Oh, yes, Mr. Gordon. That would be awesome." He hands them back to me and grins while I sign them with the Sharpie from my pocket.

"And Jimmy, you can call me Larry." I pull up the other chair and sit down in front of him.

"Thank you so much. I can't wait to show them to my Little League team. They'll be mega-jealous."

Jimmy starts talking a mile a minute about his team. I find out that he plays for the Union Bank Renegades, and he likes to pitch best.

While he is talking, I look up at Gina. She is smiling and her eyes sparkle with unshed tears.

Jimmy is now sporting a huge grin. "You're my favorite player," he says. "I want to be just like you when I grow up."

No you don't, kid. I'm a mess.

I wouldn't wish what I'm going through right now on anyone, especially a nice kid like this one. But I realize he's giving me a big compliment, so I mumble my thanks. "Just do well in school, play hard, and do what your parents say. You'll be fine."

Gina steps forward and puts her hand on Jimmy's shoulder and rubs it a little. "Jimmy, Larry wanted to come by to meet you today, but he has to get going."

Leave it to Gina to make it my idea to come.

She motions Jimmy to jump down from the table. "We're all done here." She looks down at him and smiles. "And, Jimmy, you're cleared to play baseball."

"Awesome!" he says, and gives me a high five.

"Knock 'em dead, Tiger!" I say, high-fiving him back.

The four of us walk out to the door toward the waiting room.

Jimmy's mom turns to me. "Thank you for making my son so happy. I haven't seen him smile like that since he got sick."

"No problem. Nice to meet you both."

They walk out the door to the waiting room, Jimmy clutching his baseball gear and bouncing with joy.

I turn back to Gina. She still has tears in her eyes.

"Thank you so much for doing this," she says. "It means everything to me." A tear runs down her face. She swipes at it with her hand and blushes.

"Don't be embarrassed," I say. "You're beautiful when you cry." I want to wipe another escaping tear, but I don't dare. I don't want to spoil this moment.

"I do get so attached to these kids," she says, wiping away the tear. "I'm afraid I have to go. I have another patient waiting. You can escape out this door," motioning me to a different door than the one Jimmy and his mom went out.

She squeezes my arm and gives me that electric jolt again. I put my hand over hers and give it a squeeze.

She smiles and turns to head back toward her office to get ready for the next little person. I smile at her retreating back, put on my sunglasses, and walk through the door into the hall.

Back in my car, I marvel at what I just witnessed. It seems hard to imagine that Jimmy almost died a week ago. He looks so healthy and full of energy. He obviously loves Gina and she him. How wonderful it was to see the excitement in his eyes when he realized who I was.

It was amazing that I could bring such joy to a child. I guess I'll pay a little more attention to the kids in the stands from now on.

Seeing Gina with tears inundating her smile makes me want to love her even more. I see now why she loves her job as much as she does, and how great she feels when one of her kids comes back from the brink of death. It must feel powerful and humbling at the same time. I imagine its really hard for her to lose one. I don't want to think about that.

Chapter Twenty-Two

Fenway Park never gets old. But man, it's hot and sticky today. One thing about being on the East Coast in July, it makes me really appreciate the weather in the San Francisco Bay Area. Thoughts of playing somewhere else next year appear, and my mind wanders to what it would feel like to play for the Red Sox. It would be awesome to play for such a storied and well-respected franchise, with some of the best fans in the majors. On the other hand, the press is merciless, just like in New York.

But I can't continue down this road. I need to focus on the game at hand.

I'm on the hill today, and we really need to win this one. The Red Sox have an eight-game winning streak coming into this series, and we have lost a shitload of games at Fenway in the last couple of years. And we lost last night in a walk-off at Yankee Stadium.

We need to win one or two of these games to Boston to keep our confidence up. It isn't going to be easy, and it starts with me. This is what I get paid to do, and my adrenaline surges as I warm up in the bullpen.

If I can't be pumped at Fenway Park, I'm dead, and I might as well quit the game and start selling used cars. And to add to it, I'm getting back together with Gina, at least as friends. That thought makes my blood run hot. I'm lucky to be me, right here, right now.

I walk out to the mound in the bottom of the first, and I notice the groupies next to our dugout calling to me and sticking out their tits invitingly. Looking at them, I actually think it's sad that these girls feel they need to flaunt their bodies shamelessly to try to find love, or just sex. Boy, I guess I really am changing. I would have feasted there in the past.

I smile to myself and ignore them as I throw my last warm-up pitch. Game on.

All my pitches are working perfectly. The hitters won't touch me today. It's going to be great to shove it up their asses in Fenway for a change.

I shut out all sounds, and it's just me and my catcher, Jason Gardelli. We have the field to ourselves. Everything else melts away.

It feels almost like there's an angel sitting on my shoulder sprinkling magic dust on the ball. I smile at the thought that the angel could be Gina.

Jason puts down one finger next to his left thigh for the first pitch of the game. Fastball away. I go into my full windup and throw the pitch into Jason's waiting glove for strike one. Yeah, that feels good.

After a second fastball on the inside corner of the plate for another called strike, Jason puts down two fingers. Uncle Charlie. The batter waives helplessly at it, and walks back to his dugout in disgust.

My fastball has been hitting ninety-three miles per hour on the scoreboard, and Uncle Charlie has definitely come to play. I feel comfortable, recharged, connected. I retire guys like they're little league players.

Eight innings fly by without me allowing a run. Curt Pence, the Red Sox starter, matches me, so the game is scoreless going into the ninth inning. I wonder what the contract genius thinks of my performance today. Kiss my ass, Bob!

We score two runs off Pence in the top of the ninth, giving us the lead. In the bottom of the ninth I get two quick outs. Jimmy Laird, the Red Sox leftfielder, works a walk, and Coop signals me to walk Dan Ostler, the Sox' power slugging DH.

Ninth Inning. Seventh game. I am going to win this, dammit.

Danny Gonzalez steps in. He's one of their best hitters, but he won't touch me. I have this one under control. I start him out with Uncle Charlie and he watches it fall in for a strike. Then I give him a ninety-three mile-an-hour fastball. He swings late and now I have him where I want him. I waste a few fastballs outside the strike zone, but he doesn't even twitch at them.

Time for Uncle Charley again. Ninth Inning. Seventh game.

The ball starts above Gonzalez's head. Right before the plate it dives and nicks the rear corner of the plate. He watches it go into

Jason's mitt. The umpire punches him out for the last out of the game.

The guys erupt from the dugout and mob me near the mound. A complete game shutout of the fucking Red Sox in Boston. Damn, I'm good. Now I have ten wins to go with five losses. I feel like an ace as I walk with the guys down the tunnel to the visiting team's clubhouse.

In front of our adjoining lockers, Rick and I pull off our dirty uniforms and put them in the laundry cart for the clubhouse crew to wash before tomorrow's game. After my victory, I decide to let the media guys have some of my time. Starting pitchers are supposed to do that anyway. Maybe they'll write good stuff about my complete-game shutout.

I tell them that I felt good on the mound, that I was in complete control of my game, and was "in the zone," a phrase ballplayers and the media love to use. Happily, no one asks me about my upcoming free agency. Instead, they focus only on my achievement today. I hope you like what they'll write, Bob.

Chapter Twenty-Three

In game two at Fenway, we manage to scratch out one more run than the Red Sox for second win in the series. Rick pitched the eighth inning and set them down on seven pitches. Man, he was lights out, like I was yesterday. It must be catching.

In the clubhouse after the game, Rick is riding high. "Hey, Larry, I'm ravenous, and I'm up for a big lobster." Rick licks his lips. "How about the Chart House down on the harbor?"

"Fine with me. I'm still stoked about my win yesterday, so a humungous lobster sounds awesome."

"Then the Chart House it is," he says, and finishes tying his shoes.

I put on my shirt, and look over at Rick, "Man, I felt good after my win yesterday. I wish I knew what made the difference. All my pitches were working."

"Yeah, and ninety-three on the speed gun. You taking something?" He pokes me in the ribs.

"Me? You know me better than that, man," expressing mock shock that he would say such a thing. "I just felt great. My head was in the right place, and I felt like I could pitch a no-hitter."

He laughs. "When you figure out what made the difference, bottle it and you'll make gazillions." Rick pulls a polo shirt over his head and steps into his slacks.

We amble out of the stadium and hail a taxi to the restaurant which is at the end of one of the piers on the Boston waterfront. It's an old three-story brick building, a former fish cannery that has great views of the harbor on three sides.

The late afternoon sun turns the sailboats and surrounding wharf buildings to gold. I watch my best friend stride along the pier in front of me, the sun making his reddish brown hair look like windblown strands of copper. I'm a lucky guy to have him as a friend. I often wonder why he puts up with me.

Once inside the restaurant, we are greeted by a noisy bustling scene. The downstairs is packed with hungry diners talking or devouring their huge platters of food. Everywhere waiters are on the move dressed in white shirts and black pants with white tablecloths for aprons that reach almost to the floor. Each makeshift apron is secured with an over-sized safety pin in back. The waiters seem to glide effortlessly among the tables with heavy trays on their shoulders piled high with food. Busboys scurry behind them pouring water, serving bread, or removing dirty dishes.

We give the blond sylph-like hostess our restaurant name, which is Rick Gordon, and ask for a quiet table. She winks at me, and I suddenly wonder whether she thinks we're a gay couple. Nah, she's probably flirting with me.

"Have a drink in the bar, and we'll call you when your table's ready," she offers, with a very wide smile.

I smile back.

Rick grabs me and pulls me toward the bar.

Once perched on our stools, Rick says, looking into his beer glass, "Hey, man. Were you trying to blow it at the front desk?"

"No. Not really. She just had a nice smile." Liar.

"Didn't look that way to me. Looked like you were trying to hook up big-time."

"Look, I have been fine so far," taking a swallow of beer. "Gina and I talked about that over dinner the night before we left. She's real skittish where I'm concerned, so we are doing the friend bit for now. I haven't had sex for over three weeks, and I don't mind telling you, it sucks."

"Man, that must be a record for you! Do you think you can keep it up?" Rick's brown eyes twinkle, obviously enjoying his play on words.

"Very funny." I flick a peanut at him that whacks him much closer to his eyes than I intend.

Rick recoils, frowning. "Ow! That hurt. Look, man, I'm trying to be sympathetic here."

I look around the room and take another swig of beer. "She said she's willing to continue seeing me which is great, but she laid down some ground rules."

"Like what?"

"Well, she said she doesn't want me to be a 'good boy' just because that's what she wants. She thinks it should be relatively

117

easy for me to make a commitment not to have sex with anyone else."

"Yeah, chicks always think that." Rick's crooked smile is more like a smirk.

"They must not know that us guys are slaves to our dicks," I say, but it sounds so high school.

Rick rolls his eyes at me.

I plow ahead. "She's worried about what I'll do when she's not around, like now." I take another pull on my beer. "She says I send out 'messages' that I'm on the prowl, pheromones or some kind of sexy look."

"Yeah, you probably do. Cindy told me that I sent out 'invitations' too. I had no clue I was doing it either."

I stare into my glass at the amber liquid. "She said either I decide to have sex only with her and buy into it totally..." My voice trails off. Damn, I don't like the thought of what comes next.

"And if you don't make that choice?" Rick says gently when I don't continue.

"She said we should end our relationship now." My stomach does a somersault.

"Sounds like an 'Old Tomato' to me."

"Huh?" I say, puzzled.

"It means 'ultimatum'," Rick says. "I've explained that a couple of times before. Shit, you were probably wasted."

"Gee, thanks." I pretend to launch another peanut at him but refrain.

He laughs. "My dad used that expression all the time."

"So yes, that's what she gave me, an Old Tomato. It's crunch time. I have to decide."

"What do you think you'll do?"

"I don't know. I think I'm in love with Gina," causing Rick to look up quickly. "Yeah, I have finally realized that. But, I've been a hound for a lot of years and I just don't trust myself."

"I remember that feeling. We'd be on the road and chicks would be buzzing around, and after a few beers, Cindy would begin to fade into the background."

"What did you do about it?" I'm afraid of the answer.

"I cut down on the beers when I was out with the guys, for one thing. Like I told you that day you called me over to your house, I started comparing the chicks to Cindy. You know? A side-by-side comparison. A cost-benefit analysis, I think they call it."

We laugh hysterically at pretending to be economists.

Then he says, "The chick of the moment would start fading, and Cindy would come back into focus. I usually excused myself and beat a retreat to the men's room for a nice long visit with some cold water to gather my wits."

I smile at him and ask, "Did that work?"

"By the time I came out of the john, the chick usually had moved on to other action. It was hard to do at first but got easier with every encounter." Rick's brown eyes smiled warmly at me making me feel a little less lost.

"Rick Gordon, party of two. Your table is ready," we hear over the loudspeaker. We grab our beers and head back to the front desk. One of the young girls hanging around at the desk escorts us up the stairs to the third floor where she seats us at a table in the corner, and hands us our menus. She recites the obligatory "Enjoy your dinner," and disappears down the stairs. My eyes follow her wistfully. No wedding ring.

"One other thing I did was stop hanging around with the single guys as much. Less temptation," Rick continues.

"Hmm. Well, aren't I lucky that my best friend is married and willing to hang out with me?" I pick up my menu.

"Happy to oblige," he says and winks a lopsided grin.

"When you and Cindy got married, I was afraid it would affect our friendship. I'm sure glad it hasn't."

Rick smiles. "Hell. I see more of your sorry ass than I do her cute one!"

Our waiter appears and tells us that the special tonight is lobster, one and a half pounds or bigger. Man, this is our lucky night. I order a two-pound steamed Maine lobster with drawn butter and lemon, with side orders of corn on the cob and coleslaw. Very New England. Rick follows suit.

We retreat to lighter chit chat while we wait for our food. I need a breather from the gut-wrenching stuff for a few minutes.

When the food appears, the waiter puts on a show for us by expertly cleaning the lobsters, cracking the claws and removing each piece of tail meat whole without showering us with lobster juice. He artfully arranges lobster parts on large white platters and places one in front of each of us. We don our paper lobster bibs, pick up our shell crackers, and dig in.

Once the waiter has retired, I plunge in again. "I guess this is a test, this road trip. She told me that I have no strings. That I need to play it by ear and see what happens. And I'm very uneasy about the whole thing."

"If you stick with me, you'll be safe!" Rick puts his fork down and looks me in the eye. "Buddy, you have to decide how much Gina means to you and then make a decision. I know it's hard not getting any, but if she's what you want, you gotta stick with the program."

"Easy for you to say. You can go home to Cindy and get your rocks off."

Chapter Twenty-Four

"You really think that's what it's all about? Come on, man. A real relationship is a partnership, not just a roll in the sack. It's about cherishing each other, making plans, raising kids, having each other's back. Two people as one, taking on the world together. And having sex sometimes takes a back seat to the rest of it. "

I look at him for a few minutes and then shake my head. "I never thought about it that way. I don't know if I could do that, even without the temptation of the baseball groupies."

"I'm afraid to tell you that is exactly what you have to do if you want Gina in your life permanently. That *is* what you want, right?"

"I think so."

"You 'think so?' What's holding you back? The chick thing?"

I think about that for a few moments.

"Yeah. I'm petrified that some chick will come on to me, and I won't be able to resist and do something stupid."

"Well, damn it, Larry. That's not what grown ups do. They suck it up and do the right thing even if its hard."

"I guess so." Why can't I see it as clearly as he does?

"Look, let's talk about Gina and why you want to have a more-permanent relationship with her. What is it about her that makes her special to you, other than sex, and things you have in common like jazz and playing golf?"

"I guess the thing that sets her apart from other women is that she's just as dedicated to her job as I am. For instance, she told me about this little boy named Jimmy who was brought into the emergency room last week, completely out of it, gasping for breath, and running a high fever. She stayed with him in the hospital all night until she was convinced he wouldn't die. I gather it was touch and go until they knew what kind of infection he had and could give him the correct antibiotics."

He mulls over what I just said. "Okay, so…"

"She knows all her kids' names, makes follow-up phone calls to check on them, and is very involved with their parents. She is so much more than just a doctor to her patients. I think she actually loves them." I smile just thinking about her.

"Well, it goes both ways, man. Cindy says the kids love having her as their doctor. And I've really enjoyed watching her with them the few times I've gone to an appointment."

I smile. "I actually got to meet Jimmy right before this road trip. He's a huge baseball fan so she asked me if I'd drop by her office when he was there, so I went."

I look at Rick. "It was so amazing. She actually had tears running down her face while I was talking to Jimmy."

"I guess she loves you after all," he says, smiling.

I look at him puzzled. "I don't know about that, but seeing her with Jimmy made me want her in my life for sure. She was awesome with him." I smile at the whole experience.

"So, why are you tearing yourself up so much about her? Sounds to me like she might be the one."

"I don't know, Rick. But maybe what has me hooked is… is the thought that maybe she might learn to love me the way she loves Jimmy and the others. Not as a doctor or a mother, but you should see the light in her eyes when she talks about 'her kids'. It's awesome. Maybe I want some of that, too."

"You're a goner!"

"Maybe so. I just know that I want her in my life. I just hope I can figure out a way to live up to that kind of a commitment."

He looks at me for a long time, apparently trying to figure out what else to say. Finally, he shakes his head and says, "Just eat your lobster and stop worrying so much."

I try to focus on the delicious platter in front of me. I'm down to the little claws now, so I start stripping the meat out with my teeth. I wish Gina were here. This lobster would taste even better.

Rick and I talk baseball while we finish our lobsters, pass up dessert, and I slap down my credit card. "I insist, Rick."

We wait outside while the maitre d' calls a cab for us, enjoying the moist night air and the clink of the halyards on the masts nearby which are silhouetted against the night sky.

Back at the hotel, Rick retires to his room to call Cindy. Once I'm down to my skivvies, I think about calling Gina but dismiss the idea. It'll just make me think about her gorgeous body and the wonderful things she does with it, and I'll have to retreat to the john.

I try to immerse myself in "State of Fear," but my stomach is very full and churning after all the talk about Gina. At some point, the words begin to swim on the page, so I douse the light and give in to sleep.

Chapter Twenty-Five

We lose the last game in Boston and travel to Cleveland for a three-game series against the Indians, who always give us a difficult time. We win the first game by one run. In the second one, we play well for eight innings, but lose in the bottom of the ninth inning when Johnson gives up another walk-off home run, a carbon copy of the one in Yankee Stadium a week ago.

Some of the other pitchers are going out to a club to hear a jazz trumpeter who is supposed to be hot. They invite Rick and me along. I hesitate before answering and listen to the conversation going on in my head.

Should I go? Or not?

It's Cleveland, for God's sake. The girls are probably all dogs or hooked up with some loser.

Rick says he'll go so I decide to chance it. "Okay. I'm in." I haven't been to a jazz club in months. Sounds like we'll hear some good licks.

We head out of the ballpark in two cabs. Twenty minutes later, we come to a stop in front a club called Nighttown. Rick pays off the cabby, giving him a nice tip. We walk beneath a blue awning through the glass-paned front door. This place is really nice, not at all the dark, smoke-filled jazz joint I was expecting.

Straight ahead is a long bar with artwork behind. I leave the others and step up to the counter.

"What'll you have?" the bartender asks while drying a glass.

"I'll have a good table up front near the band." I slip him a fifty and mention under my voice what team we play for.

He grins and says conspiratorially, "Leave it to me." He flags down the maitre d' and talks to him quietly. This elicits a smile from the latter, who waves at us and disappears.

The bartender turns back to me. "Why don't you have a drink. The maitre d' will come to get you when your table's ready."

I tell the others that I have arranged everything. Hey, I'm the veteran on the pitching staff. Gotta take care of the younger guns.

We order drinks and stand by the bar trying to look inconspicuous. After a few minutes, the maitre d' appears and shows us to a table in the lounge right up near the bandstand. Rick sits down to my right, Donnie Kensler to my left. The other two, Judd Johnson and Tommy Sanchez, sit across the round table from us. When I sit down I don't see that a corner of the white table cloth is on my chair. I figure it out when water glasses tip over and the silverware rattles. We all jump up and pull out our chairs to avoid the flood.

Some veteran! I feel my face flush as the whole dining room turns to look in our direction.

Donnie Kensler says, "Nice move, dumb shit."

Embarrassed, I pick up my wet menu and hide behind it. I don't want to encourage any of those jokers. This is a nice place. I don't want us to get tossed out before we eat dinner. A waiter appears with a dry table cloth and begins cleaning up the mess.

"What are you having, Rick?" I inquire when we are once again seated at the table.

"I don't think I'm up for a steak after all," he says. "I think I'll have the 'Chesapeake crab cakes with roasted corn and chipotle mashed potatoes.' Are you going to stick with your red meat concept?"

I peruse the menu and look up when I've made my decision. "Since I'm trying to change my life, I might as well start with dinner. I'm intrigued by the 'Dublin Lawyer', one of the house specialties. The sound of 'lobster meat sautéed in a mild cayenne butter cream sauce with mushrooms, scallions, and Irish whiskey served over rice pilaf' and a small salad is more than I can resist."

At the word "Lawyer," a brief vision of Gail from spring training flashes across my mind. I banish her instantly. Don't need to be wearing any drinks tonight, other than the spilled water that still wets my pants.

"Lobster twice in one week," Rick muses. "That is a change for you."

Rick closes his menu, and says, "Your choice does sound delicious, but I'm sticking with my crab cakes."

After the waiter leaves with our orders in hand, I survey the scene like I always do. Most tables are filled with couples or families, but there is one table not far away containing trouble, a group that has to be young, single girls. They're showing lots of bare skin, long shiny hair, and eager smiles. One has blond hair cascading over her shoulders and is wearing a halter top barely controlling luscious full breasts. Another with her back to me shows me bare shoulders with a strip of fire engine red fabric below.

Rick sees my shit-eating grin and follows my line of sight. "Just a reminder, bro," he says, nodding in the girls direction. "That's what you're supposed to avoid." He smiles encouragingly. I look down before I catch one of their eyes.

Damn. This is hard. But I gotta do it. I dial up my resolve, and down a little of the beer the waiter puts in front of me.

I guess the guys across the table have turned to see what I was checking out. When they spot the beauties, two backs collectively sit up a little straighter. This is not lost on the women, who start whispering to each other and stealing glances in our direction. In the nick of time, our food arrives, and our collective attention is drawn to the steaming plates in front of us. The aromas push all thoughts of the girls to the back of my mind. Maybe I can get out of this unscathed.

Over dinner we relive today's game, and then move on to talk about the players who have admitted to taking steroids. We all have varying opinions about the Hall of Fame and the steroid era. I tune it out. I won't touch the stuff. Don't want my balls shrinking. But guys cheat. Always have. Always will.

After dessert, Wallace Roney and his band are introduced and begin their first set. Roney blows a mean trumpet, and the band is really good. Mostly jazz with Motown and blues overtones. Gina would love this.

About thirty minutes into the set, my bladder starts vying with the music for my attention. When I can't hold it any longer, I push back my chair and try to crouch my six-foot-four frame down. I work my way unobtrusively to the back of the room, doing a pretty good imitation of a cat burglar. I make it to the men's room in the nick of time.

I look at myself in the mirror as I wash my hands. "Gina is who you want," I whisper to my reflection. "Keep that in mind. And do the right thing for a change."

I take a deep breath, check my hair, and walk toward the door full of confidence.

126

On the way out of the men's room, I crash right into a young woman who is standing outside the door. I apologize profusely while she bats her blue eyes at me and smiles. I recognize that shade of red, and it dawns on me that this little scene may not be an accident.

"Hi, handsome. You and your buddies are sitting at the next table to ours and I just had to meet you." She smiles broadly and cocks a hip to one side. This is definitely trouble.

She has gorgeous blue eyes and long brown hair with blond highlights, long shapely legs, and a voluptuous body nicely packaged in a bright red strapless tube of fabric. It looks like the same dress that Gail had on in the Round Up, and on this girl it leaves little to my overactive imagination.

Don't go there. Pretend Gina is here, I say to myself.

The latter thought evaporates as I hold out my hand to her. "I'm Larry Gordon. I'm with the Oakland Renegades. We lost to the Indians today."

"Nice to meet you, Larry."

All sorts of voices are screaming in my head, telling me to knock it off, walk away, don't do it, etc.

I have to see if I can handle this kind of situation sometime, I rationalize.

I visualize walking back to her table, sitting down at mine, and ignoring her for the rest of the evening. But she smiles again, and my primary decision maker is pointing right at her. I smile back at her. "You didn't tell me your name."

"Oh, Marilee Burns," she says with a giggle. "Hey, when the band breaks after this set, why don't we get a drink together? I'm sure that my girlfriends would love to meet your friends. They're your teammates, right?"

"Yes they are." I gesture in the direction of our table and she walks in front of me, swaying her hips sensually for my benefit.

Damn. I could definitely get lost in her. Take her off to another bar for that drink. Get her a little tipsy. Tell Rick to go back with the others. Blow this place, go to a hotel room, put out the 'Do Not Disturb' sign and take this luscious thing several times, and be able to sleep like a baby.

I button my jacket to cover the growing bulge in my pants. When I swipe at my brow, my hand comes away soaking. Shit. I'm sweating like a fucking race horse. This is not good.

The battle continues in earnest in my brain. I hungrily watch her moving between the tables in front of me, my eyes glued to her ass.

Wisdom fights back in the form of a voice inside my head asking, "Larry, what about Gina?"

Reality comes back with a jolt.

Sweat builds as the precariousness of the situation hits me. I should excuse myself and flee back to the safety of the men's room like Rick suggested. I eyeball this luscious thing again. The other guys would love to meet these girls if they are anywhere near as dazzlingly as Marilee is.

But Gina. Remember her?

"Sure," I hear myself say to Marilee. "Getting a drink sounds good."

You dumb shit!

When we reach the lounge, the set has already ended. The guys have pounced on Marilee's table, all except Rick who is frantically looking around, probably trying to find me. When he spots me following Marilee, he gives me a pointed look that screams only one thing: You asshole!!!

I head straight for Rick and introduce my new appendage. "Rick, this is Marilee Burns. I nearly killed her with the men's room door."

I look at her. "This is Rick Wycliffe, my best friend and stellar relief pitcher. He's saved my backside countless times."

"Nice to meet you, Marilee." He glares at me sideways.

"Nice to meet you, too." She offers Rick her hand which sports nail polish that matches her red dress. Rick tries to smile at her and then looks daggers at me.

"Marilee, will you excuse us for a few minutes?" Rick says, in an artificially pleasant voice. "I'll bring him right back. I promise."

"Sure. I guess," she says, looking doubtful. Gradually, she turns to talk to one of her friends.

Rick turns his glare on me. If looks could kill, I'd be getting the last rites. He grabs my arm with a vice grip and forcibly propels me out to the parking lot.

Once we're out in the night air, Rick yells, "What the fuck are you doing?"

I open my mouth and close it again, unable to speak in the face of so much anger.

"What the Hell happened to all that resolve? That 'I only want to be with Gina?' Did you forget all that when you 'ran into' this bimbo?"

I have never seen him so furious before, his face as red as my lobster in Boston.

"I don't know," I say, finally finding my voice. I shake my head to try to clear my brain of the chatter going on inside.

I look at Rick, but I can't stand his fury, and return my gaze to the asphalt.

Finally I say, "The problem is that I've done this scene with women for so long, it's just second nature to me. I go on autopilot. I can't help it."

Rick looks like he is going to explode, his face now purple with rage. "Yes... you... can!" he hisses through clenched teeth. "And that's a fucking cop-out, and you know it!"

I say nothing.

He goes on, gentling his voice a bit. "Larry, I have wanted to say this to you for some time, but I always bit my tongue. You gotta fucking grow up, man. You're twenty-eight years old and your acting like a fucking teenager who's trying to get laid for the first time."

I hang my head, not wanting to see the disappointment in his eyes. I feel more like I'm twelve years old, and Mom has caught me sneaking a beer.

"When are you going to start acting your age?" he continues. "Women aren't playthings you can just use and discard. We talked about this before. I think you know that up here," pointing to his head, "but your dick gets hard and you forget everything else and bang whoever is in sight. That's not what adults do."

"But I can't..."

"YES, YOU CAN, GOD DAMMIT!" he yells. Angry sparks shoot from his eyes.

I look down at my shoes. Rick walks away mumbling to himself. Finally, he comes back over to me.

"Look, you're my best friend," he says in a somewhat calmer voice. "I don't like yelling at you, but you need a big wake up call. You're trashing your life, and it fucking kills me to see you doing it."

I don't say anything for a long time. When I can trust my voice, I say, without looking up, "I know. I know. I don't like me very much either."

Rick comes over and puts his arms around me and gives me a hug.

When he lets go, I ask, "What am I going to do now?" I feel beaten and drained.

He takes a deep breath. "Okay. You asked me to help you with this so here it is. Go back in there and make some small talk with her and in the conversation drop the fact that you have a girlfriend at home and you're practically engaged. She'll get the message."

"I can't just drop her like that. Besides the other guys might be having a good time with her friends." I clutch at this quasi-legitimate but lame excuse. "Also, the band plays another set. What am I supposed to do during that?"

"Shit, this is like talking to a fuckin' two-year-old," he says, his exasperation obvious.

I flinch. His words hurt like a fist to the solar plexus.

Rick takes a long deep breath and lets it out slowly. "Just sit there and listen to the fucking music with your fucking hands folded, and go easy on the beer."

"And when the set ends?" I sound like a child, even to me.

Rick rolls his eyes. "Jesus, Larry. You're not this stupid."

I shrug and say nothing.

He throws up his hands. "Okay, I guess I have to spell everything out for you."

He shakes his head and continues in a sing-song voice as if he's talking to a child. "We all get up and you say to her, 'It was nice to meet you,' and you stick out your hand. She'll shake it, and you and I will turn and walk out of this joint. End of problem. The other guys? They're on their own."

I look at my best friend and suddenly long for Gina. "Okay. You're right. I'll do it," I say with some conviction.

Rick smiles and says, without anger, "Don't look like such a forlorn puppy. You said you want Gina. Do this and be happy about it."

We walk back to the lounge and sit down to listen to the music. Marilee is now sitting in the chair next to mine, and Donny Kensler is over at the girls' table. I watch him wistfully but sit down next to

Marilee. I smile at her but turn to watch the band intently until the piece is over, trying not to groove to the music.

During the applause, I lean over and say to her, "God, I wish my girlfriend were here. She's a jazz nut and would love this place." I look down for a few minutes so I don't have to see how she takes this.

Finally, I turn to her, but she's now talking to Hank Sutro, working her wiles on him.

Disaster avoided, at least for now. So why do I feel so shitty?

The set ends and Wallace Roney tells us we are a wonderful audience. They play an encore, and depart the stage to raucous applause, as the stage lights dim and go out. We all stand up and I turn and say, "It was nice to meet you, Marilee." I stick out my hand.

She hesitates a moment but takes my offered hand and shakes it. "It was nice to meet you too." She looks up at me wistfully and withdraws her hand, turning slowly back to Hank.

Rick taps me on the shoulder and points toward the front entrance.

We walk out the door, and I exhale deeply into the humid night air. "Man, that was hard!"

Rick doesn't respond and keeps walking in front of me toward a waiting cab.

On the awkward ride back to our hotel, I mull over what just happened.

I don't know whether Rick is still angry. He's said nothing to me since the music ended. The silence is oppressive.

Finally, I can't stand it. "Jesus, Rick. I was watching myself back there while all that was happening. I was out of control, even though there were these voices inside my head screaming at me to back off Marilee."

No response.

I turn to look at him. "I can't believe that's how I have operated with women in the past. No wonder I haven't had any lasting relationships."

"Hello!" Rick says with a little residual heat in his voice.

I ignore him and plunge on. "I never got to know any of them before we hopped in the sack, and I always lost interest pretty soon thereafter."

Again, nothing from his side of the cab.

131

I look out my side window, watching the buildings fly by.

"I guess I'm a mess," I say, finally.

After a few minutes, Rick says. "You're not any more of a mess than any other guy before he sees the light. Except that most guys usually get it a lot of years sooner. You're finally growing up emotionally." He hesitates. "And it's about fuckin' time, if you ask me."

I know I'm a late bloomer, but it still smarts to hear it said, even by my best friend.

He isn't done. "This was a wakeup call for you. In the end, you made the right choice tonight. Good work!" Rick finally turns my way, and gives me one of his lopsided grins.

I still have a queasy feeling about the events of the evening. "But what happens if I have to face this kind of thing and you're not around?"

"You'll have to deal with it on your own." He pauses and smiles. "And I'm not going anywhere, ya know."

Relief floods through me. He's still my friend.

"And besides, the next time will be easier," he says.

*   *   *

I'm on the hill for the third game of the series today against J.J. McGonagle, and the Indians get to me for three runs in six innings. I don't feel the high that I felt in my start against Boston. My arm feels tired from the get-go, and I can't keep the ball down in the strike zone. Sometimes that just happens. I can't explain it.

The bullpen holds them to the three runs but the guys can only manage to score two, so I take my sixth loss. Allowing three runs in six innings today isn't so terrible for me. Come to think of it, we also scored only two runs when I won in Boston. Why do our bats seem to go silent when I pitch?

I try to drain it all out of me in the hot steamy shower after the game, but it doesn't have its usual rejuvenating effect. I'll get over the loss by morning. I always do.

Rick and I haven't talked any more about last night. He's probably been avoiding it as much as I am. But after he comes back from his shower, he looks over at me with a smile on his face, crooked as usual, and asks, "So are we okay after last night? I wasn't too hard on your ass?"

132

"Yeah, we're fine. I guess I needed the chewing out."

"Cool," he says, and goes back to getting dressed.

I think about last night and that Rick had to rescue me from Marilee and yell at me in the parking lot. I realize he was right. I do need to grow up, and it makes me love him even more. It's as if until last night we were best friends. Today, it feels like we're brothers. He really put himself out there for me.

Chapter Twenty-Six

I get home from the road trip around eight o'clock in the evening, stifling more than a few yawns. Our flight from Cleveland was delayed for two hours because of thunderstorms all over the Midwest. I order a pizza and wolf it down with a couple of beers, before calling Gina to let her know I made it home. I get her answering machine and leave a message. Exhaustion from the long road trip asserts itself, and I drop into bed and fall asleep instantly. No game tomorrow, so I don't set my alarm.

In the morning after coming back from my favorite Danville breakfast spot, I turn on my cell phone, which I have ignored until now. There's a message from Gina, one from my agent, and one from Darren. I decide to call them back in the reverse order, saving what I hope is the best for last.

Sitting in my favorite chair, I dial Darren's cell. He says he's doing well and had called to thank me again for helping him at spring training.

"No worries, Darren. Happy to do it. By the way, the last time we talked, I forgot to thank you for the card you sent me when I was losing it on the mound. You sure had some brass balls, man!" I try to keep my voice light so he doesn't think I'm upset about it.

"Yeah, I know. I was nervous how you would take it. I even tried to get it back from the post office later that day."

"Well, I wasn't mad. I had lost my way. It was a good wake-up call. But, if you'd been here, I'd probably have given you some serious shit. But no worries, man."

"Cool. I appreciate it. And good job in that game in Fenway. You were awesome."

"Thanks. Sorry to cut this short but I got in last night from our trip, and I have a lot to catch up on. Stay focused, Darren, and don't let success go to your head." Yeah, like I do sometimes. "Good luck."

I hang up and look around at my bachelor pad with its modern sterile furniture and lack of adornment and sigh again. This place really needs Gina's touch. My body could use that too.

I push those thoughts out of my head and dial my agent. "Hi, Bob."

"Hey, Larry. What's new?"

"Not too much. Just doing my job." Ten days on the road, being tired even after a good night's sleep, an ache in my shoulder, and stacks of mail piled high. I'd like to see him try it.

"Doing your job is great. You've had some terrific outings since we last talked. Definitely moving in the right direction."

"Yeah. So what's up, Bob?" Not wanting to hear the answer, my eyes roll like I just hung a slider over the middle of the plate.

"Look, Larry, you know the saying. Your last start is yesterday's news, and, well, markets are falling all over the world. You're supposed to be setting the baseball market. Let's not forget that. So you still need to turn it up a notch."

Turn it up a notch? What does this asshole know about being sixty feet six inches from being drilled by a batted ball? He has no fucking idea what it's like to be staring disaster in the face with every pitch. I tell myself to hang up the phone. Unfortunately, I really can't. He is my agent after all.

Instead I say, "Fuck you, Bob," and let the words hang there between us.

I feel like slamming the phone down, but take a few deep breaths instead, and say, "Look, Bob. I just got home from a long road trip. I'm exhausted. I don't want to deal with this shit right now. You know how I feel. The business side of the game really sucks." Again, I fail to follow my impulse to blow him off.

"Wake up, Larry," he says. "It comes with the territory, and we have to deal with it. It's part of my job description, but it's also my responsibility to make you aware of your role in all of this. I can't do my job without you doing yours."

I get up and pace, my head suddenly gripped in a vice of tension. Bob prattles on about my bloated ERA, the number in my loss column, and how much less I'm going to make next year and beyond.

When I can finally speak without yelling at him, I say when he takes a breath, "Bob. Bob."

"What?" he asks, sounding perturbed.

135

"I've already got enough fuckin' pressure on me. I don't need yours, too. I'm doing my best. And you know I do better when the end of the season is in sight. Just watch, okay?"

"Look, Larry. Business..."

This time I hang up before he can finish the sentence. I shake my head to try to rattle away the double whammy of tension and loneliness. "Fuck the hell off!" I say to the phone. I grab a beer from the fridge even though it's ten-thirty in the morning, and flop down in my chair again.

I hate this shit. I'm supposed to set the fucking market for premier pitchers. I thought this was what I wanted, but now I'm not so sure. Who needs all this pressure? Why can't I just sign a contract with the Renegades at a more modest price and live a normal life? Even if it's only forty million or more dollars over three or four years. Who can't live on forty mill? I'm sure Bob could find a way to live with that.

And I wouldn't have to move. I could buy a big house. God that sounds tempting.

I'm twenty-eight years old. How many more years of this do I have at best? Twelve at the most? Do I really want to live with all this pressure until I'm forty? At the end of that, I'll still be a reasonably young man. I'll have to do something after I can't play ball anymore. Stay in baseball as a coach? Be a color analyst on TV or radio? Sell real estate? God, not real estate. I'd die of boredom.

I look at the clock. 10:45. Fuck it! I take a long swig.

Gina in my bed would solve a lot. If I stay here next year, maybe there's a chance I can succeed in patching it up with her. That would definitely allow me to cope with stress a lot better.

I stretch out on my black leather couch and punch the speed dial key assigned to her. It's Friday morning. I don't think she'll be home so I'll talk to her voicemail.

After two rings, there's a click. "Hi, Larry, welcome home," she says, in a cheery voice.

"Oh, Gina. Hi. I thought you'd be at work. I was just going to leave you a message."

"Nope. I switched with a colleague so she could go to a wedding this weekend. So it's your lucky day. You got me instead of my machine."

136

She sounds so upbeat, that I decide to take a chance. "I was hoping to talk to you. Can I come over?" What am I going to say? I haven't a clue.

Silence.

"I guess. Sure. Come on over," she says, but I can hear the hesitancy in her voice.

"I'll be there in about forty-five minutes."

I get up, finish my beer, take a quick shower, dress, and drive the eight miles to her house. On the way there I run scenarios over in my head. But they all seem to end in her throwing me out. I park in her driveway and check my hair in the rearview mirror. I look tired, with sad-looking eyes.

Perk up. You're about to see Gina.

I get out of my sports car and shake back my shoulders. Here goes. I could be out on my ear if I don't play this right.

Ninth inning. Seventh Game.

I put on a smile, walk slowly up the front steps, and rap twice on her door. It swings open on the second knock.

"Hi, come on in." She looks wonderful in jeans and a tee shirt. My mind races to the feeling of her arms around me, and how I felt the last time we made love. Taking in a deep breath, I look down at the floor before my eyes can give me away.

I take a chance and say, "Can I give you a hug? It's been a long time."

"I guess," she says, and steps slowly into my arms.

I hold her close, but not too tight. It is pure bliss having her in my arms again. I feel her body give in to mine a bit. A little spark of hope flickers to life and goes straight to my dick.

I relax my hold on her and back away so I can see her face. She's smiling. That's a good sign. God I hope I'm reading her right.

"Could I please have a glass of water? I'm thirsty as hell!" I'm also as jumpy as a cat.

She disappears into the kitchen, and I devour her with my eyes. Slow and easy now. Take your time.

I turn and walk to the couch in the living room and sit down, trying to collect myself. My gaze lands on the current issue of *Sports Illustrated* on the coffee table. The Indians' J.J. McGonagle and I are pictured on the cover, but J.J. is half-again as big as I am. Well, in height and weight he certainly is. What really galls me is

137

that he's pictured on top, and I'm much smaller and down near the lower right-hand corner like an afterthought. That hurts.

The accompanying article on page fourteen is entitled, "A Bumper Crop of Free Agents." There is an array of smiling faces with different colored hats staring out from the pages, all free agents after the end of the season. What a lineup. I close the magazine in disgust.

Looking at the cover picture of J.J. McGonagle makes me wish our guys could have scored a few runs off him when I was on the mound in Cleveland. I guess that's why his picture is larger than mine.

I open the magazine again and start reading the article. Milo Peterson of the Angels threw a no hitter in his rookie season, it says. Jeff Collier of the Mariners had a great postseason last year, throwing two shutouts in the ALCS. And Clint Pence of the Red Sox has a 2.23 ERA in eight post-season appearances. How can I compete with that? And I'm supposed to be setting the market for these guys, Bob? The pressure kicks in again.

The article does mention me, but the author highlights some of my less than sterling moments and a few games where the guys just didn't score many runs. Of course, the author doesn't focus on games like my recent complete-game shutout against the Red Sox. Shit, I beat Pence in that game.

A wave of anxiety hits. I close the article and lean my head back against the couch. I practice yoga breathing to calm my nerves.

I open my eyes when I hear Gina return. She hands me a cobalt blue glass with water, ice cubes, and a spring of mint in it, and sits down on the other end of the couch.

"So, tell me about the road trip. I read about your loss in Cleveland. It wasn't your fault."

I point at the *Sports Illustrated* cover. "Yeah, but I gave up one more run than that guy did. How exactly is that not my fault? My agent clearly thinks it is. He said as much on the phone earlier."

Here I am talking all about me again, when this conversation should be all about her. That's not what I had in mind when I asked to come over here.

"Larry, don't be so hard on yourself," she says, melting my self-destructive thoughts with a warm smile. "Give the hitters some of the credit. Sometimes they're just 'on', and no matter how well the ball is pitched, they can hit it." Leave it to Gina to try to make me feel better.

I gaze around her neat cheery house and mentally compare it to my place. There's a place for everything here. Even me.

I feel at home in this house. I just exist at mine.

"Let's not talk anymore about the road trip," I say. "I'll just mention that I haven't been with anyone since you saw me last. Let's leave it at that."

Gina's smile broadens a bit, but unspoken questions flicker across her beautiful face.

I'm not sure what I came here to say, but words start pouring out. "It hasn't been easy, but I guess I realized on this road trip that I really don't want to be with anyone but you."

I watch her for a reaction, but her face doesn't change, so I keep going. "I had a few opportunities but didn't pursue them."

Marilee flits across my brain again, but I dismiss her rudely. My thoughts consume me for a few moments. My lips dry up. I rehearse in my head what I want to say.

Gina waits patiently for something from me, the smile still on her face and in her blue eyes.

I reach over and take her hand. I gaze into those eyes that make me melt and decide I have to take the plunge. "Gina, I've thought a lot about what I really want, and I've decided I want to be with you. If that means being faithful to you, then I want to do that too." It actually feels pretty good to say it.

She is grinning now. "Wow, Larry. I'm amazed." But hesitation still haunts her eyes. "But wanting to be with me isn't enough. I need to be sure that you really don't want to be with anyone else. That's what love is, Larry." She looks down for a moment and back up at me, her smile gone. "Do you love me, Larry?"

Here it is: the "L" word, the big do or die moment.

Do I love her? Yeah, I do. I still worry about living up to that, but I really want to try. Of course, I've never actually been in love before. And do we ever really know if we're in it? This is all so new.

I slide closer to her and take both of her hands in mine. I look deep into her eyes. Somehow, magically, my universe goes calm, and I have the same tunnel vision I have when I'm mowing down hitters. I'm completely in the zone.

139

"Gina, I love you. I don't want any other woman. I just want to be with you. I want what you want."

I take a deep breath and say, "Yes, I really do love you."

"Oh, Larry." Her eyes now shine with tears, and her hesitation is receding by the second. She moves closer to me, but still apart. "Are you sure?"

This is beginning to feel right. I'm not nervous.

"I'm very sure. I love you, and I don't want to be with any other woman. I can't make it any clearer. I LOVE YOU, GINA!" I shout at the top of my lungs, not caring who might hear it through the open windows.

Her face lights up and a tear escapes. She looks at me as if trying to decide what to do next. Without speaking, she throws her arms around me and her lips find mine.

We kiss for a long time. My heart is pounding, but I feel a calm wash over me. I pull her closer and deepen our kiss. I feel like I'm finally home, here in her arms.

When she comes up for air, she says, "I have been so miserable without you." Her tousled blond hair frames her face and her eyes blaze blue. "I love you, too."

Somehow hearing her tell me she loves me makes me feel even calmer and happier. Unlike in the past, I don't feel like running for the nearest exit at the sound of those three words. My mouth finds hers again. I kiss her longingly.

She rests her head on my shoulder and sighs. "I love this, just sitting here with your arms around me, resting against your wonderful muscular body."

She snuggles in a little closer, and says, "Staying away from you was the hardest thing I've ever done."

She strokes my chest, electricity sparking where her fingers fall.

"I'm probably a fool but I'm a fool in love," she says softly into my neck.

She relaxes into me and her warmth radiates through my body. A strand of hair tickles my nose. I don't care. I've never been happier in my life.

She lifts her face and her blue eyes lock onto mine, holding my gaze for a very long time. I feel as if I'm looking into her soul, and I feel warm comforting white light pouring into me. My mind flashes to the scene in the hospital with Jimmy. That's the same light of love she shined on him.

140

Her lips meet mine, and I devour her mouth. When I have to take a breath, I say, "I've missed you so. You feel wonderful. But if we don't stop right now, I may not be able to control myself."

"Who said anything about stopping?" She kisses me again, tenderly at first, then warming in intensity until I want to make love to her right there on the couch.

But she stops and stands up. She holds out her hand and pulls me down the hall to her bedroom. We strip off our clothes, eyes locked on each other, and lie down into each other's arms.

I look at her beautiful body stretched out next to mine. I feel her flesh respond as I find her breasts and linger there. Feeling the soft roundness, I bring my lips to her nipples which rise and harden in my mouth. She arches her back and moans softly. My fingers stroke their way down her flat belly which lifts to meet my touch. I take my time caressing the silky flesh. I try to maintain control to pleasure her as much as possible, but my erection is painfully hard.

"I can't stand it any longer. I need you inside me." Her voice rasps with desire.

"Are you sure?" I say, and she answers by pulling me into her.

A wave of pleasure courses through my body. We move together as one, lost in each other as we give in to the passion.

All the old rhythms of that January day, before my world fell apart, come flooding back. But this is different. It is so much more intense. It feels so right. This is where I am supposed to be. And where I want to be. As we reach the apex, my world shrinks to a point of light burning intensely where our bodies merge.

I'm completely spent. I feel like I have just come home from a very long journey. I realize that I have never been happier, and I want this for the rest of my life. I stroke her hair, kiss her closed eyelids and whisper in her ear, words I thought I would never say.

"Gina, will you marry me?"

She lies there in my arms, silent.

Finally, she takes a deep breath and says, "Wow. I didn't see that coming."

Shit. I've said the wrong thing again. "I'm sorry. I guess I put my foot in it again. Please tell me you love me again so I don't feel like I've just ruined the whole thing." My heart kicks into a sprint.

"Hon, of course I love you. You just took me completely by surprise."

"Is the idea of marrying me a problem?" Now that I've stuck my neck way out of my comfort zone, I'm afraid she doesn't like my proposal.

"No, it's not a problem at all. I have hoped for this day for a long time."

It's not a "yes," but it's not a "no" either.

I kiss her passionately, and I feel the familiar heat surging again. She responds with her hands taking a languid inventory of my body. I lie back and enjoy the sensation of my skin responding to her touch. God, please don't let this stop. Let me stay here for the rest of my life.

I look into her eyes and she into mine. Our lips move closer, and in an instant, we're steaming the sheets again. We make love until we're once again sated and exhausted.

I pull back and look at her. Tears are running down her face. She looks into my eyes and nods up and down, unable to speak.

"Is that an answer to my big question?"

She still can't manage to speak, but nods again.

I pull her close and we fall asleep in each other's arms as if we've been doing this for a lifetime.

*   *   *

I wake up in the middle of the afternoon with a start. My hands are shaking and my heart is machine-gunning. Oh my God, I just asked Gina to marry me! Shit!

I look over at Gina sleeping soundly. Can I do this? What will happen when temptation presents itself?

God, I want to be the person she thinks I am. But I'm scared shitless. Why? Why can't I trust myself? What if I'm as unsuccessful at this as I am with a bat in my hand?

I ease out of bed trying not to wake Gina, and wander to the kitchen. In the third cabinet, I find pay dirt. A bottle of Chivas Regal. I pour myself a double and drop in a couple of ice cubes. I flop down onto the couch in the living room to contemplate what I have just done. Before I can take a swallow of the scotch, an unfamiliar warmth and calmness flows over my body, inside and out.

This is new.

Okay, I think. Let's look at this thing more rationally. This is a beautiful, intelligent woman whom you want more than any other woman in the world. You asked her to marry you. She wants you. She loves you. She's independent, self-supporting, caring, loving, and wonderful with children. You just made the most fantastic love of your life. Twice.

I look down at my drink, but hold off on bringing it to my lips. She wants me. And she loves me.

What's the fucking problem here? I'm going twelve innings with a sixteen-year-old inside my head. I put the drink down on the coffee table and lay my head on the back of the couch. Something's just not the same.

Calm and serenity flow over me again as I try to look at my situation rationally, without booze to carry me along. This may be the hardest thing I've ever done. I close my eyes and take a long breath. Or it might be the easiest.

Seventh game. I start to drift. Seventh game... World Series...

I'm jilted out of this strange sensation by arms surrounding my neck from behind the couch. I jerk around to find Gina smiling, her face flushed with sleep.

"I heard you talking out here so I came out to investigate."

I slump back into her arms with relief and lay my head on the back of the couch next to hers.

"I suppose I heard from my conscience," I say. "I have this voice in my head that talks to me and I talk back to it." I look at her and smile. "I didn't realize that I was talking out loud though. I'm sorry if I woke you up."

"It's okay." She runs her fingers lazily through my tousled hair. "I've been awake for a little while thinking about today, too. I'm thrilled that you asked me to marry you, but if you want to slow this down a bit while you get used to the idea, we don't have to go public with it right away." Her fingers wander down to my chest.

"I don't want to take it back, but I'm nervous about doing this," I say.

She kisses me gently on the neck as her hand explores lower.

I grab her roving hand. "How can you be so understanding?"

"I love you and I make it my business to tune into the feelings of people I love. Just like I can often diagnose what is wrong with little kids even if they don't have the language to express it. I'm good at it." She gives my neck a little squeeze.

143

I turn so I can see her smile. "What did I do to deserve you?"

"You let down your guard and allowed me to see into your soul, and I liked what I saw there. You players all have this macho façade. But I saw something in you that was different. Once I got to know you, I decided that having you in my life was worth fighting for, even if it meant I had to push you away to find out if I had a chance."

To find out if she had a chance? Now, I feel manipulated!

Why does that make me feel angry? She's only telling me what's true about ballplayers, and that she saw something more in me. I should love her for that. I guess it's just a knee-jerk reaction—something I would have felt a year ago. Probably my ego talking.

I take a deep breath and will my hurt to get lost. Shrugging my shoulders back, I smile at her, and she wraps her arms around me again.

"I was prepared never to see you again," she says. "It was the last thing I wanted. I've had a big hole in my life since January. And that day you appeared in my driveway, all I wanted to do was rush into your arms. But I knew if I did, we'd be right back where we were in January, so I hung tough."

The feel of her warm breath on my neck removes all negative thoughts.

"I guess I can live with that," I admit.

She gets up and comes around the couch and kneels on the floor in front of me, taking my hands in hers.

"And now here you are and you love me. We're engaged. It was all worth it. You wouldn't have gotten to this point if I had caved, now would you? Be honest."

I look down at our intertwined hands and smile. "Probably not."

"So, the marriage thing. Are you sorry?"

"No, I'm not," I say earnestly. "I'm just scared."

"About what?" Concern furrows her brow.

"About being able to live up to this huge commitment I just made to you. That's what."

"You can do anything you want if you put your mind to it. You know that. Let's just take it slow for the rest of the season and see how things go. Okay?"

"Okay!" I stand up and grasp her hands, bringing her to her feet, and kiss her.

Serenity returns.

Chapter Twenty-Seven

July is history, capped off by a series we took from Kansas City, winning two and losing one, bringing our record to fifty-four wins and fifty losses. The Minnesota Twins are now in town, and I'm on the hill today to pitch the second game of the series, a Wednesday 12:35 pm. start. Last night we won the first game by a big score.

I've been lucky lately and have been pitching a lot of day games. My career numbers show that I pitch better during the day, probably because the weather is warmer. Balls do leave the yard more during day games, but my pitches also have had a lot more movement. Sometimes you can't explain these things.

Today everything I throw lasers right into Jason Gardelli's mitt. I've been painting the edges of the plate, mixing up my pitches and keeping the hitters totally baffled. My mind has been clear and focused.

The Twins are now down to their last out in the bottom of the ninth. Jason and I are completely in sync, and I shake off a couple of signs only to confuse the hitters. I unleash Uncle Charlie and their final batter swings and misses it by a mile for strike three. We win sixteen to two. Not too shabby. A complete game on a hundred and twelve pitches.

Coming off the mound to greet the rest of the team, I feel elated. Tired but not spent. Coop gives me a high five, and mumbles something about seeing "the old Larry."

Down in the clubhouse, I head to the showers to hose off. Once back at my locker, I dress in my civvies and await the media onslaught.

One of the beat reporters sidles up to my locker, and says with a smile, "Well, Larry, I guess everything was working out there."

With the media, I'm usually on guard; afraid I'll put my foot in my mouth and say something stupid that will appear in the paper the next day. So I usually say as little as I can. But I decide to cut him a break today.

145

"Yeah. I felt great on the mound, really in control—of myself and the game," I say, focusing the positive. "Happy to get win number eleven."

"Thanks, Larry." He nods and seems at a loss for words. After looking at me for a few more moments, he wanders off to talk to Frank Matson who blasted two monster homers today.

After I toss my dirty uniform into the laundry bin in the middle of the room, and gather my stuff that's going home with me, a columnist I recognize from across the bay approaches me. He's a short balding man who has seen far too many pizzas and beer.

He has his pad out and appears ready to take down my every word. There goes my feeling of contentment.

"How difficult has it been to put the subject of contract talks out of your mind and concentrate on baseball?" he says with a smirk on his fleshy face.

Why does everyone have to remind me this is my contract year? Do they think I don't fucking know that?

I take a deep breath, and say, "I can't worry about that stuff. I'm hoping I can continue pitching well for the rest of the season. I'll concentrate on doing my job on the mound. The contract thing I can't control."

"So what made the difference today?" He asks.

I know but I'm certainly not going to tell this jerk about Gina.

"Check back with me toward the end of the season on the contract thing," I say instead.

I don the winningest smile I can muster and wait for the baseball gods to relieve me of this annoying guy. Go talk to Frank Matson and leave me the fuck alone.

The guy stays rooted to the floor. "What kind of money do you think you can get this winter?"

I glance up at him. "You'll have to ask my agent about that."

He still has that smirk on his face. I feel like clocking him one in his oversized gut which faces me at about my eye level. Instead, I realize that his shirt is straining mightily against its buttons, so I look away, worried that one of them might fly off and put my eye out. That could be the end to my season.

I stand up, knocking over my chair. "Look, I don't mean to be rude, but I really have to get going now." Like hell. Being rude is what I really want to be, but I bite my tongue. Don't want to see a hit piece on me in tomorrow's paper.

146

I look around for Rick. He's talking to our third baseman, Javi Vasquez, on the other side of the clubhouse. I excuse myself from the hazardous gut and join Rick. "Let's get the fuck out of here. My least-favorite columnist has been giving me the once over."

He looks over to my locker area and nods. He walks over there grabs his gear bag and mine, while I skirt around the clubhouse on the opposite side. I banter with the guys as I pass, so I don't look like I'm avoiding the fat man, who has given up and moved on to someone else. Rick and I jog through the bowels of the stadium hoping we don't encounter anyone else who wants to talk about our contract plans for next year.

After we exit the parking lot, Rick asks, "You've had this shit-eating grin on your face all day. What did you have to do to get in her pants?"

I take my eyes off the road for a moment and see a smile splitting his face.

I stifle a laugh. "That obvious, eh?"

"Yup. I could tell it the minute I laid eyes on you when Cindy dropped me off at your house this morning. And the fact that your bed hadn't been slept in was also a good clue."

I give him a smart-ass look. "What were you doing snooping around my bedroom?"

"Just needed to go to the bathroom. You were in the one in the front hall."

"Oh." He wasn't being a snoop after all.

I hesitate discussing my relationship with Gina because I'm afraid it will tarnish my wonderful feelings about last night. But he's my best friend, and I don't think Gina would be surprised if I tell him a little about it.

"I thought a lot about what you said in Cleveland, and my conscience has been wailing away at me saying some of the same things, so I decided it's time to take control of my life and confront this one head on. I went over to her place yesterday and told her that I love her and that I don't want to be with anyone else."

"Did she buy it?"

"She was wary at first, but I told her I would commit to being only with her, even when we are on the road." I smile at him. "I told her I would hang out with you. That you'd make sure I stay away from temptation."

"And she believed you?"

"Yup. She threw her arms around me. Nearly knocking me off the couch. Dragged me off to her bedroom."

Rick's grin broadens and he pumps his fist.

"And, bro, that's all you'll find out about what happened," I say.

"You don't have to tell me more. It's written all over your face and the box score today."

Should I tell him I asked her to marry me? We sort of agreed not to tell anyone until after the season is over, but what the hell.

I take the leap. "One thing I will tell you, I… uh… asked her to marry me." I'm surprised by the hesitation in my voice.

Rick's turns to face me. "That's terrific!" he says. "I'm so happy for you both! Are you telling everyone? Can I tell Cindy?" His kid-like excitement defeats my resolve.

"I don't think Gina is big on bedroom proposals. She suggested that we play it by ear for the rest of the season and keep our engagement under wraps for now. I guess you can tell Cindy, but you have to swear her to secrecy, at least until Gina knows that I've told you. And you can't tell anyone else, okay?"

My mouth is dry. Shit, I have gone slightly public with my engagement. I hope Gina isn't upset that I did that. But I'm glad I told him. It somehow makes me feel more committed to the decision.

"It's a big step," Rick says. "I never thought you'd go that far."

"Yeah, it is. I'm just nervous, that's all," I say, as I exit the freeway.

"I remember that feeling, thrilled she'd have me but scared shitless I'd somehow screw it up. Yup. Been there, bro."

Chapter Twenty-Eight

No game today, so I'm heading into Oakland for an appointment with Dr. Blackwood. It's a sunny day, and I have the top down. Yesterday we completed the three-game series with the Minnesota Twins by losing to Johan Fernandez, who had a no-hitter going into the bottom of the eighth inning. The Renegades now have fifty-five wins and fifty-two losses. We are three games ahead of the Angels, with roughly a third of the season left to play. Not a bad place to be during the dog days of August.

On the drive into downtown Oakland, I rehearse what I am going to tell Dr. B. about what's happened since I saw him last. Let's see. I followed his advice and went to Gina's and she didn't throw me out. We had dinner twice but no sex. I had an opportunity to get hooked up at the All-Star game but sidestepped it. And I got in real trouble in Cleveland and was saved by Rick physically removing me from the scene. I did a lot of soul searching and went to Gina's this week and made a commitment to her. We had sex and I asked her to marry me. That about covers it, I guess.

I arrive at Dr. Blackwood's and his secretary doesn't seem to be there today. The door is standing ajar, so I knock and let myself into his inner sanctum.

"Well, Larry, nice to see you again. Close the door, would you?" He gets up from his desk and holds out his hand. After we both settle down in the green leather chairs, he asks, "How are you doing?"

I tick off the list of events I went over in my car. When I get to the part about the engagement, I hesitate, fumbling for the right words.

"After we made love for the second time, I realized that I was happier than I had ever been, and I didn't want to be anywhere else. I decided to… I opened my mouth… I decided… hell, I asked her to marry me."

149

There, it's out in the open. I cross my legs and shift awkwardly in the green leather chair.

"Why the uneasiness?" Dr. Blackwood gives me an expectant look.

"I'm not sure. All I know is that I woke up in a cold sweat and shaking after I proposed. I decided I really do want to marry her, but I'm scared to death I can't follow through with it."

"What scares you?" He looks at me over steepled hands.

I can't look at him. My lap is safer territory.

I think for a minute. Then another.

Finally, I look up and say, "I guess I'm scared that some gorgeous babe will come on to me while we are on the road, and my dick will start messing with my head. I'm afraid I'll forget all about my commitment to Gina and do something rash."

"Why do you think you won't be able to control yourself?"

"The incident in Cleveland that I mentioned really scared me. I got so turned on and was sailing along on the anticipation of what could happen." I shake my head and think for a minute before continuing. "But I had sort of an out-of-body experience while I was in the middle of it and watched myself. I saw how easily I fall back into my old ways, and it terrified me."

I drop my eyes and focus instead on my fingers.

"That's good, Larry. The fact that you could observe yourself while you were experiencing it means you have a chance of changing your behavior."

"Yeah, but I didn't. It took Rick forcibly removing me from the scene and getting in my face to bring me to my senses." Head hanging, shoulders slumped, shame all over my face. I'm the picture of dejection.

Doc Blackwood takes his time answering. "Do you really think you are the only guy who has had to deal with their dick having a mind of its own? Hell, Larry, you're no different than any other guy."

He leans forward with his elbows on his knees and looks at me. "Yes, you've had a long history of women pitching themselves at you. And you're as good a catcher as you are a pitcher. But all of us guys have a hard time ignoring old habits when we finally choose a mate."

"So what do I do to play it safe? To keep myself from getting into compromising situations?" I ask.

150

Dr. Blackwood sits up. "What do *you* think you can do?"

Shit, why do shrinks always answer a question with a question?

"My friend Rick says I should stick with him," I say, after a painful search for an answer. "After all, he got me out of the disaster in Cleveland." I fall silent for a while, lost in my uncertainty.

"Okay," he says, revealing little about what he is thinking.

"I plan on surgically attaching myself to his side on the road."

"Well, that might work when Rick is available. But you have to learn to do this on your own, Larry. Have you thought about what would happen if Rick wasn't there?"

My stomach drops to my heels with a thud, rendering me mute.

"Look, Larry," he continues. "I'm not suggesting that you start flying solo in situations that have always led to sex. But you need to change your mind set away from 'available' to 'engaged.'"

"But how do I do that?"

"That's what we need to work on in our sessions. In the meantime, use your safety net. Stick with Rick. And give some thought to what your decision to marry Gina really means to you."

"Maybe with some more experience with Rick along, I won't be so tempted?" What I don't say is that chasing tail is fun.

"Eventually," Dr. Blackwood says, "you'll become more comfortable with your decision to be monogamous, and when you fully embrace that, you'll be able to handle other women with grace and a firm 'no.'"

"Yeah, that's what I want, but…" My voice trails off when I can't think of anything to add.

He takes a deep breath, and says, "Larry, you have lots of experience on the field with being single-minded and sticking to a game plan. Just trust yourself to be able to translate that into your personal life. 'Ninth inning. Seventh game.' I believe you said that was your mantra. Just use it when temptation comes, and you should do fine." He looks at his watch, signaling that the session is over.

I stand up awkwardly and look at him. "You have more confidence in me than I do." I hate feeling this helpless. I want to believe I can do it.

"You'll be fine. Call me to set up another appointment in about two weeks."

Ninth inning. Seventh game. Whatever!

Chapter Twenty-Nine

I'm riding the pine tonight. We are in Seattle for a three-game series. We now have sixty-four wins and fifty-five losses, and we're four and a half games ahead of the Angels.

Donny Kensler has the ball and is looking good. He'll probably be considered our ace next year if I'm not here.

Kensler blazes through the M's line-up in the first three innings, and the Mariners can't get anyone on base. His six-foot-five frame uncoils from his trademark slow wind-up, and the ball whizzes by the batter before he knows what has happened. It's comical to watch guys flail helplessly at ninety-two-mile-an-hour fastballs that bend back over the plate at the last second, and then watch them swing way out in front of a seventy-eight-mile-an-hour curveball for strike three. They just shake their heads on the way back to the dugout.

I watch the players in the Seattle lineup I haven't faced before, so I will know what they will swing at or lay off. Vince, our video guy, will have tape for Jason Gardelli and me to look at tomorrow, but I like to scope hitters out myself to form a preliminary opinion on how to handle each of them.

Danny continues to pitch well through the top of the seventh inning, allowing only a home run by Takeo Shimada that barely makes it over the right-field wall. Donny has notched ten strikeouts, but his pitch count is up to a hundred and two. On his way back to the dugout he puts his finger in his mouth, looks at it, and shakes his hand. Gotta be a blister starting. Looks like his day is done.

While our guys are at bat in the bottom of the seventh, Coop makes the call to the bullpen. Rick gets up and shrugs out of his jacket to start warming up.

After the third out, Rick trots in from the centerfield bullpen to pitch the top of the eighth. After his final warm-up tosses, he goes to work and gets the first two batters out quickly on ground balls to the infield. He's at the top of his form too. I feel confident we will post a win tonight.

Bobby Black steps into the batter's box. Rick's first pitch is a ninety-two-mile-an-hour fastball way inside, and Black hits the dirt, barely avoiding being hit. He looks pissed and shouts something menacing at Rick. He steps back into the batter's box looking like he wants to kill someone.

Rick delivers another fastball over the outside edge of the plate for strike one. He looks in to Jason for the next sign and comes set. He goes into his wind-up. At the last minute, Black calls time and steps out of the batter's box. Rick completes the pitch and glares at Black.

Rick walks around the mound, obviously fuming, and steps back onto the rubber. He nods to accept the sign from Jason, and throws a ninety-three-mile-an-hour fastball on the inner half of the plate. Black takes a huge rip at the ball, which flies off Black's bat and screams right at Rick's head. Rick tries to duck and puts his mitt up as a shield, but the ball glances off his glove and hits him in the face. He drops to the ground like a stone.

I jump to my feet and stare at the mound unable to breathe, silently willing Rick to move. He lies there looking dead. This can't be happening.

The ump signals for a time out and Jake Martinelli, our trainer, and Coop rush out onto the field. I join them dreading what I will find. Rick is not moving at all. His face and uniform jersey are splattered with blood. Jake waves some smelling salts under Rick's nose. Rick turns his head away and opens his eyes.

"Wha... happen?" He slurs his response, and his eyes flutter shut again.

Jake ignores this and says, "Rick. Rick. Open your eyes, Rick. How may fingers?"

"Four... I think," Rick mumbles drunkenly, turns to his side and pukes.

Jake folds his two fingers and looks at Coop. "Double vision. We need to get him to the hospital NOW!" Jake turns back to Rick, frantically trying to keep Rick conscious, without much success. Oh, shit. I hope that doesn't mean anything disastrous.

A minute or so later, a gate opens in the outfield, and an ambulance drives swiftly along the dirt track around the edge of the field and onto the infield grass to a spot near the pitcher's mound. One paramedic flies out of the back with a medical bag. The other two medics jump out of the front and go around to the back of the ambulance for the stretcher, which they carry over and place on the ground next to Rick.

Rick still hasn't moved since he lost consciousness. Tears struggle to break down my resistance. That's my best friend lying there, and I can't tell if he's alive or dead. And there's nothing I can do to help him.

The first EMT takes Rick's vital signs and checks his cheek area carefully, mopping up as much blood as possible with gauze pads. The three strong men, one cradling Rick's head, lift him carefully onto the stretcher on the count of three. They stabilize his head with towels and tighten straps across his forehead, his chest and upper legs.

I guess he's breathing or they would still be working on him. I feel like I'm about to throw up. This is awful. Now I just want to cry.

The paramedics lift the stretcher up, and the wheels drop down and lock, turning it into a gurney. They push it carefully toward the ambulance. I walk along with them encouraging Rick to hang in there, that everything will be alright, although I have no idea if he can hear me.

"Where are you taking him?" I ask frantically.

"Trauma Center, Harborview Hospital."

I turn and nearly bowl over Coop standing right behind me. "I'm going with him, Coop."

"Okay. I'll get one of the batboys to grab your gear," he says and signals toward the dugout.

Coop turns toward Bud Tanaka, our pitching coach, who has joined us. "You better let Blasco know he'll be starting tomorrow."

I put my hand on Coop's arm, turning him back to me. "Coop. I'm pitching tomorrow," I say forcefully. "I need to do this. For him," nodding in Rick's direction. "I'll be in my room by midnight." Good luck. It's already after ten.

As the paramedics get Rick settled into the back of the ambulance, I notice for the first time the silence in the stands. It's as if everyone has been holding their breath since Rick was hit.

I stand by the back of the ambulance looking at the empty packaging and medical paraphernalia now littering the grass near the pitcher's mound. My heart feels like I'm trapped in a bad nightmare. One second Rick is pitching brilliantly and the next he's flat on his back, bloody and unconscious. Will this cause brain

154

damage? Will his career be over? Or, God forbid, what if he doesn't survive this? I stare at the empty pitcher's mound, feeling utterly helpless.

"Okay, let's roll," shouts the head EMT who turns to me and says, "You comin' with us?"

I nod weakly, unable to talk without breaking down. The batboy runs up to me and hands me my gear bag. I stare blankly at Rick's feet sticking off the back of the stretcher in the ambulance. It all feels so surreal. I shake my head to try to wake up from this terrible dream.

I'm jerked back to reality by the impatient voice of the ambulance driver. "Well, then get in the back and strap yourself in."

I climb into the ambulance and stand there looking down at my best friend who looks like he is merely sleeping. That image is marred by the white bandage that now covers his right cheekbone and eye, and by the blood on his uniform.

One of the paramedics buckles himself in on the bench near Rick's chest so he can monitor his vital signs. I fasten a seatbelt around me at the other end of the bench. The other two guys lock the rear door and jump into the cab. The EMT working on Rick tells the guys in front that his vital signs are stable. That's good, I think. I hope.

We drive around the warning track to the outfield gate. Out the back windows I can see the crowd come slowly out of its trance, their heads following us, and they stand up and clap as we pass, as if doing the wave.

In the parking lot the driver turns on the siren. We race through the lot to the exit, careen onto Fourth Avenue, and scream northward through the heart of Seattle to the emergency entrance of Harborview Hospital.

When we come to a stop, everyone moves at once. The back doors of the ambulance fly open, the paramedics unfasten the gurney from the wall, and pull it free of the ambulance. The wheels drop down into the locked position with a click that makes me jump.

Doctors and nurses from the Emergency Room rush to greet the paramedics as they wheel Rick through the entry doors, shouting that he got hit by a batted ball under his right eye and that his vitals are stable. The whole thing seems like it is happening in slow motion, a well-choreographed precision drill team in action. The raised voices sound so concerned that I lag back a little so I don't have to experience the horror of it all at full volume.

The green-clad medical personnel wheel the gurney through another set of doors into a brightly lit room and roll him into a draped area, closing the green curtains around him. I start toward the fabric cubicle when a nurse materializes next to me and grabs my arm. "I'm sorry, sir, but we can't let you go in there. The doctors will take good care of him." She motions me back out the door.

"But…" I look toward the curtain and back at the nurse, unable to move or speak, mouth agape.

"You'll just get in the way, sir. I'm sorry. It's hospital rules." She gently nudges me toward the door and points to a waiting area off to the left. "Why don't you wait in there? Someone will come out in a while to give you an update."

I look at my watch and see that it is almost eleven o'clock. I slump down onto one of the chairs and look down at the legs of my uniform and my cleats. Suddenly I realize that I'm very recognizable in this get-up. Hell, my name is on the back of my jersey. I look around to see if anyone has noticed me but happily the room is empty. I grab my gear bag and crunch to the men's room to change into my civvies.

When I get back to the waiting room, a mother and three children are huddled together on a couch at one end of the room. The mother is crying and the children, whose cheeks are also wet, are trying to calm her down. I drop heavily into a chair as far away from them as possible and turn on my cell phone in case Gina calls. I don my shades, lean back, and attempt to look like I am napping.

I'm awakened by the tinny tones of "Take Me Out to the Ballgame." I fumble for my cell phone and hit the "Talk" button. "Hello?" I mumble.

"Larry, thank God I got you. Is he alright?"

It's not Gina. It's Cindy, her voice streaked with anguish. I have to fight back my tears. I don't want to scare her with the horrible possibilities that keep rewinding in my brain like a bad video. But I've got to be honest with her.

I drive fear out of my voice. "I don't know anything yet. I'm in the ER, waiting for the doctors to tell me what's going on."

"I'm so glad you're there with him. I saw it all on TV. I tried to call Rick's cell but got voicemail, and then called the GM's cell phone, but he didn't know anything. I really couldn't tell how bad it was from the TV coverage, but it looked pretty awful."

"Well, Black hit a line drive right at him. He deflected it with his glove but it hit him in the face. It looked like it got his cheek bone."

"Is he conscious?"

Damn, how do I answer that one? "Well, he was unconscious for a while and then came to. The paramedics gave him something. He's resting now. They're running a bunch of tests and we'll know more soon, hopefully."

"Promise you'll call me when you know something? No matter how late."

"I promise. I have a good feeling about this, Cindy. I'm hopeful this will all turn out to be okay." I just can't tell her how worried I am that he might not come out of this unscathed or at all. I hang up and try to get back into my nap.

After what seems like several hours, a doctor emerges from the ER, sits down next to me, and places a hand on my arm. "Mr. Gordon. I'm Dr. Johnson."

I swim up from my sleep and ask, "How is he, doc?" Instantly I'm afraid of what the answer will be.

"We've had a maxillofacial surgeon look at his x-rays and the CT scan," he says. "The news is somewhat hopeful. There is a slight fracture in the Zygomatic arch, but amazingly no bone fragments showed up on the films. He did, however, sustain a significant blow to the head, and the CT scan shows some swelling of the brain. We have him on a Mannitol drip to combat the swelling, and we'll have to monitor him closely for the next twenty-four to forty-eight hours for signs of intracranial bleeding."

"English please, Doc?" I ask.

He smiles and says, "The ball cracked his cheek bone just below the right eye socket, but it was a glancing blow off his mitt, from what the EMTs said. He's lucky he got his glove on it to break some of the force. It could have killed him."

I wince at that thought and swipe at the sweat now beading on my forehead. "What now?"

"He's stabilized. His vital signs are pretty normal for someone who's sustained a trauma to the head. We sedated him and lowered his body temperature with ice packs to slow any bleeding in the brain. We'll do another CT scan in the morning. If it doesn't show any internal bleeding or other soft tissue injury, the prognosis will be much better. But he'll be here for a few days at least, and maybe longer, Mr. Gordon."

He stands up and holds out his hand. "He's got the best neuro team in Seattle on his case. We'll do the best we can for him."

I put my head in my hands. I don't usually talk to the Big Guy upstairs, but this isn't usual. Please God, I pray, let Rick have a peaceful night with no further emergencies. I rarely ask you for much. You and I don't have a close relationship, at least not like we did when I was a kid. But even though I'm an adult now, I'm asking you to take care of Rick for me. Please God, he's my best friend, and I really need him.

The Doc puts his hand on my shoulder and says, "You should go back to your hotel and get some sleep. We'll know more in the morning, and there's nothing you can do here tonight. He'll be sleeping. Here's how to contact me." He hands me a card. "Take my advice and get out of here."

"Okay, I guess. But call me if you have any news." I give him my cell number. "And I'll call his wife. I expect she'll want to talk to you."

The Doc stands up, and I grab my bag and rise. "Thanks, Doc for everything you all are doing for Rick. I really appreciate it," sticking out my hand.

"No problem." He shakes my hand and disappears through the swinging doors to the ER to check on Rick and others in distress behind the green curtains.

I head out the door and grab a cab back to the hotel. On the way, I dial Cindy to report on what the doctor said.

"How is he?" she asks, before I can say anything. "Is he going to be all right? Should I fly up there tonight?"

"He's sedated and the doctors won't really know how bad his injuries are until tomorrow or the next day, but his vital signs are stable."

"Larry, just tell me exactly what happened to him and what you know so far."

What do I say to her? I can't soft-pedal it. If something is really wrong, she'd never forgive me, so I decide to give it to her straight.

"Well, the ball fractured his cheekbone, and there is some slight swelling in his brain. They won't know if there is any bleeding in his brain for the next twelve to twenty-four hours. They may know a little more in the morning when they do another CT scan."

"Oh, God," she cries. "What should I do, Larry?" By now she is crying.

"I think the doctor would tell you the same thing he told me, that there is nothing we can do for him tonight, or even tomorrow. He seems to be stable at this point, but they're keeping him sedated for the next twenty-four hours, or so. You've got three kids to care for. Why don't you concentrate on that?"

"Okay. I'll get my mom to come and stay with them and I'll fly up there as soon as I can get everything squared away here. Is there a way that I can talk to the doctor tonight?

"You can try him at this number." After I give her the number that the doctor gave me, I say, "If you can't get through to the doctor tonight, you can call the hospital as early as 7:30 am in the morning." I give her the other number on the doc's card.

"Okay, Larry. Thank you so much for being there with him tonight. I'm so worried about…" Her voice trails off into sobs.

"Try to get some sleep, Cindy, and pray a lot. We need him to pull through this."

Still sobbing, she says, "Sleep is probably out of the question, but I'll do a lot of talking to the guy upstairs. Thanks…"

The line goes dead.

At the hotel I pay off the cabby, grab my bag, and stop at the registration desk to reserve a room for Cindy for tomorrow night. I drag myself up to my room. I'm suddenly starving and order a couple of hamburgers from an all-night takeout service.

While I wait for the delivery, I make a dent in the alcohol supply from the minibar, trying to erase the horrible words the doctor told me. Once the buzz calms my mind a bit, the burgers arrive. I inhale them while I watch Baseball Tonight to take my mind off Rick, and to find out what happened after our early exit from the ballpark. Damned if we didn't score seven runs in the top of the ninth and win the game by a score of fifteen to one.

I change and fall into bed exhausted. I think about Rick's empty room down the hall and say another silent prayer for him.

I dial Gina but her cell phone goes straight to voicemail, and I wait impatiently for the beep. "Hi, it's me," I say. "I don't know if you've heard that Rick got hit in the head by a line drive in the game tonight. I just left the hospital and wanted to talk to you about what the doctor said. I guess you are on call tonight. I pitch

159

tomorrow, so I'm going to turn in now and try to get some sleep. I'll call again when I know more about Rick. I love you and miss you."

I turn off the light at two a.m. and try to grab some shut-eye. I have to be at Safeco Field in seven hours to pitch a day game. I toss and turn for an hour or so before I finally get to sleep, only to wake up several times during the night worrying about Rick.

Chapter Thirty

My alarm startles me out of a deep sleep, but I roll over, hit the off button, and hide my head under the pillow. I'm dreaming of pitching in the seventh game of the World Series, when suddenly, I sit up with a start, heart pounding, head spinning. My eyes stare at the clock in disbelief. It reads 9:30 and I have to be at Safeco Field... like a half hour ago. I bound out of bed, throw on some clothes and head out, looking like shit. Oh well, I can clean up at the ball park.

In the cab I call Coop in the clubhouse. He answers on the second ring.

"Coop," I say, as upbeat as I can manage, "I overslept a little and I'll be there in ten minutes."

"That's fine. You're not pitching today."

"Yes, I am," I say, with as much anger and determination as I can put in my voice. "I'm fine, and there's no way I'm not pitching this game. Got that?"

He's silent for several seconds, then says, "Larry, we'll talk when you get here."

"Coop, there's not discussion. I'm pitching today." I hear a click and then the dial tone.

Okay. Now I have to fight him. Just what I don't need.

I take a deep breath and dial the hospital. I'm transferred to the Neuro ICU, where Rick was relocated during the night.

"Could I please speak to the doctor on duty?" I ask the person who answers the phone.

"Who are you calling about?" she asks, her voice clipped and efficient.

"Richard Wycliffe."

"Are you a family member?"

"No, but I came with him in the ambulance to the ER last night."

"I'm sorry, sir. But we can't let anyone but family speak with the doctor."

Why do I have to fight everyone I encounter today?

I take a long breath and say, "Look, Ma'am. I know you have your rules, but he got hit by a batted ball in the Mariners game last night, and he doesn't have any family here. I'm his teammate. The ER doctor told me to call this morning to get an update."

"Well... just a minute," she says, sounding like I'm the last thing she wants to deal with right now.

After a couple of minutes, there's a click. "I'm Dr. Ginsburg. Are you Larry Gordon?"

Relief floods through me. "Yes, I am."

"I spoke with Mrs. Wycliffe this morning and she gave me authorization to talk to you about Mr. Wycliffe's condition.

"How is he?" I ask with my fingers crossed.

"We don't know much yet. He's still unconscious, so we won't know the extent of his injuries or impairment until he wakes up. Mrs. Wycliffe's coming up tomorrow morning. Maybe he'll respond to the sound of her voice. But until he wakes up, we wait."

My gut wrenches into a fist at the thought of Rick being impaired. I hate this uncertainty, but there's nothing I can do about it right now. I take a deep breath and say, "Thanks, Doc." I close my cell phone as the cab pulls up to the players' entrance at Safeco Field.

When I walk into the visitor's clubhouse, Coop calls my name as I pass his office. He's glaring.

"You look like hell," he growls. "You were supposed to be here almost an hour ago. How much sleep did you get?"

"I'm fine, Coop. I'm ready to pitch."

"I don't know, Larry. Clearly you didn't get much sleep last night."

"Skip, I thought we covered this. I'm going to pitch today. I'm your ace, and I've never felt more ready to pitch than now. I can do this, and I need to. For me and for Rick. I'm taking the ball today." Now I'm the one who is glaring.

"Look, Larry. If I let you take the hill today and you get knocked around, I'll lose the trust of the rest of the team. And the GM will have my ass."

"I understand that, Coop, but I've never been more sure of anything. I will be able to pitch lights out, and I'm going to fucking do it."

He looks at me for a very long time, a war waging within him.

162

Finally, he says, "I've never seen you like this. I guess that counts for something. My gut tells me that I should say no, but I'll let you do it on one condition. If you get in trouble, I'm yanking you. I can't afford to let your agenda become more important that winning the game. At this point we need to win every one we can."

"Thanks, Coop. I understand. You won't regret it, I promise."

"God, I hope you're right. Now get the fuck out of here and get ready."

I thank him again and head to my locker to change into work-out clothes. When the guys see me, one of them puts my music on the stereo, but it doesn't blare like it usually does, and the guys are much quieter than before most games. One by one they stop by for a blow-by-blow of my trip to the ER, I try not to make it sound as bad as it looked.

"I got a game to pitch, guys," I say when the huddle around me gets too big.

After they wander back to their lockers, I head off to the training room for my pre-game rubdown. Afterward, Jason and I go to the video room to look at the tapes of the guys we will face today. No surprises there.

It feels good to go through my usual routine, but it is also surreal that ten hours ago I was listening to the doctor tell me that Rick is badly injured and that he doesn't know how he'll come out of it. I've got to put thoughts of Rick out of my head during the game. That's going to be tough.

Ninth inning. Seventh game.

It's gonna take more than that today.

Back at my locker, I suit up for the game. Rick's empty locker next door emphasizes the hole in the room. The butterflies in my gut are more furious than usual. I take out his chair and sit in it for a while trying to feel his presence.

God, please let him come out of this with nothing really serious.

I think of Cindy who sat at home alone with her three kids last night, worried sick about Rick. It suddenly hits me that if Gina and I get married, I'll have someone to worry about me like that, which puts a small smile on my face. But I hope I never give her this much of a scare.

I finish dressing, grab my glove, hat, and chewing gum, and put on my warm-up jacket. Some of the guys and I head down the dimly lit tunnel and emerge into the glare of the rare sunlight. The roof is open. Thank God for that.

We head toward the dugout, and I pause just for a second and look around the field. It hits me that this might be the most important game I'll ever pitch. But I don't feel pressure. Instead, I'm at peace, remembering how I've wanted to pitch in games like this since I was knee-high. No wrenching gut or racing heart. Just a feeling of calm and laser-like focus on the job ahead.

In the dugout I stow my pack of gum on the ledge above the bench and try not to think about Rick in the hospital. I put on my hat, grab my glove, and head out to the bullpen with Jason, and Bud, our pitching coach.

I actually feel pretty good for having had only five-plus hours of sleep. I peel off my jacket and do my stretching routine and some wind sprints. After a few minutes of long tossing with Jason Gardelli, I increase my velocity with every throw and gradually move to the bullpen mound.

Bud's brow is furrowed with concern. "I hear you didn't get much sleep last night. You good to go today?"

I nod and start ramping up my pitching speed until I'm fully warmed up. I'm throwing fastballs in the low nineties consistently. Normally, my fastest is eighty-nine to an occasional ninety-one. But I'm throwing free and easy, not pushing myself to achieve these velocities. I can feel the adrenaline humming through my body. I know I'm gonna pitch a great game. Coop, I think your job is safe today.

Bud watches me like a hawk and, with a shrug of his shoulders, pronounces me ready.

"I actually feel pretty great," I say. "I want to get these guys for Rick."

He looks at me for a moment, and then shakes his head, as if he wants to say something but thinks better of it. "Say, did you hear about the rest of the game last night?" he asks instead.

"Yup. I caught it on Baseball Tonight while I wolfed down my takeout dinner last night." I don't own up to how late I ate. "I guess the guys got inspired after what happened to Rick."

"That's an understatement." He signals to Coop that I'm ready by raising his hat, and looks back at me. "Well, go get 'em."

"Damn right I will!" I suddenly feel a surge of energy. I pump my fist. For Rick.

164

Adrenaline is a magic drug. It makes me feel strong, that I can do anything. My feeling of omnipotence is helped by two solo homers in the top of the first inning by Matson and Hayner, giving me a two-run lead to start. This is going to be fun. I can feel a win coming.

On the mound in the bottom of the first, after taking my final warm-up pitches, I look in to Jason for the sign. Fast ball in. Here we go!

I deliver the first pitch which makes a very loud "thwack" as it hits Jason's mitt. I stare at the stadium radar gun in amazement. It flashes "94." Man, I haven't seen one of those in a long time. I set the Mariners up and down for three quick outs on seven pitches.

I cruise along on my adrenaline high for the next five innings. I have a little scare in the seventh, when I give up a solo homerun to Takeo Shimada and walk the next guy with one out. I can see Coop nearing the dugout steps but he doesn't come out. This must be his way of warning me that he meant business when he said he'd pull me.

I get the next guy to strike out on another ninety-four-mile-an-hour fastball. They're still thinking I max out at ninety-one. Fools!

So now I have two outs and a runner on when Bobby Black steps in. Perfect!

Ninth… No, I don't even need that now. Just pitch.

I chuckle to myself. I'm sure Black's been paying attention to how hard I'm throwing today. I bet he's expecting some heat on the first pitch. Let's fuck with his head a bit. I shake off Jason until he puts down two fingers next to his right thigh.

I go into my stretch, paying no attention to the runner who takes off for second base. He won't get any further than that. No one can touch me today.

I send the ball to the plate high and a little harder than I usually throw my curveball, but it falls through the strike zone perfectly into Jason's waiting glove. Black takes a mighty cut at the ball, swinging way ahead of it. He loses his balance and stumbles backward out of the batter's box. The umpire yells "Stri-eek one!"

Black glares at me for making him look foolish.

God, this is fun! Now I'll give him one of my newly potent fastballs. Black swings at it but he can't catch up to it, lunging wildly and looking almost as foolish as on the first pitch.

Jason puts down one finger again, signaling a fastball on the outside corner. Perfect.

I stretch, come set, and send the ball on its way with a little extra force behind it. The ball blazes over the outside edge of the plate. Black follows it into Jason's mitt, smiles, and steps back, thinking it is a ball. "Stri-eek three," yells the umpire and pumps his fist, calling Black out.

Black glowers at the ump for a long time, his face red, and finally decides to let it go. He turns and walks away slowly, obviously fuming.

The ump starts after him but instead shakes his head and leans down to brush off the plate.

I look up at the scoreboard. The speed gun reads "95". Holy Shit! Gotta love that adrenaline! I stand there looking at the numbers, until they disappear. Jaime Cruz runs by me and pats me on the butt. I register that Black was the final out of the inning, and head toward the dugout.

Coop comes over to me. "Great job with Black," he says, smiling. And then adds, "You still feeling good?"

"I wish you'd stop asking me that. I'm in the zone. Get outta here."

"Okay. Just remember. If you get tired, the bullpen can finish it off for you."

"No fucking way, Skip. Not today. This one's mine!"

I strike out the side on only eleven pitches in the bottom of the eighth. As I walk off the mound to my cheering teammates, I smile up at the sky, and send healing prayers to Rick. This one's for you, bro!

Our guys tack on another run on solo dinger, this time from Heath Barton, our right fielder. So when I take the mound in the bottom of the ninth, the score is three to one, Renegades.

First up is the Mariner's ninth place hitter, Jackie Bell. I strike him out with three fastballs for out number one. Next Takeo Shimada steps in. I blow a couple of fastballs by him for two quick strikes.

On the third pitch Shimada slaps the ball to Bobby Crandell, normally a routine play for him, but Shimada is lightening fast. Bobby has to hurry his throw and the ball sails wide of Dan Jackson, pulling him off the bag at first. Shimada stands on first, and Bobby gets credited with an error. Fuck!

166

Arlen Jones, the M's third baseman, is up next. He saw how I pitched to Shimada. So, I think, let's start Jones off with one of my famous benders. Jason calls for a fastball, but I shake him off. Next he puts down two fingers away, and I nod and go right into my slide step. The pitch is perfectly executed and Jones follows it with his eyes, but doesn't lift his bat. The ump informs Jones that it's strike one. Jones just shakes his head.

Let's do that again, I think, and Jason agrees. Jones swings this time but way early, missing it completely for strike two. He steps out of the batter's box and adjusts his batting gloves and his crotch. This guy is their best clutch hitter, but I refuse to give in to him.

Shimada takes off for second as I start to throw the next pitch, a slider that just misses the plate. Jason jumps up and fires a dart to Jaime Cruz at second. Shimada goes into a slide but the ball hits him on the back and dribbles into center field. As soon as Shimada feels the ball hit him, he jumps up and takes off for third, making it easily. Shit.

Ninth inning. Seventh game. Maybe I need my mantra after all. No, I'm still pitching well. This is not my fault. I'm not the reason Shimada is on third base. The infield owns that.

Jason and I decide on a fastball to finish off Jones. I deliver the ball to the plate. Jones takes a mighty cut, but the ball squibs off the end of his bat slowly towards Dan Jackson, who has no choice but to step on the first base bag. Shimada scores, and my lead is cut in half.

I'm not bothered, though. As I walk off the back of the mound, I concentrate on Rick and my mission. I throw the ball hard into my mitt a couple of times to pump myself up, but also to show the infielders that I'm not happy a run has scored. I reach down and touch the rosin bag, and walk back up to the rubber to face Ken Osaka, the M's catcher.

Okay. I've got one run in, nobody on, and two out in the bottom of the ninth. Not bad for five hours sleep. But we aren't done. The last out is the toughest. This is the most important out of my career so far. My adrenaline spikes when I think of Rick. It's the jolt I need to finish what I started.

Osaka swings at my first two pitches, a ninety-four-mile-an-hour fastball and a backdoor slider, and misses both. I clench my fist after each pitch and mumble "yes!" I've got Osaka right where I want him. Now the Mariners are down to their last strike.

I look in to Jason for the sign. He signals fastball away. No, I think. Osaka will be expecting that. I shake off a couple of signs, and Jason turns to the umpire and asks for time. He trots out to the mound and asks, quite uncharacteristically, "What do you want to do?"

"I'd like to waste a couple of fastballs out of the strike zone to get him convinced I'm going to give him a steady diet of heaters," I say into my glove, "and then drop a curveball on him."

"Sounds like a plan to me." He touches my glove with his and walks back to the plate. No back talk from him. I guess I have him convinced I can do this.

Osaka doesn't bite at either fastball off the plate, so the count is now two and two. I look in at Jason, who smiles while he puts down two fingers for Uncle Charlie. I go into my slide step and deliver the ball about head high. Just in front of the plate, the ball arcs down into Jason's waiting mitt just off the dirt.

Osaka flinches but his bat remains on his shoulder. The umpire yells "Strike three!" and punches him out to end the inning and the game.

Our entire team charges out of the dugout and mobs me on the mound, jumping up and down in our group huddle. Since we're not at home, our celebration breaks up quickly, and we head into the clubhouse.

Once inside, I yell for them to huddle up and say, "Guys, lets not forget who isn't here today," and I bow my head. We stand in our huddle frozen in place, an impromptu moment of silence for Rick.

After a few seconds, I look up and say, "Thanks for sending Rick your prayers and thoughts. He needs both while he battles this injury. And thanks for helping to make this game today especially meaningful for me."

Jason pulls out Rick's chair and sits down next to me. He looks at me, smiles, and says, "You pitched one helluva a game today. Did I see "95" on the gun? Or was I hallucinating?"

"No one was more amazed at seeing that number than I was. Shit, I haven't thrown that hard since college! What a rush!"

"Amen. What made the difference?" he asks. "Rick?"

"Pretty much. I wanted so badly to win for Rick, but it was more than that. I felt invincible out there today. I knew from the beginning of the game that they couldn't touch me, and except for Shimada's homer, they didn't."

"Nope. Good job! It was a pleasure to catch you today." He pats me on the knee and stands up, his knees crackling. He shakes them out and retreats to his locker.

I'm completely wiped from pitching a complete game, and my left shoulder is talking to me, so I ice it and dress without showering, ducking out of the clubhouse before the media are let in. I head back to the hotel, luxuriate in a hot shower, and fall into bed. No calls to Cindy or Gina. They will understand.

Chapter Thirty-One

Right after the game today, the team flies to Anaheim, but it doesn't feel right for me to leave Rick here, unconscious and alone. Maybe I'll stay over until Cindy gets here. Finish what you started, as my dad would say.

After we lose the game to close out the series in Seattle, Ramon, one of our batboys, stops by my locker. "This is for you. I meant to give this to you yesterday, but I put it in my bag and forgot about it. Sorry."

He holds out a business card. "What's this?" I ask.

"I got it from one of the Seattle batboys. He said some girl gave it to him."

I look down at the card. The name on the card is "Tiffany Dixon." Never heard of her. Turning the card over, I read, "In April, I held up the 'Marry Me' sign. Please give me a call." My heart starts thumping in my chest. I should just throw the card away, but my curiosity won't let me do it. Yesterday I shut down the M's on no sleep, and I'm still pumped. I can handle this.

I grab my cell phone and walk out into the hall where I can hear. I dial the number on the card, my heart trying to hammer its way out of my chest.

She picks up on the second ring. "Hi. This is Tiffany."

"Hi, Tiffany. It's Larry Gordon."

"Oh, my gosh! You called!" She sounds so young. Trouble.

"So you're the girl with the 'Marry Me' sign?"

"That's me." She says, with excitement in her voice. "Hey, listen. I'm a huge fan. How about meeting me somewhere for a drink so we can talk?"

Do I really want to do this? I really should go back to the hotel and catch up on the sleep I missed last night.

"Listen. Did you hear about our pitcher that got injured two nights ago?"

"I saw it on TV. It looked really awful. Is he gonna be alright?"

"I don't know. He's still unconscious. We won't know anything until he wakes up. I'm really worried about him."

"Oh, then I guess you won't want to get together for a drink?" Disappointment is obvious in her voice.

What should I do? Rick is still out. And I really should face this kind of challenge on my own. A drink with her can't be too dangerous, can it?

"Tell you what," I say. I can't get out of here for another thirty minutes at least. I'll meet you somewhere for a quick drink."

"How about O'Shaunessy's? It's about a block north of Safeco on King Street. How about 5:00? Does that work for you?"

She sounds so nice, but my heart is still pounding. Nevertheless, I say, "Okay. I'll see you then. If my friend wakes up, I'm not coming. But I'll let you know."

"Fair enough. Do you think you'll recognize me?" she asks.

"I think we'll find each other." God, I'm sounding goofy.

End this right now. "See you then," I say instead.

I go back into the clubhouse and the media are buzzing like flies. I wade through them and head to my locker.

Jim Staley, one of the Bay Area beat writers who cover the Renegades, comes over. "I've never seen you get so much velocity on your fastball as you did yesterday. What happened? Can you explain it?"

He probably thinks I've started using something, but I smile at him and say, "The thing that happened to my friend, Rick Wycliffe, really got me fired up yesterday. My adrenaline kicked into overdrive. I guess that accounts for it."

A guy from the *Seattle Post Intelligencer* sticks his head into the conversation and asks, "I know that Rick Wycliffe is your good friend. Any thoughts about what Bobby Black did?"

I decide to take the high road. "You know, when a guy hits a line drive, he can't really control where it goes. It really depends upon where the pitch is thrown. I feel bad for Black. It's gotta be difficult for him, sending a guy to the hospital in a coma. I'm sure he feels awful about it."

When the media types move on to someone else, I gather my stuff and leave the locker area, to shower, shave, and get dressed. One last stop in the washroom to slick back my hair with a little water and splash on some aftershave.

171

I look at my reflection in the mirror. Why am I meeting Tiffany? I'm supposed to be engaged. And Rick's in the hospital.

I look down as I dry my hands on the wrinkled paper towel I have been gripping in my fist. I take a deep breath in and let it out on the word "Shit!"

On the way out, I stop by Coop's office, and say, "Skip, I'm headed out to have drinks with a friend. And I'd like to stay up here tonight so I can spend some time at the hospital in the morning with Rick. Okay, with you?"

"Okay, I guess. Just call Jim Martini ASAP, so he can make new travel arrangements for you. I'll have somebody take your stuff to the hotel if you like."

"Great. Thanks, Coop," I say and walk toward the clubhouse door.

He yells at my back, "You know what the answer would have been if you'd lost yesterday."

I hail a cab and call Martini, who says he'll drop off my new plane ticket at the hotel tonight. Next I call the hospital and ask for the Neuro ICU. Now that I'm on the list, I get transferred to the doctor right away. When he comes on, he tells me that nothing has changed but someone wants to talk to me.

I can hear the phone being passed. "Hey, Larry," a familiar female voice says.

"Hi, Cindy, I say. "I'm so glad you're here. How are you holding up?"

"Oh, I'm okay. It's just that if you don't look at the bandages, he looks like he's just sleeping. His breathing is regular and he looks so calm. I keep expecting him to roll over and open his eyes when I'm talking to him." A sob escapes and she falls silent.

After a few moments, she lets out a deep breath and says, "I'm sorry, Larry. It's just so frustrating to sit here and wait for something to happen. I feel so helpless."

"I know, Cin. I know." Visions of Rick from two nights ago make me swallow hard. "Would you like me to come sit with you for a while?"

"No, thanks. You're sweet. I'm going to try to get some sleep shortly. They rolled in a cot so I can sleep near him, in case he wakes up. I'm completely exhausted. As you can imagine, I haven't had a whole lot of sleep in the last few days..." her words ending in a yawn.

172

"I know. Get some sleep. Call me anytime if you have any news. I'm staying over tonight, and I'll stop by on my way to the airport tomorrow morning. I also made arrangements for you to stay in Rick's room at the hotel, if you decide to get out of there for a while."

"Thanks, Larry. You've been my rock during this. See you tomorrow," and she hangs up.

Her rock. No one's ever called me their rock before. Feels kinda good.

Chapter Thirty-Two

I stand outside the door of O'Shaunessy's for a long time, a war raging inside my head. This is a big mistake. Don't do it. But I have to find out if I can be around a pretty woman and keep my head. There will be lots of other people around. I'll have a drink, shake her hand and leave, just like in Cleveland. Well, not quite. No Rick tonight.

Just don't forget about Gina, I tell myself. A vision of her smiling face dances before my eyes. Okay, I can do this.

Ninth inning. Seventh game.

I grab the brass handle and pull open the heavy oak door. My eyes begin to adjust to the dim interior of the room, and I see a blonde waving frantically from a booth in the back past the bar. That must be Tiffany. It's dark and sparsely populated back there. So much for safety in numbers. I walk past the bar to her table, my heart pounding and my hands clammy.

"Hi. I'm Tiffany," she gushes. She tilts her head and her blond hair drapes nicely over one of her generous breasts that are trying to escape from her pink tank top. Before Gina, I would have said something off-color and predatory to myself. Not tonight, though.

She gestures for me to sit next to her. Instead, I wipe my damp right hand on my pants and hold it out to her. She looks disappointed but shakes my hand limply. I sit down across from her at a safe distance, the thick oak table forming a reassuring barrier between us.

I try not to look at her because I'm afraid of what will happen if we should lock eyes. Instead, I survey the bar while I get myself settled. Lots of oak, dark red leather, and brass. There are quite a few people over at the bar, young men obviously trolling and chicks looking to hook up. But they're not nearly close enough to give me any comfort.

A waitress appears. "What can I getcha?" She cocks her head and gives me a long look. "Do I know you? You look familiar."

"I don't think so." I say. "I have a common face. Happens all the time," waving it off with my standard line.

"No, you probably recognize him from the newspapers," Tiffany says, in her Valley-Girl voice. "He's Larry Gordon. You know, the star pitcher of the Oakland Renegades? They're in town playing the Mariner's. He pitched an awesome game yesterday, even though the M's lost."

Tiffany, beaming, is obviously thrilled to be seen with me. Shit. The blond angel image I have of her in my mind begins to crumble.

I lean closer to the waitress and say, "It's true. But I'd appreciate it if you wouldn't spread that around. I need some privacy here." My eyes plead my case, as I slide a twenty dollar bill across the table.

She hurries the twenty into her pocket and glances from Tiffany to me, a knowing look in her eyes. "Sure. No problem. What can I bring ya?"

Tiffany says, "I'll have a glass of white zinfandel."

Oh brother. Chick wine. "Do you have any Hefeweizen on tap?" I ask, hoping they have my usual.

"I think we have that. If not, you got a second choice?"

"Heineken." It's Rick's favorite. I think of him unconscious in the hospital. I wish he were here to protect me.

After the waitress records our orders and departs, Tiffany drops her eyes and I see that her face is red. She looks stricken.

"I'm so sorry. I've never been with a celebrity before," she says. "I bet you hate going out in public. I'm sorry I kinda 'outed' you."

I think to myself that this is hardly "being with" a celebrity. We're just having a drink.

I decide to do what I came to do. "Listen, Tiffany, you held up that sign the first time I pitched here in April. Don't you think a proposal in public was a bit over the top?"

"Yeah… I guess. I just wanted you to notice me. I've followed your career in the papers, and I've had a crush on you since you first came up from the minors. I've seen you pitch here many times."

"Oh, I noticed you in April. I nearly fell flat on my face. Remember?"

She blushes and tries to cover it with a smile. "Sorry about that. I was hoping you'd notice me yesterday." Her naiveté is both charming and sexy.

175

"Girl, I was so focused on my game, I didn't notice anything going on in the stands. You could have been naked and I wouldn't have seen you." I'm not so sure about that, but I let it go.

She reddens further and looks down. At this point our drinks arrive. Tiffany pulls herself together in the presence of the waitress.

"Do you want to run a tab," the latter asks.

"Fine," I say, a little too quickly, hoping she'll leave us alone.

She gets the message and departs, leaving a nasty smirk for me.

I turn back to Tiffany and say, "When you showed up with the sign in April, I tried to find you after the game, but you'd already left."

"Yeah? Well, when the sign clearly upset you, I chickened out and went home. But I'm sure glad you wanted to meet me today," she says with a smile.

Do I really want to be doing this? I ask myself again. Yes! I've gotta find out if I can handle this on my own.

I know it's trouble, but like a moth, I go back for another shot at the flame. "So did you have something in mind for this evening?"

"Well," Tiffany says, and winks at me. "I thought we could finish our drinks, grab some dinner and... play it by ear." As she cocks her head slightly, some of her shiny blond hair falls over one side of her face. My heart kicks into a higher gear. Oh man, this is real trouble. I really should get up and go.

I could have dinner with her, and then politely extricate myself. But it would be so much easier to leave now. Not after I've eaten a delicious dinner and had a few glasses of wine, watching her flirt with me with her eyes and her body.

Just then, my mind begins to wander. Something is trying to get my attention. Gina's face flashes across my eyes. It's as if a cold knife slices through me. What the hell am I doing here? If I continue this, I might not be able to make a clean exit, and I'll throw away my future with Gina. I can't do that. I don't want... no, I won't do that.

I look across at Tiffany, and suddenly see her for the young girl that she is. A decision ratchets into place.

Tiffany's face changes to concern when she sees my smile disappear.

I clear my throat and say, "Tiffany, you're a lovely girl. I just can't do this."

She looks crest-fallen. "Why not?" she says, her voice streaked with anguish.

"For one, I have a fiancée back home."

"Oh, forget about her. You're here with me now," she purrs, and reaches across the table and takes my hand.

With my other hand, I disentangle her fingers from mine and place her hand back on her side of the table. "No, Tiffany. I can't continue this."

"Sure you can. What happens in Seattle stays in Seattle." Her smile broadens with a hint of wickedness, and she reaches for me again.

I put my hands in my lap, and say, "Look, Tiffany. This is all my fault. I never should have agreed to meet you. I'm really sorry." I slide toward the open end of the booth.

She drops her head and won't look at me. She says in a small voice, "I wanted to have a magical evening with you. I've dreamed about this moment for years. You can't leave now." She raises her head slowly. Her face is shiny with tears. Her wounded look makes me feel even more like a shit.

I will myself to go on. "Tiffany, you're a beautiful and sweet young woman and you deserve someone to have a relationship with, not a one-night stand. You don't know me at all. Save yourself for someone you love."

She takes a deep shuddering breath and shakes her head.

I look at her slumped shoulders and slowly stand up. "It was nice to meet you, Tiffany."

She looks up and nods, and I walk toward our waitress. I give her a fifty dollar bill and head to the front door.

I hail a cab, and once inside I let the bumps in the pavement calm my racing heart. Shit, I should never have called her in the first place. At least I extricated myself from the evening before she could get her hands on me. Rick would be proud of me, I think.

Once safely back in my hotel room, I call Gina but get her answering machine yet again. I leave her a message telling her how much I love her, and hit the flash button and punch in Cindy's cell number to get an update on Rick.

"What's the word on Rick?" I ask.

"Nothing's changed. I'm still sitting in his hospital room, watching him sleep."

177

"Do you want me to come down there and sit with you for a while?"

"No thanks, Larry. That's Okay. I'm exhausted and I was just about asleep when you called."

"I'm sorry, Cin." I think for a minute and ask, "When he does wake up, if you think of it, could you tell Rick something for me?"

"Sure. What do you want me to tell him?"

I inhale deeply and say, "Tell him... tell him 'I passed the test'. He'll know what I mean, I think."

Chapter Thirty-Three

Before going to the airport this morning, I head over to the hospital to see Cindy and Rick. When I get there Cindy gives me a big hug. I wrap my arms around her and hold her for a while, patting her on the back.

Finally, she shakes herself free of my arms and says, "It's so good to see you. It's been so lonely here by myself without a familiar face."

"Believe me, I know." I look at her and try not to show my concern. When we turn to look at Rick, I ask, "How is he, Cin?"

"He's still out. He has rolled his eyeballs under his lids a couple of times this morning. The doctor says that's a good sign that he might be waking up soon." The smile on her face reassures me.

"That's great news," I say and give her another hug. I hope the news continues to get better. God, I hope Rick can return to some sort of a normal life. The thought of something less scares the crap out of me.

I sit with Cindy and hold one of Rick's hands, telling him I'm here. I keep hoping he'll move or something so I know he hears me, but there's no reaction. Cindy puts her arm around me to comfort me when a sob catches in my throat.

Together we watch him sleep for about an hour before I have to leave for my flight to Anaheim. When I have to go, I look at her and say, "I hope he wakes up soon. Call me day or night when he does. I want to know."

"I will. I promise," she says.

I give Rick's hand a final squeeze and give Cindy a long hug. I barely make it to my flight on time. I run most of the way through the airport, causing some strange looks.

Once on the plane, I think about seeing Rick in the hospital earlier. I'm so worried about what kind of life he will have after he recovers from the initial trauma. My anxiety level spikes at this line of thinking, so I try to focus on the upcoming three-game series in

179

Anaheim that begins tonight. At some point in the three-hour flight, I doze off.

Chapter Thirty-Four

When I walk into the visiting team clubhouse in Anaheim, I see Darren Clarke suiting up. "Hey, Darren," I say, clapping him on the shoulder. "Welcome to The Show." It hits me suddenly that Darren is here to take Rick's place on the roster. One man's disaster is another's golden opportunity.

I see nervousness in his eyes. I remember when I was called up for the first time seven years ago. I was a basket case. The newly found mentor in me takes over, and I smile at him. "Just take it easy, Darren. Keep your eyes open, pay attention, do your work, and you'll be fine."

"I guess I am a little nervous." He blushes beet red. His blond hair, longer than I remembered it, falls into his eyes. "I've had a good year at Sacramento, and I'm hoping I can carry over some of that up here."

"Look, Darren, let me tell you something. The game is the same. Yes, coming up here is a big jump, but just pitch your game. That's all you can do." I don't want to scare him.

"Thanks, Larry. I really appreciate the encouragement."

"No problem," I say, and head back to my locker. He reminds me so much of me at that age: eager, scared, cocky, anxious, and elated, all at the same time.

Later Darren comes over and sits down in Rick's chair. "I'm so sorry about your friend Rick getting hurt. I sure hope he comes out of this okay. I feel kind of weird being called up because of something like this."

"Part of the game, man. You can't feel bad. You would've gotten the call at some point." I pause for a moment, "I'm very worried about Rick. Unfortunately, all we can do now is wait until he wakes up, before we'll have any idea what the outcome will be."

My whole body is rebelling when I think about Rick, so I say, "Let's talk about something else, okay?" I lean down to tie my shoes.

"Sure. It must be hard for you. So tell me what else is going on with you?"

"Well, you probably know about my numbers so far this year. Not what I had hoped, especially in the loss column, but all I can worry about is my next start."

Darren looks at me intently. Geez, I remember how I hung on every word the veterans said when I was a rookie, often taking them personally, thinking I had screwed up big time. He'll learn that it's all in fun and develop his macho soon enough.

"So what are you doing for fun these days?" he asks.

"Well, I've asked my girlfriend, Gina, to marry me, and she said yes!" I grimace. "Oops! I'm not supposed to spill the beans. Please don't tell the rest of the guys, okay?"

He pumps my hand. "Sure, my lips are sealed." Then in a whisper, "Congratulations, Larry. I'm glad someone finally corralled you. She must be pretty awesome."

"Yes, she is." I whisper back, and feel my face flush.

Sometimes I wish Gina didn't work, so she could come with me on the road, but part of what attracted me to her was that she is smart, professional, and independent. Who knows, maybe I wouldn't have thought she was so wonderful if she were one of the baseball groupies.

I shake my head in complete wonder. Who is this person inhabiting my body? I'm mentoring Darren, and analyzing things in a rational, thoughtful manner. Maybe I am finally achieving adulthood.

Darren makes a zipping motion across his mouth and wanders back to his locker. I continue getting ready for the game, listening to Blasco's music. He's starting tonight, and I don't even have to chart pitches. No responsibilities. Gotta make sure I don't doze off.

We cruise through the first six innings building up a big lead of nine to zip. In the bottom of the seventh, the Angels push across a couple of runs. Bud Tanaka goes out to the mound to talk to Joe. When he returns, I flag him down.

"What'd he say?" I ask.

"He says he's fine. But I told him to get this next guy or Coop's coming out. We'd like to see what the new kid Clarke can do."

"He's a great kid. I'm glad he's done well this year."

"He says it's your fault, you know. Says you told him your mantra at spring training. He says you helped him with the mental

182

part of the game. Sure as hell surprised me." He has a twinkle in his eye so I just smile.

I hear the crack of the bat, and turn to watch the ball bounce out into center field. Coop decides to make the change and strides out to the mound. Joe hands him the ball and walks back to the dugout.

I look out to left field to see Darren emerge through the bullpen door and trot through the outfield to the mound. As he prepares to throw his first-ever pitch in the big leagues, I can see him mouthing something to himself.

The score is seven to two with two outs, and Vern Ramero is on first base. Darren looks over at Ramero, and then fires a ninety-two-mile-an-hour fastball on the outside edge of the plate. The batter, first baseman Tim Pike, just watches it. The next pitch is a carbon copy but on the inside corner. Strike two.

Darren throws over to first to keep Ramero close. He steps back onto the rubber and there is a hint of a smile on his face. He makes the identical motion as when he threw the two fastballs and delivers the ball high. About five feet in front of the plate, the ball sinks like a rock. Pike realizes his fate too late, and stands there with his shoulders slumped as the umpire punches him out with a loud "Stri-eek!" Inning over.

Darren sprints back to the dugout, and the guys give him high fives to congratulate him. I make a space for him on the bench next to me, and say, "Nice pitching, Darren. That was a big-league K."

"I just stood up there, used your mantra, and pretended I was you. It worked." He's beaming from ear to ear, and his eyes sparkle.

"Welcome to the Show. But be your own person, not me. You deserve to be here."

I'm so proud of him. I like to think I had a little something to do with what happened tonight. He really is a lot like me about six years ago.

Darren also pitches a flawless ninth inning and we win seven to two. He gets lots of butt pats from the guys as everyone rushes from the dugout to form a line to congratulate the guys coming off the field.

Jason taps me on the arm and hands me the ball from Darren's last out. "Give this to the kid," he says.

When I reach Darren, I hand him the ball and say, "Hang on to this for your trophy room." Then I give him a big man hug.

When I get back to the hotel, I call Gina, fingers crossed that I don't get her answering machine. We've been missing each other the past few days, and a voicemail message just isn't the same as hearing her real voice. I wait through three rings, and then hear a click.

"Hi, Hon," she says.

"Hi, yourself. I'm so glad I finally reached you in person. I've missed you so."

"I've missed you, too. I'm so sorry about Rick. How are you holding up?"

"Oh, I'm doing okay, I guess. Like Cindy, I feel so helpless. I can't do anything for him, except maybe pray." A vision of his bandaged face appears, and I wince.

Gina sighs on the other end of the line. "I've been keeping up with his progress, such as it is, from Cindy. She calls me often, to ask questions or just to talk. She's got to be scared to death with her husband in a coma. I know I would be."

"It's so nice to think that you would be there for me if I got hurt."

"Of course. I would. I love you."

"I love you too. God I miss you."

"Yeah. Me too. But you'll be home in two days. I am cooking up lots of ways to… uh… reconnect with you then."

"Ooh. I like the thought of that. I have a few ideas myself." My dick starts to come to life.

I can hear her cell phone ringing in the background. "Hold on a sec," she says. "I'm on call and I got to see if that's the hospital." When she comes back on the line, she says, "Damn! I have to head over there. I wish I could talk longer."

"No problem. Go take care of your little guys, and I'll see you when I get home. I can't wait. I love you!"

"Love you too. Bye," and she's gone with a click.

*   *   *

We play two more games against the Angels. We win the first, and lose a hard-fought game on get-away day. We head to the airport for our flight back to Oakland, but the guys are quieter than usual.

While our plane waits at the gate, my cell phone chirps to life. It's Cindy. Before I can say anything, Cindy yells, "Larry! He's awake!"

"Thank God!" I say. Then, with much trepidation, I ask, "How is he, Cin?"

"Well, he has some weakness on his right side, but... wait... here comes the doctor. I'll let you get it directly from him."

"Dr. Singh here," a male voice says with a clipped Indian accent. "Mr. Wycliffe regained consciousness around noon. His speech is slurred and halting, and he can't grip my hand very hard, so he has some weakness in his right side. We're going to do an CT scan in about an hour to check for swelling in the brain or bleeding, and then run some more tests. It's still too soon to tell much, but we're very happy to see him awake. It's a very good sign."

"That's terrific, Doc. Thanks." Oh, man. I hope that he can come out of this without any serious disabilities.

Cindy comes back on the line just as the stewardess tells us to turn off our cell phones, that we're about to take off. I ask Cindy to say hi to Rick and tell her goodbye.

On the flight home I say a silent prayer of thanks that Rick is awake and beg the man upstairs to let him have a good recovery.

I walk in the door to my house, drop my bags, and grab a beer. After taking off my jacket and tie, I flop down on the couch to call Gina to let her know that I'm home. She's working tonight, so I leave her a message, and then I dial Cindy's cell.

"Hi, Cindy. How's he doing?" I ask, trying not to let my fatigue show in my voice.

"He's doing better. He sleeps a lot, but the nurses say they can tell he is not slipping back into a coma, because we can see his eyes rolling, and his arms and legs twitch while he's asleep. That's supposed to be a good sign."

"I'm so glad, Cin." I don't want to ask the next question, but I can't stop myself. "Can he talk okay?"

185

She hesitates a moment and says, "He has some difficulty getting certain words to come out right, often saying one word when he means something else. It's something called 'aphasia,' according to the doctor. They hope it will get better over time." She pauses. "I hate all this waiting. I worry about being away from my kids for so long." I can hear her sigh deeply. "But it's better than having him in a coma."

"Absolutely. So what's going to happen next?"

"If the next CT scan looks good, he'll be transferred out of the ICU to the regular part of the hospital. They'll probably keep him there for a few days, just to make sure that he has no more brain issues."

"Any guess on when he'll be able to come home?"

"Not really. It all depends upon what future CT scans show and his physical progress. They did tell me that as long as he continues to show signs of improvement, there's hope."

"Rick's a fighter," I say. "I'm sure he will give it everything he's got. Whatever happens, he's got you and the kids for motivation. You've always been the most important things in his life."

"Thanks, Larry. You're pretty important to him too, you know."

I blush. "Yeah."

"Well, he's waking up, so I better go. I'll tell him you said hi. That will bring a smile to his face, or at least the side we can see."

"Bye, Cin. I'll call you tomorrow. Call me anytime if you want. I'm here for you if you need me. So is Gina."

*   *   *

During our home stand we win two from Chicago, sweep a series against the Indians, and take two from Baltimore. I pitch well during my last two starts, winning one and losing a complete-game, one-to-nothing squeaker. I now have fourteen wins and seven losses. We're seven-and-a-half games ahead of the Angels, a nice lead for the first week in September. But six of our last nine games of the season are against them, so we can't get complacent.

Gina and I spend most nights together, either at her house or mine. We've now been engaged for almost six weeks, and I love coming home to her each night. She's often asleep by the time I get home from night games, because she has to get up so early on the mornings she works. It's wonderful just to be lying next to her.

We have decided on a Christmas wedding on December twenty-first. It'll be a small affair, mostly family and a few friends, at Round Hill Country Club in Alamo. We were lucky to get that date. A wedding was cancelled at the last minute for that Saturday. I feel sorry for that poor couple because it must mean at least one of them is very unhappy.

I can't imagine being with anyone else. I'm still a little anxious about the road trip to Tampa Bay and Texas in a couple of days, but I have no worries while I'm at home.

Chapter Thirty-Five

I'm camped out in Dr. Blackwood's waiting room. His secretary hasn't come in yet, and the magazines on the coffee table don't look at all interesting, except the pile of *Sports Illustrateds*. Unfortunately, I've probably read them all. The waiting room looks spare this early in the day. There are no fresh flowers, and everything is neat and tidy, as I'm the first "victim" of the day.

I can hear the doc talking on the phone just low enough so I can't decode what he's saying. Good. I don't need to tune into someone else's problems on top of my own.

I slouch down and lay my head against the back of the couch, closing my eyes, enjoying the near quiet. My mind wanders for a while and finally settles on what I really want to talk about in my session—why I'm still so scared that I'll stray, even though I'm really happy with Gina. Then everything begins to fade as I doze off to the muffled tones coming through the door.

"Hi, Larry. Come on in."

I jump at the sound and shake myself awake. Pushing myself up off the couch, I follow Dr. B through the door into his office and sit down in one of the green leather chairs.

"I'm sorry. I guess I was dozing," I say with a yawn.

"No problem. Glad to see you're relaxed." He sits down in the chair next to me and crosses his legs.

"I was so sorry to hear about Rick getting injured. How is he doing?" he asks.

"Cindy keeps me posted on his progress which is slow but steady. The weakness on his right side lessens with each physical therapy appointment, which is a good sign."

"That's great. I hope it works out well for him," he says, and then asks, "So how are things going with you?"

"Other than worrying about Rick, really well, I think. I mean I'm pitching a lot better, which should make my agent happier than it does." I hesitate for a fraction of a second. "When I'm with Gina, I don't think about other women, so that's good, too."

"Good. But am I hearing some reservation in your voice?" He leans back in his chair and folds his hands in his lap.

I will myself to relax by thinking of Gina, and words come flowing out of me. When we get to the heart of my concerns, I say, "I guess, Doc, I'm still afraid that I'll succumb to the charms of some beautiful woman when I'm on the road, and I'll do something really stupid and lose Gina for good. I really need to talk about that." I lean forward, elbows on knees, shoulders slumped. A shock of hair falls across my face, but I ignore it.

"What do you think is going on?" he asks.

"If I knew, I wouldn't be here," I say a little too testily.

"Well… from the anger in your response, this fear is exactly what we should be addressing."

I tell him about my near miss with Tiffany. He takes a sip of coffee from a Renegades mug, and asks, "What made the difference in your encounter with Tiffany? What gave you the courage to stop?"

"I suddenly had a vision of Gina, and I knew that if I continued down that road, I'd lose her, so I decided to go back to my hotel instead."

"That's good. But why do you think you saw Gina?"

I take a deep breath and let it out in a rush. "I don't know."

Silence sets in and I start to squirm a bit. Answers seem to be on the tip of my tongue and I can't seem to get the words to come out.

I can hear the tick of his office clock get louder with each passing minute. My heart races at the thought of losing Gina. How could I do something like that to her? Hell, to me? She is all I have ever wanted in a woman. Why was I chasing her opposite for so long?

Finally, I manage to say, "I guess I have deeper feelings for Gina than I've had for any woman before. And I've actually talked to her about my feelings." I smile and chuckle. "That's definitely a first for me."

"Try this one on. Maybe you opened yourself up to her, and you let her see you for who you really are. That can be very powerful… and very scary."

His words make me feel both hopeful and terrified. I mull these extremes over for a minute, and then say, "Yeah. I guess letting

189

Gina into my heart made me feel really and truly known by another person. It's like tasting a two-hundred dollar bottle of wine for the first time—you never knew that something could taste that rich and mellow at the same time."

Dr. Blackwood smiles. "Great analogy, Larry. So why do you still have the fear?"

"I guess I also realize how easy it would be for me to throw it away in a moment of weakness. That scares the shit out of me." I shift in my chair at these uncomfortable thoughts and fall silent.

Dr. B just watches me, offering nothing.

The silence begins to weigh heavily on me, so I say, "It was hard letting Gina see who I really am, but it felt good to do it. After a while I wasn't so scared. She understands me so well, and she's put up with a lot of my crap. That makes me love her even more."

"And you don't want to screw that up."

"Exactly."

"Well, you managed to avoid having sex with Tiffany, right?"

"Yeah, but I came close to blowing it, and I'm scared I might not be able to back off the next time. And I don't want to see that hurt look on another woman's face, or Gina's for that matter."

"But you never would have worried about hurting a woman before. That's a real change for you."

"I suppose it is. I didn't realize that until just now." I look at my hands, which are trembling. Finally, my eyes meet his. "Doc, I'm twenty-eight years old. I can control myself on the mound. I'm a grown-up there. Why do I revert to a fucking high school mentality when I see a pretty woman?"

He looks at me for a while, his face showing no expression, and finally asks, "Speaking of high school, what was your relationship with girls during that period?"

"I don't know. I guess I was terrified of them at first. My brothers were dating lots of girls in high school, different girls at the same time. I idolized my big brothers, and I really wanted to be like them. They were always telling me about their sexual exploits."

"And... ?" Dr. Blackwood prompts.

"I heard my brothers talking about how girls were 'just chicks.' They bragged about being big jocks on campus, that the 'chicks' fell all over them and would do anything they wanted."

"What did you think they meant by 'just chicks' and 'they'd do anything they wanted?'"

190

I ponder the question for a few seconds. "I guess I gathered that my brothers thought they were superior somehow to the 'chicks'. I assumed that they could—and did—have sex with these girls anytime they wanted. As I said, I idolized them, so I guess I adopted the same attitude toward the opposite sex."

"And does your father have that same attitude toward your mother?" Dr. B asks.

"No! He worships her. He always has. But you know teenage boys. They think their parents are fossils. Teenagers make their own way, and I followed in my big brother's footsteps."

"And how did that work for you?"

"Well, as a high school freshman, when I'd come on to girls, they thought I was just dorky and usually split before much happened. But after I grew about six inches and became the star pitcher on the baseball team, the girls started falling all over me. I thought they were there for the taking and... well... I took."

"How did that make you feel?"

"At first, I felt awkward and a little guilty. But my brothers were doin' it, so I did it too. And, Doc, the girls made it real easy. So I quit worrying about it and just enjoyed them... a lot... throughout high school and college."

"What about the nights before you pitched?"

"I rarely hooked up with girls if I was on the mound the next day. I learned that lesson the hard way. I had a few terrible games the day following an evening of booze and sex. So I made it a rule never to do either on the nights before I pitched. I'd wait until after the game when the groupies would fight with each other to have me."

"So you could control yourself on the nights before you pitched."

"Yeah, I guess so." I'd never thought about that before. "I'd lay off the booze and try to get a good night's sleep instead."

"Why do you think you could refrain from partying back then?"

"It was too important for me to pitch well. I just decided that I wouldn't do that and I didn't. It seemed so easy back then."

Doc Blackwood thinks a minute, his eyebrows knitting together. "So now that you have Gina, can't you just decide you're not going to be tempted and carry through with that? Isn't being faithful to Gina as important to you as pitching a good game?"

Wow. He's got me there. I'm stymied into silence.

191

I sit in silence for a while, breathing deeply. Finally, I say, "Yeah. I… suppose." I think for a few minutes more before continuing. "I guess if I think of it that way, I could be faithful to Gina on the road." But I don't sound very convincing to me.

"You know you can do it. You've done it in the past and you did it with Tiffany in Seattle. So, back to the original question. Why do you still have doubts?"

I think about this for a long time, trying to make some sense of my life. Things begin to ratchet into place in my brain, and I look up at him, my confidence growing with each tick of the clock on the shelf. "I guess I'm being a little silly, aren't I?" I smile sheepishly. "Of course, I can do it. Gina means too much to me to risk blowing it."

He smiles. "Good. We've made real progress here."

"You remember the mantra that I say to myself in tight spots in a ballgame? 'Ninth inning. Seventh game?'"

He nods, but doesn't say anything.

"Sometimes I say it to myself when I get anywhere near a tight spot off the field."

"Sounds like a good plan to me. It's similar to what we call in the psych business 'creative visualization.' You say your trigger words and visualize yourself doing what you want to do, which puts that image in your mind. That way, when you're challenged, it's there to help you stay on course."

"It sounds so easy, but it's not. I've tried it and failed."

"The thing is, you need to trust the process and trust yourself to follow through with your intention."

"Trust the process and follow through. On the mound and off. I'll work on that." I chuckle to myself. "You know, I've always heard people say that baseball is a metaphor for life. I guess I never realized how much it really is true."

Dr. Blackwood stands up, signaling that the session is over. I get to my feet and shake his hand. "I'll make this work on the next road trip. Thanks, Doc. I really appreciate your help."

"No problem. Let me know how it goes when you get back."

"Will do," I say, and leave his office feeling better than I have felt in a very long time. I have a strange sensation of peace inside. Maybe I am changing after all. It's about fuckin' time.

192

I call Gina after I get through the Caldecott Tunnel and she answers. No machine. "Let's go out to dinner tonight. I feel like celebrating," I say.

She agrees.

Chapter Thirty-Six

When we exit our plane at Dallas-Ft. Worth Airport, we're greeted by the blistering early September heat and humidity that this city is famous for, which is much hotter than the sticky weather we've endured the last three days in Tampa Bay. I lost a close game there because the guys' bats went silent on me again. I'm sure that Bob Jacobs is steamed about my eighth loss.

I'm not pitching in this series but Mom and Dad decided to come up from Midland, just to see me. They've always been there for me. I may be twenty-eight years old, but I owe my career to the coaching my dad gave me growing up. And Mom, she's always been the embodiment of home for me. My mouth waters just thinking about her great cooking.

I call the airline when I get to my hotel room. The agent tells me that some mechanical problem has cancelled Mom and Dad's flight. They won't leave Midland on another flight until at least 9:00 pm. Bummer. I want to go to bed early, but I also want a Mom hug.

I decide to go downstairs to the bar for a nightcap to wait until Mom and Dad arrive. I plunk down on a barstool so I can talk to the bartender. He turns out to be a nice guy and a Texas Rangers fan.

While we are shooting the shit, he cuts his eyes to the left. I follow his gaze and see a lovely young woman with very long legs walking toward us. She raises a hip, lifting herself onto the barstool next to mine, and orders a glass of Chardonnay.

Her copper hair is trying to escape from a comb at the side of her head and her long frame is nicely packaged in a green sheath with a plunging neckline revealing substantial cleavage. This is real trouble. The bartender looks at me and winks as he sets down her glass.

She chugs about half of her wine as if it were water, and puts her glass down with an "aah" of satisfaction. Then she turns her warm green eyes on me and offers her hand, "Hi, I'm April. What's your name?"

Shit. Why can't I just be left alone? She's gorgeous and sounds nice. But I'm not in the mood for this.

Ninth inning. Seventh game.

I take her hand and shake it. "Hi. Larry Gordon."

Come on, Larry, I say to myself. Be nice but be firm. She's trouble and you need to get up and leave.

She interrupts my thoughts. "Wanna buy me another drink?" She's already drained her first one.

Here's where the shit hits the fan. I know what I have to do but my mouth is anesthetized. Not good!

I order her another chardonnay. I decide not to order a drink for myself. I need to be sober to get out of this.

She starts flirting with me big-time now and occasionally pats my leg. Shit. She tells me all about herself, and I just listen and keep my hands in my lap. That's progress. Let's build on that, and get the fuck out of here.

Gina's smiling image wanders across my brain, and my heart rate slows.

Ninth Inning. Seventh game.

When the bartender returns with her wine, I ask for the check. When he sets it down in front of me, I charge the tab to my room, and step back off my barstool. She follows suit, obviously assuming we are going to my room. Allowing that to happen flits through my mind and out again.

I thrust out my hand. "Nice to meet you, April. Enjoy your drink. I need to go call my fiancée before it gets any later."

She shrugs and gives me a wistful look. After a few seconds she turns back to talk to the bartender, whose eyes brighten at the prospect of my departure.

I let out the breath that apparently I've been holding. That was dangerous but I think I handled it pretty well. This was certainly easier than with Tiffany. But I still feel like I've been through the ringer.

After I let myself into my room, I remove a small bottle of Dewars from the minibar. I plunk a few ice cubes into the glass and pour in the amber liquid. Swirling my scotch around, I think back on my encounter with April. I recognized trouble from the get-go, said my mantra, and thought of Gina. That allowed me to fend off April's advances. And I didn't even get aroused when she put her hand on my thigh. Amazing!

195

I can do this.

I call Gina and wake her up. She must have had a hard day and gone to bed early. It's only nine o'clock in California.

"I'm sorry, Hon. I didn't mean to wake you up. I just wanted to tell you how much I love you."

She mumbles, sleep slurring her speech. "I love you too."

I hear the rattle as she attempts to replace the receiver, and then a dial tone. I smile at hearing her voice and at successfully escaping from trouble.

I call Mom's cell phone and she says they're finally at the Dallas airport. I look at my watch and see that it's close to eleven. Mom says they are exhausted and they'll meet me for breakfast in the morning around eight.

No Mom hugs tonight.

Chapter Thirty-Seven

After sleeping soundly, I dress and go down to the restaurant. The maitre d' shows me to a table toward the back of the room. Once my parents arrive and I get my Mom and Dad hugs, the waiter appears and we order our breakfast. After he departs, I look from one to the other and say, "I have some big news. I proposed to Gina and she said 'yes.' We're going to be married after the season is over. But we're not telling anyone so please keep it a secret."

Mom tries to dam her tears and fails. She fishes a Kleenex out of her purse and blows her nose. Once the waterworks cease, she says, "Oh, that's wonderful, Son. I'm so happy for you and who would we tell anyway?" She sniffs and says. "I was so sorry when she broke up with you in January."

"Yeah, me too." I recall how empty I felt when Gina wasn't in my life and push the thought away. "But she says she'll have me now, and I feel like the luckiest guy on the planet."

"Well, maybe the second luckiest, Son," Dad says, smiling at Mom. "If you and Gina are half as happy as your mother and I are, you'll be a very lucky man indeed."

I squeeze Mom's hand and give them each a big smile. "Thanks, you two. You guys have always been great role models for me." I could do a lot worse than trying to be like them. "It's just taken me a long time to realize that I want what you guys have." Mom looks at Dad and blushes.

As if on cue, the waiter arrives with our food, covering Mom's embarrassment, and we dig in.

Mom looks up from her food and smiles. "So when's the wedding and where?"

"We've having it at Round Hill Country Club, just south of Walnut Creek, on December twenty-first, long after the World Series is over. We wouldn't want to jinx the team's chances in the playoffs."

197

Mom suddenly looks worried. "That's not much time to prepare." She cocks her head and gives me a look. It's obvious there is something on her mind.

The light bulb goes on in my head. "No, Mom. We don't have to get married. But we do need to have the wedding during the off season, and neither of us wants to wait another year to do it."

Mom pats me on the arm. "Well, she's a very lucky girl." She thinks for a moment and asks, "How's Rick doing?"

"Pretty well, considering he had a very serious brain injury. He still has some weakness on his right side and some speech issues. His type of injury may require a long recovery."

"Do they think he will be all right?" She asks.

"It's too soon to tell. He was flown home to a rehabilitation hospital in San Ramon yesterday." I explain to them about his aphasia and weakness on his right side. "The doctors want him to have more intense speech and physical therapy than they can give him in a general hospital, such as the one in Seattle. And he's ecstatic to be near home so he can see his kids."

"That's wonderful." she says with a smile.

"He keeps improving with all the therapy he's getting. As long as that continues, there's hope for a good recovery."

Dad asks, "What about his future? Do you think he'll play ball again?"

"I don't know," I say. "My guess is that he won't. He'd miss it, of course, but he's always loved being home with his kids. He says that's his real calling—being a father. Playing baseball lately has been just a means to that end for him."

"Are you saying he's not as driven as you are?" Dad asks.

"No, not at all. What I'm saying is that if he can't or doesn't want to step back up on a pitcher's mound—and I wouldn't blame him—I think he'd be just as happy staying home and raising the kids. Cindy could go back to work. She was an accountant until the kids started coming. But whatever happens, they'll work it out. They're an amazing couple."

Mom puts a hand on my arm and says, "I have always loved Rick. And he's been such a good friend to you."

"Mom, you don't know the half of it." Amen to that! "I wouldn't be marrying Gina if it hadn't been for Rick's good advice over the years. He's a wonderful role model for me, and he'll always be my best friend."

"Well, I hope he comes out of this okay," she says. "We all want the best for him." Dad echoes her sentiments.

"Me too," I say, with a lump in my throat.

I put down my fork and look at Mom, changing the subject away from Rick. "You know, Gina might love to get you involved in the wedding plans. As soon as I tell her I've told you, why don't you give her a call?" I write her number down on a paper napkin and hand it to her.

"Okay. I'll call her when I get the okay." Mom looks at me, her face dissolving like she is going to cry. "I'm glad she makes you happy, son," she says. A tear escapes and runs down her cheek.

Mom excuses herself to search for the ladies room, Kleenex in hand.

Dad and I chat about the Renegades and my upcoming contract talks. At one point Dad looks up, and I turn to follow his gaze. Mom is walking toward us with her mascara back in place. She sits down, and says, "There. That's better."

I catch a glimpse of Darren talking to the hostess at the door to the restaurant, and wave him over to our table.

When he approaches, I stand up. "Hay, Darren, please join us. I want you to meet my parents."

"Oh, I don't want to intrude," he says, looking embarrassed.

"Nonsense. Mom? Dad? This is Darren Clarke, the rookie that I helped during spring training. He was called up when Rick got hurt." Dad stands and shakes Darren's hand.

"Hi, Mr. and Mrs. Gordon," he says, leaning down to shake Mom's.

Dad gets another chair from a neighboring table and retrieves a place setting, too. "How are you liking being in the majors, Darren?"

"It's awesome," he says, as he sits down. "And I'm really lucky that Larry has taken me under his wing. I don't get teased nearly as much as most rookies do, because the guys know that Larry will kick their butts."

"Happy to do it," I say.

Darren orders some food, and while we all eat, he talks about baseball and his family with my parents. At some point I mention the wedding. "I hope you'll come, Darren. It's on December twenty-first out here."

199

"I'd be honored, Larry," he says. "I'll probably be back in Connecticut, but I'll fly out. So count me in." His big grin shows his enthusiasm and his youth.

"And we're still not telling anyone just yet."

"No worries, man," he says. "I've already forgotten it."

Mom puts her hand on my arm. "A wedding in December, what fun! And of course, we'll do the rehearsal dinner. I'll discuss it with Gina after its okay to call her, and we'll take care of everything."

"That's great, Mom."

After I pay the check, Mom looks at Darren and says, "It's been great to meet you. Larry has told us a lot about you."

"Thanks, Mrs. Gordon. I really enjoyed meeting you both too."

Mom looks at him and smiles, pointing her thumb at me. "He says you're going to be as good as he is."

Darren blushes and looks at me. "Thanks, man, for doin' all this for me."

*   *   *

We lose the first game of the Texas series badly and win the last two. We are now seventy-nine and sixty-two, five-and-a-half games ahead of the Angels, and we're headed home.

We arrive at Oakland Airport at around 11:30 pm and board a bus on the tarmac for the ride to the Coliseum. I locate my now dusty car in the players' parking lot, and drive home thinking about how great it was to see Mom and Dad. And I remained celibate on the trip. I feel really good about that.

*   *   *

We sweep the two series on the home stand, taking three-games from both the Red Sox and the Royals, much to the delight of the Oakland fans.

I pitch the last game in the Boston series, going seven innings of one-hit ball. The bullpen saves the one-run ballgame, giving me my fifteenth win of the season. Unfortunately, my eight losses aren't going anywhere. But my ERA is now down to a very respectable 3.23. Even so, my guess is that I won't be hearing happy words from my agent. Just more shit about the losses, the prick.

Next we fly out for a six-game road trip in Detroit and Minnesota. We win five and lose one on the trip. Unfortunately, the loss breaks a thirteen-game winning streak. And the Angels are matching us pretty much game for game, so we're still five and a half games ahead of them.

I get my sixteenth win on the road in Detroit. I'm stingy with their hitters, and our guys have balls flying out of Comerica Park in a blowout, for a change.

I also manage to avoid getting cornered by any of the groupies on the trip, and it actually feels good being faithful to Gina. I keep telling myself I'll get my reward when I get home.

Chapter Thirty-Eight

The Angels are in town for three games and we could clinch a playoff berth during this series. Since they have six more losses than we do with nine games remaining, our magic number is four, so any combination of Renegades wins and Angels losses that add up to four means we clinch the series. We win the first game reducing our magic number to two.

As I sit in the clubhouse before tonight's game, the thought of clinching has us all pumped. The plastic will go up over our lockers in the late innings, and the champagne is already on ice.

This will be the last regular-season game I will start in Oakland, because after this series we travel to Anaheim and then Seattle to close out the season. Just thinking about this game being my last start at the Coliseum makes me incredibly sad. I have played in Oakland for the last six years, and I'm going to miss this concrete tomb of a stadium. The generous foul territory here allows many more balls to be caught for outs, balls that would end up in the seats as foul balls at most other ballparks. Also, the cool air in the evenings tends to keep fly balls inside the park instead of in the stands for homers.

But most of all I will miss the guys I've played with here, especially Rick.

I call him every day to see how he's doing. He's working hard at the rehab hospital and is regaining more strength on his right side. His speech has cleared up a lot, but he still has trouble sometimes saying the word his brain is telling his mouth to say. Cindy says the doctors are really happy that he keeps progressing.

I will miss Rick the most if I get a contract with a team other than the Renegades or the Giants for next year. Bob Jacobs still says neither of those teams are a possibility, so I'm staring at a move to some other city or state.

What will I do about Gina? What if she won't move to who-knows-where with me? Can I leave her here? That feels like a total disaster for our relationship. I can't lose her again. Nothing is worth that, not even baseball.

I look up at the clock on the wall and am brought back to reality with a jolt. It's thirty minutes before game time. I can't think about all that now. I've got to finish getting ready to pitch.

Grabbing my jacket and glove, I walk down the tunnel to the field with Jason and Bud, our pitching coach. I will my anxiety about Gina and missing Rick and the guys into my mental vault, and slam the door firmly shut.

My bullpen warm-up goes well, and I take the mound with a lot of confidence. Bring it on. We're going to clinch this thing in front of the home fans. On my watch. No question about it.

I sail through the first six innings without allowing a hit. We score three runs off Milo Peterson, the ace of their rotation. I give up two walks, but both runners are stranded at first base. My confidence soars with each out. I'm in the zone. I feel on top of the world as I look in to Jason for each sign.

In the seventh with two out, our shortstop Bobby Crandell makes a routine play but airmails his throw to first into the visitors' dugout. That puts a runner on second base, but I'm not concerned. I'm the ace of this staff, dammit! A runner on second isn't going to make me lose my composure.

Vern Romero, the Angels' slugging outfielder, steps into the batter's box. I start him out with a curve, which he isn't expecting, and he watches it into Jason's glove for strike one. Next Jason puts down one finger against his right thigh—fastball away. I deliver it into his waiting mitt for strike two.

After I waste a fastball inside and tight, causing Romero to lunge out of the way, Jason puts down two fingers next to his right leg. I deliver the curve ball high and watch it drop over the outside corner. Romero recognizes the spin a second too late and swings way out ahead of the ball, getting nothing but air. The ump punches him out with a piercing "Strike three!"

As I walk off the mound, I feel that I can do anything. I'm not cocky, just confident. We're going to win this, and I'm going to be the one leading the way.

There's a hum in the stands as I make my way to the dugout. I guess the fans also know it's my last start here in Oakland. Someone near our dugout starts chanting "Lar-ry! Lar-ry! Lar-ry!" Others join in. I tip my cap to them and smile. Renegades fans are the best. Stepping down into the dugout, I have to swallow the large lump in my throat.

Our guys help me out with a couple more runs in the bottom of the seventh, sending Peterson to the showers. The score is now five to nothing. I can breathe a little easier, but I'm not taking anything for granted. Not with the Angels. No number of runs is enough insurance with these guys.

I breeze through the bottom of their lineup in the top of the eighth, and we don't score in our half of the inning, so I take the mound in the top of the ninth knowing that three more outs will clinch the title. The crowd is on its feet, and they cheer with every pitch. I get two quick outs on ground balls. The crowd is going nuts. The noise is deafening.

John Rivers, the Angels' clutch-hitting outfielder, walks up to the batter's box on the first base side. I've got to put him away for the last out. Lefty against lefty. A good match-up for me.

Jason and I start him off with a slider. I rarely throw that pitch, but with my confidence today, I can throw anything. It heads toward the middle of the plate but drops off to the right at the last minute into the dirt. It looks so inviting to Rivers that he takes a huge swing and misses by a mile.

Jason calls for another slider, and Rivers can't lay off this one either, for strike two.

Crunch time.

I look in at Jason for the sign. He calls for a fastball away. It just misses the edge of the plate for ball one. The sellout crowd shouts insults at the umpire.

Next Jason calls for the slider again but I shake him off. After a couple of signs, we agree on a curveball, which I send high. But it stays high, for ball two. The count is now two and two, and the fans—not to mention the guys on our bench—are getting restless.

Jason calls for a slider again and I shake him off. He asks the umpire for time and trots out to the mound.

"Larry, why don't you like the slider? You've been throwing it well, and Rivers hasn't been able to lay off it. Let's use it again."

For some reason, I feel like taking his advice. "Okay. We'll go with slider."

Jason returns behind the plate and drops into his crouch. He flashes four fingers away.

Ninth inning. Seventh game. I growl these words under my breath. I'm confident. I can do anything.

I step back up onto the rubber and go into my windup. I deliver the slider over the right side of the plate knee high, until it drops down about eight inches. Rivers misses it by a foot, and Jason snags it in his mitt just above the dirt.

I stand there waiting for the umpire's late call. Finally, he turns to the side and jerks one elbow back and punches the air with the other. Strike three. I look at Jason who rises out of his crouch and jumps up in the air, pumping his fist. Suddenly it hits me like a freight train. We did it. We're going to the playoffs!

The guys erupt from our dugout and mob me in front of the mound. We all jump up and down at the same time, slapping each other on the shoulders and hugging. Guys are whooping, others have tears running down their faces. For the first time in five years, we're going to the post-season. And we did it at home.

Gradually the huddle dissolves, and we wander around congratulating each other on our amazing achievement. When I get to Darren, I give him a big hug and tell him, "Soak it up kid. This doesn't happen every year. Some guys play twenty years and never get here."

He can't stop himself from grinning. "Fucking awesome!" he says.

Coop appears in front of me and says, "Nice job, Larry. You pitched one helluva game." He puts out his hand for a shake.

"Thanks, Coop," I say, taking his hand. I think of all the ways Coop has stood behind me, especially that day in Seattle after Rick got hurt. I smile at him and say, "I wouldn't want to be celebrating with anyone else."

"Well, you did it. Congratulations." He hesitates a minute and then gives me a hug, and says, "Thank you!" He turns around quickly, as if he's embarrassed by this exchange.

Thoughts of Rick flood in. He should be here celebrating with us. I really miss his company in the clubhouse. The game just isn't as much fun without him. I'm glad he's doing so much better, but I'll miss being along side of him during the playoffs. It'll be like missing a body part.

The crowd has been on its feet and cheering ever since the start of the ninth inning. Once again they start chanting, "Lar-ry! Lar-ry!

Lar-ry!" Then that morphs into, "MVP! MVP!" Which then morphs into "Stay, Larry! Stay, Larry!"

I raise my hands in the air. That brings even more noise from the stands. I begin turning slowly in a circle, savoring the adulation from these wonderful fans. The stands are still full, and the cheers keep coming.

I look around and think about not pitching here next season. It feels all wrong. Maybe I'll talk about that with Bob one more time when I see him next.

Once we get back to the clubhouse, the lockers are covered with plastic and champagne bottles are lined up like soldiers on a table in the middle of the room. I grab two and take a huge swig from one, enjoying the bubbles bursting in my mouth. I put my thumbs over the top of both bottles and shake. I point them at the closest guy to me and pull back my thumbs a little. Champagne spews out and douses Nick Hayner, soaking his long hair. He just laughs and returns the favor.

The noise is deafening and the floor gets slippery very quickly, but we don't care. I kick off my cleats and shove them under the plastic in front of my locker and dance around in soggy socks, enjoying the revelry.

While I'm drinking some of my liquid ammunition, Darren sprays me from behind, and says, "This is way cool, dude. I can't believe it's really happening."

I turn around spray him back. "It's awesome, Darren. A very special moment. The culmination of six months of very hard work. Just enjoy it. You're one of us now."

Again, I think of Rick, working hard to put his life back together. I wish he could be part of this moment. He deserves to be here so much. He's a big part of why we got here.

And Gina couldn't be here to watch our triumph either. She has a very sick little patient that she had to monitor. She DVR'd the game and we'll watch it together when I get home, if it's not too late. But it won't be the same as if she had been in the stands tonight. I really wanted to share it with her.

My impending free agency sticks its nose into my thoughts. What if she can't go with me next season? What if she decides she can't do a long-distance marriage? We need to talk about all this, and soon. Suddenly, waves of anxiety roll through me.

Jason taps me on the shoulder. "Why aren't you celebrating?"

I suppress all my negative thoughts and paste on a smile. "You're right, Jason. Let's celebrate!" I pick up another bottle from the table and take several long pulls on it, hoping the champagne will rescue my mood. Then I pour the bottle over Jason's head and pull him into a soggy bear hug. "Thanks, man, for catching me this year and watching out for my backside. It all worked out pretty well, didn't it?"

He upends his bottle over my head and says, "I had my doubts about you this year, but you put it all together, and today you were fuckin' awesome."

"You were a big part of that. The slider call in the ninth was inspired. Here's to our awesome day and to a great year." We clink our bottles and he melts back into the celebration.

Suddenly a bright light blares in my face and one of the TV guys starts introducing me. I answer all his questions politely before they move on to Coop's office for a statement. I even humor the print media, including the chubby guy whose shirt is still too tight.

About two hours later when I've had enough revelry and champagne for one night, I find my locker and retrieve my toilet kit from under the plastic and head for the showers. By the time I'm finished showering, most of the celebrating has calmed down and guys are beginning to straggle out of the clubhouse. I dress and walk out between the TV trucks to my car in the players' parking lot and drive home by myself, thinking that Rick should be sitting beside me.

When I get home, Gina is already asleep. She left me a note telling me there's a plate of dinner in the fridge to microwave if I'm still hungry. I wolf it down and crawl into bed, trying not to wake her. Before I fall asleep, I relive tonight's game and the celebration that followed. We're going to the postseason. Absolutely fucking amazing, considering how I started out this season.

*   *   *

Unfortunately, we still have two more series to play to finish out the season, three games each in Anaheim and Seattle. In Anaheim, there are quite a few rookies in our line-up, and the Angels sweep us in the series. Our team only manages to score seven runs in the three games. Doesn't mean much except for the minor effect it has on the guys' stats.

I'm pitching the second game of the Seattle series tonight. I really want to finish the season on a high note so I'm pumped up to get a win. It won't be easy as the guys and I have Felix Sanchez to deal with, the same guy I faced on opening day here in April. He and I throw shutout ball for five innings.

In the top of the sixth, three Renegade runs go up on the scoreboard on a towering blast from Frank Matson with two guys on base. That sends Felix packing.

I sail through the rest of the game to get my eighteenth win of the season. Once in the clubhouse, I talk to the media and head to the showers. I dress quickly and head toward the players' entrance with a big smile on my face. Eighteen wins. How do you like that, Bob?

Chapter Thirty-Nine

When I open the door to leave the stadium, I stop dead in my tracks. Gina is standing there with the lights from the parking lot behind her making her hair look like spun gold. She shrugs out of her backpack, letting it fall to the pavement, and I take her into my arms and kiss her deeply.

When our lips part I ask, "What are you doing here?" I realize that may not have been the best thing to lead with, so I say, "Gosh, it's wonderful to see you. This is a fantastic treat!"

She just smiles at me and shrugs. "Surprise!"

"Well, I love it. It is the best thing that could have happened to me tonight." I give her another hug and hold on for a long time.

When she loosens her grip on me, I say, "Let's go somewhere where we can get something to eat and talk. You can tell me all about how you happen to be here."

"Great. Do you have a favorite place?"

"Let's just head into the city and find someplace nice," I say and give her a squeeze. I gather up her backpack and put it over my shoulder. Hand in hand, we start walking.

"God, it's good to see you," I say. "By the way, how did you get to the stadium? Did you rent a car?"

"I did. It's in that garage up ahead." She points to a red brick building.

"Great. I'm sick of taxis." Holding hands we walk to her car, and I kiss her longingly before I help her into her seat.

We park in the heart of downtown Seattle and decide to walk around. With my arm around Gina, we peer into the windows of the closed stores, thinking about furnishing a house we don't yet own. I never knew that talking about mundane things like furniture and pots and pans could feel so good.

We finally settle in at Wild Ginger, an upscale Asian restaurant across the street from Benaroya Hall which, Gina informs me, is the home of the Seattle Symphony. According to the sign on the door, the restaurant stays open until midnight for late diners after the concerts.

We sit side by side in a booth so we can touch each other and order some of Wild Ginger's specialties—Fish Satay, Vietnamese Green Papaya Salad, Lemongrass Chicken and Wild Ginger Fragrant Duck.

"How do you know all this stuff? About the Seattle Symphony and Bena-what's-its-name Hall?"

"Well, Hon, I've been hatching this plan for some time. I did some internet research on Seattle, and that happens to be one of the factoids that just stuck in my mind." She babbles on about other things she discovered in her research. I must have a shit-eating grin on my face because I'm a very happy guy right now.

Our food arrives and we enjoy the pungent flavors of the orient. Everything smells wonderful and is beautifully and architecturally presented.

"Were you in the stands for the game? I ask.

"Yes, I got there in the third inning. My seat was in the fifth row not too far out from third base. I just sat there watching you. God, I was so proud. I never felt more in love watching you on the mound when you didn't know I was there."

I lean over and kiss her. "I love you, too!"

I let the warm feeling of her love flow over me for a minute. "Having you here is really special. The road can get pretty lonely." Understatement of the world. "You're welcome to come with me any time you like."

"I might just do that if my schedule permits."

We order dessert, and I maintain contact with some part of her body as we eat.

"I have a confession to make," I say. I watch as several emotions march across her face in succession."

"Is it good or bad?" she asks without smiling.

"I don't know how to answer that. You'll have to tell me. The thing is, I was talking to Jason in the clubhouse after the game, shooting the shit. In the course of the conversation, I referred to you as 'my fiancée.'"

I take a deep breath and study my lap. Before she can say anything, I blurt, "I know we said we wouldn't tell anyone until after the season, but it just came out. I'm so sorry. I swore him to secrecy."

210

Time to come clean with the rest. "I've also told my parents and Darren when we were in Texas, I'm really sorry I couldn't keep my mouth shut."

I don't want to look up. I don't want to see disappointment on her face. When she doesn't say anything, I finally raise my head and see love in her brilliant blue eyes, underscored by a warm smile.

"It's okay. I think we should tell everyone. It's too hard for me to keep from doing exactly what you did. Besides, we need to send out invitations next month, so people will know about it before long anyway."

"So you're not mad at me?" I sound like a kid who's been let off the hook after emptying the cookie jar.

"Of course not. I love you, remember?"

I hug her tight to me and kiss her. "How was I so lucky to fall for you?"

"Must be my brains and my charm."

"Definitely those," I say, giving her a wicked smile.

I pay the check and we drive down the hill to my hotel. We park in the garage and take the elevator up to my room, entwined in each others' arms.

I have never been happier in my life.

*   *   *

The next day, Gina is again in the stands by third base, this time in the first row. If I lean over, I can see her from my seat in the dugout, and occasionally I catch her eye and smile at her.

I suddenly remember the one topic that I don't want to deal with—playing somewhere away from the San Francisco Bay Area next year. I guess my face looks forlorn because Darren sits down next to me and asks, "Are you okay? You look like somebody died."

"It feels like it. I was thinking about the fact that I probably won't be playing on this team or in the Bay Area next year. I'll miss all you guys, but most of all, I'll miss Gina. She's here, by the way." I lean forward and point toward her. "See? She's waving at us."

Darren bends over and waves at her. "Man, she's a knockout. I hope I get to meet her."

"You can if you're quick after the game."

211

He leans forward and looks at Gina again. "You are one lucky son of a bitch!"

We get the win and I hurry back to the clubhouse to shower and dress. I tell Darren to do the same and follow me out. The media guys aren't interested in me tonight since I wasn't on the mound for this one, so Darren and I head toward the players' entrance. When I open the door to the parking lot, there she is with her sunny blond hair falling around her shoulders framing a brilliant smile.

Darren and I walk up to her, and I give her a quick kiss. "Hon, this is Darren Clarke, the rookie I told you about."

She turns her smile on him. "It's nice to meet you, Darren. This guy here says you're going to go far."

Darren blushes. "Thanks," and turns to me and nods. "You can keep her. I approve."

To Gina, he says, "Nice to meet you, Gina. I hope to see you soon, and for sure at the wedding," and turns to sprint off toward the bus.

Gina smiles. "I guess you invited him to our big day. That's great."

"Yeah, I asked him when I told him about the wedding in Texas."

I kiss her deeply. I am a happy guy. I don't want to stop holding her.

Unfortunately, Gina and I have planes to catch, so we head for the airport and turn in Gina's car. After a long kiss goodbye, she boards her plane to the Bay Area. I head off to find our charter plane.

I settle into a seat near the other starting pitchers on the team and close my eyes as the plane taxies to the runway. Once we're airborne we talk about finishing the season with ninety-five wins and sixty-seven losses and going to the playoffs. I finished the season with eighteen wins and eight losses, with an ERA of 2.99. Who would have expected that in April when my ERA was above 6.00?

After a while, I close my eyes and relive the last two days with Gina in Seattle and how much I loved having her with me. It was a wonderful surprise, something I will remember for a very long time.

Chapter Forty

This morning I don't want to get out of bed. I just want to stay here holding Gina forever, but the alarm shatters my calm. She has to go to work, so I cook her breakfast while she showers. When she's ready to leave, I kiss her longingly at the door just like a married guy.

It's 7:30 in the morning, so I transfer a load of laundry from the washer to the dryer and load the washer again. It's nice to relax and do nothing for a while after the hectic pace of the regular season. I go through the mail that accumulated during our last road trip and pitch most of it.

While waiting for the dryer to beep, my heart races as I think about heading off tomorrow for the first two games of the American League Division Series in Minnesota. I'm excited but I'm also anxious. The Twins were really tough on us this season. This is not going to be a walk in the park, more like climbing Mt. Everest. I hope we can carry over our success during the regular season into the playoffs.

The dryer interrupts my reverie, so I fold the warm underwear and put the next load in the dryer. I settle back onto the leather couch and start reading the current issue of *Sports Illustrated*. I must have dozed off because I jump when the dryer dings again.

I check my phone messages and find I have several from Bob Jacobs, my agent. Something must be happening. I pick up my cell phone and speed dial him.

"Hi, Bob, It's Larry. What's up?"

"Larry, I've been trying to get a hold of you since yesterday. Things are getting interesting, and from now on I need to be able to reach you day or night. Leave your cell phone on, please."

What's your problem, dude? A little testy today? Instead, I say, "Chill, Bob. You got me now."

"I'm starting to get off-the-record feelers from teams that will be looking for starting pitchers next year, and I need to bring you up to

213

speed. I need you to come into the office this morning, preferably ASAP?"

Jesus. I just got home late last night and we leave for the Division Series tomorrow. Don't I even get a day to myself?

"Bob, can't we do this on the phone?" I ask.

"No Larry, I need to talk to you in person."

I sigh audibly. "Okay, Bob. I can be there by eleven thirty."

Click. I guess I've been dismissed.

After folding the rest of my laundry and putting it away, I shower and dress. It's a beautiful day so I put the top down on my Lexus and head into San Francisco. After parking in the garage under the Transamerica Pyramid, I take the elevator upstairs to Bob's office, a mixture of anticipation and anxiety. Geez, I've won eighteen games this season. Why am I so uptight?

In his office, Bob is sitting behind his desk, phone propped on his shoulder. His bald spot glistens in the fluorescent lighting, and the remnants of a donut litter his desk. His face is flushed as he yells into the mouthpiece, "God dammit! How can I fucking represent you when you keep doing this fucking shit? If you expect any team to give you big money, you have to keep your extracurricular activities out of the fucking media." After a pause, he says, "Yeah, you said that the last time. This time, just fuckin' do it!" He slams the phone down and extends his hand to me. "Sorry."

I sit down in one of his black leather client chairs and try to muster a calm I don't feel. "So, Bob, tell me what's going on."

He tosses the rest of his donut into the trash and retrieves two file folders from a pile on his desk. He opens them both, placing them side by side in front of him. "Now, we can't talk specifics with teams, as you know. But my sources are telling me there's a possibility Seattle might go as high as $75 million over four years for a premier pitcher. They might even throw in a decent signing bonus, and they could offer a no-trade clause. The money's not as good as I had hoped, but a no-trade clause would give you control of your future."

A no-trade clause would give me control of my future? Duh. What does he think I am, stupid? I feel like telling the Chronicle beat writer that Bob has been talking to teams about specifics. That would get him in hot water, the prick!

Instead, reality pokes a hole in my mental rant. I can't do that. He's my agent now, and I just have to suck it up and take his shit.

Besides, spilling my guts to the media could put me on a blacklist with teams and the union.

I look at Bob, who has almost a sneer on his face. Shit-taking time. "I was kind of expecting more than seventy-five million over four years, based upon what you said before the season."

"Hold on now. I've also heard rumors about the Dodgers," he says, with a smile. "They might be willing to go as high as $90 million over four years, maybe more for five, with a larger signing bonus, but they probably aren't open to a no-trade clause."

I fall silent for a while, slouched in my chair, while Bob watches me intently. After a few moments, wishful thinking prompts me to ask, "Any discussions with my current team? I really don't want to be away from Gina for seven months each year." Maybe a miracle is possible and I can stay here.

Bob face turns impatient. "Larry, are you nuts? We've worked hard to get you a good contract for next year. Even if your GM would consider making you an offer, it would be for a fraction of what you're worth and a one-year deal at best. Your value in the market could plummet like a stone if you don't have a good year. It would be disastrous for your career."

My career? Or his?

"But I'd really like to stay in the Bay Area, and I'd be willing to take less money to do so."

"Look, Larry, wake up from whatever dream you're having and be sensible. You can't turn your back on your career now."

Yeah, I think. And you'd get a much smaller commission if I do.

"But can't you talk to our GM and at least float the idea?"

"Larry. Your personal life is your business. Let me take care of your professional life. Besides, the players union will pressure you big time to take the biggest contract you can get, in order to set the standard for other pitchers. You really don't want to experience their wrath, believe me."

I don't have an answer for that, so I steeple my hands and mull over everything he's told me.

When I don't respond, Bob says, "I'm sorry, Larry. You knew staying here wasn't in the cards before this season started. I spoke to your GM last month and he basically said 'No way,' that they'd love to keep you but they can't afford what you're worth. You need to give up on that idea. It ain't happening."

My small bubble of hope bursts quietly.

"Look, you're sitting pretty with these two feelers. Both Seattle and L.A. expect to lose key guys to free agency. Right now we'll use their interest to establish your market."

He closes the two files. "We may get offers from other teams once you're a free agent, but there's no guarantee they will be as good as these two possibilities. And the kind of money we talked about earlier this year just isn't there. The economy is headed into the tank, and attendance is way down everywhere. All free agents will take a hit this winter."

So much for a Bob's bidding war in the hundred-million dollar range. Oh well. I guess it's not his fault.

"And, Larry, no one else needs to know about any of this, especially the media. Got that?"

"Yes, Bob. I'm not a fucking two year-old." Man, I feel like throwing something at him. Good thing I don't have a baseball handy!

He looks at me with a pained expression. "Look, Larry. You finished well, which is terrific, but you've had a lot more losses than I had hoped."

There he goes, ragging on me about my losses again.

He gets up to refill his coffee mug and returns with one for me. "You look like you just lost your best friend."

"I guess I haven't told you I'm engaged to Gina." I take a sip of the coffee and savor the aroma rising from the hot liquid.

"Congratulations. That's wonderful." He smiles broadly. "When's the wedding?"

"We're getting married in December. I am afraid neither L.A. nor Seattle will be good news to her."

"Well, wait until after the wedding to tell her," he suggests.

What a shithead! If she found out that I've known about this since before the wedding and didn't tell her, she'd never trust me again. And she will find out.

I try to sound calm but I'm anything but. "Are you kidding me? I don't want to get married with an untruth between us. We've already dealt with some serious trust issues, so I won't lie to her. But this could jeopardize everything." My heart hammers the inside of my ribcage, and steam builds up in my ears. I'm starting to get really ticked at his attitude.

"So what are you going to do?" He asks, looking worried now.

"I have to tell her I'll be moving, and I guess I have to do it sooner rather than later. But I'm not looking forward to it."

"I can tell. You look like shit."

Well, fuck you too, I want to say. Instead, I swallow. "Look, I'll talk to her tonight, and I'll call you in a day or so."

I shake his hand and leave. Uneasiness accompanies me out the door.

Driving home, I mull over how to approach Gina with this news. Maybe a nice dinner in a restaurant is the safest place to begin the discussion. I torture myself by thinking of all the ways this conversation could really screw up my life.

The clock on my dash says it's one-thirty. Gina's at work, so I dial her cell, and get her voicemail. After some internal debate, I decide to leave her a upbeat message. "Hi, Hon, it's me. I would love to take you out for dinner tonight. You can pick the restaurant. There are a few things we need to discuss. Call me on my cell, and let me know where we are eating. I'll make a reservation." I take a deep breath and add, "I love you."

I hope she still loves me after I drop this bombshell.

Chapter Forty-One

When I get back to the Walnut Creek area, I decide to stop at my favorite golf course and hit a couple of buckets of balls. This should help to take my mind off the news from Bob for an hour or so and kill some time before I meet Gina for dinner.

I keep my golf clubs in the trunk of my car in the summertime for occasions like this when I need to pound the shit out of something. I've been doing that a lot this year, but today I can't seem to make good contact with the little white spheres. I spray them all over the range. Story of my life.

I'm right in the middle of one backswing, when my cell phone rings. I look at the screen and see that it's Gina. I punch the green button and say, "Hi there, gorgeous! How are you? Where do you want me to take you for dinner?"

"Larry, thanks for the invite, but I'm having a killer day. Can't we just have dinner at my place so I can get into my sweats and relax?"

There goes my idea of the safety of a public place. "Okay, if that's what you want. What time?" I hope my plummeting emotions don't get transmitted in my tone of voice.

"How about seven? That will give me some time to decompress after I get home from work and figure out something for dinner." She hesitates a minute and asks, "What do you want to talk about? Should I be worried?"

I decide to dodge the issue. I put on my most diplomatic tone and say, "It's nothing we can't handle. I'll see you at seven at your place." I wish I were as confident as I sound. I feel like a jackass, manipulating her that way.

"Larry, my nurse just stuck her head in the door. I've got to go," she says hurriedly.

"I love you. I'll see you in a few hours." But by now, I'm speaking to dead air.

I toy with the idea of going to a jewelry store to buy Gina something that sparkles and looks expensive. No, that's too obvious. Anyway, that's what guys do when they've just cheated on their wives.

So why do I feel like I have?

I decide that a big bouquet of flowers and a bottle of wine are much less incriminating. I stop at a flower shop on Main Street in Walnut Creek, and choose a couple of dozen calla lilies, yellow ones since that's Gina's favorite color.

While the florist is assembling them into an arrangement, I walk down the street to Coffee and Things, trying to look inconspicuous behind my sunglasses. I get a couple of looks but ignore them. I'm not in the mood to sign autographs today.

Thankfully, the coffee bar isn't crowded. I order a double cappuccino and buy a sliced turkey breast and avocado sandwich. With food and drink in hand, I find a small unoccupied table in the back. Two women are typing away on their laptops at the neighboring table. They don't even look up when I sit down.

A chill shivers through me, and I cup my hands around the scalding coffee. How to tell Gina about the potential offers? Either one means we will be apart for over seven months each year if she stays in Walnut Creek.

Are there any Kaiser facilities in L.A. or Seattle? Could Gina transfer to one of them? Would she even consider changing jobs? I should have talked to her about this a long time ago. I've really screwed this up big time.

I've only eaten about half of my sandwich, but I'm no longer hungry. My stomach is too unsettled to eat the rest. I grab my coffee, leaving the rest of my sandwich on the table, and bolt out of the store, my mind alive with chatter. I need to start taking care of myself and stop doing dumb-ass things like putting my head in the sand. I can't keep pretending I don't have to think beyond today. Hell, do I have such little faith in Gina or her love for me that I can't tackle a difficult subject with her?

I mean, Gina isn't some bimbo. She's a doctor, and she loves me. We're adults. We can work this out. I start to feel a little better. Maybe this will all turn out okay after all.

I finish the rest of my coffee and toss the cup into a green trash container on the way back to the florist. I pay for the flowers and head back toward my car.

I pass a wine shop and pick up a very expensive bottle of Merlot. I retrieve my car and drive back to Danville to kill some more time before dinner. I feel like a kid on his first date! Nervous. Excited. Scared shitless.

Chapter Forty-Two

As I put my finger out to ring the doorbell, the door opens and Gina steps back to let me in. She is dressed in sweatpants and a tank top, and her hair is pulled back in a damp ponytail. She wears no makeup, and weariness is evident in her blue eyes.

She looks beautiful to me.

I hand her the flowers and the Merlot which she takes from me with a smile and walks to the kitchen with me trailing behind. She puts them down on the white tile countertop and turns into my arms.

After a long kiss, I squeeze her more tightly, breathing in the floral scent of her freshly-washed hair. I hold on for a long time, not wanting to break the mood.

She goes along with it for a while but finally wriggles out of my embrace. Her hands find mine, and she asks, "Would you like a drink or shall we open that wonderful-looking bottle of wine?"

"Your choice. If you want to save the wine for dinner, a beer is fine."

I watch her pop the cap off a bottle of Gordon Biersch Hefeweizen and expertly pour the amber liquid slowly into a crystal beer glass she holds on a slant. I long to take her in my arms but will myself to put my news on the table before I chicken out.

She fills a wine glass with Chardonnay from the fridge, hands me the glass of beer, and heads into the living room. "Have a seat and you can tell me what you want to talk to me about," she says, flopping down on the couch.

I sit down near her on the couch, and my heart beats double time to her grandfather clock. I take a huge gulp of my beer, enjoying the familiar taste of the liquid, and then set my glass down on the coffee table slowly, trying to put off the inevitable for a few extra seconds.

She's had a long day, which means she's probably not in the mood for small talk, so I take a deep breath and get right to the point. "I have some news."

"Oh, yeah?"

"I'm not sure you'll be real happy about it, though."

"Well, tell me anyway."

"Okay," I say, dreading what will come next. "Bob Jacobs has feelers from two teams for long-term contracts for me for next season. I didn't want to give him any direction without talking to you first." I look to the ceiling and pray the last sentence gets me some points.

"Oh…" The smile withers on her face as the implications of my words begin to sink in. I can sense her withdrawing. "Which teams?"

"The Seattle Mariners and the LA Dodgers."

"Oh." She slumps back onto the couch.

I look expectantly at her, hoping for a glimmer of a smile, but her face is unreadable.

She sits there looking at the wine glass clasped between her hands. Finally, she looks up at me, sorrow in her eyes. "I guess I have known this day might come, but I didn't want to think about it."

She's been avoiding it too. Guess I'm not the only one. My heart slows down a bit.

As she draws a strand of blond hair back behind her left ear, her hand is shaking. "Do you have a preference?" She asks, but the light has gone out of her eyes.

"Not necessarily. And the thing is, this whole situation could change after the season is over. Teams aren't even supposed to be talking to us officially yet."

The ticking of her grandfather's clock ratchets up my anxiety level.

"I want to talk about how this will affect us," I say, even though I really don't.

Still looking at her wine glass, she says, "I don't know the answer to that." She takes a sip of her Chardonnay, looks up at me, and then down again. "You know I love my job and my patients, and I've lived in Walnut Creek all my life except for while I was in college and medical school. I really don't want to move." She looks so small, her shoulders hunched over, sitting next to me.

"I know you don't want to move. That's what makes this so difficult. The problem is that if we don't live where my home team plays, we won't see very much of each other for seven months of the year. And that would be really awful. I've seen guys try it, and a lot of them... well, it doesn't often work."

"So what are you saying?" Anxiety tinges her voice now.

I forge ahead. "Well, assuming nothing changes, I'm kinda leaning toward the Dodgers. So I'd have to move to L.A., at least for the baseball season."

She looks away and is silent for a long time. Finally, she says, "I guess I'm beginning to realize what life will be like married to a ballplayer."

"Yeah. Unfortunately, uncertainty is the name of the game. Players and their wives have to deal with it all the time. Injuries. Trades. Free Agency. None of it leads to stability." I put an arm around her. "I'm really sorry."

"I know, but I hadn't really understood all that until now." She now looks even smaller somehow, her head bowed, like she's sinking into the couch.

"But we have to talk about it and figure out how we can make our relationship work, given the uncertainties and the very real possibility that I will be playing in L.A."

She takes a deep breath and stands up. She hugs her arms across her chest, looking anything but happy. Finally she says, "I agree we need to talk about this, but it's a lot to get my head around all at once."

I want to get up to put both my arms around her and tell her it will all be okay, but her body language tells me this might not be a good idea.

I draw in a long breath, and decide to keep going, "Does Kaiser have any facilities in the L.A. area?" I ask. "If so, could you possibly transfer there?"

She takes an eternity to answer, emotions marching one after the other across her beautiful face. "Yes, Kaiser does have facilities in Southern California," she says and comes over and sits at the other end of the couch.

She looks out the window for a while, before saying, "I don't know, Larry. Moving to LA is an awful lot to ask..." Her voice trails off, leaving the room in a silence befitting our clubhouse after a tough loss. The ticking clock begins to sound like a time bomb. She leans away from me a little, and I notice that her hands are still shaking.

223

Eventually she breaks the silence. "I don't want a five-month-a-year marriage either. I may be independent, but I don't want to be married and live alone for most of the year."

That feels like another punch to my already-agitated stomach, but I choose selfish optimism.

"Are you saying you might consider changing jobs?" I ask. "Or are you saying you want to call off the wedding?" I fold my hands to keep them from shaking like hers, and swallow hard.

We sit in silence for a long time without looking at each other, the only sound being the ticking of that damned grandfather clock.

Finally, she raises her head. "I don't know. I just don't know. This is such a big change. I need some time to think. I don't want to say something I might regret."

"Me neither." I want to make her feel better, but I can't think of anything else to say.

She looks up at me, her blue eyes glistening with tears. "Look. I don't mean to be unkind, but I suddenly have no appetite, and I need time to think about this without you here. Can I have a rain check on cooking you dinner?" Tears are ready to spill from her eyes.

I don't think I could stand it if she started to cry, so I say, "Of course you don't have to cook me dinner. I know this is a lot to dump on you. You need time. I get that."

"Thanks for being so understanding." She's still looking down at her hands.

I turn toward her and say, "I love you so much. And I hate that I have upset you. But we'll have to deal with this soon. My agent is being a real prick and wants me to give him some direction. That's why I needed to bring it up tonight."

"I know…" Her voice trails off, and we sit at our respective ends of the couch, lost in our own thoughts.

Slowly she pushes her shoulders back and turns to me. Her face has lost some of its sadness and concern. She takes one of my hands in hers and says, "You know, we really don't have to decide this right now? You said yourself that you won't know anything definite until after the World Series is over. So let's put this topic on hold until we know what the choices actually are? Besides, you need to concentrate on the playoffs."

She's right, of course. We don't have to come to any decisions right now. But at least the subject of my moving is out on the table. And now I can focus on the Division Series with Minnesota.

"You're right. We don't have to decide now," I say with relief. And then, maybe a little too loudly, "Fuck Bob Jacobs!"

"No thanks!" she says, and a smile is back on her face. I squeeze her hand and smile back at her.

"So the wedding is still on?" I ask, my heart pounding.

"Of course it is, silly. You didn't think I'd call off the wedding just because there's a possibility that you might be moving to L.A. or Seattle next year, did you?"

"But you looked so sad and withdrawn when I told you what Bob said. I guess I thought the worst might happen."

She takes my hand and strokes it. "Nope. I'm still here, and so are you. Let's try to enjoy each day as it comes, until we know what the choices are. Okay?"

I pull her into my arms, and say into her neck, "I'm so sorry I got us both so upset."

"No, Larry. Don't be sorry. We need to be able to talk about things like this."

"But Gina, I've never done this before, talk about tough issues. I've always run like hell from them. I was so worried that you'd want to call off the wedding. I was so afraid it would mean the end of us."

She takes my hands in hers and smiles. "Hon, we're adults. Have confidence in our love and in yourself. We can talk anything out and trust that it won't result in the worst case scenario."

"I love you so very much," I say, "and I want this to work out in a way that is good for both of us."

"I know. Me too," she says, and kisses me.

"God, you're wonderful. I don't deserve you."

She puts her arms around me, and says, "Yes, you do. We both deserve to be happy."

She gets up, yawns, and steps toward the door. She turns and says, "Now I'm going to kick you out. I'm completely drained from my long day, and I need think about all this and get some sleep. I'll talk to you tomorrow. Okay?"

With that she ushers me out the door with a quick kiss and a pat on my butt. The door closes behind me with its familiar click.

Chapter Forty-Three

On the way home, I glance at the clock on the dash. 7:00 pm. I hope it's not a bad time to call Rick's house. He answers on the second ring. After some small talk, I ask if I can come over. He says they're in the middle of the kids' baths and getting ready for bed, and he asks if I can come at 8:00. "Sure," I say.

"You okay? You sound down."

I guess I can't hide anything from Rick. "I've got some things on my mind. But I'll survive. See you in an hour, man."

Rick's speech is so much better. The therapy is still working. Hallelujah!

I drive to Rick's house after killing some time at home watching TV. When Rick opens the door, I see he's standing up, leaning on a cane. "Look at you!" I say. "You're up and walking around." I put my arms out to him and he hugs me, the cane dangling down my back, hitting me in the butt. For a few moments, I forget about my conversation with Gina.

But the thoughts come flooding back, and when he backs off from our hug, he sees my face. "You need a drink. Beer or something stronger?" He tilts his head, giving me the once-over.

"Beer is fine," I say.

He canes his way into the kitchen and pours me a cold one. "Hey, you got to come carry this," he says. "I'd probably spill it."

I take the beer from him and head to the black leather couch in the family room. Rick lets himself down carefully into one of the side chairs.

Cindy appears and gives me a hug. "Ricky and Larra are doing their homework, and Bobby is tucked in and probably already asleep."

They named Larra after me. I was honored when they told me they wanted to do that. She's grown into a lovely nine year-old who takes after her beautiful mother. Sometimes I think she runs the household. Ricky Junior is ten, and quite a little leaguer. He wants

226

to be a pitcher like his dad. He's a good kid and my godson. Bobby is six and came along as a surprise baby. He's spoiled rotten by everyone, especially Rick.

Cindy taps me on the shoulder while I am musing to myself, "What do you think of our guy walking around? Yesterday, he got clearance from the physical therapist to walk unassisted. He wants to lose that cane so badly that he won't rest."

She sees my face and her smile fades. "Are you all right?"

Do I look that bad? "Why don't you pour yourself a drink," I say, "and I'll explain everything."

When Cindy emerges from the kitchen, glass of wine in hand, she sits down next to me on the couch. Rick breaks the ice. "So what's with your weird voice and mopey face?"

"I should be elated because Bob Jacobs told me the Dodgers and Mariners may make me good offers when I become a free agent." I fill them in on the details of my meeting.

"That's terrific, buddy, but why..." Rick's lopsided smile morphs to concern. "Oooh, I get it. You're worried how Gina will take it."

"I was coming home from her house when I called you earlier."

"So what did she say?" Cindy asks.

"She isn't keen on the idea of moving or having a long distance relationship either."

"Oh," Rick and Cindy say in unison.

Turning to Rick, I say, "For all the reasons you can imagine, I really don't want the long distance gig either. At least, Rick, you live where your team is. You're only gone a couple of weeks at a time during the baseball season."

"She could come to where you are most weekends when your new team is at home," Cindy says. "That's what Rick and I did before we had kids. It's a lot of traveling for her, but you could see each other that way."

"Yeah, I suppose. But that's no way to start a marriage, and she's on call every few weekends, so her travel opportunities are limited."

Cindy takes a sip of her wine, and says, "That's a toughie."

No one says anything for a few moments.

Cindy smiles at me and says, "You and Gina will work this out. You guys are made for each other."

"I hope so, Cin," I say. "The way we left it was that we won't deal with it until we know exactly what the choices are, which means after the World Series is over. We're going to enjoy the time together we have now and try not worry about what will happen until then."

"Probably a good idea," Rick says. "You leave for the playoffs tomorrow. You need to concentrate on that without any distractions."

I swallow hard. It must be tough for him to encourage me to focus on baseball, when he can't play and may never play again. I decide to ask him about that. "Hey, Rick. What do the doctors say about your recovery?"

"Well, they're happy with my progress. My speech is almost back to normal, but I still don't have a lot of strength in my right hand. I'm facing the real possibility that I might not be able to pitch again." He shrugs.

"How do you feel about that, bro?" Never pitching again? My God, that would be awful. I can't even bear the thought of that happening to me.

He looks at me and smiles crookedly. "I guess I'm okay with that possibility—hell, it's really the probability. A miracle could happen and I get my arm strength back, but that seems unlikely, so I have to accept it and move on."

"What do you think you'll do?" I ask.

"To start, I'm going to become Mr. Mom. You know, like the movie? Actually, I would love that almost as much as playing ball. You know how much I love being with my kids."

"And I'm planning on going back to work in any event," Cindy says. "Bobby is in school all day this year, so I'm looking for an accounting job. I've got a few leads."

"That's great," I say. I look at Rick. "But couldn't you get a job as a coach, or something?"

"Right now I need to concentrate on my therapies to try to regain as much strength in my right side. When I have achieved as much as I possibly can, then I can think about somehow getting back into baseball, or doing something on the outside. But for now, my number one job is to get strong and be a good husband and a father to my kids."

"And it's now my job to support the family," Cindy says.

"Sounds like a good plan to me," I say.

228

After I drain my beer, I get up to leave. "Thanks, guys, for listening. You're the best. I love you both."

I give them both hugs and leave, waving to my two best friends in the world.

Chapter Forty-Four

I head to the ballpark this morning to work out and get in some in some light throwing to keep my arm in shape for the playoffs which start in Minnesota tomorrow night. I jog out to the outfield warning track which thankfully I have to myself. I run some wind sprints and try to meditate to the rhythmic pounding of my feet, breathing in the cool air.

I look around at this concrete mausoleum that has been my home for the last six years. Damn, I wish there was a way for me to play ball here for a few more years. I could take a lot less money and stay with the Renegades. Maybe I'll call Bob. Nah! Bob will give me all the reasons he gave me yesterday that staying here is a very bad idea.

Shit. I know he's right about one thing. The opportunity to make big bucks as a pitcher has been a dream my whole life. I can't turn my back on it now. I guess I have no choice. I have to accept a contract to play somewhere else or quit baseball and do... what? I don't know how to do anything else.

I am only twenty-eight. I'm near the top of my game. I can't walk away from what I have worked so hard to achieve. Gina has to understand that.

I head into the clubhouse to work out in the gym. I make myself concentrate on my body and what I need to do to stay in top shape for the playoffs. We're flying out later this afternoon, so I've got to go home soon to finish packing for the trip.

We are considered the underdogs in the American League Division Series against the Minnesota Twins. They have the home-field advantage because they had a better won-lost record than we did this season, so the best-of-five series starts with two games in the Metrodome in Minneapolis. My pitching schedule means that I am not pitching either of the games in the Metrodome, for which Bob will be grateful. Some of my worst disasters have occurred in that miserable ballpark. I'm just along for the ride to cheer the rest of the team on.

*   *   *

We arrive in Minnesota to a cold, crisp fall day with a frosty bite to the wind. We check into our hotel. After I unpack my toilet kit and hang up my clothes, I call Gina on my cell phone to let her know we arrived safely. For once she answers the phone.

"Hi, Hon, we made it okay and I'm relaxing in my hotel room." I take a deep breath and say, "I thought a lot about our situation on the plane. I feel really optimistic that we'll be able to work something out for next season."

"I know. Me too."

Neither of us speaks for a while. I listen to the noise on the line, not knowing what to say.

Finally, she says, "You just concentrate on encouraging your team to do well there. We'll make this work."

I smile, and relax a little. "Gina, I love you!"

"I love you too. That's what makes all this uncertainty bearable. I miss you."

Chapter Forty-Five

We have the day off today and we're completely astounded. We won the first two games in Minnesota, and we're two to zero in the Division Series over the Twins, a team that killed us during the regular season. And we did it at their stadium where we almost never win. I got home last night late and stayed at my house so I wouldn't wake Gina up in the middle of the night.

After I play a round of golf at The Bridges in San Ramon this afternoon, Gina calls to say she's on her way home from work, so I head over to her house. When she opens the door, I become alarmed. I'm expecting a big smile since I've been gone, but she has a flat expression on her face, and she looks exhausted. After I give her a big kiss, I ask, "What's wrong? Oh, no. One of your little ones?"

She nods. "We almost lost a little girl when you were in Minnesota. She took a turn for the worse again today, but the nurse on duty just called to tell me she's doing better. But she's not out of the woods yet."

She inhales deeply and lets it out with a whoosh. "The thing is, it brought home to me just how much I love what I am doing here, and how much I really don't want to leave." Tears are brimming in her eyes.

My good mood from our two wins fizzles like air from a freed balloon.

She looks into my eyes and must see the deflation. She looks away at her hands and takes a long time before saying, "I'm not sure that I can go with you in January when you move to L.A. or Seattle. I have a knack with these difficult cases, and I have the perfect job here now." She looks so sad, and I pull her to me, as if my warmth and my arms can cheer her up.

I pitch tomorrow so I need to deflect these negative emotions as soon as possible. "I know you love what you do, but we agreed that we didn't need to make any decisions until we know what the choices are. Has something changed?"

"No. It's just that it's hard not to think about what a wonderful job I have here, and how difficult it will be either to give it up or to live apart from you. It gets me down when situations like today arise."

"I know. I know," I say into her hair as I rock her in my arms. I can't think about next year now. I need to focus on my next start which is tomorrow night. "Hon, I have to turn in early. We can talk more tomorrow after the game," I say, and head off to bed. She joins me after a few minutes of turning out lights and checking windows and doors, and welcomes me home properly.

Before we fall asleep, she wishes me good luck and promises she will be at the game early, as long as her little patient doesn't take another turn for the worse.

Chapter Forty-Six

I arrive at the Coliseum around noon, and the clubhouse is already lively. The guys are so happy to be back in our own ballpark. Like the rest of the team, I try not to think about the possibility that we could win the series tonight.

We've been in this position before. We beat the Yankees twice in Yankee Stadium four years ago. All we had to do was win one of the three games here at home. But we failed. Same against the White Sox the next year. Some in the media say we are cursed because we haven't been able to get beyond the Division Series in recent times. I aim to break that curse tonight.

I'm facing the Twins' lefty Brad Shakley. He's had our number the past couple of years, so we know this game will be a tough battle. I have a good warm-up, and Bud reminds me to take it one pitch at a time. Never too early to tell myself, "Ninth inning. Seventh game." Let's go get these guys.

I take the mound before a packed Coliseum crowd, and I feel great. I'm loose and ready for the game to start. This place is not often filled, but when it is, my adrenaline pumps that much more. I find Gina and my parents behind our dugout and give them a nod. Mom and Dad flew in last night for the rest of the Division Series. I feel like I can do anything with them in the ballpark.

I look around at my fellow players and tip my head. They return the nod, indicating that they are ready to go too.

Let's roll!

In the top of the first inning, I give up a single to Ron Dunn who is quickly erased on a fielder's choice. Joe Thayer touches me for another single but I get the next batter to ground into a short-to-second-to-first double play, and the Twins come up empty.

Adrenaline zings through my body as I walk off the mound. On the top step of the dugout, I look up at Gina, who smiles and winks. I can't help but grin back at her.

We don't score in the bottom of the first. In the top of the second, after I get the first two outs, the umpire gift wraps a walk to a lowly Twins rookie. I don't let that bother me, and get the next batter to hit a ground ball right back to me. I throw a strike to Dan Jackson at first for the third out. Gina pumps her fist as I step into the dugout. With Mom, Dad, and Gina in the stands, I feel like I can pitch a shutout.

When we come up to bat in the bottom of the second, Javi Vasquez strokes a home run to right field. The guys leap up and watch it clear the fence with plenty to spare. Javi is mobbed when he finishes his trot around the bases and walks down the dugout steps.

Jay Jamison lifts a single to center, and Jaime Cruz doubles him in for a second run. Two to nothing. I feel a calm wash over me. I've got a job to do, and I can do it.

In the top of the third, I find my groove, and the ump begins seeing things my way, giving me the benefit of the doubt on a few close pitches. My luck holds and I have a one-two-three inning.

In the bottom of the third, Heath Barton hits a towering home run over the center field fence, scoring Seve Castro ahead of him, to bring our lead to four to nothing.

I sit quietly on the bench with my left arm in my warm-up jacket, as the other guys dish out high fives and butt pats. I've gotta stay focused.

In the top of the fourth inning Terry Fisher touches me for a solo home run. So much for the shutout, but we're still in good shape. Then, in the top of the seventh inning with two outs, Justin La Pierre gets ahold of a fastball out over the plate that he strokes to right for a single. Terry Fisher steps in and drives a double to center field moving La Pierre to third base. God, I hate pitching to Fisher. The guy owns me tonight.

I walk around the mound to regroup. Ninth inning. Seventh game.

Back on the mound I deliver a fastball that fails to break. Ron Dunn slaps it into right field for a single which scores La Pierre. Now it's four to two. Shit. I gotta get it together. Our lead is expiring rapidly.

I settle down, taking deep breaths after every pitch, and get the next batter to hit a line drive to Javi Vasquez, who looks La Pierre back to third base, and tosses the ball to me. Two outs. I take a spin behind the mound to catch my breath. Now I just need to get Nick Packo. Ninth Inning. Seventh game.

I step back up onto the rubber and see the one-finger sign from Jason. I deliver a fastball that just grazes the outside edge of the strike zone, and hits Jason's glove with a healthy pop. Strike one. Then Jason puts the same figure down but points to the other side of the plate. I throw another fastball in on the hitter and he fights it off foul. Strike two. Now for Uncle Charlie. I go through the same motion as the last two fastballs but uncork a curveball which dances high and then loses steam and drops over the plate for strike three. Ring him up.

When I walk off the field, Gina waves at me and mouths, "I love you." I smile back at her. Whatever happens, it will be okay.

When I sit down, Coop strolls over. "Larry, you've reached a hundred and ten pitches and this game is too important to take any chances. I'm bringing Clarke in next inning."

I look up at him for a long while and finally decide not to argue, although I am disappointed. "Okay, Skip," I say.

I can still get the win if the bullpen holds it. You can do it, Darren, I say under my breath.

I go into the clubhouse so that Jake Martinelli, our head trainer, can tape ice packs on my shoulder and arm. As soon as he's done, I head back to the dugout. When I am seated in my accustomed spot, I look at the scoreboard, nervous as a cat. It's two out and nobody on in the top of the eighth. Good work, Darren. Now get this last guy.

Darren throws a perfect ninety-four-mile-an-hour fastball on the outside edge of the plate. Joe Thayer, the Twins catcher, watches it cross the plate for strike one. The next pitch is a nasty slider that Thayer swings awkwardly. Next Darren throws a fastball inside, which Thayer fights off. The end of his bat makes contact, and he pops the ball up to Jaime Cruz at second for the third out. A one-two-three inning. Good work, Darren. Three outs to go.

Things get even better in the bottom of the eighth when we load the bases. Nick Hayner works a walk, forcing in a run. Jaime Cruz drills a double to right field driving in two more, bringing the score to seven to two. That's a lot better. Some real breathing room.

Judd Johnson takes the mound in the bottom of the ninth to finish the game. Three more outs and we win the Division Series, and I get the win. This is what I have worked toward my whole life. My heart pounds thinking about what this means to our team.

We are all up on the steps of the dugout, willing Johnson to pitch the inning of his life. The crack of the ball hitting a bat and sailing into center field for a single has everyone on edge, but it's followed by a double play and relief. Then Jason Jones turns on a nasty slider for another single. Shit! This anxiety is agony.

Luis Robles steps in, and we are hanging on every pitch. Strike one, yes! Ball one, damn! Strike two: elation. Ball two, then ball three: nerves ajangle. Robles fouls off a few more pitches, tantalizing us even more.

Then Johnson delivers a fastball on the outside edge of the plate, and Robles hits it off the end of the bat, sending a high fly ball toward right field. The ball seems to float suspended in midair. We're all frozen like statues on the top step of the dugout. Our eyes follow the arc of the ball's flight, and we hold our breath. We see Heath Barton camped out under it. Finally, the ball begins its slow descent and finally comes to rest in Barton's waiting glove for the third out, ending the inning, the game, and the Division Series.

We explode from the dugout to join the guys on the field for our tribal huddle, jumping up and down and hugging each other's backs with Johnson in the middle. We're overjoyed with our sweep.

At the edge of the huddle, I jump up and down with these guys I've played with for the last few years. I love these guys, and we're going to the American League Championship Series!

I look around and see that the stands are still full. No one has left and the fans are cheering and high-fiving their neighbors for a full twenty minutes after the final out. Some of our guys run along the sidelines slapping hands with the fans on their way to the dugout. A group of guys circle the stadium to a standing ovation, but I just waive to the fans, spinning around like a top.

This is what we all live for. We won the Division Series convincingly. We're going to the Championship Series to try to win the American League pennant and the right to play in the World Series. Fucking awesome!

I walk over to the stands to where Gina and my parents are standing and clapping. Standing on tiptoes I give Mom and Dad awkward hugs. I lift Gina over the railing and give her a kiss. "Thanks for being here tonight. I sure needed your help."

237

"Oh, Hon, you didn't need me. You did it on your own," she says, smiling broadly.

"Yeah, but it was wonderful knowing you were in the stands and cheering for me."

Eventually the guys start leaving the field in twos and threes. The fans begin to pack up their gear. The love fest winds down, and I open the gate so Gina can go back into the stands as the last of the guys head for the tunnel under the stands.

Plastic sheeting covers the lockers when we enter the clubhouse. Open bottles of champagne are set out on tables. I grab one and we revert to being little boys, shaking the bottles and spraying each other, while we jump up and down in a very wet victory dance.

The merriment is being recorded by TV cameras decked out in the plastic raincoats that they wear when rain threatens. Everyone is wet and happy. Someone yells, "We broke the curse!" and we all pick it up and chant as we jump up and down.

After the cameras and the press leave, I shower and change into street clothes. I'm ravenous and grab something to eat from the tables heaped with food that the clubhouse manager Steve Fox and his crew have laid out for us. Darren joins me, and we talk about what we are going to do while we wait for the American League Championship Series to start next week.

Just then everyone looks towards the door as the families begin flooding into the clubhouse. Gina and Mom and Dad pick their way through the throng and give me hugs and congratulations. We stand there in a small circle with our arms around each other and smile a lot. This is the best moment of my career, and the three people who matter most to me are sharing it with me.

I squeeze Gina, and say to our small circle. "Pretty cool tonight, eh? We're going to the ALCS. No more curse!"

"This is awesome," she says. "You pitched great tonight."

"Thanks. I really felt in command. I knew we were gonna win it from the start."

"Congratulations, son," Dad says, looking very proud. "That was really fun to watch."

"Thanks, Dad. It was wonderful knowing you and Mom were here, giving me inspiration." I look around at the circle, and say, "Actually, there's one more person who should be here. Rick. I wish he were here to help us celebrate."

"Hey, you big lug." I hear from behind me.

I turn around and look into the big brown eyes of my best friend. I'm elated and speechless.

"Wouldn't have missed this for anything," he says, and moves slowly toward me, one hand on his cane and the other around Cindy.

My heart swells at the sight of him. "Man, am I glad to see you here!"

I let go of Gina and step aside to let Rick and Cindy into our circle. Rick steps in, a little unsteady on his feet, and gives me a hug. "We watched the whole thing from the press box. It was awesome! Man, you pitched great!"

I give Cindy a hug and the six of us try to talk over the din in the clubhouse.

When the festivities wind down, we head out through the gray-painted bowels of the Coliseum to the players parking lot. Gina took BART to the game, so I put one arm around her shoulder, and we walk slowly to my Lexus so that Rick and Cindy can keep up. When we get to my car, I give Mom and Dad a hug and hand them the keys to my car. They say that they'll see us tomorrow for lunch. Their treat.

Gina and I walk with Rick and Cindy to their car which is parked a couple of cars away from me. I look at Rick, still standing thanks to Cindy, and hug him once again, this time for a long time. "Man, I'm so happy you are doing so well."

"Yeah, me too," and he takes a step backward toward Cindy. She helps him into the passenger seat, and comes back around the car to where I'm standing.

There are tears in her eyes. She swipes at them with a trembling hand. "He insisted he had to come to this game. I tried to talk him out of it but he wouldn't take no. He wanted to see you pitch today." She smiles through her tears and gives me a hug.

"I'm so glad he's doing well enough that he could come," and hug her back.

"Don't get too happy. This took a lot out of him." She leans down to look through the window at Rick and laughs. "He's already asleep. You can come over tomorrow and rehash the game with him. He'd love that." She pats me on the chest and gets in her car.

As Gina and I drive to Walnut Creek, we are consumed by our thoughts. I don't know where I will be next season, and I won't know anything for two to four weeks, so I tell myself to chill out and train my attention on the wonderful woman by my side.

Also, I have to start focusing on the upcoming American League Championship Series which starts next week. We don't know who we will be playing yet because the other American League Division Series isn't over. It will either be Detroit or the Yankees.

Chapter Forty-Seven

Mom and Dad have decided to stay in the Bay Area for the first two games of the American League Championship Series, which we play here in Oakland. They're settled in at my house, and Mom has cleaned the whole thing, including washing the curtains, in addition to insisting that she do my laundry for me. I feel like a kid back home again. And I love staying at Gina's, so it's a win for all of us.

Even though Detroit had a better record than our team did during the season, we have the home field advantage in this series, because the Tigers got into the post season as the wild card team. Advantage us. They beat the Yankees in the other Division Series, so they're going to be tough, even though we had a winning record against the Tigers during the regular season.

Unfortunately, we lose the first game badly after blowing a three-to-nothing lead. So we're already in the hole one game to none. I'm on the mound tonight for game two.

Gina, Mom, and Dad are sitting in the first row behind our dugout with Gina sitting between them. My heart warms to see her there as part of my family. I give her a wink. She waves and wishes me good luck with her eyes.

I tear myself away from her smile and head to the bullpen to warm up. I chant, "Ninth inning. Seventh game," to the rhythm of my strides.

The fans are here earlier than during the regular season, and the noise in the stadium is much louder than the usual pre-game hum. I can feel the tension and expectancy in the air. I hope I can do my part to fulfill their hopes. This is a must-win game for us, or we'll be down by two games when we fly to Detroit for Game Three.

As I walk to the bullpen in left field, an older woman with short blond hair yells at me, "Knock 'em dead, Larry!"

I see her there a lot. She must have season tickets. I give her a smile, and she wishes me good luck. I suddenly have a flash of what she must have looked like at Gina's age. This woman must have been a knock out when she was young.

I chuckle to myself and continue on to the bullpen. I drop my mitt on the bench and jog onto the outfield grass to do some stretches and sprints before starting to throw. I feel good today, and my warm-up goes very well. Really well, in fact. I bet I'm throwing ninety-two or ninety-three miles per hour.

My heart is pounding like a machine gun. This is the most important game I've ever pitched. The whole world is watching. We're down in the series by a game, and we have to win this one.

I throw a few more fastballs that really pop when they hit Jason's glove. The pitches are effortless, and I feel like I did in the game when we clinched the pennant.

I have a nagging worry that I'm being a little too cocky, or I'm pushing too hard, or maybe I'm too amped up. I stop in the middle of my warm-up and take a walk around the bullpen mound. I take in few deep breaths and let them out with a rush to try to slow my heart rate and calm down a bit. It's hard during a post-season game to stay calm, and so much is riding on my performance in this one.

"Are you a little too wound up, Larry?" Bud Tanaka asks, while I take a couple of swallows from my water bottle.

"I don't think so," I lie. It's the postseason. Everyone is amped up.

"Well, I know you know this but pretend this is the regular season and just pitch your game."

"I know, Bud. Let me do my thing, okay?" I know my job. He doesn't need to remind me.

He looks at me but says nothing more, and after I throw a few more pitches, he raises his hat to let Coop know that I'm ready.

We walk to the dugout, where I stow my gear and take a few more drinks of water. My heart is still pounding, so I try to meditate until the game starts.

Finally, we take the field, and I finish my warm-up on the mound. When it's time, the umpire says, "Play ball."

When I step onto the rubber, I look around the stands. The place is sold out. A buzz goes through the crowd. "Okay," I say to myself. "Here we go."

Ninth Inning. Seventh game.

I retire the first eight hitters in a row, although the Tiger batters are very patient at the plate. They work the counts deep, and I have to throw a lot of pitches to get those eight guys out. I get the job done, but it isn't easy.

Then, with two outs in the top of the third, Brandon Orry, hitting ninth in the Tiger's batting order, steps up to the plate. I owned him during the regular season, but his four-for-twenty-three record against me apparently means he is due. He works the count to two and one, and on the next pitch he tags me for a solo shot into the left-field stands.

Crap!

I walk around the mound and grumble my mantra, trying to calm myself.

Curtis Hendersloot, the Tigers' lead-off hitter, steps in and, after waggling his bat like a guy on speed, strokes a double. Shit! My heart rate spikes, and I have a sinking feeling in my gut.

I try to regroup, but I walk the next two batters, loading the bases. Fuck! I walk off the back of the mound, grab the rosin bag, and throw it sharply into the dirt. It releases a little puff of powder as it hits the ground. I scream inside my head to "get it together, NOW!" My heart is racing and I'm sweating bullets.

Ninth inning. Seventh fucking game!

Back up on the rubber, I throw a couple of pitches for strikes, but Emilio Consuelos, the Tigers' most dangerous hitter, strokes my next pitch towards Javi Vasquez at third, who dives and knocks it down. He jumps up and guns it to home plate, but Jason's tag is late, allowing Hendersloot to score and the other batters to move up a base. Now it's two to nothing Detroit. Fucking awful. I walk around the mound again, trying to reclaim some of my pre-game confidence.

When I step back onto the rubber, I glare at the next batter, Carlos Sanchez, the Tiger's second baseman. He gets me off the hook by grounding the ball back to me, which I throw to first to end the inning.

Walking off the field I'm furious with myself, but I try to push that thought away as I plunk down on the green bench. This can't be happening, but it is. I stab my left arm into the sleeve of my warm-up jacket and try to slow down my hammering heart while I watch our guys come up to bat.

In the bottom of the inning with one out, Jason Gardelli works a walk, and Seve Castro singles Jason to second. Some of the guys stand up and move to the steps of the dugout. Maybe we can get back one or both of those runs I just gave up. But Heath Barton hits a ground ball to the shortstop, and the Tigers turn a double play to end the inning. Bummer.

In the top of the fourth, Tiger's catcher, Jorge Gonzales, likes my fourth pitch a lot and sends it into the stands. Shit! I can't buy an out. It's now three to nothing. This is a fucking disaster!

My heart hammers in my chest. I walk off the back of the mound in an effort to calm myself down and clear my head of any negative thoughts. After pitching the rosin bag into the back of the mound, I walk back up to the top. I kick at the rubber in disgust and growl into my glove, "Ninth inning. Seventh game. God dammit!"

I manage to get the next two batters out, but then I cough up a walk, a double and a single, allowing two more runs on aggressive base running. It's now five to nothing.

How is this possible? How did I let this get away from me? I beat these fuckers twice during the season, and I had a no-hitter going into the eighth inning in one of them. My world is tumbling down around me, and I can't seem to do anything about it. I shake my head in disgust.

Coop walks out of the dugout while I'm feeling sorry for myself. When he reaches the mound, he looks at me and says, "Larry, it's not your night tonight." He holds out his hand for the ball.

Embarrassment eats at my innards, but I put the ball into his outstretched hand, and say, without looking at him, "Sorry. I did the best I could tonight."

"Yeah. It happens to all of us. That's baseball." He pats me on the back and turns to watch Tommy Sanchez jog in from the bullpen.

Standing there while Sanchez jogs toward us, I chastise myself. We really needed a win tonight, and I let the team down. I stay rooted to the mound, still in shock over what I allowed to happen. And it happened so fast.

When Tommy steps onto the mound to relieve me, I have no choice but to turn and walk to the dugout. It feels like I'm going to the guillotine. I focus on the ground as I walk. When I get to the dugout, I don't make eye contact with any of the guys. I don't want to see the disappointment in their faces. Thankfully, they leave me alone.

I can't say as I blame Coop for taking me out. I'd have taken me out too. I stunk out there. Shit, I guess I left all my good stuff in the bullpen.

Sitting in the dugout I watch Tommy Sanchez get the final out but it's five to nothing, and they're all earned runs—and all mine! Disgusting performance. Absolutely fucking hideous.

I gather my stuff and flee into the clubhouse. With ice packs on my pitching arm, I think about watching the rest of the game on the big screen TV that I bought for the clubhouse couple of years ago. But even though I don't want to be around the guys after that pathetic showing, I have to. I let them down big time, and I have to own up to it.

We do squeak two runs across in the bottom of the eighth inning, but it's too little and way too late. We lose the game five to two, and we're behind two to nothing in the series. I get to add a post-season loss to my stats. Won't Bob Jacobs just love that?

I get dressed and suffer the media onslaught. Everyone wants to know what went wrong on the mound tonight, and what will happen to my free agency prospects after this awful performance. I say as little as I can get away with and take my lumps. After what seems like an hour, they desert me for some of the other guys.

When I emerge from the stadium, Gina and my parents are waiting for me. I hang my head in sadness as I hug each of them in turn.

Dad says, "You ran into a buzz saw tonight."

"No, Dad. I just didn't have it. I had to battle the whole time. I'm telling you, it was no fun." I shake my head.

"It's okay, Larry," Gina says. "It's not the end of the world." She smiles at me and puts her arm around me.

"I know that," I say, and go silent for a few moments. "But, I had such a great warm-up in the bullpen, and I thought I'd have a really good game. But I was awful." I feel like I let my family and Gina down, and the city of Oakland too. The world feels as dark as a bedroom with all the blinds closed and the lights off.

Mom gives me another hug and just holds on, like she used to do when I was a kid and something didn't go my way. This allows a crack of light to seep in.

Gina strokes my arm while Mom is holding me. When Mom lets me go, I ask Gina if I can drive her home. Mom and Dad can follow in my Lexus. Dad loves driving that car.

245

"How could I let the team down that way?" I ask Gina, as I turn the key in the ignition of her BMW. "I had such a good warm-up. I was on top of the world when I took the mound. Then everything just fell apart in the third inning." I shake my head and grip the wheel tightly as I drive.

"Hon, stop beating yourself up," Gina says, rubbing my arm for encouragement. "The Tigers did a really good job hitting tonight. And you threw reasonably well. It's not entirely your fault, you know."

"I know, but I still feel responsible."

"Whatever it is, it's not the end of the world. We have each other."

"Yeah, but for how long?"

"Now Larry. We agreed," she says. "We're not going to talk or even think about next season until the World Series is over."

"I know. I guess I'm just down, and all the negatives are chirping away in my head because of that. I'll be quiet now."

She lays her head on my shoulder and closes her eyes. We drive on in silence.

When we get to Gina's house, Mom and Dad give more hugs, before taking off for my house in their rental car. I'm so glad they came, but I'm sorry they had to see me suck. They're taking off early tomorrow to fly back to Texas.

My cell phone rings again as we walk into the house. I look at the display and see that it's Bob Jacobs. I can't face a tirade from him right now so I turn it off.

Gina pours me a beer, and I down about half of it quickly, hoping it will take the edge off. I'm too keyed up to sit, so I pace around her living room sipping my beer and succumbing to my negative thoughts.

Gina must read this as she sits down on the couch. "You know, in the broad spectrum of life, this is just a blip. After all, nobody died." She smiles up at me, and somehow that makes me feel a little bit better.

"I know," I say. "It's not a disaster, but it's been a helluva bad night. I let our team down. I put us in a two-game hole in our ballpark. I'm so angry at myself for doing that."

"Getting angry at yourself isn't going to change the result. So, come over here and sit with me."

I hesitate and decide I really don't want to take my frustration out on her. Breathing in deeply, I sit down next to her and she takes me in her arms.

She says into my chest, "Take a deep breath and start looking forward, not back."

We sit there entwined in each other's arms for a long time. Finally, I take her hand and we head back to her bedroom. I tell her I'm too upset to make love, and she understands. When she slides under the covers, she kisses me goodnight and falls asleep almost immediately. I guess she had a hard day too.

I stay awake for a long time rehashing today's debacle and my part in it.

Chapter Forty-Eight

We are all sitting in the dugout in stunned silence. Not that we'd be able to hear each other even if we wanted to speak. The sound raining down is like that of a jet engine. The Motor City is roaring for its first pennant in a quarter-century.

When we landed on the tarmac in Detroit on Saturday night we were hopeful. Teams have come from two games down in the ALCS before, and we really felt like this was our year.

But we didn't hit in game three, probably because of the frigid temperatures we had to play in, and the Tigers won it four to zero. Tonight, we showed some pretty good heart, going into the ninth with the game tied three to three. But we gave it up in the bottom of the inning. Our ALCS was over in four straight games.

Amid the Tigers' celebration, I look up and see Darren walking dejectedly off the mound, and I wait on the top step of the dugout to meet him. He was so damn good for us after he got called up. Without him, we wouldn't have been here. He's been nails after he stepped in for Rick.

But we all hang sliders occasionally, and Emilio Consuelos jumped all over the first pitch Daren threw in the bottom of the ninth, and did what cleanup hitters do, sent it over the fence for a walk-off home run. Just like that, the Tigers are headed for the World Series, and we're going home. We're all heartbroken.

Darren smiles at me briefly, and we grab our gear from the dugout. While the ear-splitting celebration continues out on the field, we make our way back to the visitors' clubhouse.

When Darren and I walk in, the feeling and noise level in the clubhouse stands out in stark contrast to the last game of the Division Series. There is no plastic hanging over our lockers this time, no music is playing. There are the usual reporters hovering around like vultures, looking for interviews. Everyone feels deflated.

When the media guys see me, they all swarm around me like bees. Everyone wants to know about my prospects for free agency. I tell them to talk to my agent, Bob Jacobs. I'm sure he'll love that. Bob will probably hang up on them, the prick.

When they realize that they won't get anything newsworthy from me, they go off to talk to Darren. Poor guy. He'll have to get used to dealing with the media after a painful loss. Might as well start now.

We continue dressing in silence, punctuated only by the occasional comment about what went wrong. It feels like we've all been punched in the gut.

Coop comes out of his office while we're dressing, and asks for quiet. He doesn't really need to, because no one is talking much. All we hear are the sounds of people dressing or packing their bags for the trip home.

When he has our attention, Coop says, "Well, guys, we can dissect what happened forever, and it won't change the result." He stops for a minute and looks around the room at the sea of guys in various states of undress.

Then he smiles and says, "Remember, we weren't expected to make the playoffs at all when we began this year. You guys stepped up and produced a winning season with a bunch of young players and a few veterans. You guys not only won the Western Division you made it to the ALCS. You all should be very proud of yourselves for that."

Yeah, I think. Some of us didn't step up when we needed to. Anger burns through me again.

Coop looks around, making eye contact with each of us. "You guys are a great team. This just wasn't your time to win it all. That time will come, so don't beat up on yourselves. It won't help you, and it won't help the team. We have to put this behind us and get on with our lives." He stands up and smiles at us all. "I expect to see most of you at spring training, fit and ready to play."

With that, he turns and goes back to his office to get ready for the flight home to Oakland.

Yeah, I think. Most of these guys will be here next year... but not me.

*   *   *

The mood is somber on the charter flight back to the Bay Area. No one wants to talk about what just happened. We did so well in the Division Series against the Twins who had given us a lot of trouble during the regular season. We had a much better record against Detroit, but they flat-out humiliated us in the ALCS. Our mediocre pitching and non-existent hitting allowed them to beat us in straight games. In short, they wanted it more than we did. We choked, and our baseball season has come to an abrupt and unfortunate end.

I think about the fact that this is the last flight I will be taking with these guys. I turn to the window so no one will see my brimming eyes. My whole life is going to turn upside down, and I have very little control over what will happen. I will miss these guys so much, especially Rick. He's shared my journey for almost a decade. It feels like I will be losing a part of myself next year.

The tears overflow, and I wipe my eyes with a napkin from under my empty beer glass.

Am I doing the right thing? Should I try to stay in Oakland?

No. I've been down that road before with Bob. It's a no-win situation.

Why does this hurt so badly? And when did I get so emotional?

A voice inside my head says, "That's easy. When you opened up your heart to Gina."

But the thought of leaving this team, of playing somewhere else, maybe in the other league, hurts so much. I wish I could go back to spring training and do it all over again. But I don't want to go back to the macho self-absorbed Larry that started this season. I really don't like that guy. And that would mean I'd lose Gina. That would be so much worse.

Somewhere over Iowa, I doze off. I am jolted awake when the plane touches down in Oakland.

250

Chapter Forty-Nine

We arrive home at four thirty in the morning. Though I'm exhausted, I manage to drive home to my house without incident. I drop my bags, strip down to my underwear, and fall into bed. My exhaustion overcomes any thoughts of what happened in Detroit, and I sleep until after noon when my doorbell rings.

I put on a pair of pants that I find on the chair in my bedroom and shuffle to the door in my slippers which were miraculously next to my bed. I look through the side light window and see Gina standing there. She has a strained smile on her face.

I open the door and spread my arms. She puts down the paper bag she is carrying and walks toward me. I pull her to me and kiss her deeply. I leave my arms around her and say, "I'm not a happy camper. I hope you have some good news to cheer me up."

A pained look flashes across her face, but she wipes it off almost instantly. "We'll talk about that in a minute. First, do you have any coffee in the house? I could make us some."

"I think so. That sounds good to me. I just woke up."

She looks at my beard and uncombed hair, and smiles. "I think I figured that out." She turns and follows me into the kitchen.

I find the coffee and plug in the coffee maker. I find a filter in the cabinet above and put it in the brew basket. She rinses out the glass coffee pot, and fills it. She pours the water into the reservoir and closes the cover. Then she spoons coffee into the filter and swings the filter basket closed.

She wipes her hands and says, "There. We did it. What a team!" She puts one arm around me and we stand in the middle of the kitchen, arm in arm, as the coffee maker starts making spitting sounds, followed by gurgling noises. Soon the rich aroma of coffee fills the air, and my stomach begins to alert me to my hunger.

As if on cue, she walks back to the front hall and retrieves the bag she brought. From it she pulls eggs, bacon, and a cake box.

When she opens it, I see a coffee cake with at least an inch of crumbles on top. "Oh, baby. You're a life saver!"

I reach for her but she dances away, saying, "None of that. I need to make us breakfast." She chuckles, "Though it's really lunch for me."

She fries the bacon and cooks the eggs in some of the bacon grease. She sets the coffee cake on the only platter I own, and we sit down at my dining room table across from each other.

Losing hasn't hurt my appetite, and when I've devoured most of the delicious food on my plate, I look at her and ask, "So what news do you have to tell me?"

There's something in her eyes I've not seen before. I try to gauge her mood. Her body is tensed, and she looks guarded, almost afraid.

"I guess the best way is just to say it." She takes a deep breath and lets it out slowly. "This morning I got a call from my boss asking me to come down to the hospital to meet with him. I had no idea what he wanted. All sorts of scenarios ran through my head in the car on the way down there, and I was nervous when I walked into his office. I'll spare you a blow-by-blow of our conversation." She takes a deep breath and looks me in the eye. "Larry, I have been offered the job of Assistant Chief of Pediatrics at the hospital."

My initial excitement for her quickly fades as the implications of what she just said sinks in. She can't move with me next season if she takes this job. A jolt of panic assaults my entire system. I certainly wasn't prepared for this news.

But I also realize it's a great coup for her. I decide to go with that thought first. "That's wonderful!" I say. "Congratulations, hon. That's a real achievement for you. I'm so happy for you." I take her hands in mine and squeeze them gently.

She draws her hands back, and says, "You know that means that if I take this job, I'm not going to be able to go with you next season."

Another jolt of anxiety hits me, but I don't change course. Instead, I say, "But it's what you've worked toward your entire life since medical school."

"That's right," she says and then looks into my eyes. "Just like you've worked your entire adult life toward a big contract at the end of this season, which will take you away from me. It's not a good situation for our relationship."

252

Oh, no! Is she going to break it off? I couldn't bear that.

After taking several deep breaths, I ask in a flat voice, "So what are you saying?"

"I'm saying that I think I want to—no, I need to—take this job." She won't look at me, and her shoulders slump.

"So, we'll have to live apart next season." I say, hoping to sound encouraging, but not feeling it. My mind starts to race out of control. I don't know if I can take this the day after our team got eliminated from the ALCS.

What if I can't stay faithful to her when I live in L.A. or Seattle, hundreds of miles away? That scares the shit out of me. And I'm not sure I have enough strength to avoid the constant temptation. It'll be like being on the road for the whole season. Suddenly, I feel sick.

She interrupts my thoughts. "Yes. We'll have to be apart for most of the year, which I don't like either. I will be able to come to you once or twice a month, and we'll see each other when your new team plays one of the teams here in the Bay Area. I don't like that scenario but we have to face it."

What do I say to her? I can't tell her that I'm afraid I'll screw some bimbo if she's not around, but that's precisely what worries me. So I approach it another way. "Are you confident that our relationship can withstand so much time apart?"

She thinks a long time before responding. "That's my biggest worry." She looks down and focuses on her hands. "To be frank, Larry, I think I can hold up my end of the bargain. I'll be busy starting a new job, and I'll have a lot more responsibility as Assistant Chief. And I've lived many years without a social life, during med school, internship, residency, and for quite a few years before I met you. I know how to do that."

She looks up at me. "My real concern is that you won't be able to avoid temptation, when I am far away."

That's Gina, a mind reader, in addition to all of her other skills. She certainly knows me well, often better than I know myself.

I think about what she said for a long time. Finally, I say, "I have to admit that I'm worried about the same thing."

She reaches over and takes my hand. "So how do we solve this dilemma?"

"I have no idea," I say. "It's truly an impossible situation. I can't see any way out. We'll have to live apart. But I hate even the thought of that."

"Yeah. Me too," she says, and looks down at our joined hands.

I take her other hand in mine and turn to her. "It doesn't change how I feel about you. I still love you so very much, and I'm so proud of you for your new job. I still want us to get married, even though we won't be able to be together much of the time."

She still won't look into my eyes. She says, looking down at our joined hands, "That's what makes this so hard. I love you with all my heart." She stops, as if frozen. "I think we should put the issue of the wedding into the same place that we put the issue of your contract, and deal with that when we know what's actually going to happen. Okay?"

"But we're still engaged right?"

She looks up and smiles. "Yes, we're still engaged. But picking a wedding date will depend upon a lot of things that we can't decide on until we know where you will be playing. But I won't cancel the reservation at Round Hill in December until we know what we are doing."

Her smile evaporates and she looks down again. She withdraws her hands and places them on the table in front of her. After a few moments she says, still looking at her hands, "You hurt me deeply once, Larry. That almost destroyed me. After that, I thought I'd never find love again."

"I know. I'm so sorry," I say, remembering the pain I caused her.

Finally, she looks me in the eye and says, "And if you do it again, Larry, it will break my heart for good. There'll be no going back from that."

I swallow down hard. "I know. It would destroy me too."

There it is. The ball is firmly in my court now. I know what I have to do to protect our relationship, and I want to do it. But can I?

A year ago, I'd be running out the door as fast as my feet could take me. I'd consider myself well out of the situation and looking forward to my next fuck. Another day, another conquest.

But that's not me anymore. I love Gina. I love who I am when I'm with her. I'm not that self-absorbed jerk who fucked when he felt like it and gave no thought to the person on the receiving end. I care for her, and I feel my feelings now. I don't run from them anymore.

Gina is everything I want. I have to honor that. But man, it's going to be hard.

I look into her beautiful blue eyes. She smiles, and my heart melts. With a smile to match, I say, "I will be true to my word. I want only you, and I will be faithful to you, even though we won't be living together. I give you my solemn promise."

I get up and pull her into my arms. My lips find hers and linger there for a long time.

When she pulls back, she looks into my eyes and says, "God help me, but I'm going to believe you. I couldn't bear not having you in my life, even if I can't have you full-time."

"We'll figure this all out," I say, looking into her blue eyes. "Besides, baseball is nothing if it's not fickle. I could get traded back to the Bay Area. I could get injured and go on the DL. And, to be realistic, I really only have eight to ten years of baseball ahead of me, at the most. You have at least three or four times that long to practice medicine. We'll find a way to make this work."

She turns her sunny smile on. "Let's see how this all plays out. You don't have a contract yet, and we have a few more weeks before you'll know where you're going. Let's just enjoy each other in the meantime, and deal with it all when we have something concrete." She hesitates and then says, "I'll tell my boss tomorrow that I'll take the job."

"That sounds like a good plan. Something might come up to change all this. I'm glad we'll be 'enjoying each other', at least for a little while. How about we start right now?"

I stand and pull her down the hall to the bedroom. She doesn't resist.

Chapter Fifty

The first day of free-agent eligibility is today. Bob Jacobs has filed the necessary papers with the Commissioner's Office, beginning the five-day exclusivity period during which only my current team has the right to negotiate with me. As Bob constantly reminds me, a deal with my team is not going to happen, so I have to suck it up and wait to see what presents itself.

As usual, I try to wait out the uncomfortable times with Rick. His recovery continues at a good pace. He's doing much more vigorous physical therapy and has regained some more strength on his right side. He no longer walks with the cane, though he still has a slight limp. He teases us all by substituting hilariously funny words for the ones we expect him to say, but his tendency to say the wrong word is essentially gone. It's just his wicked sense of humor talking when he does it now.

He has settled into his role as a stay-at-home dad, now that Cindy has a job with an accounting firm in Walnut Creek. I'm over at his house today killing time with him.

"I love taking care of my kids," he says. "It's great fun watching them grow up and blossom. I love getting them to their games, doing the laundry, helping them with their homework, etc. I want to be the kind of dad that my father never was to me."

"But don't you miss baseball?" I ask.

"Not as much as I thought I would. I miss the camaraderie in the clubhouse, but I don't miss the pressure to perform. I'd rather be here with the kids, helping and guiding them to be happy with their choices in life. I didn't get that, so I want to make sure that they do."

"Any thoughts about playing again?"

"To be honest, I'm not thinking about it. I'm happy with my life now. And so is Cindy. She gave up a lot when we had kids, and she had to quit work. She loves being back in the business world." He looks at me and flashes one of his lopsided devilish smiles. "And our sex life has gone to a whole new level! If I'd have known this would happen, I'd have encouraged her to go back to work a long time ago. She's a new woman."

"I like it. But you'd better not tell her you told me this. I don't want her to be embarrassed every time she sees me."

"Don't worry, bro. I don't even think she would mind that I told you. She adores you, you know. Especially since Seattle. She also likes that I'm not hanging around in bars with you anymore."

"Yeah. I'm getting boring, aren't I?"

"No, you're growing up—finally!" He flashes me a smile. "Now we just need to get you a couple of kids to really ground you."

"Let's get me married first, please?"

I suddenly remember what Gina told me last night, and I fill him in on Gina's new job. "So we're going to live apart next year. I don't like it, but it is what it is."

"Can you handle that?"

"I'll have to. If I don't, I'll lose her. I can't afford that. I love her too much to hurt her that way ever again." So why are my insides in an uproar?

I change the subject. "Enough about me. How about a game of Madden?"

"Okay. You know, my physical therapist said that playing video games is really good for my eye-hand coordination. So while I'm beating your ass, I'll be doing my PT homework."

We quit when we've won the same number of games, calling it a draw. It's about time for Gina to get home from the hospital, so I take my leave. Rick and I agree to continue our match tomorrow or the next day.

Chapter Fifty-One

To kill some time during my wait for Bob to get some firm offers, Gina and I are driving to Carmel for a couple of days. The weather down here is spectacularly clear and sunny, so we decide to stop in Monterey and hike along the headlands for a few miles.

The ocean is dotted with whitecaps, and seagulls wheel in the fresh breeze, screeching their raucous hellos. They touch down on dry land when the prospect of a meal presents itself. We feed them some leftovers from our lunch at the small French bistro we found in town.

After walking about a mile, we sit down on a bench to watch two sea otters floating in a bed of seaweed, with something resting on each of their stomachs. I pull out my binoculars to get a better view.

"Hmm," I say. "That's odd."

Gina, who is leaning back with her eyes closed, enjoying the warmth of the sun on her face, says, "What's odd, Hon?"

"I'm watching those two sea otters and each one has what looks like a flat rock on its stomach. I wonder what they're for."

She doesn't stir from her languid sunbath, but says, "Just keep watching. You'll see."

I follow the playful creatures through my binoculars for a few minutes. Pretty soon, one of them turns over and dives down into the waves and is gone for a long time. His friend seems unconcerned, so I decide I shouldn't be either. In a while, the first otter emerges, still clutching his stone in one arm, and something else in the other.

"Hey, he just came up with his stone and a dark blue shell, and he's rolled onto his back. It looks like he's catching his breath," I say, still looking through the binocs.

"Just wait. He'll put on his show in a few seconds," she says, still not looking away from the brilliant sun.

"Okay. He looks like he whacking the shell against the stone."

258

I watch as the otter cracks the shell, picks off the broken pieces, and sucks or chews some of the innards out, looking very pleased with himself. He cracks the rest of the shell open and cleans it out, tossing pieces of shell into the water as he chews. The mother of pearl inside the shells flashes brightly before the shells sink into the shadows of the seaweed.

"That is so cool," I say. "The otters are amazing. Oh look, the other one has just gone down to the bottom."

Gina sits up and holds her hand out for the binoculars. I pass them to her and she watches as the second otter repeats the same water ballet the first one did.

"I never tire of watching these guys do their thing," she says. "I think we should name them. The guy—he's the bigger one—I'll call 'Larry,'..."

"And the lady can be 'Gina,' I add, smiling as I interrupt her.

I lean over and kiss her.

I look into Gina's eyes for a long time. She just smiles at me. I'd give my eighty million-dollar left arm to know what she is thinking. She's smiling so it must be good.

"I love you so much," I say into her fragrant hair. "I'm reminded of that every time we are together."

Gina goes back to scanning the water with the binoculars. "Oh look! 'Larry' is going deep again," she says and hands the binocs back to me.

"No. Keep 'em for a while. I'm just content to sit here and watch you."

After "Larry" comes up again and eats his next treasure, Gina reaches out and takes my hand and pulls me closer to her. I put an arm around her and close my eyes to soak up the warmth from the sun and Gina.

My phone jars me out of my reverie. I look at the screen and see that it's Bob Jacobs, the very last person I want to talk to now. I turn the phone off and settle back against the bench, holding Gina.

She opens her eyes and asks, "Who was that?"

"Oh, nothing. My fucking agent is harassing me, as usual."

"Wow. There's a lot of anger in your voice. Want to tell me what's going on?

Do I really want to go into this now? Not really, but I don't want to keep secrets from her either. So I swallow and say,

"I am really fed up with him, Hon. All he's interested in is getting as much money for me as he can, but really it's about maximizing how much money he will get, and he has no consideration for what I want at all. I've asked him many times if there is a way for me to stay here in the Bay Area, and he always bats it away with a wave of his hand, as if what I want is of no importance. I feel like I'm no more than chunk of money to him, and I feel dirty and slimy after every interaction with him."

"I'm so sorry, Hon." She snuggles closer to me.

"And then you know what he said?" I ask, and squeeze her tighter as a fresh breeze lifts her hair. "When I told him I didn't want to be away from you for the season, he patted me on the shoulder, and said, 'You'll probably be in L.A. There are lots of gorgeous sexy women there. And like Las Vegas, what goes on in L.A., stays in L.A. Ya know what I mean?' He had a disgusting smirk on his face. I had to swallow hard to keep from vomiting. I was really furious, so I got up and left before I did something stupid that would get the cops involved."

"He is a jerk. And what he said was outrageous! I'm really sorry you have to deal with him." She's silent for a few moments, and then asks, "It sorta sounds like getting a huge contract is not as important to you as it was earlier this year. Is that true?"

How can she read me so precisely? I guess that's what being in love means.

"It doesn't seem so important anymore," I say. "Not since we've been back together."

I slowly scan the horizon, trying to regain the calm I felt a few minutes ago. I look down at her head resting on my shoulder and kiss the top of her head.

"I feel truly alive in only two places in this world. One is on the mound. But even more, I feel happy and alive when I'm with you. Like sitting here in this gorgeous place with my arms around you, naming otters, and doing nothing. This is so important to me, that I would consider taking a whole lot less money to stay in the Bay Area."

She sits up and looks at me. "Really? Is staying here a possibility?"

"Hell, I don't know. I can't seem to get Bob to get his head around that idea, so unless a miracle happens, I guess I'm stuck with moving somewhere else."

"Larry, let me tell you something. This isn't slavery. Bob doesn't own you. He can't make you go somewhere else." She sits up and turns to me. "Maybe you need to consider getting another agent. It's not too late. You haven't signed anything, right?"

"No, I haven't agreed to any deals or signed anything. But if I fire him at this late date, he'll probably sue me."

"So settle with him. Pay him something to make him go away. It may be expensive, but your happiness—our happiness—is more important than money."

I pull her back into my arms. "Does that mean you won't think less of me if I take a lot less money than I could get from say the Dodgers?"

She looks up at me. "Larry, how much money you make is not at all important to me. You should know that by now. I want you to be happy, first and foremost. If that means taking less money, then do it. It's not like we're going to be homeless. Besides, I would be able to have my husband with me most of the time. That's better than any amount of money to me."

"I don't know," I say. "I've worked so long and hard to get to this point in my career. I'd have to think very hard before turning my back on a big contract."

"Last I checked, any contract you sign will still be in the tens of millions," she says and smiles those sea-blue eyes on me.

"True." I smile sheepishly. We ballplayers lose site of the real value of money when big numbers are thrown around. Gina and I would still have plenty of money between us.

"Anyway, you don't have to decide right now. Let's just enjoy this place and hold each other. Just keep in mind that you're in control of your destiny, not Bob. Do what makes you happy. You need to decide what that is. And, Larry, we'll be fine either way."

"Thank you," I say, and hold her more tightly. "I guess you're right. It'll all work out. I am confident of that." But I guess I'm not because I ask, "We are still engaged, right?"

"Of course, silly. You worry too much." She snuggles back into my arms and closes her eyes.

We sit a long time, listening to the crash of the sea against rocks, feeling the spray in the air, and listening to the "keer" of the seagulls. Gina's warmth radiates from her body into mine, flowing straight to my heart.

I look around me at the late-afternoon sun glinting off the waves, the otters putting on their show, and the waves crashing against the cliffs. I marvel at how lucky I am to be here with her, and how close I came to losing her in January when I callously blew off her suggestion of a more permanent relationship. She was right to walk out on me. What was I thinking?

Jesus, I was a mess. I was so self-absorbed, shallow, and thoughtless back then. I physically shiver at the thought, even though the day is pleasantly warm in the Indian summer sun. Gina stirs at my shiver but settles back in my arms.

I close my eyes and relive the months after Gina left, which I spent searching for myself and making so many mistakes. An image of Rick's crooked smile floats into my brain. What would I have done without him to keep me out of trouble? And how can I ever thank Rick and Cindy for showing me a better way to relate to women?

The first half of this year was so painful, but I have to make myself embrace these thoughts and not flee from them. I think about Gail in Phoenix and my gin and tonic shower. And I cringe at my impotence with Crystal, how embarrassed I felt, and how scared I was that I might have something wrong with me.

Then there was Tiffany in Seattle. What a sweet girl, whose only fault was in thinking she was in love with me. I will never forget the look on her face when I told her I had a fiancée at home. It will make me think twice before I say anything that might be hurtful to Gina. I never want to see that look again.

I have changed so much since January. I didn't realize how much until today, sitting here holding Gina, and looking out at all this beauty. Instead of being antsy to get going, I feel calm and content, probably for the first time ever. Though I don't know where I'll be playing, I feel that it will all work out fine.

When a late afternoon breeze comes up, Gina and I retreat to our car and continue on south to Carmel for the night. Tomorrow I'll even go shopping with her, and enjoy it. Just being with her will be enough.

Chapter Fifty-Two

The glorious beauty that is San Francisco spreads out below me. The noonday sun is ablaze, rare for a December day. The Golden Gate Bridge, stately in its majesty, stands as a red silhouette against the blue of the sky and the bay. Small sailboats skip across the water bouncing off the whitecaps kicked up by the fresh breeze.

Beauty like this is to be savored, but no such luck for me right now. The brilliant scene is not enough to blot out my inner turmoil. Somehow I thought all of this would be resolved by now, but it seems I've been wrong all along, so why not again. I certainly didn't anticipate being summoned by my agent to the Top of the Marc, the bar with spectacular views of San Francisco on the top floor of the Marc Hopkins Hotel. Baseball's Winter Meetings are going on in the ballroom downstairs.

I look at my watch again and groan. Bob was supposed to meet me here two hours ago, but as usual the plan has changed. Something about trying to draw a fourth team into what he now says has become a "bidding war." It's funny. Back in January, the thought of such a thing was all I could live for. Now, all I want is my life back.

I want to snuggle up next to a fire with Gina, to feel the softness of her skin and caress the inside of her thighs. Not to deal with all this free agency bullshit. And that's all it really is.

This team? That team? Bonuses? Clauses? Setting the market for others? Players who aren't even born yet? And I can only imagine the pressure that comes my way once I sign my name on a big deal. Hell, the Dodgers' verbal offer that Bob went over with me on the phone a couple of days ago had my head spinning. I don't think I even want to know what the proposed offers look like from the Mariners, Diamondbacks, and Angels, and whoever else has joined that circus. I can only imagine what the fully written contracts would look like—probably a stack of paper three feet thick. Who wants to look through all that shit?

Fuck this! Baseball used to be a joy. Now, it's a real hassle. A fucking pain in the ass.

Gina's new job starts next month. She can't wait to get started. I've got to get my situation resolved, because she's got enough on her plate to worry about. But neither one of us is exactly itching to get the long-distance thing started.

"Excuse me."

I'm stirred from the inner darkness of my brain by a very attractive older woman in a sharp black suit with short blond hair and a smile I've seen somewhere before. I can't place it, though. I'm sure the three beers I've had while waiting for my dickhead agent to show up aren't helping.

"Hi, my name is Gail Landon. You're Larry Gordon, right?"

"Guilty!" I say smugly. "And unless you're taking drink orders right now, I'm not sure I'm the greatest company."

"Oh, well, I'm sorry to hear that. No, I actually recognize you from the ballpark, even without your hat."

I stare blankly.

"Well, we've talked a few times before games and so forth. I sit in the first row just beyond third base. I usually say something encouraging to you when you walk by me on the way to the bullpen to warm up. Now I just want to wish you good luck and say thanks for the years you've given to our team. You've brought my husband and me some very happy times."

"Why thank you. I appreciate that. I do." She does look familiar. I know. She's the one who must have looked like Gine twenty years ago. I look at her and smile. "I remember you. What are you doing here?"

"I've been over there having lunch, and I noticed sitting alone all this time looking at that very expensive watch every so often."

I look down at my watch for the fiftieth time today and smile. "Yeah, my fiancée gave it to me as an engagement present."

"Engaged? You should be radiating happiness. Why do you look sad? Could you use a friend?"

Without waiting for my answer, she puts her purse on the table and slides into my booth, pulling a leather briefcase in behind her.

She's got to be fifty years old. She can't be hitting on me.

"Listen," I say. "I'm in a foul mood, and you really won't like talking to me."

"Well, Larry, I'm a sympathetic listener. And I'm a lawyer. I represent athletes." She gives me an appraising look. "Let me guess. Your agent, Bob Jacobs, told you he'd be here a couple of hours ago, but he's downstairs trying to drum up interest to make the market go up. He told you this whole thing would be over by now, but in reality, you're beginning to realize that it's just getting started." She smiles. "How am I doing so far?"

A waitress arrives with another beer for me, and looks at Gail who orders a glass of chardonnay. I take a sip of my beer and think about how I should answer her.

I certainly wasn't expecting a woman to plop herself down in my booth, read my mind, and know everything about the process of free agency, let alone one who's old enough to be my mother. But what the hell. I'll play along.

Instead of answering, I search my mind for her name. Shit, I've had a lot to drink! Time to embarrass myself. "What'd you say your name was?" I ask.

"I'm Gail Landon." Suddenly I flash on the lawyer who doused me with her gin and tonic in the Roundup at spring training. This is most definitely a different Gail. The thought of Gail in the tight red dress makes me wince. I guess I should've been nicer to her.

The Gail across from me taps me on the hand. "And you, Larry Gordon, should remember me, not just from our conversations at the ballpark, but from that day at Bob Jacobs' office last year when he took you on as a client."

Suddenly, a light flickers on inside my head. Bob introduced me to the others in the office that day, and I remember an agent who was a nice looking older woman. She wasn't hot, so the old me paid no attention to her.

I come out of my reverie and say, "Oh, Gail. Yes, now, I do remember you. That's right. You were a new agent at Jacobs Sports Management then. Bob said you were a rising star, and that you were going to be a force in the profession. You still with JSM?"

"No way!"

"Really? What happened?" I play with the rim of my glass but refrain from taking another sip. This is beginning to sound interesting. The last thing I need to do is further cripple what little judgment I have left with more alcohol. At least talking to her passes the time waiting for dipshit Bob.

"Well, let's just say that you're not the only one with issues regarding Mr. Jacobs."

"Oh, really? Tell me about it." This is getting fascinating.

"Listen, Larry. What I'm going to tell you is off the record and could get me in a lot of trouble. So I'm gonna deny I ever said it. But the reason I left JSM is that Bob came on to me one evening in the office in March.

"No shit! That dirt bag! I didn't think he'd make a pass at someone he worked with. He's been married for a long time." Realization dawns in my brain. Shit! That explains a lot about his nasty comment about "what happens in LA stays in LA."

"Yeah, well he did." She looks around and raises a hand. "Where is that waitress? Geez, for what they charge here, you'd think they'd have better service."

"Let me go get your drink," I say and start to get up.

Gail puts her hand on my arm to stop me and says, "No, she saw me. She'll show up with my wine eventually. I'm not that desperate."

I sit back down, and my eyes encourage her to continue.

"So, back to Bob Jacobs. The man doesn't take no for an answer very easily, if you know what I mean. Anyway, after that 'incident,' I decided I needed to go my own way, so I resigned. He was pissed, but I didn't care. I started my own firm the next week. I've got two clients, both in the minors."

"Two clients? Can you survive on that?

"Good question. I don't know if we're gonna make it, but I couldn't keep selling my soul by working for a man with more hair on the top of his head than scruples in his psyche."

We both laugh. Bob would really be pissed at that. Nothing like trading here's-why-Bob-Jacobs-is-an-asshole stories to kill the time. I glance at my watch and notice that he's now three hours late. No calls or texts, either, according to my cell phone. What an arrogant prick!

"Well," I say, "I have my own issues with the man, too."

"You mean other than him leaving you here hanging for hours?"

I chuckle in agreement. "Yup. I guess the main one happened when I met with him a couple of weeks ago. I'm engaged to a wonderful woman. She's just been appointed Assistant Chief of Pediatrics at Kaiser in Walnut Creek, so I'm concerned about how my going to a new team is going to affect us. Jacobs had the balls to

266

tell me I didn't need to worry about being apart from her, saying that what happens when I'm away from her stays there and she'll never know. That's the absolute last thing I wanted to hear from him."

"So why are you still with him then, Larry."

I'm stymied. A simple question, really. Why am I still with that jerk? All he's done since this entire process started is insisted on a strategy that directly benefits him, with no consideration of me.

"I guess because I thought he was the best," I say.

"Well, he is one of the best agents in the business at getting players the most money they can possibly get. But the thing you need to ask yourself is whether money is really the most important thing. The money issue's always going to be there, but it's not what's going to create your happiness, and you can't lose sight of the things that will, like being with your fiancée. The reality is that the pressure that comes with signing your next deal will be very intense if you don't have reasons other than money to feel happy about it."

The cocktail waitress makes her way toward our table with Gail's glass of chardonnay.

"Listen, Larry," Gail continues. "What if I were to tell you that you could have it all? Maybe not all the money that Jacobs can get you but enough so that you'll never worry about money again, all the while maintaining your happiness. What would you say to that?"

I take a last sip of my beer. Before I can answer, Gail interjects again. "What would make you happy, Larry?"

My heart skips a beat at the same question Gina and I discussed overlooking the Pacific in Monterey.

Gail looks at me with warm brown eyes that remind me of Rick's. He would tell me that I ought to do what's best for my relationship with Gina.

"What would make me happy?" I take a deep breath and smile at her. Might as well answer truthfully. "What would really make me happy would be to stay with my team, get married to Gina, buy or build a nice house in the East Bay, and in a few years start having kids."

"And Bob has you convinced that it'll take every last million to get that?"

"Pretty much, at least until Gina talked some sense into me recently. She said that money doesn't mean anything unless I am happy."

"Smart lady. So I take it your current team can't afford to match any of the deals that Bob has been cultivating."

I laugh. "No. I'd be lucky to get them to pay half the amount the Dodgers have thrown around."

"I also assume that you would be willing to take considerably less than that, or a shorter term contract, to stay with your team, correct?"

My cell phone chirps to life. I have a text message from Bob. "Lots of teams interested in you. Can't meet with you today. Call you tomorrow."

I look at Gail. "Fucking Bob just blew me off. I don't believe him. He ordered me here five hours ago, saying it was urgent, and now he can't meet with me."

Gail chuckles. "Standard operating procedure for Jacobs."

"Yeah. I feel like I've been slimed again."

"Look. Let's move this discussion to my room. You never know who might see us and report to Bob. He still thinks he's representing you."

She gathers her things and we take the elevator down to her room on the fourth floor. Once inside her room, she smiles at me and puts her laptop on the desk. While it warms up, she gets out a calculator and a pad and pen, arranging her office away from home. She is in business mode, and my heart begins to thump in my chest at the possibility that something may come of this chance meeting.

When she has her workspace set up, she says, "So let's be creative here. What if we proposed a front-end loaded contract for, say, $15 million for the first year? That ought to set a pretty good market price and keep the player's union happy enough."

"Okay. Sounds good so far."

She punches some numbers into her calculator and then continues. "And if we say $10 million for the second year, and $8 million each for the third and fourth years, that would come to $41 million total for the four years. My guess that's probably close to half the Dodger money."

"Bingo!" Damn, she's good.

"We could add some performance bonuses, such as winning more than fifteen games, All-Star appearances, the Cy Young, etc. Do you think your team might go for that?"

"Yeah. I think they might. At least I hope so."

She starts typing notes of our conversation on her computer.

My heart sinks. I've never heard of a player offering to take so much less than they're worth before.

"Worried about the money?" She's reading my mind again.

"Not so much about taking less money. It's just that I've never heard of anyone taking such a cut in pay before."

"That doesn't mean it can't be done. Your team would be getting a huge bargain, and you'd get to live with your wife. It's a tradeoff, Larry. Is it worth it to you?"

"That's the real question, isn't it?"

Gina appears in my mind. She looks so beautiful and whispers she loves me. How can I ignore that? I recall our conversation by the ocean in Monterey. She wouldn't object at all. Suddenly, my brain clears, and it all sounds so right.

I look at Gail, and smile. "Yes, it is definitely worth it to me."

"Then we have our answer, don't we?"

But what will my dad say? What will Rick say? Doubts start my heart racing again.

"Larry, it's your choice. Your loved ones will support you no matter what you decide." How does she do that? She's a fucking mind reader.

"But what will I say when people and the media ask me why I took so much less money than I could have gotten on the free agency market?" My pulse kicks up a notch, and then backs off. "I guess I can say something like 'my family is much more important to me than the money.'" Sounds rational.

"Exactly."

"And I'm pretty sure the guys on the team would be happy to have me back."

The tension begins to drain out of my body, but my heart is still racing. It feels... so right, but this is all moving so fast.

"And Larry, don't forget that $41 million plus incentives isn't chump change."

I feel a shift, as calm washes away my inner storm. "Gail," I say. "Let's get this done."

"Okay, I guess we'd better get our act together immediately."
She picks up her cell phone and says, "I'll try to get through to your
General Manager right now. What's his name?"

"Dick Franklin." I sure hope he's willing to listen to reason.

Gail pulls out a list of suite numbers for each team, and dials the
number for our team's suite. When someone answers, she says, "I'd
like to speak to Mr. Franklin."

Chapter Fifty-Three

"Mr. Franklin, my name is Gail Landon. I'm with Larry Gordon here in the Marc Hopkins. We have a proposal that I think you'll want to hear. Can you give us five minutes of your time?"

She listens for a few seconds and says, "That's great. We're in room four twenty-nine. See you in ten minutes."

I jump when the door bell rings. Gail opens it, and Dick Franklin walks in. I introduce him to Gail.

Once we're seated, Dick asks, "So, Larry. What brings you here with Ms. Landon" He has a smile on his face, and I take this as a good sign.

Gail explains my predicament to Dick. He looks surprised and says, "Larry, can you please tell me why you are so desperate to stay here with this team?"

"Well, sir, my fiancé has just been offered the job of Assistant Chief of Pediatrics at Kaiser Hospital in Walnut Creek. It's what she's worked toward her entire adult life. I can't ask her to turn that down and go with me to L.A or somewhere else. And I don't want the kind of life we'd have if I went there and she stayed here. So I am asking you to consider the deal that Ms. Landon will outline for you, which would allow me to stay here with the only team I've ever played for. I really want to play here for the next four years, sir."

"And how much are other teams talking about? I know the Dodgers are interested in you? Just a ballpark figure. I don't want you to violate any confidentiality agreements."

Gail answers for me. "It's in the eighty to ninety million dollar range, four year deal, standard terms, might include a no-trade clause." I look at Dick and nod.

He shakes his head. "That's way out of our range," he says, looking at me. "But I suppose you know that, and that's why I'm here." He does a double take. "But you're represented by Bob Jacobs, aren't you?"

271

I look at Ms. Landon and smile. "Not anymore."

"Does Bob know that?"

"No, but if you like our proposal, I'll fire him immediately," I say, smiling.

Gail jumps in. "We can talk hypothetically. If we can't come to an agreement in principal, then Larry and Bob can pursue the Dodgers' or any other teams' deals."

"Okay…" His voice trails off while he's thinking. Finally, he says, "This is very unusual. I can't believe this."

"So, can we talk specifics?" I ask.

"Let's do just that," he says and looks at Gail. "Hypothetically, that is."

She outlines our proposal. I'm really impressed with her. She knows her stuff, and Dick is listening with rapt attention. Fucking Bob will explode if this works.

When she's done, I look at Dick and ask, "So what do you think?"

"Well, it's creative. I'll give you that. I'm a little worried about the $15 million for next year. I'm not sure I can spring that much cash."

Gail thinks for a moment, and then says, "What about a side agreement that defers some portion until the last year? But we'd probably have to tell the League and the Players Union about that."

"Yes, I'm afraid we would have to tell them."

I can see the wheels turning in his head. Finally, he asks, "What if you loaned some of the money back to the team, say $7 million, and we could make it due and payable at the end of your new contract?"

I look at Gail, and she says, "If it's okay with Larry, we could do that."

"Fine with me," I say, eagerly.

"Let's not get too excited yet," Dick says. "There's a lot still to be worked out. For instance, we could put some additional performance incentives into the last two years that could allow you to earn forgiveness of the loan. How does that sound?"

Gail jumps in. "I'll do some research on how to structure all this, but I think we can at least sign a letter of intent that's valid for a short period of time while we negotiate the exact language. Does that work for you, Mr. Franklin?"

"If it works for Larry, it works for me. I'm old fashioned. A handshake would be good enough for me, but I'm accountable to the ownership group, so we have to make it airtight. A letter of intent will suffice, as long as we can wrap this up with all the lawyers in the next week or so."

"It works for me," I say, a little too enthusiastically. Oh my god, I think. This could really work out.

He stands up and shakes Gail's hand and then looks at me. "Larry, I was really sorry that we were going to lose you. You were a big part of getting this team to the ALCS this year. I never thought there would be any way in hell that we could keep you. I really have to hand it to you and Ms. Landon for coming up with a win-win for both you and the team. Welcome back."

Ms. Landon says, "Shall I draft the letter of intent? It won't take me too long."

"By all means," Dick and I say in unison and laugh at each other.

Dick reaches in his pocket and hands his card to Gail. "I hope you'll excuse me, but I have other business as well. Email me the Letter of Intent. I'll look it over and get right back to you."

We all stand and shake hands. Dick gives me a man hug and hurries out the door.

I get up and start pacing, noticing the understated décor in muted beiges, while Gail types away on her computer. When she's done, she stands up and says, "It's on its way to Franklin. While we wait, can I call room service for something for you to eat or drink?"

"I'm too nervous to eat anything. I'm not sure how long it would stay down. But a beer would be great. Ask them if they have a Hefeweizen?"

"Happy to." She picks up the receiver and orders my beer and a glass of chardonnay for herself.

While we wait for room service, I go back to pacing. My feet take me to the large window in the sitting area. Looking on the City spread out below me on this clear December afternoon, I watch a ferry out on the bay headed to Marin County. People below on the sidewalks are doing their Christmas shopping, and Alcatraz is sitting on its rock in the middle of the bay, looking like a boarding school in the blazing sun rather than a prison. I hope with all my heart that I can stay in the Bay Area, at least for the next four years. I want to be here to share scenes like this with Gina.

273

I'm brought back into the room by a two-toned ping from Gail's computer. She motions me over to where she's sitting. With my fingers crossed behind my back, I look over her shoulder at the monitor. I follow along as she reads the words aloud. "All fine. Discussed it with the Managing Partner, and they're on board. Now fire Bob Jacobs!!!"

Chapter Fifty-Four

I get out my cell phone and speed dial Bob Jacobs' cell phone. This feels as good as my first day in the Majors. After a few seconds I hear, "Larry, I can't talk now. I'm in the middle of..."

I cut him off. "You damned well will talk to me. I'm calling to fire you."

Dead silence on the other end of the call.

I plow ahead. "I gotta be honest with you, Bob. This isn't working for me. You've never listened to what I want. All you have cared about is the almighty dollar, and not my dollars, just how much you'll get out of it. I've told you almost every time we've talked that I want to stay in the Bay Area. You always told me I was full of crap and forged ahead with your own agenda. And all you've been doing since the season is over is playing your little power trip games and jerking me around. Well, I've had enough. There is more to life than money, and you won't get me what I want, and that sucks. So you're fired!"

Loud laughter forces me to hold the phone away from my ear. When he calms down, he says, "You can't be serious, Larry? Fire me? That's ridiculous. Let's just talk this out."

"No, Bob. I've made up my mind. And you know as well as I do that our agency contract expired the moment I filed for free agency."

He doesn't speak for a few seconds and then asks, "What's wrong? Have you signed with some team that I don't know about? I'll sue you for everything you've got if you have."

"No. I haven't signed with anyone. I just can't work with you. You can sue me if you want but you have no grounds. I haven't seen any contracts or signed anything from you. You're no longer my agent."

"Good luck with that, you asshole. I'll sue your ass. You'll be done. You don't realize how much power I have, do you?

"Frankly, Bob. I just don't care. I'm done with you. I'll text and fax you my termination, and follow it up by snail mail. As of right now, you are no longer my agent."

"Yeah, well fu…"

I punch the off button so I don't have to listen to one more word from that asshole.

I look at Gail and ask, "So what's next?"

"I'll email Franklin that you've fired Bob." He'll sign the letter of intent, and I'll have to get the signed copy from him. Then you sign it, and I'll make a bunch of copies for both sides, and we'll be done for the time being."

When she returns with the signed letter of intent, I stare at Dick's signature, not quite believing that he actually signed it.

"You have to sign here," she says, pointing at a line at the end of the letter.

I do my best to sign even though my hands are shaking, and hand it back to her. She makes several copies on her portable printer and leaves the suite to deliver the signed copy to Franklin upstairs.

It hits me with full force. I'm staying in the Bay Area and with my team. It's a dream come true. If winning the World Series is greater than this, I'd be completely surprised. I can't wait to tell Gina!

I look at Gail and smile. "Well, I guess you're my agent now," I say, reaching out to shake her hand. "How can I ever thank you for what you've done for me and for Gina? And on such short notice!"

She smiles back. "You happened to catch me—or rather, I caught you—at a really great time. I'm happy I could help you out." She looks at me and winks. "I'll be sending you a fee agreement tomorrow. We'll talk about my bill when this dies down."

On the elevator ride down to the lobby, I think about Gina and how happy she will be. I want to do something to show her how I feel about her, so I ask the concierge where I can find a jewelry store. She directs me to a corridor in the hotel with boutiques along it, one of which is a very nice and obviously expensive jeweler.

I walk in and a sales person steps up to me. "Good afternoon, sir. May I help you?"

"I want to see engagement rings," I say. "Something three or four karats, emerald-cut."

Chapter Fifty-Five

Today is the five-month anniversary of Gina's and my first date after we started talking again, or so she informed me when I called to ask her to meet me at Fleming's at 7:00 pm. She said she was tired from a long day at the hospital, but I kind of insisted, and she agreed. Fleming's is the perfect place for me to tell Gina my big news. With the ring in its velvet box in my jacket pocket and a wrapped gift under my arm, I walk into the familiar restaurant and head for the maitre d'.

"We have your booth ready in the back room as you requested," he says and ushers me to our table. When I turn to thank him, he asks, "Special event tonight, eh?"

"Absolutely! And if you see my fiancée and me dancing, I'd appreciate complete privacy until I let you know." I hope he doesn't think I'm going to make love to her in the restaurant. Actually, I don't care what he thinks.

I feel my jacket pocket to make sure the ring is still safely there and slide into the booth to await my angel. I hide the gift on the floor next to my feet.

In about five minutes the curtain is drawn aside and in she walks. The waiter takes her coat and Gina turns to me, taking my breath away. She seems to have a golden glow surrounding her, and I'm suddenly speechless and on the verge of spilling tears of joy. I am also grinning from ear to ear, probably looking like a tool, but I don't care. My whole life has just walked through that curtain.

Sliding out of the booth, I pull Gina into a hug. "My god, you look beautiful tonight!" I say, inhaling her perfume-like scent. Her body molds itself to mine, and we stand there kissing and holding each other for a long time.

She pulls back and looks at me. "You look different tonight. I'm not sure what it is but you look... I don't know... peaceful."

She reads me so well. No wonder she is so good at diagnosing little kids. She is so intuitive and tuned in. I'm a lucky guy. And I do feel peaceful. She nailed it.

We sit down and our meal is superb as usual. After dessert is cleared away, I wink at the waiter and he disappears, closing the curtain behind him. I lean down and retrieve the gift from the floor beside me and put it in my lap.

I look into Gina's eyes and say, "I have some good news to tell you."

I set the wrapped gift on the table between us and say, "I've had a very interesting day today. As you know, I went to the Marc Hopkins this morning to meet with Bob. He wanted me to be there so that if he got a firm contract offer I would be available to go over it with him and make some decisions. I waited in the Top of the Marc for what turned out to be close to five hours. He didn't call or text me, just left me hanging, waiting for some word from him."

"Really? What an asshole!"

"Yes, he certainly is. But it's not important. Anyway, while I was waiting, a woman came up to me and introduced herself. Now don't get the wrong idea. She's about fifty, and used to work for Bob, so she knew who I was. Anyway, the long and the short of it is this."

I push the gift closer to her.

She looks at it for a long time, but doesn't open it.

"Open it. You'll like it, I promise."

She pulls the box closer to her and begins unwrapping it carefully, as if it were bone china, her hands shaking a little. When she removes the paper, she looks at me quizzically and picks up the box containing a Larry Gordon bobblehead that the Renegades gave away this past season. When she sees my name on the box and our team's logo on the doll's chest, her eyes widen. She turns to me and her blue eyes twinkle. "Does this mean what I think it means?" Her eyes fill with tears.

"It does. I signed a letter of intent this afternoon. All that is left is some minor details to be worked out and my signature on a full contract."

She grabs my arm and squeezes it tightly. "That's wonderful, Larry. But how did all this happen, and so fast?"

I tell her about firing Bob and about the talks Gail and I had with Dick Franklin. I also tell her about the creative contract deal Gail negotiated.

By now Gina is grinning. "She sounds wonderful. I assume she's now your new agent?"

"Yup. And I am lucky to have her. Did you know that jerk Bob made a pass at her when she worked for him? I guess that explains his offensive comments about me screwing around on you, doesn't it?"

"You are so much better off not working with him, even if you have to pay him off to get rid of him." She scoots over closer to me and puts her arms around my neck. "Oh, Larry. I am so happy right now. Everything is working out perfectly for us."

As I kiss her deeply, I hear the strains of one of my mom's favorite songs, "Unchained Melody," by the Righteous Brothers on the Muzak, but this is an orchestral version. I slide out of the booth and walk around to the other side, bow, and hold out my hand to Gina. "May I have this dance?"

I take her in my arms and treasure the feeling of her in my arms. "I need your love, God speed your love, to me," I sing in her ear.

When the song ends, I drop to one knee and look up at her. "I didn't propose to you properly the first time, down on one knee. Gina, my angel, with my whole being I want to be your husband. Will you be my wife?"

Before she can answer, I reach into my pocket and pull out the velvet box. When I open it, I look up at her and see tears running down her cheeks, making wet parentheses around her smile. She pulls me to my feet and says, "That's the kind of proposal I have dreamed about all my life. And, of course, I'll marry you!"

I take the beautiful ring out of its box and slide it onto her ring finger. Amazingly, it fits perfectly. I look into her eyes and say, "After I signed the letter of intent today, I visited a jeweler in the hotel and bought this for you. If you don't like…"

"Don't like it? Are you nuts? It's exquisite!" She throws her arms around me and kisses me warmly. "I love it and I'll never take it off. Ever!"

I take her hand and walk to the curtain. The waiter is right outside. "Sir, we need a bottle of your finest champagne. This beautiful woman has just agreed to be my wife."

"Right away sir!" He grins at us and winks at me.

When the champagne arrives, I raise my glass, "To the most beautiful and loving woman in the world!"

We click our glasses and sip the bubbly liquid, our free hands entwined.

She raises her glass, and turns her blue dazzle on me. "And to you, Larry. You've grown so much as a person this year, and I'm so proud of you. I can't wait to be your wife."

Chapter Fifty-Six

We had a beautiful wedding in January at Round Hill Country Club. The December date just didn't work out and luckily the Club had an opening the next month, so we took it. Gina looked like an angel, and my family and some of the guys from the team helped to make it perfect. Rick was my best man, of course.

We actually bought a house right down the street from where we got married, and we moved in a few weeks after the wedding. Gina loves her new job, and I'm headed off to Phoenix for spring training next week.

Looking back over the past year, I have grown to accept the part of me that caused Gina to leave me. Gina was right. I needed her to shake up my world, so I would be forced to take a look at my life and change what needed to be changed.

I owe so much to Rick for sticking with me all these years while I was trying to ruin my life and helping me to turn it around. He's got a broadcasting gig this season as a part-time color guy on our team's radio broadcast. He will do only home games so he won't have to be away from Cindy and the kids. His great sense of humor and baseball insights will make him a success. I'm happy for him.

And I have Gina by my side. It's not just my world anymore. It's ours. And it couldn't be more perfect!

Baseball Lingo and Definitions

Big Team/The Bigs/The Show: Slang for a major league baseball team (as opposed to minor league team), or playing in the big leagues.

Cy Young Award: An award given after the end of each baseball season to the best pitcher in each league, as voted on by the Baseball Writers' Association of America.

Dinger, Bomb, Homer, Go Yard, etc.: All are slang for home run.

Foul Ball: Any ball hit by a batter that is not between the first and third base lines. If a foul ball is caught before it touches the ground, the batter is out. Once the ball touches the ground it is a dead ball (no longer in play) and the batter is assessed a strike.

Full Count: Three balls and two strikes on a batter is called a full count.

Grounder: Any batted ball that bounces on the ground.

Hat: A baseball cap. Players never refer to one of these as a cap.

Madden: A video game series developed by Electronic Arts Tiburon for EA Sports. The game is named after Pro Football Hall of Famer John Madden. It is played on either the PlayStation or X-Box consoles.

Pop-Up/Pop the Ball Up: A ball hit by a batter high in the air usually in the infield area.

Pitches:
Fastball: A pitch thrown primarily with the index and middle fingers that reaches velocities ranging from the high 80's to the low 100's in miles per hour, a pitchers fastest pitch. The two fingers can hold the ball along the seams or across the seams, often called a "two-seam" or "four-seam" fastball. Each grip gives different movement to the ball.

Curveball: A low velocity pitch, typically in the 70-80 MPH range, thrown by placing the middle and index fingers on the top of the ball and twisting the hand as the ball is released, causing it to drop or curve dramatically when it reaches the plate. Often called Uncle Charlie, a bender, a rainbow.

Slider: A pitch halfway between a fastball and curveball in velocity, which breaks laterally as well as down. It is thrown primarily off the index finger but with the middle finger next to one of the long seams and slightly off center of the ball.

Changeup: A pitch thrown with the same arm action as a fastball but slower, also called an off-speed pitch, thrown with middle and ring fingers on top of the ball and the thumb and forefinger touching on the side to form a circle, often called a "circle change". Also can be thrown with three fingers across the seams and the thumb and pinky on the smooth leather on the underside of the ball. This is called a "three-fingered changeup."

Rookie: Any player who has fewer than 130 career at bats in the major leagues, or 50 innings pitched for a pitcher, or more than 45 days on the 25-man active roster of any major league team or teams.

Scoring Position, Runners in Scoring Position: A runner who has reached second base or third base is said to be in scoring position because a batter hitting a single has a good chance of scoring the runner.

Scout: Staff members in an organization who scout out potential players for the organization. Scouts visit high schools and colleges who have players that might fit the needs of the organization. Scouts evaluate players according to the criteria set by team management.

Spring Training: In Major League Baseball, spring training is a series of practices and exhibition games preceding the start of the regular season. Spring training allows new players to audition for roster and position spots, and gives existing team players practice time prior to competitive play. Spring training typically lasts almost two months, starting in mid February and running until just before the season on opening day, traditionally the first week of April. Pitchers and catchers report to spring training first because pitchers need more time to get their pitching arms back to game-ready strength after several months away from baseball. The position players arrive a week later. Teams primarily located in the eastern half of the country train in Florida ("The Grapefruit League"). The rest train in or near Phoenix, Arizona ("The Cactus League").

Stolen Base: A base runner may attempt to run to the next base while the pitcher is in his wind-up or when another fielder is not paying attention. If he touches the next base before a fielder can tag him out, he has "stolen" that base.

Strike Out: A batter strikes out when he has three strikes on him— any combination of three swings and misses or called strikes (pitches in the strike zone as determined by the umpire).

Tag Up and Score: When a is runner is on a base, if the batter hits a fly ball into the outfield, the runner may touch the last base he has safely achieved (tag up) and wait until the ball is caught. Then he can run to the next base before the ball is thrown to the base the runner is running to. If he gets there before the ball arrives and is not tagged out, he is safe and may stay on that base. If the runner is on third and a fly ball is hit, and he gets to the plate before the catcher can tag him out, he scores a run.

Three Up, Three Down: When a pitcher starts an inning and retires the first three batters he faces.

Uncle Charlie: A slang name for a big breaking curveball.

Walk-Off Home Run: When a batter in the bottom of the ninth inning hits a home run that puts the home team ahead, the game is over immediately, and the home team wins. That homer is called "a walk-off home run." If a batter in the bottom of the ninth inning hits any other type of hit or draws a walk with the bases loaded that wins the game, it is often called a "walk-of hit" or even a "walk-off walk."

Wheelhouse: The area of the strike zone where the batter likes to have the pitch delivered, which is slightly different for each player. Typically most of a player's hits are on pitches delivered to his "wheelhouse."

Walk/Work a Walk: A walk is achieved when a batter receives four pitches outside the strike zone. When a hitter is patient, not swinging at ("taking") pitches out of the strike zone, and fouling off pitches in the strike zone, he runs the count full. If the pitcher misses the strike zone for the fourth time, it is said that the batter has "worked a walk".

Yard: ballpark, or stadium.

ACKNOWLEDGEMENTS

First of all, I would like to thank the Oakland Athletics. A's baseball has been my passion since I was fourteen years old. My family and I lived in Kansas City, Missouri, when the Philadelphia Athletics took that Midwestern city by storm, largely because the A's were the first major league team of any sport to be located there. I reconnected with the A's when I moved to the San Francisco Bay Area from Boston in the mid 1970's and rekindled my love of the A's. As a season ticket holder, I find joy in the Oakland Coliseum, watching my guys do what I would have loved to do, but for the lack of a Y chromosome, and probably talent.

I would also like to thank James Simmons, Brad Kilby, and Jeff Gray, who are either current or former ballplayers in the A's organization, for their time and their insight into the life of ballplayers on and off the field. Their input and friendship has been a godsend to me, particularly James Simmons who read an early version of the book. He also read the latest draft and agreed to give me a quote for the back cover.

My profound thanks go to Rick Hurd, a national baseball writer and former A's beat writer for the Contra Costa Times, a newspaper in the San Francisco East Bay Area. He edited the last three versions of Contract Year, and has become my good friend. His insights into the world of baseball behind the scenes and his considerable editing skills have made Contract Year a much better and considerably shorter novel.

I also would like to thank Tom O'Connell, President of O'Connell Sports Management, located in Tampa, Florida, whom I found via the Internet. He was gracious enough to read the entire novel (not just the scenes with Larry's sports agent as he requested), and his input into the role of a sports agent and Major League Baseball's many contract rules have been invaluable.

I am also indebted to all the people who read various drafts of Contract Year, among them Sandy Vance, former Los Angeles Dodger pitcher, and his wife, Dee Vance, who is my friend. Sandy's insight into the mindset of a major league pitcher resulted in a major rewrite of the book. Others who have read entire drafts of this novel are my friends Jean Georgakopoulos (who copy-edited the final draft), Sandy Olsen, and Vivi Wiitala, and my brother Ned Laird. I thank them for their input and support.

Without my writing sisters—Jean Georgakopoulos, Eva Dunn and Anna Froker—I could not have written this book. Their friendship and input along the way have kept me going on many occasions. Likewise, the support and encouragement of my writing teacher and mentor, Clive Matson, author of "Let the Crazy Child Write," was vital to the conception and early drafts of this novel.

Finally, I would like to thank my husband, Ralph Hylinski, who read many versions of Contract Year with an eagle eye, finding typos that everyone else missed, and my wonderful daughter, Ginger Clark. Without their love, understanding, and encouragement, this novel would not have been completed.

Bee Hylinski wrote this novel as a labor of love for the game of baseball. Before becoming an author and professional editor, she was a tax, estate planning, and probate attorney, Mayor of Moraga, CA, and an artist. She enjoys cheering on her beloved Oakland Athletics and lives in San Francisco Bay Area with her husband.

Made in the USA
Charleston, SC
10 July 2012